DOCTOR HEARTLESS

J. SAMAN

Cover design: Lori Jackson

Photographer: Rafa Catala

Model: Jorge

Editing: My Brother's Editor & Emily Lawrence

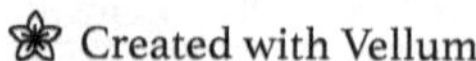 Created with Vellum

PROLOGUE

I can't shake it. This restlessness. An anxious stirring that overtakes my body, quickens my heart rate, and compels my muscles into action. It's as if I've forgotten to do something. Something big. Important, maybe. Something vital.

The oven is off and so is the stove. All the doors and windows are locked. Hell, the alarm is on. My keys are in my purse, and my cell phone is plugged into the outlet beside my nightstand. So no, it's not any of that. I've done everything I should have. Nothing is lost or forgotten or even missing.

And I'm not in danger.

It's the middle of the night. Somewhere close at least, and I can't fall asleep. It's this feeling that's keeping me awake. Feeding my unease as it churns the boiling acid in my stomach. I blow out a breath, trying to shake the urgent thoughts that will no longer be silenced. *Listen to us, dammit,* they demand, and for once, I do.

Some might call it intuition. Some a conscience.

For me, it's the voice in the back of my mind.

My stupid meter, and it's firing on all cylinders. It's not the first time my mind got its rocks off by shouting, *you couldn't be any stupider if you tried.* Not the nicest sentiment in the world, but not wrong either. *How long are you going to take this? How many times does he need to screw up or lie through his apology or treat you like you're nothing better than a cockroach he stepped on before you've had enough?*

Yep, it's all coming out tonight. No holds barred.

A growl slips past my mashed lips before I can stop it, and I can't decide who I want to hit more, me or my husband. Flopping onto my back, I stare up through a pinched brow at the vaulted ceiling of our bedroom, the ceiling fan twirling around and around, circulating the stale, miserable air around me.

Stale and miserable. Just like my life.

The cool sheets, which are nothing if not expensive and soft, rub my skin raw. The blanket fashioned from silks and satins is smothering me. The memory foam pillow, a brick. I roll over again and for a contemplative moment, stare at my husband's sleeping form. His breathing is heavy, not quite a snore but not quiet either. The sort of breathing that tells me he's in a deep sleep.

Of course he is. What would he have to be sleepless over?

He'd have to have a heart or a conscience or actually give a shit about anyone other than himself for that to happen.

My husband went out tonight to a charity dinner of some kind and came home drunk. He doesn't typically do that. Drink. Not since shortly after we were married anyway. But when he does, all the burning acrimony he tries so hard to hide from the world lashes out.

And I'm its prime target.

He's smart enough not to have lipstick on his collar or perfume on his jacket. Hell, I don't even know if he cheats, though I wouldn't be shocked if he does. "I go out and this is what I have to come home to," he had snarled, meaning me in my yoga pants and oversized T-shirt, my hair up in a ponytail, and my face void of makeup. "Can't you at least attempt to look like the beautiful woman I married instead of this ugly trash?" It went on from there until he stormed off to his putting green in the back with a glass of something, and I went to bed.

Well, pretended to anyway.

Then he came in, woke me up with his mouth and his hands and his body. Thousands of dollars of counseling talked me into staying, into working on our marriage and allowing my husband to put his hands on me and his dick inside me whenever he wants.

"It'll keep the passion alive. When there's passion, there's hope," my therapist had said.

And yet, every time he touches me, I'm revolted. I must have lain there like a dead fish because that's exactly how I feel. Dead. Lifeless. Soulless. That last one might be the worst of all. There was a time when I thought I'd die without his love. Now I realize his love was a weapon. One he wielded proudly, claiming my best pieces as his trophy while leaving me scrambling over my leftover parts.

What life is there when you're reduced to missing pieces and leftover parts?

I hate my husband for the woman I've allowed him to turn me into, and as I stare at his unconscious form, I wonder if killing him in his sleep would stick me in prison or if a jury of my female peers—the ones whose husbands have stolen their souls—would vindicate me. It would be justice, they'd claim. Only at this point, I don't feel much of anything.

Not enough hatred to kill him. Not enough pain to yell. Not enough sadness to cry.

I'm empty. *Soulless!*

But my husband is as untroubled as it gets.

Confident that this trophy wife will still smile at his handsome face and kiss his cheek in the morning. I watch him for a moment longer, then I tell him, "I don't love you anymore. I don't think I have for a very long time."

Silence.

The man doesn't even stir. How unsatisfying. Maybe if he gave a fuck? Put up a fight? No. Not even then.

I clear my throat, raising my voice. "I want a divorce. You'll thank me for this one day when you find another poor, unsuspecting woman to demoralize and destroy." I snort, rolling my eyes, already feeling sorry for her. "I'll do my best not to hate you. I won't even bad-mouth you to the tabloids or news networks when they come knocking. We'll claim irreconcilable differences when we both know the truth. You're a wolf in sheep's clothing."

I sigh, satisfied that I said my piece.

Climbing out of bed, I spot my alarm clock. Midnight. Sharp. Well, what are the odds of that? I don't want to spend a new day in this house. I don't want to spend any more wasted minutes in this life. In this bed. With this man.

How can a man who claims to love you endlessly treat you worse than the dirt stuck in his golf cleats? I used to matter. I was his world, and he made sure I and everyone else knew it.

Walking into my closet, I tug a duffel bag down from the top shelf and start filling it with whatever I come across first. I have zero ideas about what I'm packing, but whatever. Who cares? I obviously don't. Fucks to give abandoned me months ago. Instead, I bring meaningless stuff into my meaningless life, and when they don't fill the void, I hang them up in my closet.

Staring down at my bag, I wonder why I'm bothering.

Because you don't want to end up homeless and naked.

Yep. I suppose that sums it up.

I zip up my bag, now filled to the brim, and walk into our bedroom. Staring down at my husband, who is still dead to the world, I smile at him. "I'm leaving and I'm not coming back."

More heavy breathing. "Don't fight me, okay? I just want a clean break. A life for myself. You'll realize I'm gone when you go looking for your coffee and breakfast tomorrow, so I better get cracking."

Slinging my bag over my shoulder, I walk out. With absolutely no idea where I'm headed or what I'm going to do next.

1

S ix months later

SINCE THE DAWN of man and the beginning of time and the advent of bar hookups, I've never had an issue scoring a woman. That's not even arrogance. It's a simple, stupid fact—a byproduct of my last name and the size of my bank account. But one I've been grateful for over the last nine years.

The last time I cared enough to put effort into meeting a woman, I was eighteen.

The night I met my wife.

Now, at thirty-three, the game has changed, as have the stakes. I've already met and lost the love of my life. No other woman will ever compare to her. This, I already know. It's why I've never cared to look beyond her. Why when she died, sex became a matter of need rather than desire. A sick pleasure I hate indulging in.

Even all these years later.

"Good evening, Dr. Fritz," the valet greets as he opens the car door for me, the cool autumn air biting at my face as I step out. "Will you be needing your car again tonight, sir?"

I certainly hope not. "I'm not sure."

"No problem. I'll park it in the residence lot in one of Dr. Fritz's spots for you."

I grin at that. He's referring to my brother Carter, who lives in the residence here at The Ritz. But considering every single one of my four brothers and our father is a doctor, we all fall into the Dr. Fritz title.

"Thank you, Gerald. I appreciate that." I shake his hand, tipping him a large bill as I do. "Have a good night."

"Thank you. You too, sir."

Grudgingly, I enter the opulent lobby, but instead of going up to the counter, I trudge into the bar. *The* bar. The one I just so happen to always frequent out of convenience and habit when I reach the point of no return. Carter living next door is a bonus, and on a typical night, I'd likely meet up with him or one of my other siblings.

But not tonight.

"Are you waiting on someone to meet you, Dr. Fritz? Dining with us perhaps?" the hostess with the pushed-up nose and heavily made-up eyes asks me, her fake but nice-looking tits thrust in my direction.

I shake my head. "I'm just heading to the bar."

She eyes me up and down. "I didn't think you'd be back this soon," she says, and my eyebrows crease. So soon? It's been... five months since I've made the solo trip here. "I'm off at midnight. If you're interested in some fun."

Every time I come in here, I consider taking her up on what her eyes—and tonight her mouth—have been offering me all along.

But then I couldn't return to this bar.

"Not tonight."

She frowns but doesn't hover on it, turning her focus to the people standing behind me, anxious for a table at a restaurant that's typically reserved weeks in advance.

I stroll through the crowded restaurant, averting my gaze from the curious patrons who spot me, staring, murmuring, likely speculating. I call it the casualty of being an Abbot-Fritz in Boston. Our city. If my entire family wasn't located here, I'd heavily contemplate moving elsewhere to escape it. Unfortunately, as it is, I can't go anywhere without being recognized.

Only when I reach the bar do I suddenly understand the hostess's comment when the bartender, Gabe, greets me with a surprised and amused grin. "Luca!" He gives me the bro shake. "I didn't expect to see you back here tonight. Hell, I thought you'd still be in bed with the woman you left with last night. She was the hottest thing I've seen in a while."

Luca. Gabe thinks I'm Luca. My twin, who obviously came here looking—and finding, even though that surprises me—a hookup last night. You'd think in all the years both Luca and I have known Gabe, he'd be able to tell us apart. Clearly not.

Only Luca is no longer with whatever woman he found last night.

He's with Stella tonight, taking my daughter to Dave & Buster's for games and dinner and then back to his place for a sleepover. Because my brother gets it. All of my siblings and even my parents do. I'm human, and therefore, unfortunately, have needs. Needs that eventually supersede what my hand can provide me.

Instead of correcting the bartender, I just shrug up a shoulder.

It's not the first time I've been mistaken for my identical twin. Likely not the last and on nights like these, it's easier to put on an act and pretend I'm him. The flirt. The playboy. The easy-going guy everyone adores.

Instead of me.

The quiet one. The grump. The heartsick man who never found his way back after losing his wife.

It also means if I'm photographed, I'm photographed as him. Not me. Luca doesn't care, but I do. Because the last thing I want is for my teenage daughter to see me in tabloids with a strange woman she'll never meet.

"The hottest thing you've seen in a while, huh?" slips out, if for no other reason than my inwardly teasing my brother. I doubt he looked all that closely. Women come on to him, and he responds because he too has needs, but he never sees them. They're not the one he wants.

"Well, she was," he replies with a sly grin, his eyes now tracking beyond my shoulder, following whoever is heading this way. "Damn. I might need to amend that." He bites his knuckles as if he's in pain, then goes about pouring me a drink I didn't order. Top shelf. Expensive as fuck. Bourbon, when I'm more of a vodka man. "Shit, now that you're here, I won't stand a chance."

"I'm sorry?" I question.

He bounces his head to my left as he sets my drink down in front of me, then walks in that direction with a wink. "I get first shot."

Before I can stop it, natural curiosity takes over, and I glance to my left. And sure enough, a woman slides onto a stool three seats over, her face cast toward the wood bar, her dark blond hair, the color rich and golden, covering the majority of her face. All I can catch is her slim nose and the delicate hint of a profile. And her body. There is that, encased in a form-fitting yet modest black dress. Petite. Firm. Subtle curves.

Just how I like them.

But her most prominent feature—the one I can't turn away from—her full, pouty lips are tipped down in the most melancholy of frowns. Her heart visibly aching, outwardly bleeding across the bar she sits in front of.

I focus back on my drink, hating the emotions her sadness stirs in me.

I miss my wife. I still haven't learned how to live without her.

Gabe engages the woman, talking and making her laugh, though I can't hear much of what he's saying. Just bits here and there, but before I can stop myself, I slip my phone out of my pocket and dial up my brother.

He picks up quickly, the eardrum rupturing noise on the other end only made worse as he shouts, "Why the fuck are you calling me?" into the phone.

"Just checking on things," I tell him in a low tone when he and I both know that's not true. "How's Stella?"

A point he proves as he growls, "Stella is great. We're having an awesome time." Another growl, then I hear him tell Stella to stay wherever she is, and he'll be right back. Suddenly, it's quieter. "You're not doing anything wrong, Landon. You're allowed to go out. Meet women. Enjoy yourself. Have fun even."

I drag my glass up to my lips and take a sip, hating how it slides so smoothly down my throat when I'd rather feel the bite of something harsher. "I know," I lie.

He puffs. "You don't know because if you did, you wouldn't be calling me on your night out to check on Stella."

"They think I'm you."

He laughs. "Even better. Turn on the Fritz charm, smile so your facial muscles don't atrophy from lack of practice, and get laid."

"Like you did last night?"

"Oh shit. You're at that bar. I should have warned you. I left with that woman, but as per usual with me, nothing happened with her. I just couldn't..." He clears his throat, his voice dropping. "Reese would want you to live your life."

I don't know how to do that anymore hovers on the tip of my tongue before I swallow it down with another sip of Luca's favorite bourbon. Luca's favorite. Tonight, I'm him. Not me. Because the not so simple question is, would she? Sometimes I'm not so sure after what I did.

"I mean it, Lan. Stow your emotional baggage for a night and remember what living actually feels like."

I roll my eyes, hating how he called me Lan. He did it on purpose, to get a rise out of me. "Tonight you get to be the single dad, and I get to be the playboy? Is that it?"

He laughs. "Now you're talking. I gotta get back to our girl. You've got all night, Landon. Use it."

He disconnects the call with that demand, and I set my phone face down on the bar as I let his words burn a hole through my brain. I glance around the bar, flittering from one woman to the next. There's a group of them at the far end, all making eyes at me. Soft, hypnotic jazz and low lighting sets a seductive tone as come-fuck-me eyes and flirty smiles that do nothing for me hit me from every direction while I do what I can to resist the temptation.

I don't make it long.

A few more seconds at most before I lose the battle I was hardly fighting and turn back to *her*. The woman on my left. I watch, mesmerized for some unexplainable reason, as she pulls her phone from her purse only to scowl at the thing, shake her head, and then shove it right back in. She growls, curses, laughs, then shakes her head again.

Dragging some green concoction in a towering martini glass to her lips, she nearly downs the whole thing in one swift go before licking the remnants from her lips. Then, as if she senses me staring, her head whips in my direction, and I'm met with huge, doe-like hazel eyes, and every single breath I had trapped in my lungs flees.

Holy shit.

I swallow thickly, my throat dry, words failing me.

And not for the first time in my life, I genuinely wish I were my brother.

Any of the other four of them because they're so good at this—talking to women—and I'm terrible. I haven't wanted to make small talk or listen or pretend with any of the women I've temporarily fallen in bed with. But, staring into her eyes that somehow manage to strip me bare, I want to know all her thoughts. All her hidden words. Every secret she's terrified to tell another living soul.

She smiles at me—a breath of dawn after the stormy night—and now I'm the one frowning. I hate this. Her barely concealed sadness pisses me off. I'm not here tonight to wallow in misery—that's all I ever fucking do—I'm here for a few brief moments of pleasure. For that reason alone, I should turn away. Pick up one of those other eager women to get lost in for a few hours.

But her eyes, they won't let go.

They pierce through me, attacking my armor. Which is why I do what I always do when feelings stir inside of me. I shut it down. Only I don't—*can't*—look away either. That is until Gabe comes back, breaking the spell I'm cast under.

"You want another, Luca?"

Right. I'm Luca. Not Landon. What would Luca do when faced with a beautiful woman? "Yes."

He pours me more of Luca's bourbon before strolling over to the woman, dropping his elbows on the bar top, and leaning in as close as he can.

"And I take it you want your second half?"

"If that's okay?" she replies, her voice soft, sweet, Southern—more twang than drawl.

"Left it right here for you." Gabe's eyes skim back and forth between the sexy stranger and me as he pours her second martini of the night from a pre-filled shaker that had been set on ice. "I see you've met my friend."

She shakes her head, her gaze casting back to mine. "Not yet."

Well, hell.

"That's Luca. Lucky bastard," Gabe mutters that last part under his breath as he slides her glass toward her and walks away.

She twists to face me, and before I can stop myself or think twice, I rise out of my seat and move into the one directly beside her, catching a hint of her perfume as I do. She was beautiful before, but up close she's incredible, and my heart kick starts in my chest.

"Rough day at work?" I ask, then inwardly cringe. Not only does it sound like I'm judging her for drinking the way she is, but it's a dumb as fuck pickup line.

She laughs, the swirls of green and brown in her eyes sparkling. "No. No work for me today."

We both lift our glasses like they're going to save us from this awkward, intense moment. She smiles. I smile back. We stare.

"Looks like we're having a drink together," I remark.

"Looks that way."

I do a slow sweep down her body before returning to her eyes. "Lucky me."

"We'll see about that," she replies, then laughs, shaking her head as if she can't believe she said that out loud. "Wooh, it's been a long day, and I'm horrible at this. Pretend I didn't say that."

Like hell I will.

"I'm Elle."

"I'm..." I hesitate.

"Luca. Yes, your bartender friend told me."

I don't correct her. I nod, but as the lie passes over me, I'm hit with the all too familiar twinge of guilt. I don't enjoy lying to anyone, but remembering the sadness in her eyes before I sat beside her makes the feeling worse. The feeling doesn't last long, though. It's quickly overpowered by something else—trepidation—as she studies me curiously.

I can see it all unfolding before my eyes. The way my name zips around in her head, the flicker of her gaze as she examines me closer. I'm waiting for it. For the recognition to come while wishing I hadn't been stupid enough to sit beside her.

"I feel like I've seen you before."

Yup. Here it comes. "Maybe I have one of those faces."

She tilts her head, knowing that's not it. "Are you a golfer?"

"A golfer?" I parrot, nearly on a laugh.

"A professional athlete then?"

Now I choke. "No. Not an athlete. Is that your type?" I ask, changing the subject before she keeps going and figures it out.

"You're amused by me, but you shouldn't be. You have the build of an athlete, the sexy confidence of one too."

My eyebrows hit my hairline. I don't know if it's the alcohol or if she's generally this unfiltered and bold, but it's certainly unexpected. It quirks a smile on my lips. A genuine one. Something others before her have tried and failed to make appear.

"Anyway, no," she continues. "Athletes are definitely not my type. Not anymore."

"But sexy, confident strangers? What about us?"

"As long as you're not a professional athlete, I'm all for sexy and confident. My ex was a professional athlete." She tries to say this matter-of-factly, but there's no mistaking the contemptuous undertone mixed into her angelic Southern twang. She blusters out a sigh. "I have no idea why I'm telling you that."

"Want to talk about it?"

She shakes her head, her finger toying with the delicate edge of her glass. "Not even a little bit. The last thing I want to do right now with a hot stranger is think about life stuff and even less to talk about myself."

"Now I'm a hot stranger?"

"Just sayin' it like it is. My nana, rest her soul, would have tanned my hide for doing otherwise. Plus, this delicious cocktail is loosening my lips."

I blink at her, leaning in. "Wanna know a secret?"

"Sure."

"I like sexy, confident, hot women. It's why I came and sat down beside you."

A hint of a blush blooms across her cheeks as her eyes darken. She gives me a flirty smirk that goes straight to my dick. "Then I guess we have something in common."

"Guess so. I take it you're visiting Boston?"

She laughs sardonically. "Just moved here actually. As in tonight. New town, new job, new life. How did you know I wasn't from around here?"

Now it's my turn to laugh at her teasing lilt, my gaze dragging hungrily across her. "Exactly how Southern are you?"

"Very Southern. So Southern my home state is practically its own country and only a hundred miles separate where I grew up from Mexico. But you're asking me questions about myself, Luca, and I believe I already clarified that's not a subject I want to chat about."

"That doesn't give me much to work with."

She raises a challenging eyebrow at me, angling her head in my direction. "We could always talk about you."

My finger drags along my lower lip. "What do you want to know?" I ask cautiously. I can't tell if she already knows something personal about me and is trying to play the game where she pretends she doesn't or if she's genuinely curious.

"Do you come here often?"

I grin at her cheeky line, taking a sip of my drink to hide it. "I've been known to."

She reaches for her glass and does the same with her own smile. We do that staring thing again, unable to look away. It's just us, nothing else, the bar floating into the background, and I'm captivated.

"Because this is where you pick up women?"

I lean in a little more. "Does that bother you?"

She thinks about this, her gaze dancing around my face, so I return the favor, taking in every detail. The way her hair tumbles around her in thick, glossy waves of smooth honeycomb. The innocence to her large, round eyes, almost too big for her face. The light dusting of freckles adorning the bridge of her petite nose only visible up close. The delicate beauty of her high cheekbones kissed with a heart-shaped freckle just beneath her right eye. Then there are her lips. Lush and bow-shaped and insanely kissable.

Each of these features individually isn't anything all that impressive, but on her they flawlessly coalesce, giving her stunning beauty a seductively sweet look. The all-American girl next door with a siren's temptation. A total vixen.

"Surprisingly, it doesn't," she declares after a quiet beat. "I could go for being picked up. It's been a while. Is this how you typically do it? Judging by the women at the end of the bar staring at you like you're a juicy steak, I'm guessing you don't have to work all that hard for it."

"It depends," I muse, setting my glass down on the bar and dropping my hands in between us. They flirt with the gap between our legs, so close to her bare knees, testing the waters. "Sometimes I do have to work for it. Others not so much."

She cocks a playful eyebrow, her lips curving up, making her eyes sparkle against the dim overhead lights. "Hmmm. And where do I rank on that scale? Am I making it too easy for you, Luca? It's been a while since I played this particular game. I'm not quite sure how it all works."

I grunt, staring down at my hands for a beat, the small smile and the thrill of the chase I had going plummeting as a fresh wave of guilt slams into me. I should have told her the truth from the start, corrected her when she called me Luca, but it's too late for that now.

"Nothing about you is too easy. It took all my nerve to come and sit beside you."

Her eyes widen at that, incredulous, but her honesty seems to draw some of my own to leak out. She's real. I don't know her, but somehow, I know that. She's not those women and maybe that's what drew me over to her despite her sadness I want no part of.

"Is this all you wanted to do? Sit beside me and chat?"

"No. Not even close. I don't come here for the conversation."

My eyes coast along her face, watching her with an uneasiness that wasn't there before. I just basically set my cards on the table, waiting to see if she'll pick them up and play a round with me.

She sucks in a rush of air. "And you sat beside me?"

A ghost of a smile teases my lips. "I did." I blink at her deer-in-headlights expression. "Did I insult you?"

"No," she sputters. "Does it make me a total hussy if I admit I like that more than I know I should? You have no idea how long it's been since a man looked at me the way you are."

"You're beautiful. Any man who doesn't look at you this way is a fool." I shift ever so slightly on my stool with a purpose that makes her breath hitch. Her scent reaches me first, light and floral as it curls around me, forcing me to take a deeper inhale than I'd like. My cock jerks in my pants, my insides quickening with anticipation.

I want this woman. More than I can remember wanting anyone in a very long time.

Desire burns a path through my body, warning me to walk away before I do something I can't undo. But the devil in her eyes keeps me rooted in place. It's playing with my own, reminding me how long it's been since I've lost myself in a warm, willing body.

Here goes nothing.

My lips skirt past her face, heading directly for her ear. A shiver courses through her as she does everything she can not to squirm. "How much have you had to drink tonight, Elle?" I whisper, my warm breath brushing her sensitive skin.

"The one your friend just poured is my second drink."

"Do me a favor then?" I swallow, releasing a shuddered breath that would be embarrassing if I wasn't so keyed up by her proximity. "Don't have any more." My face slips back, hovering a few inches away from hers as I stare into her eyes. "I want to take you upstairs and fuck you all night. And I need you sober for that."

She swallows. Hard. "And this is something you want to do now?"

A dirty smile spreads across my face. "Yes. If that's what you want?"

2

Luca's words zip around in my head over and over like a deranged pinball as I stare at him, a little surprised. I expected him to flee with his good sense the moment I unleashed a touch of my crazy. Instead, he studies me with a barely-there smirk and a dark gleam to his wicked, half-mast eyes that can only be described as flagrant lust.

I'm not even sure that makes sense, but that's still how he's looking at me. Like there are no other women in this bar—there are dozens, all staring at him, might I add. Like I'm the most beautiful and interesting woman he's ever encountered—I highly doubt that, though I have always considered myself a catch. Like there's nowhere else he'd rather be right now than sitting beside me—I already know that's not true since he just propositioned me for sex and told me he's not here for the conversation.

That last part alone should have made me smack him, but seriously, what good has talking with a man done for me lately? Action and flagrant desire might be where it's at.

Because that... *that* right there. That look of unrestrained attraction and interest is doing unbelievable things to my belly.

It's clenching and coiling and swirling and swooping—all because of this one look. That one bold offer. I cannot remember the last time a man made me feel this way. Looked at me like this. Flirted with me so openly.

He's not even overdoing it, though it's hardly subtle, and we haven't exactly shared a lot of words yet.

But screw it.

I'm free to behave in all the wrong ways, answering to no one but my conscience.

I want to continue this with him because the heat pooling low in my belly is playing tricks on my mind. It's filling me with the cloying taste of shared lust. It's spoon-feeding me ridiculous rationales that never fail to appear brilliant in the moment. Things like, maybe one night of no-strings, hot sex with an attractive stranger is exactly what I need to put my past behind me and start fresh. Makes total sense, right? Besides, this guy didn't come to this bar and sit beside me hoping to find the love of his life.

No, he's seeking meaningless fun.

Something I hadn't considered until he sat down beside me.

I've never had meaningless fun.

I've never been careless or silly or wild. That was always Cat. I've been careful and planned and organized.

And look what all that got me.

My marriage officially ended today.

Four years of a relationship, of my life, are over, and I'll never be able to get them back.

I'm overwhelmed with the oddest concoction of elation and heartache and fear and anticipation. So much so that my thoughts have been racing all day, on the plane and in the cab ride and upstairs in my room. It's why I came down to the bar, hoping alcohol would put a stop to them.

So here I am. Just moved to a new town in a new state, about to start a new job—one I seriously do not feel comfortable with or qualified for—and I'm only now figuring out who I am without being David Chambers's wife. And the best part, I think I like her. She's like a badass demon on a power trip laced with speed, out to take her life back. Well, at least that's the story I'm selling myself. It nearly gets me through all the anxiety and fucking panic I have coursing through my blood.

I made it through my childhood and went to college. And where did that land me? Right before I graduated with my master's in education, I met and fell in love with David Chambers—older, pro-athlete, charming, and gorgeous.

About two years later, I started eating shit and smiling through it daily. I transformed who and what I was several times over so I could be the wife he wanted. The wife he needed. And finally, when his apologies were no longer enough. When the trinkets he bought me did nothing but make me violent. When the thought of his touch made me ill. When I could no longer stand my reflection in the mirror.

I left.

So yeah. This new life? It's all about me.

Starting now. Starting here.

With this stranger.

He's been waiting for my response to his question. And again, I replay his words in my mind. *Yes. If that's what you want?* I face him head-on, square my shoulders, and tuck away the nerves that threaten to overrun me and ruin this whole operation.

Evidently, Luca grows bored waiting on me because the next thing I know, his hand is on my thigh, just above my knee.

My eyes close, my head falling back because *what the hell?* I have chills. They're running up and down my arms, and all he's doing is touching my leg. My chin dips. My head twists.

Mint green.

That's the color of his eyes fanned with dark lashes. The color should be cold, but the intensity in those beautiful eyes suddenly heats my blood, flushing my cheeks. He has a small brown freckle in his left iris, which adds a hint of character. His jaw is the strong, chiseled from stone type—smooth, even at this hour in the evening. It makes me wonder if he went home and shaved before coming out. His chestnut hair is wavy, slightly unruly on top, and short on the sides. But the way a small lock of it flops affectionately onto his forehead—like it can't help itself—is what softens his angled, streamlined features.

He's insanely hot. Staggeringly so. Tall, even sitting beside me in the chair, with broad shoulders and muscles barely contained beneath his nondescript charcoal slacks and black long-sleeved button-down. The color seems to make his eyes even lighter. Almost colorless. I've never seen anything like them.

He smiles, those eyes feasting on each of my features one by one, and all the sparks I haven't felt in more than two years? Well, yeah, I've got them now. My skin is zinging like it's a methed up version of Fourth of July fireworks.

Luca's smile grows, and I realize it's because I've somehow drifted closer to him. So close our mouths are almost touching. Nearly kissing. Right here, out in the open.

"Is that a yes?" he hums, his bourbon-infused breath caressing my lips.

Is it? I still haven't answered.

I survey him, dragging myself back and forcing a sober once-over. I don't get the serial killer vibes from him. He wants me sober, which means he doesn't want to take advantage of me. It also means he's cautious, careful with his lovers. Stupidly, this makes me trust him when I likely should know better.

I blink at him.

"Yes." No regrets. No holding back. One night to wash away the bad juju of my past and start this new life on an uptick.

Sucking in a deep, tremulous breath, I say, "I have a room here at the hotel."

Now it's his turn to suck in a deep breath. I don't think he was expecting me to go straight there. He was probably waiting for me to tell him off or nervously ask if we could spend more time talking. But I don't need to talk to him if I'm never going to see him again after tonight.

Luca stares at me, those iridescent greens trying to read everything I'm desperate to hide. He says nothing. Doesn't lean in to kiss me. Instead, his hand slides slowly up my thigh, over the hem of my dress until it's resting over mine. His fingertips, warm and rough, gently run along the bones of my fingers. The texture of his skin against mine is like magic.

A jolt of electricity courses through me.

His hand twines with mine, knotting our fingers together. It's so intimate, this position we're in. His face right here, his hand holding mine, and I inhale the spicy musk of his heady cologne. My heart is beating so wildly in my chest, I know he can feel my pulse thrum through my palm.

"Are you okay with this just being tonight?" he asks gently.

"That's all I want." Truth.

"You sure? Because that's all I have to offer."

There's so much behind that statement. Curiosity burns at me, but he doesn't owe me explanations just as I don't owe him any. I wonder how many women he's done this with. How many women told him they only wanted one night and then sought more in the morning. His looks alone could make a nun's panties wet and have her second-guessing her love of Jesus.

"Then we're two peas in a pod."

A chuckle slips past his lips as he stands, releasing my hand. He tugs his wallet from his back pocket, drops a couple large bills on the bar, then retakes my hand. Quick steps rush out of the restaurant, through the opulent marble lobby, over to the bank of elevators.

"This one." I press the button that will lead us to my floor. Just as the doors part, I ask, "How many women have you killed?"

"What?" A burst of a laugh flies out of his mouth.

"Okay. That was the answer I was looking for."

His eyebrows pinch together.

"If you had casually said none or simply tilted your head at me like I was crazy, I wouldn't have gotten on the elevator with you."

"So now that you know I won't kill you..." He leaves that hanging as we both glance at the empty waiting car.

"I'm thinking I'd like to have some fun tonight."

"Thank fuck."

The doors shut behind us, and he keeps quiet. Not trying to fill what should be an awkward silence with useless banter. Maybe because it's not awkward. Tense might be more apt for what's zapping between us. The best kind. The kinetic kind you feel tingling up your spine while it surrounds you in a hazy mist.

The moment the elevator ascends, his hand releases mine, favoring my waist instead as he tugs my back to his chest. My head drops back, falling to the space just beneath his chin. A perfect fit. Firm lips press into the back of my hair, and I smile to myself, knowing he can't see it.

A contented hum vibrates my chest just as I spin around in his arms, surprising us both with my bold move. My fingers climb up his jaw, cupping his face and drawing him down until our lips crash together. This is no tentative sample first kiss. No gentle brushing of our lips to test if there's a spark.

This is gasoline on a forest fire.

The moment our mouths meet, we combust. Hands in hair, lips moving, bodies pressing. It's messy and hot and completely uninhibited.

Beyond sexy. Utterly unexpected.

Balling up the fabric of his shirt, I clench it in my fist so I don't rip it from his body right here in the elevator. Before I've even had a full taste of his tongue, he sinks his teeth into my bottom lip, dragging it out and sucking on it.

"God, that's insanely good," he groans.

I release another hum, this one huskier, needier as I press deeper, right into his hard length. The hand around my waist draws me in closer, flush against his chest, his other hand snaking up my spine to thread through my hair. My soft breasts squish against him, my pelvis rolling ever so slightly, desperate for friction where I ache the most.

Lips part on a gasp of air before he immediately dives back in, greedy for more of this kiss, and just as my tongue slides against his once more, the elevator dings, and we jump apart like two teenagers caught by their parents only to realize we've reached my floor.

I'm so turned on right now, I could die. I'm high on this man. Don't know how any of this happened, but it did. That was the best make-out session I've ever had, and it lasted all of thirty seconds. We have this moment. Tonight. That's all there is to this, but I'm already feeling greedy over it, wanting time to slow so I can savor every single second of what I know is yet to come for as long as possible.

"My room is just down the hall," I tell him.

Luca glances up and frowns, dismayed by how long this hall is. I get it. We're talking miles. It'll take decades for us to reach my room, and we're just too damn impatient. Reaching down, he slides a hand across my ass and lifts me. I yelp, caught off guard, my hands gripping his shoulders, afraid he'll drop me.

"Don't worry. You're not going anywhere until I let you." His mouth fuses to mine once more, his tongue slipping inside. Tilting my head, I deepen it, and wow, it's even better. "Hang on," he breathes against me.

"What?" squawks past my lips just as he takes off at a full sprint down the hall. A startled scream quickly turns into an airy laugh as I bounce against him, clinging to him for dear life. "I could have run. You didn't have to carry me."

"I like you pressed against me better."

"Hadn't thought of that." I shift closer, my warm, wet mouth trailing a path of open-mouthed kisses along his neck. He shudders, suppressing a groan. "This is me," I whisper as we approach the second to last door on the left.

"Key," he grounds out as my body rocks into his.

"I've got it." I lean back to swipe the plastic keycard along the flat circular panel above the door handle. The lock disengages with a grinding of gears and then I open it, hopping out of his arms at the same time. The door shuts with a heavy click behind us and suddenly, we're alone in my dark hotel room with nothing but our breaths between us. "Do you... um... want something to drink?"

He shakes his head, taking a step and placing his hand on my hip. He leaves it there, almost as if he's waiting for me to make the next move.

"Say something," I command softly, sinking my teeth into my lip, suddenly nervous now that we're here.

"You're beautiful," he murmurs. I blow out a breathy laugh, ready to retort with you probably say that to all the girls when he cuts me off with, "You are. It's not a line. We're not doing that, remember? You're beautiful, Elle. A hell of a lot more than that, actually. Tell me what you want, and I'll give it to you."

I inhale a tremulous breath, hold it for a few beats, then release it slowly, my eyes never wavering from his. "I want you to strip me naked and make me come."

In the next second, he's back on me, all over me. His hand in my hair, the other unzipping my dress as his mouth ravages mine. Kissing and sucking, feasting on my tongue before dropping to my neck. My dress slips past my lace-covered breasts, around my stomach, over the slope of my hips, and down my legs. I let it fall, pooling at my feet. Now I'm standing before him in just my bra, panties, and heels.

He scours every inch of me in the darkness, the only light filtering in through curtainless windows. It's with his gaze still on me that his hands come up, cupping my tits, his thumbs scraping against the lace over my nipples. I moan, my back arching away from the wall he now has me pinned against, thrusting myself deeper into his hands.

I kiss him again, our tongues dancing and swirling, licking and sucking, teasing and tasting. Undoing the clasp in the back, he removes my bra, sneaks a peek at me, then returns to my mouth as his hands knead, pinch, and caress me. I have no clue how long we do this for, probably because his mouth is a journey and a destination I'd love to both explore and live in.

But my body needs his attention, and he must sense this because in the next breath he pulls back and drops to his knees.

My fingers dive through the strands of his thick hair, cupping his head and holding on as he takes one of my peaked nipples into his mouth. He bites down, not hard, but with enough pressure to elicit whimpers and moans from my lips. He switches off, playing with both of my breasts before he trails lower, his mouth and tongue wetting my feverish flesh.

"Luca?" I pant, but it's a question, and he pauses, glancing up at me with a frown. "Are you... um—"

"Going to eat you out? Yes. I am. I'm dying to, actually. Unless you don't want me to."

I shake my head back and forth violently, but it's not a no. "I'd really like you to." My voice shudders and quakes, same as my body, because holy Devil's Night, it's been so long since someone has done this to me.

Luca slides my panties down my legs, helping me to step out of them one leg at a time. My fingers roughly pull on the strands of his hair as he kisses the top of my smooth mound.

Then he props my leg over his shoulder and licks me from my opening to my throbbing clit.

"Holy shit!" I cry out, my back bowing as my pussy grinds deeper into his face. It makes him smile against me like a smug bastard before he does it again and again. Plunging his tongue deep inside me, fucking me with it before replacing it with his fingers and focusing that talented tongue on my needy clit. He flicks it, sucking on it while his fingers pump in and out of me, over and over, curling, finding my spot.

It's wet and loud and oh so good. I'm a woman on the edge of losing her godforsaken mind, and I couldn't be happier about it.

He doesn't stop or slow down. The pressure intense and exquisite until I spasm around his fingers, writhing against his lips. He watches me, utterly entranced, and likely amused by how fast and hard I just came for him.

I have no shame right now, though.

He delivered on exactly what I asked of him, and I already know there's more yet to come.

Literally.

When he knows I'm done, once he's wrenched every last ounce of pleasure from my body, he rises, scooping me back up into his arms and walking me over to the bed. Laying me down, he climbs over me, his mouth hungrily attacking mine. He's still dressed, and I'm completely naked beneath him, my heels slipping to the floor. My hands make quick work of his clothes, my heavy eyes held captive by his hard body.

"I need you inside me," I moan softly, sitting up and running my fingers along the grooves and ridges of his chest and abs. "God, your body. The way you make mine feel." My chin rises, and my eyes lock with his. "I need you inside me," I tell him again, my empty core clenching with urgency.

Instantly he goes for his wallet, and my eyes feast on his hard dick as he rolls the condom on, my tongue jutting out to moisten my lips. Luca climbs back over me, kissing a trail up my body until he reaches my mouth. Long legs wrap around his waist, tightening on his lower back in a silent plea. *Now. I need it now!*

He doesn't make me wait. His cock slides into me and nothing—goddamn nothing—in this world has ever felt so good. My eyes close, and my head falls back on a loud moan.

"So good," I pant. "You feel so good." And big. God, he's big. I feel perfect and full and fucking decadent.

"So do you," he breathes, his voice etched in pleasure and pain.

I open my eyes, drop my chin, and let go. Let him take command of my body.

Luca glides in and out of me slowly at first, savoring the way this feels. Nearly all the way out of me before thrusting back in to the hilt. Time and time again, capturing every nerve ending with each incredible slide.

And when we've both had enough of slow, when our breathing is uncontrollable, and my hands are searching frantically, and we're building up to something explosive, he pounds into me. Hard, powerful thrusts that frazzle my mind and have me gasping for air. He gives me everything he's got, our bodies moving together in perfect synchrony.

"Yes," I cry, my eyes rolling back, my fists grappling with the sheets, his skin. "Just like that. Right there. *Oh god.*"

He pumps harder, deeper, one hand on my breast pinching my nipple, the other on my hip. He fucks me without mercy, the bed banging into the wall, the sound of skin against skin our lewd soundtrack.

My body convulses around his, my back bowing completely off the bed as I cling to him, nails digging in. He stares in awe as I fall apart beneath him, then follows me, tumbling over the edge into the most perfect abyss. A husky growl sears past his lips, his grip on my hip bruising. The heavy weight of his body collapses onto me before rolling to his side so he doesn't crush me while I hold on to this bliss for a moment longer.

Panting, our breathing ragged, a smile slays my lips.

I giggle, and he peeks open an eye, staring at me with his own dopey, sated grin.

"That was fun. Can we do it again?"

His eyes meet mine, something hazy and dangerous burning in them. "I have all night to do it again," he tells me, but I know that's not what he was thinking. He's likely wondering if I'll turn out to be like the others. Begging for his number or pleading for a second round.

My heart is already a casualty of war. The last thing I need is for it to string any foolish hopes on another man who will mistreat it.

I have to remind myself of exactly what this is.

Sex.

One night with a man I know I'll never see again. And no matter what, I have to remember, that's exactly what I asked for.

3

___

Finishing off the last of my chardonnay with a hefty gulp, I set my glass down on the counter and take in my new surroundings. Home. I mean, sort of. It's a rental, but it's mine for the next year at least, and no one's name is on the lease but mine. And instead of feeling alone, or lonely, or lost, or miserable, I feel good. Maybe even... happy? Sure. Let's go with happy.

I totally deserve happy.

"We all do," I tell my wineglass because right now, I feel like it truly understands me. Like we're in this madness together.

I arrived here early this morning after very little sleep. My body is sore in an extremely intimate, wonderful way. In a way it hasn't been sore in years. Luca was everything I never knew I was missing in a lover.

Confident. Attentive. Giving. Fun. Passionate.

He wasn't kidding when he said he had all night to do it again. We did. Again and again and again. But then, around 4:00 a.m. or so, he snuck out on me while I pretended to sleep. I let him go, afraid of the awkward goodbye and how I'd feel about it.

Whatever. It's done. And it was worth all the pesky feelings I immediately pushed away.

I checked out of the hotel and came straight here, met the owner, and got the keys. She recently refurnished it, and it's an outstanding cross between Pottery Barn and Country Living. Fitting for my Texas girl heart.

But really, this place is the first thing that has felt right in my life since I married David. Our house never felt like my home. Probably because he already owned it when we met, and we only lived there a few months out of the year. We spent our lives existing out of suitcases, rental homes, or hotels. Being the wife of a professional golfer is not an easy one. Hardly as glamorous as it's made out to be. It was all sacrifice on my part. If I wanted to see my husband, that's what it took. Following him around from location to location, from tournament to tournament.

But that's all behind me now.

I can finally find myself again. Live my own life by no one else's dictation. And just as that wondrous thought flitters through my head, my phone vibrates. It's face down on the counter, but instinctively I know who it is. My beaten-down heart knows. It's why my rhythm tumbled from regular to light speed. I hesitate, staring at the now still rectangular device. The one that's seriously out to get me. *Damn him!*

Like a woman who absolutely knows better, I flip the fucking thing over and read.

I'm sitting here in our home, what was once our home, staring out at the remains of the sun over the intercoastal, and I know beyond a shadow of a doubt, I let the love of my life become my ex-wife. How did this happen to us? When did I become so careless? I'm sorry, Elle. It's so late and probably means so little to you at this point, but I mean it. Because I love you. I fucked up and I don't know how to fix this because my mistakes were many and you were right to walk out the door. But yesterday should've never happened.

I should have stopped it. Please call me. I'm dying here without you.

Staring at his words, I read them over and over and over again. And I wait for it. For that tidal wave of regret to hit me. For the urge to get up, leave this house, and hop on a flight back to Florida. It doesn't come. Funny how insignificant words feel when it's too late.

So empty.

A text, not even a call with a voicemail. No action. That's David. Passive. At least when it came to me. Not his career—no, there he was all ambition. Where were these words a year ago? Six months ago when I walked out that goddamn door? Maybe if he had put up a proper fight, he could have stopped it.

I grin wickedly as the swell of true freedom comes curling its way up my belly. I turn up the sound on my Alexa device. Kings of Leon blares out of the speaker, and I bop my head to and fro. Only... it's not really giving me what I want. I have too much restless energy to burn off, and I'm in the mood to dance it off. To shake my ass and pour myself another glass of wine because I don't start my new job until Monday, and tonight is only Saturday.

I don't even have to get up and exercise tomorrow if I don't want to. "Ha! How awesome is that sauce?" I ask the empty room of waiting boxes. "Alexa, play..." Crap, nothing comes to mind. "Something fun I can dance to?" I shrug at the tall black cylindrical device, curious to see what this wizard of modern machinery will come up with.

Two seconds later, Taylor Swift is singing her heart out to some song I've heard on the radio, and I laugh. Why not? I can't tell if it's the wine or the freedom giving me a nice warm tingly buzz, but suddenly, my robe is feeling like an extra layer I don't need.

I shirk it off, tossing it over the back of the barstool in my kitchen as I make my way over to the refrigerator. I'm only in my bra, panties, and hot pink fuzzy knee socks because Massachusetts is cold this time of year at night, but it hardly matters at the moment.

I could dance around my kitchen naked, and no one would be the wiser.

Pouring myself another topper of Chardonnay, I close the fridge with my hip, causing the contents inside to rattle. I take a sip, staring around my new digs with an analytical eye. Boxes. I have like ten boxes and just how on earth did I accrue all this stuff? Most of it is clothes, I know. Clothes I should have donated because I am one hundred percent positive I'll never wear another collared golf shirt again. Or a tiny tennis skirt. The designer yoga pants I'll keep because let's be honest, they're damn comfortable.

But everything else from my former trophy-wife life?

Au revoir!

Turning the music up louder, I let myself go. My hands fly above my head, my hips swaying back and forth. I jump all around, sliding this way and that as my pink socks skid across the smooth wood floor. I do my best to belt it out along with Tay-Sway, using my fist as an imaginary microphone, even though I don't know the lyrics all that well.

I don't care, and I doubt Tay does either.

We have something in common, she and I. Evidently, she's never ever getting back together with her ex and that makes two of us.

I love it when things like this happen. When the perfect song comes on at the perfect moment, and you realize fate could be a real thing. That maybe even though life kinda sucks, some higher force out there gets your misery, and they're letting you know you're not alone. Or maybe I'm just a little drunk at this point. Two nights in a row of drinking is not my usual thing, but again, whatever.

Lifting my glass of wine to my lips, I take a sip just as the doorbell rings. The unexpected sound startles me, jostling the glass in my hand and spilling about half its contents onto the hardwood floor.

"Shit," I mutter. What a waste of wine.

Staring down at the mess on the floor, I decide to let it go when the ringing persists. Quickly throwing back on my bathrobe—since I'm practically naked—I abandon my spill and scurry over to the door.

"Who is it?" I call out because I'm not expecting anyone. My friend Bridget is home with her husband and kids right now, and she's the only person I know in this town. Hell, she's the reason I'm even here.

"Um. Yeah. My name is Landon Fritz. I live next door. I have one of your boxes, I think."

Oh. I pause, my hand on the doorknob. The problem with this house I'm just now discovering is that there's no window to peer out into the front porch, nor is there a peephole. And the door is thick as hell—the man sounded like he was speaking to me from space. I glance down at my purple robe and fuzzy pink socks. This is not exactly how I wanted to meet any of my neighbors.

Too late now.

I flip the latch on the deadbolt, unlock the doorknob, and open the door against the cool Massachusetts wind. My eyes land on the box first, which is nowhere even remotely close to the way it no doubt was when the shipping company picked it up. The left side is completely dented in, the clear tape on top and bottom barely in place. In fact, the bottom half must've been mangled up into a ball.

One corner of the box appears to have been... chewed on? And is also... wet?

"Did you kick it off a bridge before deciding to try and eat it for dinner?" I ask, tilting my head as I examine it further. The man does not laugh, though I can't help my small incredulous chuckle at the state of my box.

Especially considering what's in it.

Unfortunately, it's labeled. My housekeeper in Miami was very literal and old-fashioned, and she always referred to my undergarments as unmentionables. So that's what this box says on the top of it in big bold black letters. ELLERY'S UNMENTIONABLES. A box that I—and I'm positive this neighbor—now know contains all of my panties and bras.

Panties and bras I would rather this stranger not see.

"No," is all he says, but the thickness of his rough, rumbling timbre mixed with a deep whiskey baritone has my eyes drawing up. And up. And oh my God. I stare at him, unable to blink. How much did I drink tonight? Or maybe I'm having a stroke? Or this is a dream, right?

This is obviously a dream.

Why else would Luca, my one-night stand, be here holding my box?

"Is this a joke?"

"No." Again with that word.

"Why did you say your name is Landon?" He did say that, right? I'm nearly positive.

"I, um..."

Oh my holy hell, did he give me a fake name last night?

"Wait, are you Landon or Luca?"

"Listen..." He growls, clutching the box tighter. "Yes, I'm Landon. Luca is my twin brother. But..." He trails off, angry and frustrated. I stare up into those glaring green eyes, as if I'm the problem here. No, that's not even strong enough for the magnitude of his scowl. It's more as if I'm Hitler reincarnated, and I just kicked him in the nuts.

What the hell is going on? How did he know where I live?

It's as if I'm watching an invasion of aliens land on earth. This cannot be real. This cannot be happening.

"How did you get my box? Did you follow me?"

"I didn't follow you. I live next door."

And he's not happy about that either. His expression and tone tell me the prospect of being neighbors is a hazard of epic proportions. Honestly, I'm not that jazzed about it myself. He was supposed to be one night and gone. Never to be heard from or seen again.

Most definitely not part of my fresh start.

But wait...

If he's Landon and Luca is his twin, then I slept with his twin and not him? I study him closer. No. That's not right. This is him. I'm certain it is. I may not know his twin, but my body recognizes him. Not only that, he's not pretending he's never seen me before. As a twin myself, I know what being identical is like. What people mistaking you for the other is like.

That's not what this is.

This was him pulling a con on a woman who didn't know better.

I stare a little harder into his eyes and yes, there's that freckle I noticed last night. This is him. No doubt in my mind.

I blink, rocking back as I attempt to put all the pieces together. I should have Googled him, but I didn't. Again, one night and a fresh start. Also, I didn't know his last name until now. He looks so much taller than he did last night. Maybe it's my lack of heels, but wow. He's huge. Landon Fritz has to be at least six-three if not taller.

Landon Fritz. Luca Fritz. What the fuck?

Adjusting the large awkward box in his arms, holding it tighter to his chest—arms and chest I explored last night—he glares almost accusingly. His green Henley matches his eyes perfectly, only dark-rimmed glasses frame those gorgeous eyes tonight. Those are new to me, as is the colder than ice expression he's giving me.

"You lied to me."

"You live here?" he replies instead of addressing my accusation. "That whole thing about moving to a new town? This is what you meant?"

I nod numbly, chewing furiously on my bottom lip. I'm not sure what to do about this. He blows out a blustery breath, his head falling back as he stares aimlessly up at the night sky.

"Fuck," he hisses.

"Yeah. Fuck. That's what we did not even twenty-four hours ago, and that's exactly what this situation is. Why did you lie to me about your name? About who you are?"

His chin drops. "It's a long story, and if I tried to explain it to you, you wouldn't understand."

Well, that pisses me off. I shift my weight onto my right foot, crossing my arms over my chest. "Try me. I may talk slow, but I can assure you, I'm not."

He grunts. "That's not what I meant. Listen, I'm sorry I lied to you about who I was. But in fairness, I wasn't supposed to see you again, so truly, what does it matter?"

Right. I guess he's right about that. But still... "You told me you were someone else before we had sex. I said your name. Your brother's name. What we did..." I shake my head. "The sex might not have meant anything but lying..." I shake my head again, at a total loss for words. I feel cheap and used and gross and stupid.

Everything I've felt for the last two years of my marriage to David.

I take a step back, needing distance from this cruel, deplorable man.

"You're such an unbelievable asshole! Who does that? Who pretends to be their brother while picking up women?"

He glances toward what I presume to be his house and then back at me. "You don't know me, okay? You don't know who or what I am here. But others, they do. They know everything, and I did what I had to do to protect myself and my family."

My eyebrows furrow. That doesn't even make sense.

"You're right. I don't know you, nor do I want to," I blurt out because I'm not sure what else I'm supposed to say at this point. His lack of remorse is killing me. "I can't believe I thought you were sweet and charming. I thought you were a decent guy. You're none of those things. You're a user and a liar."

"You didn't talk to me long enough to determine if I was any of those things." He glowers at me, his tone harsh and unforgiving. "You got what you wanted as much as I did. What difference does it make who we said we were?"

Because by lying you make me feel worthless. Not even good enough to deserve your real name. Only I can't make the words come out.

He grunts again. "It doesn't matter. It's probably better if you think of me this way."

"Fine. We can make it like it never happened. That was in a different town, in a different place. We were different people." I snort derisively. "Obviously."

His chin drops, and his eyes meet mine. I don't know what that expression is now. It's not anger or disappointment necessarily. It's not relief either. All I know is that the smile from last night is gone. And so is the man.

In his place is this surly, heartless person, and I can't stand it.

He just stands here, gripping my box as he does a sweep of my ensemble. He finds my socks first before lingering on the hem of my robe, and once he locates my eyes, he's even more displeased than seconds ago.

"I'm sorry," he apologizes, not sounding sorry at all. "My brother's dog is staying with us, and he got to your box before I could stop him."

Right. My box. "Your identical twin brother? Is that the one you mean?" I sneer. Wait... did he say *us*? Is he married? Is that why he used his brother's name? Holy shit. Did I just become the other woman? Is he so callous and disgusting that he cheated, only to sneak out and come back home to his wife?

The backs of my eyes and the tip of my nose burn with tears and humiliation. I didn't shed a tear in front of David, and I'll be damned if I do now in front of this stranger.

But before I can formulate a response. Before I can take my ruined box from his large, partially outstretched hands. Before I can even grow more irate about his lack of remorse over lying or damaging something that doesn't even belong to him, or the crappy way he's treating me, a loud, heavy bark catches my attention. A startled shriek rips through the air, and it takes me a second to realize that sound came from me. My eyes widen as a giant black bear comes barreling across the front lawn in my direction.

"Gulliver. No!" Landon yells. "Stop. Gulliver!" The dog doesn't listen. It's a beast on a mission. Landon awkwardly juggles my box as he attempts to shift his position and grab ahold of the dog before he reaches me.

He fails.

The box goes flying in the air, crashing onto the stone front step, and smashing open with all of my bras and panties strewn every which way.

But all of that is more of an afterthought as Gulliver slams into me, knocking me down onto my back just inside the threshold of the house. The dog climbs up, getting right in my face, his large paws planting themselves on my chest. He barks playfully, licking my cheeks and nose like I'm made of hamburgers.

I giggle, trying to push the love lush off me. My best friend growing up had a dog like this. English Mastiffs are my absolute favorites, and this one is the epitome of a gentle giant. But he is a giant. Gulliver indeed. A heavy one. With nails that are digging into my flesh.

"Come on, boy. You've already gotten us into enough trouble." Landon tugs once, but this dog is persistent. "I think you've had enough fun for one night. Off," he commands with the same shrill tone he's used on me tonight.

Landon finally manages to drag the overzealous dog begrudgingly off me, and I use the sleeve of my robe to wipe my face. My smile is uncontainable for exactly one more second. That's when two things happen simultaneously.

One: My phone rings from inside.

Two: A cool breeze hits my skin. My fully exposed skin.

I realize that's likely fucking David calling, but more irritating than that is how my robe is now sprawled wide-open and my asshole new neighbor is getting a front-row view of me in nothing but my unmentionables.

Awesome. What nightmare would be complete without this?

4

In my previous life, I must have killed a priest. Or a nun. Or maybe Jesus himself. Because I'm forever tortured in this one. It's like life has a vendetta against me. A secret pledge to make anything that could potentially be good—wonderful even—bad.

Not just bad. Awful. Fucked to the worst degree.

You'd think there would be a limit on that sort of thing, but evidently, there isn't.

I stand immobile except for my hand that's restraining Gulliver. I'm like a coach trying to hold back a prizefighter from flying back into the ring for another round, and Gulliver is not happy about being kept away. He's going nuts. Barking and lunging with his front paws kicking wildly in the air as I'm forced to contain him by his collar.

He's half choking, sniffing, while making that strangled noise dogs make, but it doesn't seem to bother him.

"Fuck," is all I can manage because even though I try looking away, I can't.

I stare for exactly three full seconds. Three solid seconds longer than I should before I finally tear my gaze away. Three seconds of pure, unrestrained heaven. Of flashbacks to last night in rapid succession.

Of all the ways I took her, how she tasted on my tongue, the sounds she made.

Now, I can't get the images out of my head. My new neighbor—I can't even go there yet—is still on her back in her thin, white, lacy panties and bra with her small, perfect tits spilling out of the top. Her long, honey-colored hair is strewn about. Her cheeks are flushed. Her lips parted.

She's the ultimate vision of sex.

My live-action porn, only better. *Definitely better.*

It's why my eyes are now trained up on the gutters lining her roof.

Her body is like... nope. Not gonna think about what her body is like. Because I'm already sporting a chub from those three perfect seconds. Any more introspection into our shared night, and I'll very obviously be in trouble.

But Gulliver. My youngest brother Oliver's dog. He unequivocally knows a good thing when he sees it and did what I've been desperate to do since the moment I laid eyes on her again.

He licked her. He de-robed her. He climbed on top of her like he was staking a claim to the entire male population.

I mentally shake myself. The hell is wrong with me?

Truth, I think I just need to get out more. That's all this is.

Her phone is ringing from inside her house, but if she notices it, she doesn't seem to care. Elle scrambles to sit up, closing her robe and tying it off.

Then she races to gather up her scattered garments, and I follow suit, feeling guilty about this predicament and what happened with her box. Except... I spot a red lace thong. And a hot pink one. And a baby pink one that has tiny pink and white polka dot bows up the string in the back of it. And something black that is basically assless, which goes to show you they have created panties I haven't even begun to imagine yet.

Except now that's precisely what I'm doing. Imagining them. On her.

My eyes flitter about her underwear, some hanging from a bush, others littered about in every damn color of the rainbow. Then back to her. Her cheeks are dusted in pink, but I can't tell if it's embarrassment or anger.

She doesn't bother peeking up at me, though I know she can tell I'm staring.

"Do you want help?" I offer. I had meant to help, but then I realized I'd have to touch her panties and bras and that ended that.

"I think you've done enough," she snaps. "Just go."

"Elle—"

"Shut up," she seethes, visibly at the end of her rope. Her eyes sear a path up to mine. "Just shut up. Don't say my name. You don't know me, and I sure as hell don't know you. Now go!"

I stumble back a step, unblinking, still holding on to Gulliver, who's finally calming. Fuck.

She returns to her underwear, shoving thongs and bras into the box, hoping, praying I'll just leave. I should. I need to. She hates me and has every right to. But more importantly, I need to let her. Last night was last night, and this isn't that. This is the real world. My world.

A world where the only woman in my life is my daughter because I killed the only other one who mattered.

Before I can do something else stupid, like apologize again, I storm off.

Gulliver resists me as I drag him back into the house and slam the door shut. For a dog that's typically well behaved, he's throwing a toddler-sized tantrum now.

"Knock it off," I demand. "Do you have any idea what you just did? The trouble you got us into?"

Only it wasn't Gulliver's fault. It was mine.

If she didn't hate me for giving her Luca's name instead of

mine, she certainly hates me now that my brother's dog disrobed her on her front porch.

I saw her last night, but that was in the dark. Tonight with the porch light on her...

I release Gulliver, who quickly books it through the house, scurrying over to his water dish in the kitchen. He laps it up like he hasn't had a drink in years.

"You deliver her package?" Stella calls out as I drift toward her voice. She's sitting at the bar in the kitchen, her face in a book and a half-eaten cookie on her plate, though her milk glass is empty.

"Yes." I walk over to the cabinet and take out a glass, filling it with ice and water from the door of the Subzero. My back is to my daughter as I do, but I can feel her staring into me. "Gulliver got out. I must have left the door open a crack without realizing it."

"I didn't notice. Sorry. Was she nice?"

"How did you know she was a she?"

Stella snickers. "If the name on the box wasn't a dead give-away, only a woman would have a box labeled unmentionables. Such a weird way to call your underwear."

True, and when Elle saw the label, she rolled her eyes derisively, so I wonder if she was even the one to write it. It's sort of prudish, and I already know there's nothing prude about that woman.

"So, was she?" Stella presses when I don't answer.

"What?"

"Nice, Dad. Was she nice?"

"You thinking about dating her?"

She snorts at that. Stella came out to us a few months back. One night at dinner, she told me she was a lesbian, and I hugged and kissed her, told her I loved her no matter what, and that I was proud of her for telling me something so important. I explained I don't care who she loves as long as she's happy.

That seemed to give her confidence because she went on and told the rest of our family, including her aunt and uncles, my parents, and her BFF Layla, who also happens to be Oliver's girlfriend Amelia's little sister.

Everyone had the same reaction I did.

"Yeah, Dad," she smarts. "I'm sure she's of a perfect age for me to date. You're deflecting."

"Since when do you care about whether or not our new neighbor is nice?" I persist.

"Since now. Just tell me."

I turn around and catch the small smile she's failing to contain as it finds its way to her lips, her blue eyes—the same shade as her mother's—sparkling. It's almost as if she knows something I don't, but I can't figure out what it could possibly be. There were no photos taken of me with Elle last night. I Googled and had Luca check as well. It's why we go to that damn bar. People may recognize us there, but they already have enough wealth and influence and ego of their own to bother showing off a Fritz spotting.

So it's not as if Stella knows I was with her last night.

"I didn't exactly talk to her long, Bellas."

"Is she going to be my new Roberta?"

Ah, now I understand why she's asking me all these questions. Roberta was the previous tenant of that house, and, well, Stella's nanny, I guess to some degree. Since my mom was diagnosed with recurrent breast cancer several months back and has been recovering from surgery and dealing with chemo, she doesn't come by as often in the afternoons to be with Stella while I'm working. Roberta had been that person, more just ensuring Stella lacked nothing, occasionally hanging out, but then she moved.

Now Elle is next door.

"No. She won't be your new Roberta." *Over my dead fucking body.* "We'll have to figure something else out with that."

I take a sip of my water, hoping she gets the hint and stops asking me about her. I knew I was getting a new neighbor when I ran into Sarah Cutty, the woman who owns the house. This is a small town. A suburb of Boston, yes, but still a small town. The type where everyone knows everyone and their business—especially my business.

It's one of the few things I hate about this place.

But what Sarah failed to mention is that the new neighbor is the same leggy woman with soulful hazel eyes and bee-stung lips I slept with. That I lost myself inside of.

I foolishly assumed the woman moving in would be a hundred and ten with a gray bun on top of her head and reading glasses perched on the end of her nose like Roberta was or maybe even a family since the house is big. Too big for one person.

I saw the moving van pull up. Some box storage company arrived this morning with her stuff, and that's precisely when I left. Saturday mornings Stella likes to ride horses at my parents' compound, and I like her having one-on-one time with her grandmother.

What I didn't consider was Gulliver. Oliver took Amelia and Layla, who lives with them, away this weekend, and Stella loves Gulliver, so we offered to take him.

Only somehow one of Elle's boxes found its way to my front porch. And when I arrived back home, her box was mangled, nearly beyond recognition. Hence me being forced to knock on her door to deliver said ruined box. I hadn't readied myself. The last thing I expected was to see her again. And the absolute last thing I expected was to feel this painful twist in my chest when I realized who she was.

I've felt guilty from the second she believed I was Luca. All last night while we talked. Flirted. When she cried out his goddamn name and not mine. Guilt. It's certainly not new for me. It's my closest companion and darkest nemesis.

But this sort of guilt is different than my norm.

Because last night when I was with her, I wasn't a single dad, heartbroken and ruined and so miserable with everything, I can hardly stand my reflection. I wasn't quite Luca either, but I was certainly more carefree than I can remember being since Reese died.

Elle was fun and beautiful and fuck, she felt so good.

Could tonight have gone any worse?

But I'd rather have lied to Elle about my name than have had Stella find out what I was up to.

"I'm not a baby, you know," Stella interjects, snapping me out of my reverie.

"I know you're not." I cross the kitchen, dropping my elbows onto the counter beside her. "If anything, it's because I worry about you spending so much time alone."

"The kids in my school are lame."

I grin. "I know, but maybe you'll find a group this year."

"Doubt it. Highly doubt it."

"You need females to talk to about stuff, and I'm not very good at being a woman."

Stella laughs at my lame dad joke as I knew she would, dropping her temple onto my shoulder. "I have Grandma and Aunt Rina for that stuff. And now Layla and Amelia too."

But you don't have a mom. And that's my fault.

"I'm going to bed," she announces just as a yawn slips past her lips. It's Saturday night. She spent her Friday night with her uncle and tonight at home reading. As much as I hate to admit it, at thirteen, she should be out more. Going to the mall or having sleepover parties with friends. She has Layla, but Layla is a year older and in high school.

Stella is in eighth grade.

Part of me wonders if my permanent bad temper and universal dismay for the world is rubbing off on her.

She gets up, shutting off the kitchen lights, and I follow her, my glass of water in hand.

Gulliver trails along, the click of his nails on the floors filling the silent dark house as we ascend the stairs. "Night, Bellas. Love you." I kiss the top of Stella's head as we reach her door.

"Night, Dad. Love you."

My baby. Some days, she's all that keeps me going. My perfect girl. I just wish I could make it easier for her. All of it. The missing half of her soul where her mother should be.

Gulliver enters her room right on her heels, having taken to sleeping at the foot of her bed. "Watch over our girl," I tell him just as Stella closes the door in my face, giving me the teenage eye roll I've come to expect from her right before she does.

I head straight for my bedroom at the end of the hall. Setting my glass on my nightstand, I flop down on my bed only to sit straight back up when my neighbor's bedroom light flicks on, casting a yellow shadow across my floor. How could I have forgotten her bedroom window faces mine? I groan, wishing our houses weren't as close as they are. Big houses built on long, narrow lots.

Typically there's a tree separating us, but this time of year, the leaves are falling, and her light shines directly into my room from a mere thirty feet away.

Flashes of her on her back, her panties and bras strewn about, flicker unabatingly through my head. Then it morphs. Me on my knees, her heeled foot dangling over my shoulder as I tasted her.

Shit. I run a hand through my hair, clenching the back of my neck in a tight squeeze. I need to get a grip and fast. I force myself up and off my bed, brushing my teeth and getting ready for bed, toeing off my jeans and throwing my long-sleeved shirt in the direction of the closet.

Her light is out by the time I draw back the sheets and slip into the comfort of my cool bed.

But in the darkness that surrounds me, everything is amplified.

Which is probably why I can hear her crying.

Even a house away.

Jesus. She's crying. Did I do that?

No. I don't have that sort of power. *Do I?*

Climbing back out of bed, I drift over to my open window, pressing my fingers against the screen, unable to stop myself from listening to her even though I know it's wrong. My head falls against the mesh before I can stop it. The wire crossbar pattern digs into my skin. It's cool tonight, but not cold. Pleasant, and it seems I'm not the only one who likes to sleep with their window open.

Gasping sobs climb their way out of her house, carrying on the breeze into mine. They're suffocatingly beautiful. Achingly sweet. Painfully exquisite.

They breach my divide and enter me. Burrowing into places I wish she didn't have access to. I saw her heartache last night. Watched her frown. It disturbed me then, and it disturbs me now. Is this about her ex or something else? And why do I want to know so bad?

What is it about her?

A woman I barely know.

I close my eyes and draw in a deep, shuddering breath. Her sobs pull at me. Find the dark spot I've systematically shut down over the years. I don't want to feel what she's feeling, but I can't force myself to walk away either. That sweet, bubbly, beautiful woman who is all sunshine, honesty, and dry humor is drowning in sadness.

Is her world as ugly as mine? I hope not. Then I think of Stella, and a reluctant smile curves up the edges of my lips. My bright light. My sun.

My hand comes up to my chest, rubbing the tight spot the sound of Elle's tears elicits. And even though this feels wrong, like I should shut my window and give her the privacy she thinks she has, I can't. Because I know that pain. I understand the tortured thoughts that accompany it. They've become my most intimate friends.

That crying is heartbreak.

It's, I don't know how I found myself here and I'm scared. It's, will my life ever be right again? It's tragedy in its most intrusive form.

A jagged knife slices me directly through the heart. And for just a few moments, I allow myself to bleed with her. But once those few minutes are up, I close my window, lock it up, and get back in bed. Setting my mind straight. I have no space for someone like her in my life. No desire for it either.

So she can go right along hating me.

I'll make sure of it.

5

"**U**gh." I hate everything. As happy as I'd been before that cursed doorbell rang, I'm just as miserable now, lying here in bed on Sunday morning. Tomorrow is my first day of school, and I'm so excited about it. At least, I should be.

I'm going to be teaching.

A gift of a job I do not deserve nor am qualified for but will happily take and kick its ass.

But all my enthusiasm has evaporated, drained out of me.

My parents got their claws into me first. Evidently, David had called them and given them the skinny on my exodus. Bastard wasn't even fighting fair. He knew I hadn't told them yet about our divorce. I was saving that for Thanksgiving. You know, drop the big bomb while indulging in turkey and mashed potatoes. That might sound cruel, and before you judge, my parents always liked David more than me. Let me amend that. They always like any man with money and connections more than me.

Hell, they like their freaking financial advisor more than me.

To say I have a strained relationship with my family is an understatement. It's been that way all my life, except for my nana, rest her soul. Whatever twin-bond Landon and Luca have, I don't share with my own. We're strangers, opposites with the same face. I haven't seen her and have barely spoken to her since my wedding—one of the many, many reasons we don't keep in touch.

The long and the short of my conversation with my parents went like this:

"We spoke to your *husband*, and he said he'd welcome you back with open, loving arms if you leave whatever bad situation you've gotten yourself into in Boston and return to Miami. He's set to leave for the Ryder Cup soon and needs you with him. Divorce is a sin, and you have to take it back." That was my mom, and she does not have a religious bone in her body.

"Yes, sweetie." That was my father, and he's never called me sweetie in his life. "He can't win the Ryder Cup without you. You're the hope America is riding on." He chuckled at his miserable pun. "He said you were his good luck charm. You're lucky he still loves you, Elle. Not many men would be willing to take on a woman like you."

I was tempted to ask, have you met my sister? Every guy takes her on without realizing the death-defying leap they're taking and half of them end up in a shallow grave—not literally. At least I don't think so.

I mentally rolled my eyes at them as I finished the last of my wine and cleaned up my new kitchen. I ignored the direct barb as best as I could. Their love has always been small and conditional.

"Maybe you should have advised David that treating me like smeared dog shit on the bottom of his shoe wasn't the way to keep a wife. Considering I better fit the role of verbal punching bag than lover or spouse, I'm sure he can find someone else to accompany him and help win his precious cup."

Am I bitter? You fucking bet I am.

Because what the hell?

I mean, aren't parents supposed to be on your side? Yes. They are. But mine never were. The moment I met David, they pushed me down the aisle. He's rich, successful, handsome, and charming. Did I mention rich? It was like Elle had found herself a golden ticket in the form of a man, and anything else was superfluous.

Completely overlooked.

Like me.

"Don't be crass, Ellery. David is under a lot of stress with his career. A career that has provided nicely for you. You'd think the least you could be is supportive of your *husband*. People make mistakes. He regrets the way he spoke to you."

I snorted. Right. The way he spoke to me. Like it was a one-time thing. And what about the hundreds of other times? What about the rapid deterioration of my soul, a soul he claimed like the grim reaper and crushed beneath the sole of his golf spikes? If he didn't play well, it was my fault. If he did play well, he could have done better, and again, it was my fault.

He never physically hurt me because that leaves evidence behind.

No, he was a vampire, siphoning the life and blood from my body, only he did it slowly, systematically, alternating it with periods of love and devotion so I wasn't sure if what I was seeing, experiencing was real or just imagined. He was good at that. Messing with my head. Only after the first two years of our marriage, after his success climbed higher and higher, all that love and devotion died, and I simply became his metaphorical punching bag. The thing he used to belittle and cut at in order to make himself feel better.

This was the moment I literally contemplated throwing my

phone across the kitchen to see if it would crash through the glass sliding door or just fall to the ground and break. Aren't marriages supposed to be two-sided? Aren't love and respect in said marriage supposed to be two-sided? I couldn't wrap my head around the idea that my parents didn't even *care* that my husband had treated me so poorly.

Why did it all fall on me?

Why was it my responsibility to make our marriage work when he never tried?

Why did David have no culpability in this?

Because he earned the dollars, and I didn't? Who gives a fuck?!

Money and stress are not excuses to treat someone like they're nothing.

"Mom. Dad." I took a breath, debating whether or not I should tell them everything. Explain to them what a soul-sucking, selfish prick my husband was. Clue them into how the 'stress' of his career turned him into a mean, belligerent SOB. To this day, I've never told a soul how evil and cruel that man can be. How eviscerating simple words are when they're slung from the mouth of a man you love, who claims to love you. Instead, I said, "I don't love him anymore, and I'm done with our marriage. We finalized our divorce on Friday. It's done and so are we." There. Eat those apples.

Silence. They were freaking silent.

"You're making the biggest mistake of your life, Ellery. What will you be if not David Chambers' wife? A history teacher is a lowly profession, meant for mothers or spinsters. It's not even a career. You're nothing but a disappointment. Cat is everything you're not."

"You mean a liar and a thief? I know."

"A daughter who cares about her family. You're nothing without David. Go back to him now before it's too late."

That was the official moment my heart broke.

Because I can be so many things. I *want* to be so many things. And I'm not disappointed in myself. I'm proud. I left an awful marriage and a bad situation. Honestly, in leaving David, I feel like I can do anything with my life. This is my renaissance. The same idealistic way you ask an eight-year-old what they want to be when they grow up, and they reply with pop star or ballerina.

What limits do I have on myself now?

None. I can do this new job for a year or two or however long I want. I can save money, and I can move to freaking Paris or Brazil. It doesn't matter. Because my life is open to me.

I get to call the shots. Not David.

And whatever bullshit my parents were spewing about Cat was just that. Bullshit. She and David were so equally matched, if they ever bred children, they'd be scarier and more vicious than anything any paranormal author could conjure.

I hung up on my parents. Two minutes later, David called, obviously my parents having clued him into my conversation with them.

This was the point in the night where he professed his love for me. Again. Told me just how sorry he was. How he'd never meant to hurt me and that he'd never treat me poorly again. Only, I'd heard the exact same speech before. Several times even. And while he was delivering it last night, I know for a fact that the golf channel was on. He was watching highlights of himself because that's what he loved to do most.

Narcissism at its finest.

But it also meant he wasn't all that broken up about losing me. He just didn't want to deal with our divorce becoming public—something it hasn't been yet because we kept it quiet —and him looking bad.

I discovered this was his main reason when he threatened to bash me to every news network and trashy magazine rag in the country and take me back to court to fight the money he gave me in the divorce. I told him to go for it. Fuck his money. I have a job. And I have a savings account from before David and I married—albeit small.

He can trash me if he really wants to be that petulant.

Add to that the encounter with Landon.

Landon. Not Luca. No. That I didn't expect. Especially when it was the opposite of how he was when we met. Then again, he was looking to get laid, so obviously the man I met last night is the real Landon and the one who took me to bed in the hotel was an impostor.

That messed with me on a whole other level.

I Googled him last night. Both of them. All kinds of things came up about the Fritz family. Billionaires. Bachelor playboys. Boston royalty. Their faces were splashed everywhere—a gorgeous group of men too. But with it, I remember why he was familiar to me. I had met Luca Fritz at some charity event David went to in Baltimore. It was a passing hello and four years ago.

But it wasn't Luca I slept with. It was Landon.

My new neighbor and all-around heartless asshole.

So yeah, I don't want to get out of bed this morning. My face feels puffy, and I'm still reeling from my pity party that left me in miserable tears—I blame the chardonnay for that. But instead of wallowing over the fact that I'm alone in this world, divorced at the tender age of twenty-seven, living in a town I know nothing about, and have only one friend to my name, I pull my raggedy ass out of bed, get dressed, and head to the local garden center. There, I purchase myself a boatload of bulbs.

And it is with these beautiful bulbs that I now find myself digging through the dirt beds of my front lawn. Sure, I don't own this home, but my landlady gave me the green light to plant, so that's what I'm doing. Because I'm determined to still be living here in the spring when these suckers bloom. When all these beautiful multicolored tulips, crocuses, and daffodils sprout.

Wiping my forehead of the sweat it's accrued, I sit back on my haunches and survey my work. I might have gone a bit overboard with the planting, but can a person go overboard with flowers? They're pretty.

For the last hour and a half I've been toiling in the September sun, I've forced myself not to peer over at Landon's house. It's been a challenge, let me tell you. First of all, these houses are super close to each other. Like, the side of my house is less than thirty feet from the side of his.

It's a problem.

At least for the way my mind likes to wander to our night in the hotel. He may have been ruder than sin last night, but unfortunately, when he looked at me, I still felt that spark. There was heat in his eyes, even before I disrobed.

It's been so long since I felt anything that remotely resembled a spark or electricity or even freaking attraction. *So. Long.* I've been a starved woman left alone on a deserted island with no food or water to satiate me. So this whole not peeking next door to see if I can glimpse the hot neighbor who screws like a dirty demon and admittedly wants nothing to do with me?

It's not going so well.

My eyes have a mind of their own. Like right now as I squint, trying like a crazy woman to peer in through his window for a chance to spot him. Hell, I don't even know if he's home right now.

Dammit, did he have to lie to me? Did he have to be so cold and unfeeling? I hate him for what he did and how he treated me after, and yet I'm intrigued by him. But any intrigue I feel is a ruse. It's part of the lie he propagandized. I've had enough of men mistreating me. The last thing I need is to go looking for more in a man like Landon Fritz.

Dignity, Elle. Right. *You don't need men. They need you.* Obviously. Of course.

I square my shoulders and resume my digging, only to gasp out a loud, startled shriek when someone asks, "What are you planting?" from directly behind me.

I twist around and peer up, shielding my eyes from the intrusive sun. My other dirt-covered hand goes to my chest to calm my racing heart. It takes me a second to focus until I realize I'm staring at a young girl with stormy blue eyes set atop round, rose-tinted cheeks and full, pale lips. Her chestnut brown hair is nearly down to her waist in soft mermaid waves, and she's wearing a cropped green T-shirt that hits right at her waist, jeans, and a big, bright smile.

She's beautiful in a very classic way.

Like a starlet from The Golden Age of Hollywood.

She also looks insanely familiar, though I'm positive I've never seen her before. "Hi," I squeak. "You scared me."

"I did. Sorry. Wasn't exactly what I was going for. But I saw you digging, and I was curious. I'm Stella," she introduces, extending her hand to me.

Very proper for a girl who cannot be older than twelve or thirteen. "So very nice to meet you, Stella. I'm Ellery, but you can call me Elle."

I stand, staring helplessly down at my dirty gloved hands, and then hastily remove them so I can shake her tiny one. I study her a moment longer as we shake.

"I live there." She points to Landon's house. "You met my dad last night."

Well, that explains why she looks so familiar. I can't help it. I blush. I had sex with this girl's father not even two days ago, and last night he saw me mostly naked again. Does she know? I doubt it. I can't imagine Landon goes around telling his daughter that sort of thing. I hope.

"You look just like your dad."

She smiles even wider at that, releasing my hand and surveying my flower beds with a scrutiny that tells me she's no stranger to planting in the soil. "He says I look like my mom."

Her mom. Jesus, is he actually married? Am I going to meet her mother, his wife?! How could he cheat like that? I feel sick as I say, "Oh, I haven't met her yet."

Her smile instantly evaporates. "You won't. She's dead. Died when I was four."

Well, shit. Now I feel bad. For so many reasons I can hardly begin to think of them all.

"I'm sorry. I have a real knack for sticking my foot in my mouth."

Stella shrugs up a small shoulder. "It's fine. I'm used to it. So you're planting bulbs? You should come see my garden in my backyard. I have all kinds of things, though most of it is dying off now that we're at the end of the season. Once the pumpkins and kale are done, I'll be down to what I grow in my greenhouse."

"You have a greenhouse?"

"Yeah. My dad designed it and had it built for me."

"Wow. I'm super jealous. Do you grow just vegetables or plants too?"

She giggles lightly. "I grow both, though I end up donating most of the produce and things to local food banks. You can come see it. Some day after school would be fine."

I stare at her for a moment, wondering what I should say in response. I highly doubt her father wants me anywhere near her, let alone in their home. Not just that, but the more distance I place between myself and him, the better. But she doesn't have a mom, and she's asking to show me something that's clearly special to her. And special to me because I absolutely love growing things.

Speaking of, I wonder if she goes to the middle school I'm going to be teaching in.

"I'd love that," I tell her, curious if it will actually happen. Probably not, I decide. Kids her age throw out things and rarely follow through. "But how come you don't use any of it yourself?"

"I wish I could, but I don't know how to cook, and my dad isn't a lot of help with that."

I open my mouth to ask her more about that when someone calls her name.

Both of us whip around to find Landon standing in the middle of his front lawn, watching us. His expression is neutral enough, but his eyes, they are steel narrowed in at me, sending a chill up my spine and making my heart beat just a touch faster.

"We have to get going to the compound," he tells her.

Compound? What the blip is a compound?

Stella whirls back toward me. "I gotta go. We have Sunday dinner at my grandparents' place."

Well, I guess that explains it. But a compound? Yeesh. Billionaires indeed.

"It was nice meeting you, Stella. I'm sure I'll see you around."

"I hope so." She beams at me before running off, straight past her father, who is unmoved, and back into the house.

I twist in Landon's direction, propping my fists on my hips and tilting my head. All attitude. Challenging the asshole. He hasn't said a word to me. All he's done is eviscerate me with his darkened eyes as energy swirls between us like the coming of a storm. I squint at him, ignoring the spine-tingling jolt I feel when I'm near him.

"I'm dressed today, so if you're looking for a different visual from me, I'm sorry to say you're not getting it." I wave my hand up and down my body like a game show hostess and even do a little twist for him.

He scowls, his eyebrows tracking in as his gaze does a slow

sweep of me, taking in my bare feet, dirty yoga pants, and haphazard shirt. His scowl deepens, and I swear to God, if he makes a disparaging comment about how I look, I'll march over there and smack that scowl right off his face. With my dirty hand.

Unfortunately, this broody, growly thing he has going on also makes him look insanely hot. Life can be so unfair sometimes.

"You get your fill yet?" I bark when he still hasn't moved or said anything or stopped staring as intensely as he's staring. Like he's picturing me naked. And just the idea that he is shoots a rush of heat straight to my core.

God, he's such a jerk.

A sexy jerk who manages to make my traitorous nipples hard, but still a jerk.

He puffs out a breath, shakes his head at the ground, and without a word, spins around and marches off.

"Nice chatting with you," I yell after him, smiling at the hint of a grumble I catch. And because I can, I stare at his ass as he goes. It's only fair. I'm positive he was staring at my boobs a little longer than he should have.

I sink back down to the ground, replacing my gloves and diving back into the earth with gusto. Aggravated. Annoyed. Stupidly turned on.

I'm glad he didn't say anything.

It's just as well. Perfect even. The last thing I need is for my hot sex god of a neighbor to engage with me.

6

One hand grips the wheel, the other the back of my neck. Stella is sitting beside me, staring down at her phone and listening to something that sounds like a mouse dying on the car sound system. I'm more agitated than I was even last night. The sight of Elle—gorgeous and furious—has been driving me mad the entire ride to my parents'.

Just looking at her was a struggle.

Fucking her was supposed to alleviate the mounting itch burning through me. That's what happens every few months or so. I go out, meet a random woman, and then I'm good for another few months.

That hasn't happened with Elle.

That itch has grown. Multiplied. Taken on a life of its own.

The way the afternoon sun accentuated the hints of gold running through her hair. The flush in her cheeks. The flecks of emerald and whiskey in her eyes. The way she digs into me because I'm an asshole, and I deserve it. I lied, and she's pissed, and she has no qualms about letting me know it.

And I like that about her.

I knew it was only a matter of time until Stella sought her

out—she was already far too curious—and the fact that Elle was planting in the front beds was too much of a temptation for my little green-thumbed girl to pass up. I had been watching Elle too. The woman was digging and planting like tomorrow wasn't coming. Fierce determination lit her features as if she was setting out to prove a point and settle a score.

But every few minutes… like clockwork… she'd glance up at my house.

This is not how it was meant to be.

I was supposed to be done with her yesterday morning when I walked out of that hotel room.

Not still thinking about her.

I do my best to push it all aside as I pull down the long driveway, past the gate that leads into my parents' estate. "Grandma said I could pick out a horse for Christmas."

I cringe at that before I can stop it.

Not the horse, who would stay here in their stables. But the Christmas part of it.

My mother had told me when Stella got into riding that she'd buy her a horse for her sweet sixteen. Now it's for this Christmas, and Stella is only thirteen. My mother is worried she won't live to see Stella turn sixteen, and my insides tumble around with dread.

Her recurrent breast cancer is taking its emotional toll on all of us.

I can't lose my mother.

More importantly, Stella cannot lose her grandmother. She's Stella's only real, consistent mother-like figure. Rina does what she can, but my baby sister works long shifts as an ICU nurse and has a life of her own. My mother occasionally comes over after school to spend time with Stella—when she's feeling up to it—and goes riding with her every Saturday morning.

Stella has already lost so much. I cannot bear the thought of her losing more. Her very beloved grandmother.

"That sounds wonderful. Do you have a horse in mind?"

"No," she says as we pull around the circle that leads to the front of the main house. "She said this fall we could scope some out." She pauses here as I set my Range Rover in park. "Do you think it's because she's sick?"

My daughter is too smart. Too observant.

"I think she knows how much you love riding and wants you to have a horse of your own. I also think she wants to see you have that. To see you riding a horse that is just yours, that you'll love."

"But she'll get better, right? I mean, that's why they're giving her chemo and did that surgery?"

My chest pinches, and I reach out, grabbing a strand of Stella's impossibly long hair, giving it a gentle, playful tug. "I hope so, Bellas. I hope so. She has the best doctors in the world working to make that happen."

"Like you?"

I grin at that. "I'm a cardiologist, but yeah, like me. Like all your uncles and grandpa too."

"The new neighbor, Elle… she seems nice."

Now she wants to talk? When we're sitting in the damn driveway?

"Uh-huh."

"I wouldn't mind if she were my new Roberta. She wants to see my garden and greenhouse."

I shake my head. "I don't think that's a good idea. We know nothing about her."

She rolls her eyes. "Duh, Dad. That's why you *talk* to her instead of glare."

Nope. Not gonna make that mistake again.

"Whatever," she continues. "It was just an idea for Mondays and Wednesdays when you work late."

"I said we'd figure something else out, and we will. The last thing we need is to invite some strange woman into our lives."

"Yeah, I can see how that would be a horrible thing—"

A knock on her window cuts Stella's words off, followed by Gulliver jumping up, scratching at it.

"Down, Gulliver," Layla squeals, struggling to draw the massive dog back from my car. That beast better not have scratched the paint. "Come on, Stella. I have things to tell you. So many things, and we have to do it before dinner because Amelia is already telling me how we have to get home early because 'Oliver has an early morning at the hospital,'" she mocks her sister's voice.

All thoughts of Elle clear Stella's face as she flies out of the car, getting mauled by Gulliver, who's acting like he hasn't seen Stella in years, when Oliver only came by this morning to pick him up. Stella rubs at his head and behind his ears, and the dog turns to mush in her hands.

"Girl, Universal was epic," Layla immediately launches into. "Have you been? Harry Potter world was the coolest, though the plane might have been my favorite part. Have you ever flown on a private jet? You probably have, right? I mean, you're Stella Fritz. But this is all new to me. And damn, do you think I'll be Layla Fritz when Amelia actually does marry Oliver? How does that sort of thing work for sisters?"

Stella only shrugs because that's how she and Layla work. Layla is all energy and boundless enthusiasm, and Stella is the quiet one, more comfortable in the background than front and center. They're like sisters and best friends and cousins all mixed into one. They also both know what it's like to grow up without a mother, though Layla unfortunately lost both her parents when she was six, only for Amelia to leave college to come home and take care of her since. They struggled for years to get by, and now Oliver spoils them both rotten.

Hence the private plane to Florida for a weekend at Universal Studios.

"She hasn't stopped talking," Oliver muses, coming up

beside me, Amelia tucked under his arm, her engagement ring —that started out as fake and is now more of a placeholder— sparkles against the porch lights. "All weekend and it hasn't stopped since we got home."

"Maybe they spiked her butterbeer with speed," I quip, and both of them laugh.

Layla is still going, telling Stella about something I'm not even listening to as she drags her into the house.

"Carter sent a text," Oliver informs me as the three of us head for the door. "He said Mom isn't having a great night."

I nod, thanking him for the heads-up. "Having Grace here probably helps."

"No doubt," Rina, my baby sister, says, jogging to catch up to us, her boyfriend, Brecken, by her side. "I think Carter and Grace need to tell Mom they're having a baby. It'll mean everything to her to know she has another grandkid on the way."

Grace is Oliver's lifelong best friend and extremely close to my family. When her engagement to another guy fell apart, she ended up mistakenly knocking on what she forgot was no longer Oliver's door. Carter had bought the place from Oliver when Oliver and Amelia bought a house together. Grace and Carter work together as OB-GYNs and then ended up hooking up and accidentally got pregnant. Not that they're unhappy about it. They're head over heels for each other.

"And what about you two?" I ask because I'm the asshole and I can. "When can we expect your wedding announcement? Since we're all about doing things for Mom."

Brecken flips me off, and Rina just rolls her eyes, nudging her shoulder into me. "I'm in no rush. We're already living together. Who needs marriage?"

"I do," Brecken demands just as Oliver and I say, "He does."

"Whatever," she grumbles. "That's not happening now, so you can quit giving Brecken ideas." Pushing past us, she jogs straight into the house. She hates that question. Well, any question that is about her life or her future or her relationship.

Brecken grins. "I'm going to steal her away to Vegas at some point, get her drunk, and make her marry me."

"Very romantic," Oliver deadpans. "You could just try giving her a ring and telling her it's fake. Worked for me."

"God, men suck," Amelia asserts, but she pops up on her tiptoes to kiss Oliver's cheek. "Good thing you're hot and kill bugs for us or we'd systematically eliminate you from the planet." She gives him a wink before running off into the house as well, likely to make sure Layla and Gulliver aren't causing any trouble, which at least Layla never does. My parents are absolutely insane for their adopted granddaughter.

"Dickwads," Kaplan, our eldest brother, calls out to us as he comes out the front door, an unlit cigar hanging from his mouth, a glass of what is likely scotch in his hand. He's flanked by Luca and Carter. Carter approaches to meet us, while Kaplan and Luca stride off to one of the side porches.

"Took you fuckers long enough to get here. I wasn't sure how long we were going to stay. Grace hasn't been feeling well," Carter says, sipping at what is also likely a scotch.

"Seizures or pregnancy?" Oliver immediately asks, a note of concern in his voice. Grace is epileptic, though controlled, but I know Oliver worries about her, especially now that she's pregnant and can't take a lot of medications should she need them.

"Shhh. No one else knows yet, asshat." Carter glances over his shoulder to find the coast all clear before turning back to us. "Pregnancy. Do you think if Grace were having seizures I'd be standing here with a drink in my hand telling you she's not feeling well?"

"I'd fucking hope not," Oliver growls.

"She's fine," Carter placates. "She's in the kitchen with Sophia, who's making her eat."

"You need to tell everyone already. At least tell Mom."

Carter shakes his head. "Grace wants to wait until her twelve-week ultrasound, so we know everything is okay with the baby before we do that. Both of us being OBs is a blessing and a curse. We know everything that can go wrong. Soon, though. Only another few weeks."

Dropping his arm over my shoulder, he drags us to join Luca and Kaplan on one of the many chairs out here on the vast porch. Kaplan lights his cigar, then uses his lighter to help Carter do the same with his, puffing on it as thick plumes of cloying smoke drift up into the air. The rest of us find seats, except me. I sit on the railing of the porch, my eyes cast out to the dark grounds, illuminated only with the soft glow of in-ground lighting and the occasional lamp. Off in the distance, I catch the faintest sound of gurgling water from the fountain in the side garden.

"You have a good weekend, Landon?" Kaplan drawls, though I can tell by his tone there is nothing casual about his question. A point he proves when he follows that up with, "I heard you finally got your dick wet."

I flip him off without answering, making him chuckle as he and Carter puff on their cigars.

"You went out? To the bar?" Carter questions, and I only nod, still not bothering to look at any of my brothers or Brecken. "I would have met you for a drink."

"Same," Brecken says. "Rina was working nights all weekend."

I don't reply, but I don't have to.

"That's not why he went out," Luca answers for me.

"I got that, asshole, but I could have met up with him *before* he met up with whatever lady came onto him," Brecken finishes.

Only, Elle didn't come onto me. I came onto her.

Something I never do. Usually, I just sit at the bar and wait, and it happens for me.

Not with her, because she was different from the start.

I don't have it in me to tell my brothers anything about that night. About how I met someone who is rattling me if for no other reason than we had chemistry in bed, and she now lives next door.

"Was she good at least?" Kaplan persists, and this time I don't bother with flipping him off. I just ignore him altogether. "You're broodier and more miserable than usual, which means she must have been."

And fuck. That... That right there. That fucking *hurts*.

Because me being fully mute means I'm stewing, and me stewing means I'm so emotionally broken that I can't handle having good—let alone great—sex with a woman who isn't Reese because the guilt I feel about that overwhelms me. And everyone here knows this.

I don't want to be like this.

To still feel this perpetual guilt. A guilt that goes so far beyond grieving and heartache, it should have its own category and special name. But I don't know how to stop it either. My wife is dead because of me. Stella doesn't have a mom because of me.

There's no reconciling that, and there's no getting over it.

I stopped pretending to smile through it years ago, and now they accept that this is just how I am and what you see is what you get. Well, they accept that most of the time. But Kap's right.

I'm broodier and more miserable than I typically am.

"Back off," Luca clips out.

"You twinning up on me? Does that mean I can't give him the speech?" Kaplan presses.

"No."

That's Oliver.

"Absolutely not."

That's Brecken.

"Definitely not from an asshole who's never loved and lost

and looks like he's Stella's younger brother," Carter teases Kaplan, who looks the youngest of us despite being the oldest.

"Fuck off with that already. I look my age."

"No, you don't," Luca and Oliver say in unison.

"I have T-shirts that look older than you, brother," Luca finishes.

"Bullshit you do. Besides, you're in no place to talk about anything when it comes to age. How much younger is Raven than you? Eleven years, is it?"

Luca chuckles. "That was lame. Not even a good comeback."

"Whatever, twatwaffle. I want to hear more about this lady Landon refuses—"

"Speaking of Raven, I heard you're stalking her again." Carter shifts to Luca, interrupting Kaplan while kicking his feet up on the coffee table.

I guess now we're even. I gave Carter advice when he came to me after getting Grace pregnant, and now he's saving me by obviously changing the subject.

"She's not even home yet, and you're already all over her. Didn't you fly to New York to see her perform?"

"I'm not answering that," Luca dismisses, but the way he says that finally has me shifting my aimless gaze away from the garden over to him. "She's moving back home soon, and then I'll be able to see her whenever I want." He's frowning, and I have to imagine the reminder of the one he let get away coming back home isn't something he wants right now.

"Did she return your flowers? Again?" Oliver asks.

"What flowers? No clue what you're talking about. If you listened to her interview, she never names who sends her those with every performance."

Oliver rolls his eyes. "You think stalking her around all over the world is a good idea?" Oliver continues. "I hear women really love it when you do that. Especially scorned women who are likely to kick you in the nuts if they see you."

"Fuck you, fucker. Stalking as we all unfortunately know is often violent, and nothing I'm doing is violent."

Unfortunately, we do all know because Rina was stalked when she was in college, and it did turn violent. Violent as hell.

"Yeah, how about we don't talk about stalking?" Brecken grits out, thinking about the same thing we all are.

"Agreed." Luca nods, staring down at his tumbler as he swirls the liquid in his glass. "Besides, if Raven didn't still love me, she wouldn't still be scorned."

I can't help the minuscule smile that quirks up the corner of my mouth.

"Is that what she told you? Because last I checked she wants nothing to do with your ugly ass," Kaplan smarts, blowing smoke rings up into the air before dipping the end of his cigar in his drink and bringing it back up to his lips.

"And you talked to her?"

Kaplan grins at Luca. "Maybe I have. I'm not the one our lovely, young Raven hates above all others."

"One day, Kap, you'll unwittingly fall in love, and then your world will end because she'll own your heart and your balls."

"Sure," he agrees dismissively because he doesn't actually agree with that at all. "I'll get on that right after Landon meets another woman and falls in love."

My insides clench, twisting my black heart—the useless lump of necrotic tissue in my chest that has been a never-ending source of misery and irony in my life. A heartless heart doctor.

I stand up, done with this. "Then I guess you're safe, Kap. That'll never happen to me."

7

When you haven't worked many days in your life—and none in the last four years—your first day is fucking terrifying. Especially when you're presented with eighteen middle school students who are staring at you like you're either the bane of their existence or the answer to their prayers.

It's disarming.

We'll leave it at that.

Because I find myself standing in front of the whiteboard that doubles as a SMART board that I'm slowly learning how to use and staring back at these blinking eyes.

Did I mention I was hired to be the world and US history teacher?

Still, I hadn't considered I'd get a job that quickly. I mean, I knew I'd need one. But one hour after signing my divorce papers just didn't feel... realistic. It was. The school year had already started, and the school needed someone who could start immediately. My bachelor's is in history and my master's in education. And Bridget, my only non-David friend in the world, who happens to be a math teacher here, vouched for me.

This was about a week ago.

Which brings me to today.

My morning began like this: I walked into the school front office and was immediately ushered into the smallest office in the history—catch my pun—ever. "We have two wellness classes scheduled for you today," the main secretary, Laura, informed me as I took in my new digs. "Obviously you'll still have your regular history classes, but we're so excited you're taking this on for us."

"Um. I'm sorry. What?"

"Wellness," she said, like it all made so much sense. It didn't.

Evidently, I'm now responsible for wellness classes. As in a combination of sexual education (that comes a bit later in the semester thankfully), nutrition, mind-body wellness, and pushing the state's anti-alcohol and drug campaigns.

"So, I'm teaching wellness besides my history courses?" No one mentioned wellness when I interviewed for the history position. Then again, it was a quick phone interview, likely to make sure I wasn't psychotic and had more than two brain cells to rub together. I didn't have time to fly up here prior to starting since my divorce was literally being finalized. I'm sort of regretting that now.

"Yes. And we're so grateful you're young. We need someone the kids can relate to. The old teacher reminded me of my great-aunt Ester if you know what I'm saying."

I didn't know. I like history. I don't like teaching a bunch of pre-teens about sex.

Especially when my sex life as of late is the definition of a joke. A shitty ex-husband and a one-night stand with an asshole who gave me his brother's name instead of his own.

"The staff meeting is on the third Tuesday of every month at seven a.m., and since it's the second Monday of the month, the meeting will be next week. But tonight, as I'm sure you know, is our parent open house, so you'll likely get to meet some of the other staff and teachers around the buildings then. Plus, the parents, of course. How wonderful is that? On your first day here."

Right. Awesome. I want to vomit everywhere.

"Let's get you off to your first class," Laura said with way too much excitement in her voice and pep in her step. "I'm sorry we couldn't get you in before today to learn your way around your room, but I'm sure you'll pick everything up quickly."

At least I wasn't being thrust into sex-ed on the first day.

Just wellness. And how hard could that be?

It was nearly seven-thirty by the time I entered my classroom. I logged into the computer and played around, doing my best to learn the SMART board touch screen thing. By eight, my classroom was filling up for my eight-ten class. Pre-teens filed in one by one, talking and laughing and taking their seats and generally ignoring me while studying me at the same time.

With each new student, my heart rate went up five beats per minute. By the time the class was full, it was pumping at a solid one-eighty, and I was positive I was either going to pass out from the anxiety or die on the expensive floor from a heart attack.

Did I look like this when I was in middle school?

I'm guessing not. Because the girls—despite their uniforms consisting of brick red, gold, and black tartan skirts, white button-up blouses, and black jackets monogrammed with the school emblem—are all model gorgeous. The guys all men-children, tall, handsome, and built like they live in the gym. I thought puberty hit boys later than girls, but clearly I need to catch up on my wellness.

I couldn't figure it out.

None of these kids were awkward or self-conscious. There

were no goth girls sitting in the back eating their hair. Even the geeky boys and girls were super adorable in an emo, hipster way.

I stood on shaky legs, my palms and cleavage sweating. I was desperate to wipe my hands on my pants, but I was positive the moisture would show on my powder blue capris. I had to swallow three times and clear my throat twice before I could speak without betraying my nerves.

I'm not a wellness teacher.

I'm barely a history teacher.

I made a mental note to find Bridget and yell at her for talking me into this madness.

I introduced myself. Explained why I was in their class instead of their regular teacher and informed them I was taking on the role of wellness and history teacher for the year. I elucidated how I was planning on following the curriculum with my own small twists to update it, then I dove into my totally off-the-cuff speech about the beauty and importance of wellness.

A hand rose in the air almost instantly. "Are you a board-certified doctor?"

"No," I replied. "I have a bachelor's in history and a master's in education."

Another hand. "How does that make you qualified to teach us about nutrition and exercise? Because my mom's life coach tells me I need to work on eliminating carbs and intermittent fasting if I want to reach my ultimate weight goal."

I wanted to find that life coach and strangle them.

"Nutrition and *health*," I stressed, "are all things I'm very committed to and studied extensively in graduate school." That was kind of a lie, but they had no clue.

And so it went. I spent the first twenty minutes of my very first class dodging the bullets these over-privileged students launched at me. Evidently, the previous teacher who taught this before me often lamented about how wellness was a crock of shit and in her day, people smoked, drank, and ate butter by the pound, and no one was worse for it.

I'm keeping my opinions to myself on that—you know, since she dropped dead of a heart attack. My day did not improve. My history classes ended up being worse than my wellness classes. Especially this one.

"It says online you're married to David Chambers. Is he going to be teaching here as well?" The girl holds up her cell phone, showing me a picture of myself with David.

"Why is your last name different than his if you're married to him?"

And here we go. Fuck the internet. It really is an ugly, nasty bitch. I mean, only when it's out to get me, that is. "I do not answer questions about my personal life. They are not pertinent to your education and therefore irrelevant."

That's my new party line. I receive a collective knowing grin for that, like they have the inside track on my miserable life. Maybe I shouldn't have said that? Maybe that somehow undercuts my role as an authoritative presence?

Teaching sucks.

Luckily all my classes are on a rotating schedule, so I don't have to see these kids again until Wednesday.

"How about we divide into pairs and discuss how imperative trading routes were for the people of ancient Mesopotamia. Write them down and I'll look through your answers after class." Yep, that sounds brilliant. Totally something a teacher would say.

The bell rings twenty minutes later and all the students rise, collecting their belongings. "I'm looking forward to meeting your parents at the open house tonight."

I get some noise, and then the last class of the day empties. I drop into my chair across the room, my head falling back and my eyes closing as a heavy, relieved breath escapes my lungs. How I'm going to make it through the year, I don't know.

I like the idea of teaching. I like the idea of educating young minds.

I get there's first day razzing. That the first day is always the hardest.

That's all that was. Tomorrow will be easier. It has to be.

I spend the next few hours going through everything here. Setting up my classroom and organizing my materials. Printing out handouts for parents—for both my wellness and history classes. And when it's all finished, I take a moment to breathe, knowing the storm is about to come.

"Rough first day?" A voice startles me, and I bolt upright only to find that it's Bridget. Thankfully not the principal.

I stand, reorganizing my papers for the fifth time. "About what I expected, actually. But it's one thing to expect something and another to live through it."

Bridget perches herself on the corner of a student's desk. Her dark brown curls look like they're at the end of a long day. She pushes up the bridge of her glasses and offers me a hopeful smile. "It gets better. It always does. Just don't let these kids know they got to you. They live for that and will torture you for it. Just wait till you meet their parents."

"Thanks," I deadpan. "Because it's not like I was at all worried about that before."

She laughs. "I'm sure you'll be great. At least the open house comes before you teach their kids about sex."

"Speaking of, did you know about this wellness bullshit I'm in no way qualified to teach?"

"I sure did." She gleams at me. "Mrs. Hastings somehow was teaching it, and she'd been around since condoms were made out of sheep intestines, and I think it's safe to say had never put one on an actual penis. Imagine learning safe sex from someone who's old enough to be your grandmother."

Touché.

"Thank you again for getting me this job. I was planning on

yelling at you, but I'm happy to be here and have this opportunity."

"Thank Mrs. Hastings. She's the one who dropped dead."

A little more than a week ago, I had called Bridget at midnight crying. I had indulged in one too many drinks—clearly it's turning into a pattern. "Please tell me you're waking me up in the middle of the night because you're finally signing the papers." That was how she answered, and I knew I'd made the right decision in calling her. I told her I had, just that moment, and she replied with, "Are you psychic or just gifted with the best timing in the history of the world?"

She then proceeded to explain how Mrs. Hastings, the school's history teacher—and apparently wellness teacher—dropped dead and that they needed someone to fill her role ASAP. Somehow I got the job. I then secured my rental house and started packing up my life.

"Still, I owe you a glass of wine and a meal," I tell her.

Her eyes light up at that. "Oh, if you're cooking, and I don't have to clean up or try to deal with getting the twins to eat while I manage a few bites of lukewarm food, then I'm there."

I snicker. "You've got a deal. I'll make you anything you want."

"God, I love you." She rises off the edge of the desk. "Okay, get your game face on, babe. The vultures, otherwise known as the overly opinionated and super nitpicky parents of your enti-tled kids will be here any second. I'll come by after it's over and give you a lift home since you don't have a car yet."

She casts me a wink, then leaves my classroom, but I'm ready for this. I am. At least as prepared as any hot mess brand-new teacher can be on her first day at a prep school for the rich and elite. And for the most part, I hold my own as the night goes on.

That is until Landon fucking Fritz walks through my door.

There are so many things I hate about this moment, I'd find it difficult to rate them in order of importance if they didn't all center around one person. Ellery Chambers. Or is it Wilde as the plaque outside the door said?

I can't stop myself from glaring at Stella's new history and wellness teacher while she talks, presenting her syllabi to all the parents in the room and discussing her plan for the year. They're eating out of the palm of her hand, and half the women in this room don't eat, or like other women who are prettier than they are—which she is. The men are worse. They're unabashedly staring at her—regardless of their wives being right by their sides—clinging to the way her perfect tits show off just the tiniest hint of a lace bra beneath the cream silk of her blouse.

A lace bra I likely saw scattered on the ground outside her house the other night. Or possibly the same one I removed from her body in the dark of her hotel room. And now my cock is getting hard in my scrubs, and let me tell you, scrubs hide nothing.

Other than when I first entered the room and noted her

shock, the woman hasn't acknowledged me. I might as well not be here for all the attention I've garnered. I'm Patrick Swayze in *Ghost*. I'm here, but am I really?

I wasn't prepared.

Considering her reflected surprise, I highly doubt she had Stella today in her class. I'm not sure if I'm grateful she was equally blindsided or not. I came here straight from the hospital and haven't even had a chance to shower or change clothes or eat a meal or to see my daughter and ask how her day was.

Does Stella even know that her teacher is our new neighbor?

The neighbor I had sex with—that part I know she definitely doesn't know. The neighbor I absolutely despise for being so sweet and bubbly and perfect when I know it's an act. It has to be.

She's cried herself to sleep both nights since she moved in.

How does she do it? How does she put on this front? Smile through the bullshit? Or is her sadness just a temporary blip, a red herring I'm falling for, and she's actually, truly like this?

I can't decide which is worse.

All I know is that I'm annoyed. And turned on, which is annoying me further. Perhaps even more than her full-on laugh and glowing smile at something nimrod Chad Vandelay just said when we all know he's not nearly that funny.

My fists clench, and I grumble under my breath.

"No. That's definitely not part of the curriculum."

She's still laughing. He's smiling at her like a sexual predator.

Some weird noise escapes from my larynx.

"I'm sorry, did you say something, Dr. Fritz?" she asks with that saccharine voice, all sunshine and fucking unicorns. *Dr. Fritz.* Not Landon.

Every head in the room swooshes in my direction.

I glance down at the sheet in my hand. "What is your teaching experience prior to coming here?" Expectantly, I look back up at her.

She frowns. Turns red. And I realize once again, I'm a supreme dick. But how can I not be? I've trained myself to be numb, but with her I can't help but feel again. The throb of a fresh wound after the lidocaine wears off. It's awful.

Elle clears her throat. "If you're interested in discussing my résumé, Dr. Fritz, I'm sure we can do that at a more opportune time, or please feel free to email me to schedule an appointment during my office hours. But for now, I think everyone here is anxious to get home for the night and would prefer discussing their children and this school year."

I get the *two can play at this game* raised eyebrow and the *you're a fucking asshole* glare.

Another grumble hits my lips and once more I'm quickly overlooked.

One more set of parents filter in and out of her room, going to their children's last classroom—as I should be—and yet I can't make my feet move. I can't work my limbs. Stella has always been an A student and frankly, I don't need to meet with her art teacher to know she'll receive a top-rated education this year.

It's why I pay a college tuition for middle school.

But with this new group, I stay rooted in place, staring. At her.

My unremitting presence drives Elle mad. She was hoping I'd leave like everyone else just did, but I'm still here, hovering in the background, pressing upon her every cool nerve that I want to set on fire.

Does she have any clue?

I was in control.

Now I stand by my open bedroom window at night listening for *her*. Thinking about *her*.

Elle giggles at whatever nonsense Richard Hargrove just said to her, her hand reaching out and squeezing his forearm, and my lungs collapse, nearly choking me. She's temptation and everyone in here knows it. All it takes for them to want her is to look at her. Her laugh. That smile. An impossible piece of hidden lace.

Fucking vixen.

Which is why the second the class empties, everyone in the building now heading home, I pry myself away from the wall I was clinging to and cross the room with slow, measured steps. Elle busies herself with her computer, shutting everything down. The presentation on the SMART board flickers off, and she's organizing papers that don't require organizing.

But she knows.

She feels me.

I can practically see her pulse racing in her neck as I reach the other side of her desk and stare down at her, compelling her to glance up at me. Finally, when she's out of things to do and can no longer resist the temptation, she puffs out a breath, rolls her shoulders while planting her hands on her desk, and meets my steadfast gaze.

"Why are you still here?"

Because I have to know. "Did you know who I was the night at the bar?"

"What?" She blinks incredulously at me, not expecting me to ask her that.

"You heard me."

She shakes her head, standing upright, aggravation pouring off her. "You mean when you told me you were your brother? How could I have known you?"

"Because you said that night you thought you recognized me. You fell into bed with me quickly too, without a lot of talking or questions. Now you're not only my neighbor but Stella's teacher. I need to know if this is all just one big, fat coincidence or if you're up to something else with me."

A laugh belts past her lips. It's the kind of laugh that suggests I'm crazy, but I'm not. I'm an Abbot-Fritz, and people have done worse to get to us. Oliver's ex stalked him and Amelia all over Boston, going as far as trying to break them up, and when that didn't work, she attempted to get Layla kicked out of school. A woman Kaplan had a one-night stand with broke into his place the following night to steal stuff, including the used condom. Luckily, she was caught before she could use his sperm to get pregnant. Rina's psycho ex-boyfriend attacked and kidnapped her.

Money breeds greed and madness in people.

"You're serious?"

I stare at her, unmoving.

She huffs. "No. I didn't know who you were. I had thought you looked familiar, but it wasn't until after you showed up on my doorstep and told me your last name that I realized it's because I actually met Luca once years ago at a charity thing. I'm most certainly not up to anything with you, Dr. Fritz, and that's how I intend to keep it. If money and assholes were my thing, I'd still be married."

Money and assholes. She mentioned her ex was a professional athlete. Chambers. That was the name on the box Gulliver ruined. I bet her husband was David Chambers.

Satisfied, I rip my gaze away and stroll toward the door.

"Are you always going to be this rude?" she calls after me, and I stop in my tracks, my head rolling over my shoulder to find her. She shrugs, a half-smile pulling up the corner of her mouth. "If so, I'd just like to know that ahead of time. You know, so I don't try to borrow eggs or sugar and make sure I schedule our parent-teacher conferences as a Zoom instead of in person."

"Are you always this sweet and friendly?"

She frowns and shifts her weight, momentarily glancing away because I already know the answer is yes, and I don't think she wants to admit it. But I'm also learning that lying isn't her strong suit, and she tends to say what's on her mind when pressed.

"Are we sticking with honesty?" I ask, letting go of my question to her. I don't need to know more about her or what makes her smile or frown or tick.

"Yes."

"I wasn't trying to be rude, per se. But you're the fourth tenant in five years to move in next door to me. People don't usually stay long there, and I never found a reason to become friendly with them as a result." *And other than Roberta, the one time I did, he turned around and tried to sell pictures and a story to The Boston Globe.* I heave out a breath. "I'm not a friendly person on a good day and frankly, I can't be friendly with you. That night..." I swallow. "That night was..." *Unexpectedly perfect. Everything I've been missing.* "Not something that can ever happen again. So if you're looking to borrow eggs or sugar, Mrs. Bellows on the other side of you is very nice and accommodating. And as far as parent-teacher interactions, emails and Zoom work just fine for me."

"Huh." She tilts her head, scrutinizing me in a way that makes the back of my neck break out into a cold sweat. "So it's you and not me then? Alrighty. I'm not sure what to say to that. It's amazing to me how different I thought you were, but obviously you were playing a role to get laid, and this is who you truly are. No eggs or sugar. Emails and Zoom. Got it. Have a good night, Dr. Fritz."

Her cool tone and sharp words pull me up short. Most likely because they're true.

I'm not the man she met that night. Not anymore. But I was with her, and it wasn't all an act. Sure, I told her I was Luca, and yes, in pretending to be him—it relaxed me—but with her...

With her, I was someone I haven't been in a very long time.

Someone I thought died along with my wife.

My heart rate spikes, pounding painfully in my chest. That sweat on the back of my neck does nothing to cool me as my blood burns me from the inside out.

I need to get home. I need to eat some dinner and check in with Stella and take a shower. I need to leave this room where Elle is now rounding her desk, her purse on her shoulder, along with her laptop bag.

She's back to ignoring me, shutting down her room, and when she moves to brush past me to turn off the lights and leave me behind, instinct eclipses sanity, and I grasp her arm, stopping her.

"What are you doing?"

Good question.

"Why do you care if I'm rude to you? I thought you hated me."

Turbulent hazel eyes meet mine. "I do. But I've had enough meanness hurled my way to last a lifetime. I think it's safe to say I'm over it by this point and frankly, meanness doesn't suit me. I just moved here. I know one person in this town other than you and even if you're not exactly my favorite person, you're still my neighbor."

My grip on her arm tightens so she can't pull away. "What does that matter? That I'm your neighbor? You thought we'd do book club and gossip on the sidewalk like besties?" I mock.

She grits her teeth. "No. You don't have to worry about that. I genuinely dislike you, which I know was your goal with me. Especially with how you've spoken to me tonight. But I had been hoping..." She trails off on a bitter laugh. "It's stupid. Maybe it's the Southern girl in me or the one who automatically searches for the best in everyone or who *is* always sweet and friendly, as you put it—a character flaw I should have killed off by now considering how many times people have disappointed me—but I was hoping I was wrong about you. Clearly I wasn't, and that's all there is to it."

There's so much in her little statement it's making my head spin. But I can't focus on that. After the way I've treated her, why would she ever want anything to do with me again? Nothing else can happen between us. She's the kind of woman you don't work out of your system. She makes you crave her. Hang like a fool on her every smile, word, and laugh. She has you coming back for more until she's an addiction you worry you'll never be able to quit.

But the feel of her soft skin beneath my hand. The way her chest is rising and falling, pushing her tits up with every inhale. The scent of her perfume. The way she stares into me—as if she's still clinging to the hope I'll prove her wrong and be the guy she wishes I were.

My fingers twitch against her arm. I should release her and run from here, but instead, I'm tightening my grip. Marching forward, thrusting her back until she crashes into the wall, and slamming my mouth down on hers like I've been possessed.

I must be.

I can't be kissing her. Not my daughter's teacher in her school—that's an automatic off-limits. Not the woman who looks at me like she wants me to be more than I'll ever be.

I can't kiss her.

But I am.

Because I had to fucking kiss her.

And she's kissing me back, gasping against my lips as my tongue dives into her mouth. A sweet, little, breathy moan escapes her when our tongues touch, her hands getting lost in my hair. Her purse and computer bag slam into my side, but it does nothing to stop us or bring sanity back into our minds.

My hands fist on her silky blouse as I angle my head, deepening the kiss and pressing her harder against the wall. I want to rip her pants off, wrap her legs around my waist, and fuck her raw right here. Hard and fast. Desperate and angry because I'm both things right now.

My hand slips down to her waist, gripping her, nearly taking action on my thoughts when a sound breaks through my lust-induced haze, and my brain takes over, wrenching me back from her. I take a step and then another, both of us panting, chests heaving, eyes dark and feral.

I glare at her, and she glares right back. My sexy little vixen.

"Elle, you ready to go?" a woman calls out seconds before she enters the room and finds us both like this, not touching, but a visible mess as we stare at each other. "Oh. I'm sorry. I didn't realize you were still with a parent. I didn't mean to interrupt."

Fuck.

"You didn't," I bark out and take off, plowing past the other woman and out the door without so much as a backward glance at either of them.

What did I just do?

9

Elle

Landon kissed me. Why would he do a thing like that? And why the hell did I allow myself to not only kiss him back but enjoy it?

"What the hell was that?" Bridget asks, bewildered, practically reading my thoughts.

I clear my throat, straighten up away from the board, and will my heart to slow. I can still feel his lips. The powerful, hungry kiss he just planted on them is making them tingle and swell.

"My rude neighbor," I tell her because even though I likely should have said a student's parent, it was obvious there was something else going on between us.

"Holy shit." She gasps as I shut off the lights. "You live next door to *Landon Fritz*?"

The way she says his name with a hint of reverence has me frowning. Sure, he's hotter than anyone I've ever seen before. Especially as he stands tall in green scrubs that match his eyes, his broad shoulders and muscular chest, abs and arms on delicious display because his scrubs do jack all to hide them. But come on.

I don't respond, but I don't have to. This is Bridget, and she's already all over me as we leave the building, heading for her car in the parking lot.

"And wait," she stops abruptly, the door to her car now ajar and the interior light on. "What do you mean he was rude? Did you already have an encounter with him before tonight? You just moved in like forty-eight hours ago."

I say nothing, and a smile spears her lips.

"You've been holding out on me, Ellery Jane. I want details." She points a stern finger at me over the roof of her car before slipping in the driver's seat and starting it up.

As she drives, I explain everything that happened during the encounter at my front door, all the way through meeting Stella outside while I was planting bulbs. I don't mention anything about the hotel or the kiss in my classroom tonight. First, my friend is tenacious and will be hungry like a bear waking up after hibernation. Second, neither of those things should have happened. I mean, not now that I know who he is and that he's a total jerk of a man.

He's not only my neighbor but my student's father.

Yeesh. I just kissed my student's father like his mouth was made of crack and I needed a fix. I imagine what I just did is a very fireable offense. Especially at such a prestigious school. And he's a Fritz. Double yeesh.

Score for Ellery, putting her job in jeopardy on day one.

I do my best to keep my flush down to a minimum while I regale her with my sorry lack of clothes and the way he glared at my skimpy panties. Bridget is practically crying, she's laughing so hard. She's actually doubled over against the wheel as we pull into my driveway.

"It's not that funny." I smack her shoulder.

"Oh no," she says through the tail end of her amusement. "It really is." She's wiping at the tears streaming down her cheeks, her glasses sticking into her forehead. "That's fucking awesome. I cannot believe Landon Fritz has already seen you mostly naked. Women in this town—hell, all over this city and the freaking world—would kill for that chance, and you didn't even have to try."

Yep. Now I'm blushing. I turn away, hoping I can get control. Landon has already seen me in a lot less than my bra and panties. "You're being a brat."

"I know. It's just so... damn, it's perfect. I mean, I'm not shocked he's rough with you. He's rough with everyone. He barely speaks to anyone, and if he does, it's very curt, monosyllabic words. He keeps mostly to himself, trying to stay out of the spotlight, likely because of Stella. And after what happened with his wife and the fact that he's a single dad raising a kid, most people do leave him alone. But the people in this area have a real hard-on for the Fritz family. The Abbot-Fritzes I should say, since they're two powerful families combined into one. They're the equivalent of our royal family, and we cyber-stalk them as such."

I frown at that. I've had enough of being in the spotlight with David, and it's seriously the last thing I'd want again. I don't blame him for keeping a low profile. He had said that night on the porch that he used Luca's name to protect his family. I bet he used Luca's name with me so that if we were photographed together it was with him as Luca and not Landon. That way Stella wouldn't know what he was up to.

"What happened to his wife?"

Bridget turns to me, her expression filled with sympathy. "I don't know much. Just that she died several years ago. A car accident, but it was messy. I remember it was winter, and she skidded off the road and ended up in a lake." She licks her lips, her eyes all over me as she says, "She drowned before they could get her out."

Bridget gets out of the car, but I take a second before

following her, lost in this revelation. My chest clenches painfully tight.

Jesus. The poor man. I hate that this softens me some to him considering how heartless he's been with me, but it does. There's no way it can't. And just as I think that, I glance toward his house, finding him taking out the trash.

He looks up at that exact second. Staring directly at me as if he could hear my thoughts all the way across the lawn. Our eyes lock, and my breath catches. My stomach does a quick loopty-loop, my face already feeling the heat of a flush for getting caught staring. He tosses the bag of trash in his bin that's already on the curb, then folds his arms across his chest. He's showered and changed since I saw him earlier. His hair is damp, pushed off his face, and he's wearing gray sweatpants, a Harvard hoodie, and his glasses.

His gaze is intense as he does a long, languid sweep of me. And with each pass, his eyes narrow further. He's staring at me like I'm the devil of his nightmares. Hard. Cold. Almost spiteful.

I don't understand it.

What could I have possibly done to make this man dislike me so?

Landon and I continue to stare each other down until he finally breaks the spell I'm under and storms back into his house, shutting the door behind him and turning off his porch light. My stomach swarms with relief. Fuck, that man is so intense.

"Wow," Bridget whispers as we walk into my house. "I can't tell if he hates you or wants to fuck you. Christ on a cracker, that look he was giving you was turning me on, and I'm a very married woman."

"It's hate," I reply. He may have wanted me on Friday, and he may have planted a kiss on me tonight, but I know better. That look in his eyes doesn't lie. "Most definitely hate."

~

"This place is super adorbs," Bridget says, staring around my kitchen as I pour both of us a glass of wine.

I give her a sideways glance. "Adorbs?"

She shrugs. "It's what all the cool girls say."

"When they're thirteen."

Another shrug as she accepts her glass and sits on one of the stools at the counter. "Who do you think I teach?"

Fair enough.

"What was your first night here like?" she continues, trying to tread carefully with that delicate question. "You were living in the house with him, right? It has to be weird not living with him anymore."

She's referring to the fact that I was still living in the house with David. After I left him, I stayed in a hotel for a week. I had no real place to go. It was the start of the golf season and David was going to be away a lot at tournaments through the spring and summer. He told me to stay at the house while I thought about our marriage, that it was big enough for both of us.

He spent those months angry, and we did the dance of avoidance like pros.

I stayed in the guest room on the opposite side of the house.

But sleeping in this house alone is weird. Sad, lonely, kind of heartbreaking, and weird.

"It's fine, I guess. I'm getting used to it."

She takes a sip of her wine, then sets the glass back onto the stone counter, her gaze never wavering from mine, her expression one that reminds me of my mother and not in a good way since I can't stand my mother. "You don't have to put on a brave face. It's totally and completely normal not to feel okay. Not to *be* okay."

"David's been calling and texting me."

Her jaw pops open as her brown eyes widen.

"It's like once he received the final documents of our divorce, it actually sank in that it's over. I don't get it. I mean, he signed the damn papers, though when he did it, he was drunk and pissed off."

"The prick's trying to win you back?"

I take a long pull of my wine and nod. "Yeah. I think he is. He was mean the first night I was here, but since then he's been effusively sweet and apologetic. Claims I'm the love of his life, and he wants to reconcile. Start again fresh. Promises he's a changed man. My parents are in on it, which only makes it worse."

Bridget leans back in her stool, her fingers drumming softly against the base of her glass. "Are you considering it?"

"No. It would be a mistake. He's done this bullshit before."

"Are you asking or telling?"

"Telling. It would be a mistake. I know it would."

"But?" She arches an eyebrow, and I roll my eyes.

"But nothing. Stop staring at me like that. It's over. We're divorced. I just..." I stare up at the ceiling. "I never thought we'd end like this," I admit. "We were David and Ellery. So goddamn happy and in love for two years. The man bought me flowers and my favorite candy every time I got my freaking period. He always went above and beyond with my birthday, finding new creative ways to surprise me. He was goddamn perfect."

"Until he wasn't."

My chin drops, my throat clogging up as I stare across the room and out the back window. "Until he wasn't."

"Cheers." Bridget raises her glass, and we both drink them down, finishing them off. "Now you can fuck your neighbor."

The last drop of alcohol decides to descend my trachea instead of my esophagus, and I cough violently, choking and sputtering.

"Oh. My. God."

I turn away from her as I continue to die.

"You did, didn't you? You already had sex with him?!" she shrieks.

I spin back to her, my face like a forest fire. Once I'm able to breathe, I snap at her, utterly incredulous. "How can you know that? There's no way you can possibly know that."

"Please, bitch. I lived with you for four years in college. I know your tells like the back of my hand. If you hadn't slept with him, you would have given me a look or laughed. Instead, you choked. You're crap at lying and hiding things. Besides, the looks you two gave each other were obvious. There was far too much heat between the two of you for it to have been a random rude neighbor thing. Spill it. I need to know ev-er-y-thing." She fans her face with her hand. "I cannot believe you slept with Landon Fritz. He's so... *hot*. Like epically hot. How—" She holds up her hand, cutting herself off. "No, wait, *when* did this happen?" She sighs, shaking her head. "Just start at the beginning and spare no details."

"This is why I didn't want to tell you."

"You didn't. But you're about to. Talk and while you're at it, pour me another glass."

"I'm not telling you what happened."

She points at me with one hand and her glass with the other as I pour. "Pour yourself one too."

I shake my head. "Alcohol has already gotten me into enough trouble."

Bridget cracks up, smacking her thigh as she laughs her head off at me. "Oh, this just keeps getting better and better. You have to tell me about Landon. You can't drop a bomb like that on me and not give me the goods."

"I didn't drop the bomb on you. You figured it out."

She waves me off. "Semantics. Was he good?"

I sigh, my forearms collapsing onto the counter. The truth is, I want to talk about our night together. And Bridget is all I've got. Plus, she may love her gossip, but she'd never repeat to anyone anything I tell her. I've told her plenty over the years about David, and if she wanted to blather that about, she would have. She didn't.

"He was incredible."

She lets out an audible moan. "I knew he would be. He just has that look about him, ya know? Silently screams god in the sack. Go on. Was this the night you moved in after he saw you in your bra and panties?"

I shake my head. "It was the night I spent at the hotel *before* I moved in."

Her eyes explode with surprise and interest.

"He was at the bar. Picked me up with like ten words, and before I knew what I was doing, he was in my room, and we were going at it."

"Hot. Like super freaking hot. No wonder he was staring at you like that tonight. He was totally hate fucking you with his eyes."

Hate fucking me. How unfortunately accurate.

"Well, we both agreed to one night, and that's all it was. All it will ever be. He showed up tonight and was not nice. He made it clear we would not be friends or friendly and that whatever happened between us would never occur again."

She scrunches her nose. "What a dick. Why does he have to be so dickish? Do you want a repeat?"

"No!" I exclaim, setting my glass down. "Repeats lead to things I have no room for. I can't even handle my ex-husband."

She takes a sip, contemplating this. "Did you tell him your story? About what happened with David? About your parents or your sister? Or... Erika?"

I shake my head, and we share a small commiserative frown. "Of course not. I didn't even know he had a kid until I met her. I only told him I'm newly single."

Her expression turns grim, and she reaches out, taking my hand and squeezing it. I stare down at the counter, my heart aching. "You two have a lot in common. In the worst possible way."

"I know." I just didn't realize the extent of it until tonight.

"Don't fall for him, Elle," she pleads with a concerned tone, her eyes soft and earnest. "He's the definition of emotionally unavailable, and you have an awful tendency to fall fast and hard, and he's a prime target."

"Not gonna happen."

"Good. Because I'd hate to cut a bitch if he breaks your heart."

I roll my eyes. "Stop talking like your students. I'm fine. No hearts breaking here. He's the last man I'd ever want to get involved with, not that I'm looking for something like that, because I'm not. Trust me. I doubt I'll talk to Landon Fritz again beyond parent-teacher stuff."

But right as I think it, believe that what I'm saying is the truth, that flicker of doubt—and worse, disappointment—lurks somewhere deep and dark. And that scares me most of all.

I am the poster child for *all good things must come to an end*. It's actually my motto. It keeps me real. It reminds me shit isn't actually a fairy tale and the real world is a total motherfucker. But on today's dose of all good things come to an end...

"You've been avoiding me," Luca says as he jogs the last couple of steps to catch up to me right before I enter my favorite coffee shop in town.

It's not just you I've been avoiding. But instead I go with, "Is that why you drove all the way out here on a Saturday?"

He nods, giving me his signature I know everything smirk. "Yes. Mom called me. Said you were in a particularly shitty mood and told you to leave to gain perspective."

"Mom never used the word shitty."

"You're right. She said you were being more of a grump than she's seen you be in years. She was worried, and the last thing Mom needs right now is to be worried about you while she's undergoing treatment."

"Great. Thanks for the extra dose of guilt. It'll go perfectly with my morning cup of coffee. Does this mean everyone else is coming too? Yet another Landon intervention."

His eyes widen, glancing around the street, ensuring no one overheard us, but other than a few early risers going about Saturday morning errands, it's pretty empty out here.

"You are in a shitty mood. Shittier than normal. What's going on?"

My hands drop to my hips, my gaze landing hard on the sidewalk between us. It's been two weeks since I kissed Elle in her classroom. Two weeks of completely avoiding her while being acutely hyperaware of everywhere she is. When she's working in the garden in the front, I don't go outside. When her bedroom window is open at night, I make sure mine is closed. Even when I take out the goddamn trash now.

I can't stand it. Any of it.

I think about her.

So much more than I should and in so many ways beyond just trying to avoid her.

Her laugh. Her smile. Her voice with that accent. Her smart, sassy mouth that calls me out on my shit when no one other than my family ever does. Every damn time I take my cock in hand, it's her face and body that surface behind my eyes, and no amount of trying to change the image or willing it away works.

Stella freaking raves about her as a teacher. Talks about how they go on nature hikes around campus, and she gives them recipes she's trying out and does yoga and meditation with them. And in history, she just talks to them, tells them stories without using notes or textbooks, but they learn so much.

Until I figure out how to stop thinking and fantasizing about her, I'm avoiding her. And being shitty, as my brother so politely pointed out.

Someone crosses the street in our direction, heading for the coffee shop we're lingering outside of. I wait until they enter, and the door shuts behind him before I say, "She lives next door."

His eyebrows crease. "What? Who?"

"The woman I met in the hotel."

It takes him about three seconds to put the pieces together, and then he laughs. Like doubled over, hand braced on the side of the building for support laughing. "Shit," he sputters. "That's priceless." Then he halts his laughing. "Wait, is she—"

"No," I interrupt, already knowing what he was about to ask. "It was a coincidence. She thought I was you, remember?"

"Right. I assume she knows the deal now?"

"She hates me for it."

"She'll get over it."

I shake my head, frustrated by the way he says that. "I don't want her to get over it. I like her hating me."

Luca's eyes roll dramatically at me, sarcasm dripping from his voice as he says, "Of course you do. Why on earth would you ever want a beautiful woman with whom you already have fantastic sexual chemistry to live next door to you and not hate you?"

"Because I don't do that."

"My question was fucking rhetorical, asshole. You should want that. You should want all of that any chance you can get it."

I shake my head. The more distance and animosity I place between me and her, the better it is for all of us. "There's more." Now I look around, but no one is paying us any attention. For once. "She's also Stella's teacher."

And just like that, my brother loses his shit again.

Laughing so loud we're catching the attention of passersby. He's wiping tears from his eyes, noting my glare, and holding up a conciliatory hand when I know he's not the least bit remorseful.

"Sorry," he lies. "That's just too damn good. But wait, does that mean you can't fuck her again? Is that like some rule or law?"

"You're a dick," I grumble, turning away from him and opening the door to the coffee shop. Luca is hot on my heels as I knew he would be, taking the lead and ordering our coffees from the pretty barista. As with every woman Luca encounters, she simpers, blushing like a virgin on her wedding night.

Luca is like that, and I don't even know how he does it.

I live in this town and see this woman frequently enough, but she's never looked at me like that other than maybe the first time I walked in here. It's all so easy for him when being normal feels nothing short of impossible for me. It's been so long since I've felt anything other than pain, grief, and guilt that I don't even remember what it's like to take a breath without their insurmountable weight on me.

I turn my back on him, locating a small table off to the side of the counter, and a few minutes later, he joins me, handing me my large mug of black coffee. I blow off some of the steam, taking a tentative sip and generally ignoring the way my brother is studying me. He doesn't have to look too hard. Hiding anything from him is impossible.

A point proven when he says, "This is really torturing you."

I open my mouth to argue, to tell him I'm not tortured by her, just annoyed it's a thing, but soon enough it won't be, when the door chimes and in walks a staggeringly beautiful woman with honey-colored hair piled on top of her head in a messy bun and eyes that change color—more green to brown or brown to green—depending on her mood.

She's wearing tight as all sin yoga pants that show off every muscular curve of her shapely legs and ass and a goddamn loose-fitting crop top that hits right above her belly button.

And just like that, my cock springs to life.

I grunt, forcing myself back to my coffee, but Luca is

mesmerized, a knowing smirk on his lips as his eyes dance back and forth between Elle and me. I shake my head at him, and his smile grows as he goes back to watching her, marveling at her, ever the amused devil.

"Elle," the barista greets and great, she comes here often enough for the barista to know her name. Now I have to find a new favorite coffee shop. "I didn't think I'd see you here this early."

"I took an early yoga class down the street," she replies, approaching the counter and staring up at the board over the barista's head. "What's good today?"

"Do you like chai?"

Elle shrugs, gnawing contemplatively on her lip as she continues to study the thing like she's expecting to be tested on it later. "Indifferent."

"How do you feel about espresso?"

"Right now?" she snorts. "I need it more than sex."

Fuck. That's it. Both women laugh, and I reach out, grabbing Luca's arm, begging him. He just chuckles an in your dreams I'm not doing this laugh, already halfway out of his chair as he shrugs off my grip and heads for the counter. For Elle.

"Morning, beautiful," he says to her, and she spins in his direction, gawking at him as if he's an alien from another planet. Which makes sense since that is certainly not a greeting I'd ever bestow upon her, even if I'm thinking it.

"Um. I'm sorry. I think I must have misheard you. Or had a stroke on my walk here from yoga?"

He laughs, leaning into her, dropping his elbow on the counter, and encroaching on her space. Damn him. I have half a mind to get up and leave. I should. That's exactly what I should do. But I can't make myself move. My fists are balled up on my lap, my jaw clenched tighter than a drum even though I know. I know he's just doing this to get a rise out of me.

He'd never touch her now that I have. It's been our twin—hell, with all our brothers—rule never to pursue a woman any of us has ever messed around with. That's not even why he's doing it. But still, the thought of it. Of someone else...

"Well, considering your pupils are equal, round, and reactive, you have no facial droop, are standing equally balanced on two feet, and not slurring your words, I think it's safe to say you didn't have a stroke on your way over here."

She tilts her head inquisitively, staring straight up into his eyes, and then a smile bursts across her face. My stupid chest tightens reflexively.

"I met you once. I don't know if you remember. It was a few years back. I'm Elle." She extends her hand, and he shakes it. "It's very nice to meet you, Luca Fritz. The real Luca Fritz, that is."

I roll my eyes, and she peers around Luca, catching me do it before returning to him.

"Did you know you don't have a freckle in your eye?"

He laughs. "Did you know you're one of few people on this planet who have caught that? It is *very* nice to meet you, Elle, and yes, I do remember you now. It was at some charity thing?" He glances over his shoulder, grins like a son of a bitch at me, and then back to her with a wink he makes sure I don't miss. "I never forget a pretty face. Please, won't you come join us?" He turns to the barista, pulling out his wallet and dropping a twenty on the counter. "That's for her coffee. Obviously, you need to make her something with espresso in it."

Elle blushes but laughs in a good-natured way that makes me hate her even more.

"I'm not sure that's such a good idea—" She starts to object when Luca cuts her off with a sharp shake of his head, guiding her with a hand on her back to our table the second she has her coffee in her hands.

"Nonsense. It's a fantastic idea. I know Landon will be *thrilled* to have you join us."

"Motherfucker," I hiss out, my hand gripping the side of the table so hard the wood creaks and our mugs sway. Two seconds later he deposits Elle—a woman who looks just as unhappy to be sitting with me as I am with her—in the seat he vacated, asking a neighboring table if he can borrow a chair before scraping one over.

"Now." Luca claps his hands, his gaze flittering back and forth between us. "This is fortuitous, isn't it? We were just talking about you." He gesticulates at her.

I kick him under the table, but since he's my goddamn twin, he knows it's coming and scoots his foot out of the way so all I do is hit the leg of his chair. Unfortunately not hard enough to tip the bastard over.

Elle raises a dubious eyebrow at me, her eyes sparkling as rays of sun shining through the window hit them at the perfect angle. I hate being this close to her. I can practically feel the warmth of her skin. Smell the hints of her shampoo or body lotion or whatever that incredible fragrance is. Note every perfect line of her face.

Every synapse in my body is firing, making me feel strung out. Edgy.

"Is that so? I can only imagine what was said." She smiles coyly at me. The woman is being fucking coy, and that smile— *just fuck.* She turns her penetrative stare back at Luca. "I hope you didn't sit me down to offer up some kind of crazy twin ménage scenario."

"What?" Luca chokes, the sip of coffee he was just taking spraying right back out of his mouth, narrowly missing us as it coats the table in splattered mocha-colored drops.

"It was in a book I recently read, but really I just wanted that"—she points at the spittle of coffee running down his chin—"reaction to happen." She smiles, sitting up just a bit straighter, looking entirely too pleased with herself. "Payback and all since I know you knew about the whole name switch-a-roo. And since I can already tell you're the one with the bigger ego of the two of you, you should know I would have gone to bed with a garden hose that night if it got me off. It had nothing to do with the guy and everything to do with starting my new life out on an orgasm."

I rub my hand across my twitching lips, falling back in my chair, utterly floored. My eyes blink so many times I'm shocked I'm not damaging my contacts. Her mouth. Her dirty, impertinent mouth. The one smiling at me like the evil temptress she is.

Damn vixen. Now I remember why I kissed her in her classroom.

Every time she opens it, it not only takes me completely by surprise but makes me hard as a rock. The only thing I can think of to stop it is to shut it up, and the only way to shut it up is to kiss it. Or fuck it.

Jesus. This is why I've been avoiding her.

Whenever those hazels cut to me, I get chills, and any time she speaks, I respond just to keep her talking to me longer.

I drag a hand through my hair, squeezing the back of my neck that's loaded with tension. She takes a sip of her coffee, seemingly satisfied with the way she just put both of us in our places.

Luca is completely stunned, staring at her like she's a rare hundred-carat pink diamond in a pit full of rubble. Seriously, he's about to go all *Blood Diamond* on my ass and kill me for her. Neither of us can think of anything to say back, any possible retort dead on our lips, because let's be honest, what the hell can anyone say back to that?

She stands, taking her to-go cup with her. "Thank you for the coffee, Luca. This absolutely made my entire morning." He gets a wink, I get a blown kiss, then she's gone, walking out of the café. The only thing missing from that was her dropping the mic.

He turns to me, a smile on his lips like I've never seen. "Yeah. I get it now. You're in a lot of fucking trouble with that one."

Thanks. Tell me something I don't know.

11

"All right, y'all, let's get this moving. It's a beautiful fall day. The air is cool, and the leaves are falling, and we're going to get our nature on." That's when everyone groans. I can never tell if it's from the y'all or the trying to talk middle school. Either way, they move their butts into gear, which is the equivalent of a teacher win in my opinion.

Basically, I'm rocking at this teaching thing.

Even if sex education starts in four motherfluffing weeks!

Bridget says I just have to follow the curriculum, but have y'all ever tried to put a freaking condom on a banana in front of a group of snarky as hell thirteen and fourteen-year-old kids? Yeah, didn't think so. It's a Shakespearean tragedy—or comedy—in the making.

We wind our way around the grounds of the school, following a path that cuts through the woods in a giant loop that leads from one side of campus to the other. If we veer right at the fork halfway through, we'd be heading in the direction of Wilchester Prep high school, where most of these kids will be attending next year.

I've never lived in New England. In fact, I've only ever lived in the Southern half of this country, so fifty-five degrees in the middle of September is a new thing for me. Even when the kids remind me it's not usually this cold this early into fall. Shockingly not an unwelcome thing, though. I'm enjoying purchasing sweaters and jackets and fleece-lined leggings and boots. God, so many boots.

But the kids like to tease me because I've taken to wearing mittens and a hat on our hikes. I tell them my Southern blood has yet to acclimate to their cold weather, but I'm thinking once it drops below freezing, we'll be getting our wellness on indoors.

"What kind of tree is that?" Justin Thomas asks, walking right by my side. He likes to do that. He's fourteen and already way too flirty for a kid his age.

I give him a side-eye, noting the tree he's questioning. "Some kind of pine tree?"

He gives me the same flirtatious grin he always does. "You're a teacher. Aren't you supposed to know that kind of stuff?"

I snort. "History and wellness teacher, Justin. I'm hardly an arborist."

"How much longer?" Mandy Vandelay whines from the back of the pack.

I check my watch just as we reach the clearing that will circle us back to our side of campus. "Three more minutes, Mandy. You can make it three more minutes."

"I'm not so sure about that," she grumbles. "I can see my breath. That means it's too cold out."

"I can smell your breath," someone else comments. "And it ain't pretty. Did you swallow a dead cat before our walk?"

Everyone laughs, and I hold my hand up. "What's the rule?"

They collectively moan. "No teasing, lying, cheating, or over pleasing," they all repeat in unison, making me smile. Talk about a life lesson, especially that last one.

"And?"

"What happens in wellness stays in wellness."

"You got it." Now I'm beaming. "And look, here we are." I swipe my ID badge along the keypad to unlock the door and hold it open for the students. After the last student enters the building—it's always Mandy Vandelay—I follow them all up to the room just as the final bell for the day rings. "Nicely done today, ladies and gents. Grab your stuff and you can head on out for the day. I'll see y'all tomorrow. If anyone tries the pumpkin muffin recipe I posted on our group chat, let me know. Or better yet, post pictures. Maybe if we get enough, I'll create a Pinterest board for all of us."

"I made the butternut squash quinoa last night with my mom. It was amazing. Even my little brother ate it, and he eats nothing."

"Oh, that's fantastic, Katie. Did you happen to snap a pic?"

She nods her head like a bobble doll. "I'll post it to the chat when I get home."

"Thank you. I appreciate that. Can't wait to see how it turned out. Have a good night, y'all. And remember to write in your journals and post your entries so I can read through them before next class."

The class empties, and I leave my stuff in my room while I scoot down the hall to the ladies' room. But the second I open the door, I come to a screeching halt when I catch the sound of crying quickly followed by a soft whimper. Whoever is in the stall shuffles, raising their feet up and trying to pretend they're not here.

I walk over to the counter, grab a couple of tissues, and hold them under the door of the stall.

A sigh. Then a, "Thank you," as the girl takes the tissues from my hand.

"You okay?"

Sniff. Sniff. "Uh-huh."

"It's just us in here, and I'm a fantastic listener."

"Miss Wilde?"

"Yes..." I trail off, scrunching my eyebrows at the familiar voice, trying to place it. "Stella?"

A second later the door unlocks and out comes pretty Stella Fritz, her face tear-soaked, her eyes red and puffy. She's huffing and puffing and trying for brave as she quickly loses the battle and falls back into a fit of tears, covering her face with her hands.

I gently place my hand on her shoulder, unease skating across my skin and through my veins. "What's wrong, honey? Did something happen?"

It takes her forever to talk through her tears, but finally, after a few wet hiccups, she clears her voice. "I got my period," she whispers it so low I have to strain to hear her.

"Oh. Okay." Well, that's a relief. "Is this your first one?"

She shakes her head in her hands. "My sixth. But I didn't expect it. I had my last one two weeks ago and... and..." And she breaks down again.

"Honey, what? You have to tell me or I won't know how to help."

She doesn't stop crying as she spins around, and that's when I see it. The large stain visible even through the thick material of her skirt. Not to mention the streaks of red all down the backs of her legs.

"It happened in class, and everyone saw," she wails.

"That happened to me once," I tell her, turning her back around and prying her hands from her face. I walk her over to the sink, turning the faucet on to cold and wetting some paper towels. I hand them to her so she can press them to her face. "I was in eighth grade too, in science class, sitting in the back of the darn class. I bled right through my jeans and all over the chair I was sitting in. Right next to the boy I was crushing on too. It was a total nightmare. I had to race out of the classroom, but of course, everyone saw what my butt looked like."

She pulls the sodden paper away from her face, staring at me with those large blue eyes of hers. Obviously I've never seen her mother, but she looks so much like Landon right now with the way she's staring at me, it makes me jumpy. Her father is someone I have to actively force myself not to think about and, more often than not, it doesn't go so well.

I haven't seen him since the coffee shop Sunday morning, but that doesn't mean he's far from my thoughts. Foolishly I hope he'll seek me out. Why? I truly don't know. He hates me, and I don't care for him all that much, and we fight cruelly. It's not the makings of anything healthy and, for that very reason, I know I need to blacklist him from my brain.

It's a work in progress.

"What happened after everyone saw?"

I shrug. "It sucked." I smile, and she giggles lightly at my minor swear. "But you know what? People teased me about it for that day and by the next, something else happened, and no one cared anymore. It happens to all of us ladies at some point. Truly, it does, and to this day, I'm positive no one else remembers it but me. The next year that boy gave me my first ever kiss, so clearly it didn't mean that much to him."

"It happened in English. The one class I have with every single hateful girl in my grade. They were awful."

I can imagine they were. I've heard some of the girls in the school, and if this is how they are now, I cringe to think of them as teenagers or even adults.

Anger burns my throat, but I keep my tone light and my words careful. "Stella, life lesson time. Anyone who makes fun of you instead of helping you isn't the kind of person you want on your team." And I will find out exactly who those girls were and keep an eye out.

"I know. But they all laughed and made fun. Said that

maybe I'll finally start to grow boobs now that I got my period. Everyone stared and laughed harder."

Little bitches. "Yeah, that part sucks, and I'm sorry that happened to you. But those girls? What are they to you if you don't like them? Their opinions are meaningless and hold no power over you unless you let them. You just have to find your people."

She shifts her weight, staring down at the pale blue tile floor. "I don't really have that here. They call me princess and think I'm weird."

In the two plus weeks I've been teaching here, I have yet to see Stella with any friends. Not in the halls. Not at lunch. Not even outside in between classes. She's alone. Always. And it breaks my heart. Stella is quiet, kind of nerdy, reading by herself instead of sitting with the other girls and gossiping about boys. In the long run, she's better off for it, but it makes her the subject of ridicule because she's beautiful and an Abbot-Fritz, and jealousy at the age of thirteen—at any age—is real.

"You just haven't found the right ones yet. Girls like them feel that by making fun of others no one will see the ugly they're trying to cover up. By tomorrow or the end of the week, they'll be on to something or someone else."

She sniffs, wiping her nose with wet paper towels.

"Don't tell my dad, okay?"

I think about that for a minute. "Do those girls harass you regularly, or was that just with this?"

"They used to try to be my friends, but I knew it was because of my family and not because they liked me. Since then, they switched and turned mean. But it's not like they're threatening me or anything. They're just nasty. Please, though. I don't want to bring my dad into this."

"Okay. For now, this will stay between us. But that's subject to change."

She nods on a heavy swallow.

"Now, let's get you sorted out. Do you have a pad?"

"No. I left all my stuff in the classroom."

And her teacher never even came to look for her? The hell?

"All right. Stay put. I'll be right back."

I give her a wink, then I fly out the door, down the hall to my room. I close everything down and grab my purse and sweater I keep here because my room has a tendency to get cold. Then I go for the English class I think I've seen Stella walk into before and sure enough, her stuff is where she left it. And the room is completely empty.

Not even two minutes later, I'm back in the bathroom with Stella, who is hiding once again in the stall. "Here, hon. I have a pad you can use, some makeup wipes to clean up your legs, and a sweater you can tie around your waist to hide your skirt."

"Thank you, Miss Wilde."

I snort. "Stella, it's after school hours, and I'm not only your neighbor, but we're in the middle of a girl emergency. I think you can call me Elle."

She doesn't reply, but a few minutes later she exits the stall, looking a million times better. She even has a hesitant, albeit slightly embarrassed, smile on her lips. "Thank you, Elle."

"That's what friends are for. But my advice if you get irregular periods is to keep an extra pad on you—hide it in your shoe or somewhere on you—as well as keep a sweater or something in your locker that you can tie around your waist. Or you can always text or call me, and I'll come running."

Now that embarrassed smile turns broad and genuine, her eyes sparkling. "Thank you," she says again, and I give her a hug before handing off her school stuff.

"How are you getting home?"

"It's Wednesday. My dad works late on Wednesdays, so I typically walk home if no one in my family can pick me up."

"Wonderful. I'm hoofin' it too. You can keep me company."

"How come you don't have a car?" Stella asks as we finally—after two miles—reach our street.

"Just haven't gotten around to buying one yet. The reason I picked this house is because it's close to town and close to the school. Besides, I get four miles of exercise in a day this way."

"Something tells me after the snow comes, you're going to want that car."

I snicker. "Something tells me you're right." We stop on the sidewalk in front of her house. Their house is larger than mine by a lot, but still not what you'd think of when you think Fritz.

She juts her thumb over her shoulder. "My dad bought this house when I was only a few months old," she says, almost as if she's reading my mind. "My mom and dad had just graduated college, and my dad was about to start medical school at Harvard. I think he's regretted buying it ever since. We have that large fence, but it's not always enough. Paparazzi used to camp out on our lawn for weeks. He's threatened multiple times to buy us a place with more privacy, better security, but I don't think he could ever sell this place. He has about fifty different sketches and designs for his dream home, but they just kind of sit in his office, untouched."

My breath catches. "Because of your mom?"

Her eyes glass over even as she smiles. "My mom loved this house." She shrugs a shoulder. "Or so he tells me."

"She must have been very special."

"Wanna come inside? See her picture? Check out my greenhouse?"

I hesitate for so many reasons. I'm dying to check out the inside of Landon's home. To catch more of a glimpse of the compelling man who feels like a mystery I should never attempt to solve. But my curiosity about him, my intrigue, is why I should say no.

Bridget was right.

I need to keep my distance. He's far more tolerable when I

can't stand him, and the more I'm around him—the more I learn of him—the more I worry I'll soften my hard disposition.

But looking at Stella, her oh so hopeful expression, knowing the shitty afternoon she's already had and the idea of her going into that big house all alone...

"Sure. I'd love to come in."

I'll just have to make sure I leave before Landon comes home.

However, as I step over the threshold, I wonder if I just made the mistake of my life. This house. It. Is. Everything. Everything I was afraid it would be. Perfect. Gorgeous. Expertly decorated and finished with the highest-end touches naturally. It screams wealth and money without being over-the-top.

But who cares about that?

It's the homey feel of it. The way there are shoes sitting in a neat row by the side door in the mudroom—since that's where we entered. The smell of vanilla and something masculine, like Landon's cologne. The way the furnishings are comfortable and accessible and inviting without being pretentious and forbidden. The number of pictures lining mantles and walls—all family.

Stella is everywhere in this home.

It's a living, breathing tribute to her and the love her father has for her. It's his way of saying your mother might be gone, and we had you very young, but you're all we ever wanted. If I was ever curious about Stella's mother's appearance, I don't have to look far.

Her face is nearly in every picture. Holding Stella. Kissing Stella. Smiling at Stella.

She is a reminder of love. Enshrined for eternity. Gone, but far from forgotten.

And no matter how hard I try, I cannot contain how choked up it makes me. I can feel the ache as it weeds through me, planting roots and setting up shop. I hold in tears, but it's an act of sheer will. One I barely master.

I lost my best friend to Lake History in the Badlands of South Dakota. History. Do you feel it? Why I took up said profession? That's not entirely why, but it holds a place too. Her parents took us to see the national parks when we were fifteen. My parents never did anything special with Cat and me, so this was the trip of a lifetime. Erika and I shared a tent, and when I woke up one morning alone, I went searching. It didn't take me long. Her body had washed up on the shore of our campsite.

I still don't know what happened. All I can assume—hope—was that she sleepwalked out of our tent sometime overnight while I slept and went for the water.

Awake or asleep, I'll never know.

Intentional or accident, again, I'll never know.

Her parents stopped talking to me after that day. They blamed me for not waking up to stop her. Hated me for surviving when she didn't. Erika was my star and their shining light.

All I know is that I lost my best friend that day, and Stella lost her mom in a lake, and I hate that I feel that connection, but I do. It makes me want to tuck her under my mended wing and promise I'll teach her how to fly one day because that's a talent we all need, and everyone deserves a person in their corner teaching them how.

"That's her," Stella says when she catches me standing by a picture of newborn Stella in the arms of her mother with her father smiling at them both like they're his sun right by their side. Honestly, it's his smile that's holding me here. None of his smiles I've seen have come close to this.

"She's gorgeous."

And that's no lie.

"He keeps them like a shrine."

I jerk around, startled by that.

Her blue eyes are bold. "I don't remember her, but I know he wishes I did. It makes him sad that I don't, but I was too young."

Oh. That's insanely tragic, and I hurt for both her and her mother *and* her father. I love that he keeps these pictures for her like that. So Stella knows just how deeply her mother loved her. She obviously loved her with her whole heart, so the idea of Stella not remembering her...

"Does that hurt?" I ask before I can stop it.

She blinks at me. "No one has ever asked me that before, but yes. It hurts. I know it hurts my dad. I'm told stories, and I see pictures, but I don't remember anything other than the police coming and a lot of photographs being taken whenever I went anywhere."

An Abbot-Fritz.

Stella is an Abbot-Fritz. A Boston princess whether she's aware of that or not.

Her father does a good job of sheltering her. I didn't see much about her when I Googled him. But it's clear if she wanted to change that, she could have five million social media followers by tomorrow.

"Can you show me your greenhouse?"

She guides me through the house I'm desperate to explore more of but don't get the chance. And I won't even get into their grounds in the back because day-um. I'm led through a garden of fall flowers and plants, all beautiful and lush and vibrant, to a large glass structure near the fence line on the opposite side from my house.

"My dad designed it for me," she tells me as we stand before it. "He sketched the whole thing out for me and had it built. He and my uncles even helped. It's fully heated, so I can come out here in the winter."

My heart is so full with that.

"It's a whole other building." And by the looks of it, she

could feed an entire village with what she grows. This thing is massive.

"I like to read in here so..."

Oh, Stella. How lonely are you?

About as lonely as you've been for the last few years, jars into my head.

The moment we enter the space, I'm immediately intoxicated by the scent of earth. Warm, but not hot. Dirt and plants and herbs and flowers and fruits and vegetables. Some in pots. Some in raised beds. Some in planters. There's a freaking sprinkler system overhead that is set to water the whole damn place.

And in the corner is a nook.

Beanbag chairs and a small desk with a lamp because there's electricity out here.

I meander my way through, inspecting everything, and once I reach her desk, I hear her call out, "Will you teach me to cook? Like lessons? I see your recipes in our class chat. I know you know how. We talked about it that day when I met you. I can pay you if you want. I have money."

I spin around, staring at her from across the twenty or so feet that divide us. Alarm bells ring in my head, but I push them aside and focus on her. Not him. "I don't need your money, Stella. But is that what you want? To learn how to cook?"

She nods, her eyes filling with wonder. "More than anything."

I can't deny her, so I don't even try. "If your dad is okay with it, I'll teach you anything you want to learn."

A smile breaks free across her face seconds before the greenhouse doors open, and her father walks in. Not happy at all to find me here.

12

Landon

My heart is racing like crazy right now. Strong beats pumping the blood through my veins. My last two patients of the day were a husband and wife, and they canceled this morning. I was grateful. It allowed me to leave work earlier than I typically would on a Wednesday.

Summer rolls and shrimp lo mein for Stella—it's her favorite. Sushi for me because I can eat it while looking over patient charts.

Only, I knew before I arrived home what I would find.

I watched Stella bring Elle inside on the cameras I have set up. The rest of my drive home, I deliberated what I should do. My entire walk through our house and out through the yard to the doors of the greenhouse too.

What the hell was she doing here?

Why would she come?

For Stella... or for me?

That's what drove me mad, right up until I opened the doors and saw the answer for myself. She was not there for me. And when I should have felt relief—part of me did—the larger part of me felt this inexplicable rush of anger. Of heat.

Goddammit, why *wasn't* she there for me?

And why did I care that she was staring at me like a street kid caught stealing? Nervous yet defiant.

I turn my glare away from the bane of my existence over to my daughter. "Hey, Bellas. What's going on here?"

"Elle walked me home from school, and I wanted to show her my greenhouse."

Elle walked her home, but there's more to it than that. I can see it in the way Stella swivels around to ensure Elle meets her eyes. To ensure whatever message she wants to relay, Elle reads. And the second I see the recognition of it flicker over Elle, I know the two of them already have secrets I'm not privy to.

"Great," I say when I think it's obvious from my tone I find it to be anything but.

"Dad?" Stella turns back to me. "Elle likes to cook. Remember, I showed you some of those recipes on our wellness chat. She's going to teach me how."

Fuck.

"How about you go inside and start your homework. I'll be in in a few minutes. You'll see Miss Wilde tomorrow at school."

I can feel Stella's frown, her unhappy face imploring me. She wants to ask if Elle can stay for dinner but knows enough not to ask in front of her. If it were Layla, I wouldn't hesitate to say yes or even offer it myself. But Elle is not Stella's friend. Elle cannot be Stella's friend.

Stella straightens her spine and clears her throat, likely throwing me a death glare I can't meet because I'm too busy, locked in a visual duel with her wellness and history teacher.

"Sure. Of course. Good night, *Elle*," she emphasizes her name, showing me there's more to this than a student-teacher relationship. "Thank you again for everything today."

"Always," Elle promises, and I hate that fucking promise more than I hate her being here.

A blink of an eye. A wrong word. A patch of ice. That's all it takes. Doesn't she understand that? There is no always. There is no forever. And certainly not with her.

Stella scurries out, attempting to force my gaze to hers one last time, and I finally relent at the last second before she brushes by me. "Don't be a jerk," she hisses under her breath so only I can hear.

Her words hit me like a sucker punch. Still, I make no promises.

I watch as Elle steels her spine, her chin lifting contemptuously. She's gearing up for a battle I have no interest in fighting. I've already lost. Which somehow is more than I can tolerate from her, so I decide maybe I should go a few more rounds because I'll be damned if I allow her to chip away at more of me.

"I wasn't planning on being here when you got home. Stella said you work late on Wednesdays. Usually not home until after seven."

"Typically, I'm not. What are you doing with my daughter? You don't belong here."

She makes some kind of annoyed sound in the back of her throat, folding her arms over her chest as she leans back against a table full of potted plants. "You know what I'm doing here. Don't make it out to be more than it is. She invited me in to see her greenhouse because gardening is obviously something she and I both have in common."

"Doesn't mean I want you here with her."

Pain flashes across her face before she quickly tries to tuck it away. "Why did you say that?"

"Because I'm an asshole," I tell her simply so she knows. It's not an act. It's a fact she can rely on. "What happened today with her?"

She shakes her head. "Nuh-uh. That's something you'll have to get from her. I will not betray her confidence in that.

She was not a threat to herself or to others, so I'm not obligated to say a word."

"I don't like you having secrets with my daughter."

"Sucks to be you then."

Damn her.

"She asked me to teach her how to cook, and I'd like to, Landon. I think it would be good for her."

I take an involuntary step forward, my blood heating, my body humming with a steady cocktail of endorphins. "You're in no place to tell me what is good for my daughter."

She puffs a sigh, her head falling back as she stares up at the glass ceiling, muttering something I can't hear under her breath. It's likely a dig at me, so I don't ask.

The problem is, I know she's right.

Stella has wanted to learn how to cook for years. My human dumpster will eat anything she gets her hands on, but I'm not stupid enough to pretend I don't know why she wants to do this. She even subscribed us to a mail order thing for a while that shipped boxes of food and recipes to follow. But she was only eleven then, and I wasn't much help, though I tried to be. I offered to have someone cook our meals for us in the past, and Stella dismissed the idea.

I should kick Elle out—out the door and out of our lives— but now there's no way I can. Stella's obsession with her has me grasping at straws, searching for loopholes when I already know there are none. Stella is making her move, and as always, it's checkmate because I'd do anything to make her happy.

Even if it'll cost me dearly.

"She knows how to make enchiladas," I throw out. Carter taught her that since it's his specialty.

"And what else?" Elle challenges.

My parents don't cook. They have Sophia, their personal chef. She's been with the family for years. That's how I grew up, so I don't know how to cook either. Reese did all of that, and if she were still alive, Stella would be doing that with her mother. Not seeking misplaced attention from a virtual stranger. The truth remains, no matter what I do, I can't bring her mother back, and one day when Stella realizes she should hate me, I hope she clings to this. I'd build her a thousand greenhouses. Hire a James Beard winning chef to teach her.

But she wants Elle.

"Why do you care? What's in it for you?" I question instead, shutting the doors behind me for no real reason other than I don't want Stella to watch as I prowl toward her teacher like a tiger after its prey.

Elle visibly swallows, taking a step back and bumping into the table behind her, her hands flinging back, grasping on to the edge as it shakes. Her pupils dilate as if she knows I'm thinking about stripping her naked and devouring her.

I make you nervous, Elle. I make your heart flutter. Your skin heat. Your pussy wet. Fuck, I can practically smell how turned on she is as I get closer. See how aroused I make her as it darkens her eyes.

"I know what it's like to lose someone you love and feel like you have no one else."

That's when I freeze. Dead in my tracks. The blood that was funneling south turns to ice in my veins.

"You're not her mother."

Hackles rise. "I'd never try to be. But she needs a friend."

"You're her teacher. Fourteen years her senior. Are you that out of options?"

She lets out a humorless laugh as she folds her arms over her chest and glares. "Yeah. Maybe I am. Maybe my only friend has a family of her own. Maybe I ran out of a bad situation and now I find myself here with not a whole lot going on other than my job. But Stella asked me to help her learn how to cook, and she has a greenhouse you built for her, loaded with fruits and vegetables. I like cooking. I like Stella. I don't like you. With your permission, I'd like to teach her how to cook."

"I can't have you here, Elle. I can't smell your perfume in my house when I walk in the door. The last thing I can tolerate at the end of a long day is how your smile makes your eyes more green than brown or the way your hair looks when you play with the ends of it—the way you're doing now."

She releases her hair instantly, her hands going back to the table, but it makes no difference. It's already mussed. The way it looked after my hands ran through it. Sexy. Disheveled.

"Believe me, the last thing I want is to be anywhere near you."

I do believe her, which is why I'm taking another step, anxious to prove her a liar.

Suddenly I'm hovering over her, my size and proximity a likely weapon when she's the one disarming me completely.

"So how do we solve this?" My voice is a whisper, the sound husky. Hoarse. I want to wrap her hair around my fist and yank her toward me. Spin her around in place and spank her ass red. Her pussy would drip for me, but only after she begged me to would I fuck her like the world was ending, putting us both out of our misery. Or maybe that misery is all mine.

"You trust me—"

"I don't."

"I won't hurt her."

But she has so much power to. More than she even knows.

My hand comes up, my fist curling until my knuckles graze the soft flesh of her cheek, gliding up along the fragile bones poised beneath her silky skin. Every night I jerk off. To her. Her alone. The way she stares up into my eyes. Headstrong. Sure-fire. Brazen. Her gorgeous mouth. Those full lips. My cock slurping between them.

I want her in a way I don't remember wanting anyone. Not... fuck, not ever. And how do I reconcile that? I loved my wife in ways I will never love another woman. But she and I... we were easy. Flawless.

Everything with Elle is difficult. Blemished. And yet I crave her in this moment more than my next breath. The breath that's already ragged. Corrupt. Needy. *My vixen.*

My knuckles flatten out, curling up into her hair, and her breath hitches. "Stella goes to your house."

"All right."

"Only two days a week. No more."

"Fine.

"I need you to sleep with your window closed." Because though I've had mine locked, I still stand beside it, straining to hear if she's crying. Desperate to catch a glimpse of her. *Who makes you cry, Elle? Who possesses those tears and how do I make them go away?*

She shakes off my hand at that, not pleased at all with me. In fact, I think her hand is ready to fly. "You spy on me?"

My hands fall to the table, right beside hers, pinkie to pinkie as I bracket her in. My nose hits her neck, just at the base of it, right where it meets her shoulder. I take a deep inhale as I slowly glide up. She hates me, and yet she's not pushing me away. Slapping my face the way I deserve. No, she's trembling against me. And not in fear.

"Landon." My name on her lips. It's a demand for answers I'm not giving, but her voice is not as smooth or in control as it was. It vibrates through me and that deep, dark abyss in the pit of my gut suddenly doesn't feel as bottomless as it did seconds ago.

"I haven't in over two weeks," I tell her, my hot breath brushing against her skin.

"But you did?"

"I did. I listened to you cry."

Another inhale, this one right under her chin, and her body

shudders, shaking desperately against me. One hand flees the table, grasping my hair in a punishing fist when my tongue sneaks out, stealing a taste. She moans, and I grunt, my cock throbbing in my slacks. Her breasts press into my arm and fuck, I fucking hate her.

I hate her so goddamn much I'm crazy because of it.

I hate her for being in the hotel that night. For moving in next door. For being irresistible to me in ways I don't comprehend. For befriending Stella and me not being able to say no. For being right that Stella needs more than I can give her. For being this sweet, bubbly person when I wish she were nothing short of evil.

Truly hateable.

I steal another taste, and then I'm retreating, walking back step after step. Her cheeks are flushed, and her eyes are a wild, angry, stunning storm.

"You can't touch me again."

I smirk at that. If I want to touch her, I will, and we both know she'll like it. "With any luck, I won't have to see you at all."

She straightens, moving now around tables and pots, heading in my direction. Toward the exit. But I don't want her to go. I want to take her mouth with mine. I want her to beg for me. To cry out my name. *My* fucking name. Not Luca's.

Somehow I'm blocking the doors, and I don't even know how I got here.

She stands right before me, mere inches separating us, until she's forced to crane her neck to meet my eyes. She smirks, and I know I won't like what's to come next.

"I don't cry so much anymore at night. I'm usually busy doing other things. With my window open."

Motherfucker.

"Stella can come over on Mondays and Wednesdays," I tell

her, returning my focus to Stella or this will only end one way. "Those are the best days for me since those are the days I work late."

She swallows and nods. "I'll take care of the groceries, and she can bring anything from this greenhouse she wants to use. You'll even likely get dinner out of it."

I shake my head. "I pay for the groceries. That's nonnegotiable."

She rolls her eyes but acquiesces with a shrug. "Fine. I'll send you a receipt for whatever I buy."

I shift to the side, forcing myself out of her path. She needs to go. I'm barely hanging on.

The door opens, and a welcome blast of cool hits me, brushing my hair back off my face and dragging reason back into me.

She falters by the door, her back to me. "For the record, you're nothing like your brother. Even when you were pretending to be him. I liked the man I met in the hotel better than either of you in real life." Then she's gone, running out into the darkness of my backyard.

Me too, I think.

I liked being him with her. That guy. The one who reminded me of me from days long forgotten.

Which is why I let her go. It's why I allow her to walk back into my house and tell Stella the plan. I watch as they speak in my kitchen, and Stella jumps up and down with a squeal I can hear even from out here. She gives her a hug, and Elle is laughing. Smiling at my girl. Making her happy in ways I try to and likely fail at more often than not.

Stella needs a woman in her life, and with my mother being sick and my sister working long hours and in a serious relationship, and Layla and Amelia doing their own family thing with Oliver, it seems Elle is her best option.

Stella needs Elle, and I need to let that happen.

I just have to figure out a way to keep my distance when keeping my distance seems to require a herculean strength I already know I don't possess.

13

"Why won't you call me back?" David asks as I set the phone between my ear and my shoulder, as I gather everything I need for class. He texted it was an emergency, and because I'm gullible, I answered when he called and now, I'm regretting everything.

I should hang up, but I'd rather deal with this once and for all.

"Because there's absolutely no reason to. We're divorced."

"And I've told you that's a mistake. It should have never happened."

"And I've told you I disagree. That it absolutely should have happened."

"Don't talk to me like that, Elle. We took vows. Vows I took seriously."

"David, I don't know what to say to you anymore. You signed the papers. You agreed to the terms. I don't see why you keep calling me. I've held up my end of the agreement and haven't said a word to reporters about anything."

And they've been calling me too. Word got out about the divorce when someone found our court documents and since then, it's been a never-ending stream of calls. Thankfully, no one has shown up on my doorstep. Yet.

"I don't care about agreements. I love you. Come back to me. Please. We can work all of this nonsense out. Make it like it never happened."

"That's not what I want anymore. I tried that, David. I tried that for more than two years. I did everything I could think to do to make you show me the love you claimed to feel. To make you treat me with respect instead of like a doormat. No, worse. You treated me worse than a doormat. I went to therapy. Couples counseling—without you, might I add. I read dozens of books. I changed my hair, lost and gained weight, stopped talking back. I lost myself, David, trying to be who you wanted me to be, and it's not okay. You didn't care we were over for six months. Suddenly you do?"

He huffs into the phone, and I know that huff enough to know he's building up a fireball of anger along with it. "I lost an endorsement because of you. Do you know what that means for me? For my career? Do you have any idea all that you've cost me already?"

"Why would you lose an endorsement over getting divorced?"

"Because it was with a restaurant chain who believes in family fucking values, Elle! That's why. Our divorce is a stain on my reputation. Is that what you wanted?" His voice booms through the phone, forcing me to pull it from my ear.

Six months ago, that voice would have had me trembling. I would have apologized and said whatever I needed to say to abate his anger. But this isn't six months ago, and he can't do anything to me now other than yell. His words no longer hurt, and I no longer fear what he's capable of.

"I'm sorry to hear that, David. Maybe if they'd known the real you, they wouldn't have taken you on in the first place."

"You're such a selfish, spoiled bitch. You always have been.

Couples fight. Grow up. I never hit you or mistreated you. You had everything your heart desired and then some."

Except being treated like I mattered by the one person who mattered to me.

"You think this temper tantrum you're pulling will get you what you want from me? Haven't I already given you enough? You had no problems spending my money or taking it when it suited you. This isn't over, Elle. You are my fucking wife—"

That's when I hang up.

I don't think David knows where I live, but it's not exactly hard to find. The lease is in my name. Frankly, my parents would be the first ones to tell him anyway. They're as furious with me as he is. Couples fight. I nearly crack a smile at that. Nearly.

Maybe my dick would stay hard if it wasn't forced to fuck you every night. You're so stupid, every time you open your mouth it's like fingernails on a chalkboard. You ungrateful little cunt. You can't even make and serve a meal without fucking it up.

That last one was just the beginning after I accidentally overcooked the roast. He picked up the slightly too well-done food and tossed it across the kitchen, splattering grease and meat and vegetables everywhere. The platter shattered. He continued to stand there, yelling at me, berating me, telling me how worthless and stupid and ungrateful I was. Forcing me to clean it all up on my hands and knees. Making sure I got every last spot of food or chip of the dish. He didn't care when I cut my finger on a shard and bled. That was yet another insult to him. Another reason to call me stupid and clumsy and careless.

There was no laughing off the meal or saying don't worry, babe, we'll just get takeout tonight. It wasn't even ruined, just more well-done than he liked.

I told my mother, and she blew it off. Told me it was my responsibility to make a nice home and cook well for my husband. *It's your job to be the best wife you can be for him,* she had said. What about me? Didn't I deserve him to be the best husband he could be for me? That wasn't important to her, though.

Speaking of... Jesus.

"Hi, Mom," I answer, already guessing David sent her a text or something. This is insane.

"Do you have any idea what you're doing to the people you claim to love?"

Awesome.

I pace around the island in my kitchen, already needing to leave for school, but not wanting to talk to them as I walk. I like to start my day on a positive note and dealing with my ex-monster and my unloving, greedy parents isn't that. Thankfully my sister washed her hands of me years ago or I'd have to deal with her too.

"Why don't you just tell David to fuck off? I did."

"Ellery Jane Chambers, you will not speak to me that way. I am your mother. David has officially cut us off. Completely. The car is gone. We can't pay off the credit card. Now our condo is threatened."

I shake my head at that. "What are you talking about?"

"He was giving us a hundred and fifty grand a year, Ellery, and now that's stopped because you divorced him!" she screams into the phone, furious in a way I've never heard her before. My stomach tightens, and my heart pounds.

"Why would he give you that kind of money?" I knew absolutely nothing about this.

She clears her throat, trying to rein in her voice, when my mother is clearly on the edge. "Because we had a deal with him, but now that deal is over because you walked out. It's over. We have nothing left. Nothing to use as leverage since I can't even find the—" Her words cut off sharply.

"What? What can't you find? What leverage?"

"Listen to me, Ellery. Your father and I need that money.

You will do as I say and go back to him. After all we've done for you since the day you were born, you owe us."

I want to ask why they even need his money. Last I checked, Dad retired early with a full pension. I'm also tempted to ask what they've done for me, because it hasn't been much, but I keep my mouth shut. All I had in the world was Erika until I lost her. I didn't have my sister, and my parents couldn't be bothered with me. Hell, they hardly acknowledged my existence. When I lost Erika, everything fell apart for me. I got myself a cheer scholarship to the University of Miami and left without looking back.

Then David came along. Swept me off my feet. Made me feel seen and special and loved in a way I never had before. My parents made an effort to be involved in my life after I said 'I do,' and I wasn't stupid enough to wonder why. Now that reason is even more glaring.

"I'm sorry, but I won't go back to David. I'll help you figure something out or maybe I can even help with some of your bills, but David and I are over."

"Then you leave me no choice."

And then my crazy mother hangs up on me. I'm reeling, spinning her words around in my head. Clueless about what she means by leaving her no choice, but there isn't a whole lot she can actually do about this. I'm not going back to David.

We're divorced, and this is over.

They can't touch me. They can't get to me here.

Still, I can't help the trembling in my hands as I close and lock up my door. The burning sensation in my nose from tears I will not shed over them. I take another steadying breath.

I usually like to go to the coffee shop in town before I head to work, but now I don't have time. What I really need to do is buy a car, but now, after all that, it feels wrong to use my settlement on anything. My salary at the school is all I'm using right now, but it's not enough to buy a car. I suppose I could lease one.

Maybe I should send my settlement money to my parents and be done with the lot of them. For good.

Suddenly my scarf feels like it's strangling me as I rip it from around my neck, only to drop my keys. I move to pick them up when the first of the tears hit my cheeks. I am *not* crying. I'm just... a little flustered. But it'll pass.

All of this will.

I dip into a squat, snatching my keys and giving myself a second to catch my breath. And when I stand up, wipe the damn tear from my cheek, and turn around, I squeak out a surprised yelp, nearly dropping my keys for a second time.

Landon is parked in front of my house in his black Range Rover, the passenger window down and his green eyes fixed on me as he leans over the console in my direction, studying me. Great. Exactly what I need to start this day off on an even more stellar note.

"I'm not in the mood to fight with you today."

"Are you okay?" he calls back instead.

"Why wouldn't I be?"

"You looked upset."

How on earth could he have seen that? Was he watching me when I came out? How long has he been parked there?

"I'm fine."

His hand grips the wheel, and he turns to face the front windshield, but he doesn't drive off. His jaw is locked tight, and he looks like he's stuck in some kind of indecision I can't understand.

Unfortunately, I have to walk to the end of my walkway and down the sidewalk, past his car, and I silently plead with him to drive away. Of course he doesn't. Landon Fritz doesn't seem to do anything I want him to. And when he does, I hate him all the more for it.

"Do you need a ride?" he asks just as I make a show of pretending like he's not sitting in his car watching me with an intensity that has the hairs on the back of my neck standing at attention.

"No."

"Elle, get in the car, and I'll drive you to work."

"I'm fine."

"So you keep telling me, but I can see you're not. Come on. You're already late."

"Where is Stella?"

"I dropped her at school already, but I had to run back here to grab my laptop. Please get in the car."

"No, thanks."

"I won't speak if that helps."

"You hardly ever do."

I hear him chuckle lightly and that sound has me stopping to look at him if for no other reason than because the last time I heard it was that night in the hotel. Not since. Not once since because the man does not laugh or chuckle or smile hardly ever.

"Then it shouldn't be anything you aren't already used to." Suddenly I hear the click of his car door, and he's out of his seat, rounding the front of the car and opening the passenger door for me. He's wearing scrubs a shade lighter than his eyes —no glasses today—but those scrubs expertly mold to his muscular body. His dark hair is still damp from his shower, brushed back, revealing more of his handsome, chiseled features.

The morning light of the fall sun hits him just right, and in this moment, he's the hottest man I've ever seen. How terribly unfortunate that is. My knees are about to buckle at the damn sight of him. Is this what swooning feels like? Couldn't he be as ugly as his attitude?

I stare at him, wary, but also unable to look away. My heart skips a beat.

"Did you take out a squirrel or a cat when you dropped off Stella? Is that why you're suddenly in a good mood and being nice to me?"

He gives me a don't be ridiculous look as he motions once again for me to get in his car.

"I thought you said with any luck we wouldn't have to see each other."

"And with any luck, after this we won't. But you're making my daughter happy by doing something special for her, so the least I can do is drive you to work."

I don't budge, and he growls, at the end of his patience with me.

"Fine, consider it payback for doing a very large favor to me by spending two afternoons a week with Stella. Now come on, before we're both late."

"Fine. But this is a one-time thing. Don't start getting your hopes up that you'll have the pleasure of my company every morning."

He smirks, his eyes sparkling. "Shame. How will I ever live without that? Now move your ass."

I hop in the car, place my bag and purse on my lap, my scarf on the seat beside me, and he shuts the door behind me. The interior is smooth and dark and smells like him. Like man and spice and earth and sandalwood. I take a deep inhale just as he gets back in, and I can only hope he didn't catch me doing it.

"I'm shocked you're doing this for me. I feel like I should check your temperature, but you're the doctor here. I already know it's out of your way toward the highway, and you're not known for being all that chivalrous."

Again with that chuckle, though this time he rubs at his bottom lip as if he's trying to hide his amusement. "I was raised by a mother who absolutely believes in chivalry and manners.

She would have been appalled if I hadn't stopped. Especially with you looking as upset as you were."

He pulls away from the curb, heading toward the end of our street. "I was raised by a mother who believed my presence in her life to be superfluous and of no value until the day I married David. Then I had value, literally it seems. I'd take your mother over mine any day."

"Is that what has you frowning today? It's not a look I've seen on you often."

"I frown plenty."

"No. You're the happiest person I've ever met—or maybe friendliest is more accurate. However that works, nothing seems to hold you down for long. What happened with your family this morning to make you look so sad?"

I stare into his profile. "Suddenly you want to get to know me?"

We come to a stoplight in town, and he shifts to face me as we wait for it to turn green. His eyes bore into mine. "You haven't figured it out yet? Why I don't want to do that?"

"Because you're attracted to me, and you don't want to be?"

"Because I'm *drawn* to you, and I don't want to be."

He starts off again, the light having turned green, and we fall into silence. I fumble for a follow-up but come up with nothing. He's drawn to me, and I feel that. I see it. We have so much chemistry we could blow up a lab. But at the heart of it, he doesn't want to be. I tip my head down to hide how much that bothers me when it shouldn't.

I don't want to be drawn to him either.

But my reasons and his feel very different. His seem more like a natural extension of himself. Something he'd never consider changing. Not for anyone. Mine waver, fluctuate, and if something genuine came along, despite my recent circumstances, I'd jump at it. Life's too short not to.

To him, that notion is abhorrent.

So instead, I just stare straight ahead, sitting stiffly, breathing his scent in and out as the car drives me to work. But just as we're two blocks from the school, I feel his eyes on me. More alive than ever as their penetrative heat clings to the side of my face, imploring me to react. To look back at him.

And I do. So very helpless to resist where he's concerned.

David never looked at me the way Landon is looking at me now.

It's possessive and mad, feral and agitated. But it's also tender. Like he has to look at me, absorb everything about me so he can keep it for himself. Cherish and hold onto it because we both know there will never be anything else between us. All this fire and passion and ache have no home. No outlet.

Both of us such damaged souls, you'd think we'd be that for each other, but no. That seems like such an impossibility. More heartache in the making.

Suddenly something catches his attention while breaking our spell. His head whips around, and he slams on the brakes, sending us both careening forward. His hand shoots out protectively, catching me and holding me back along with my seat belt.

"Shit," he mutters, nearly having blown right through a red light and into oncoming traffic. His hand leaves my chest, and I try to catch my breath. He runs that hand through his hair as I pick up my purse and bag that had slid off my lap and onto the floor. "Are you okay?"

And like he can't resist, his hand comes back for me, brushing hair away from my face as he caresses my cheek, checking me over. After he tried to save me.

No. Today I am not okay.

A cascade of chills rolls down my body, and I force myself to pull away from his touch, such easy pickings where he's concerned. "I'm good to get out here."

"Elle—"

But his objection gets lost as I hastily unbuckle my seat belt and fly out the door, clutching my bags in my hands as they smash into me while I run like the coward I am. He'll break me in two if I let him. So vulnerable and easy to destroy, he'd do it without even breaking a sweat. I can't let that happen. Not again.

So I run. Up through the school grounds and into the building. It's only as I reach my desk and stow my things away that I realize I forgot my scarf in his car.

Dammit.

14

She left her scarf in my car two days ago. Two days. And like the creeper I am, it's found its way to my bedroom.

Into my nightstand and then my bed.

It's losing some of her fragrance, and I wonder if that's because I've smelled it as often as I have. I haven't messaged her about it. Haven't said anything to Stella either, when I so easily could just hand it off to her to return to her teacher.

Her teacher.

I've been waiting. Curious to see if Elle will call or text, requesting I return it.

Or worse yet, if she'll seek me out and do it in person.

It's late now, and I should be asleep, but as I hold the damn scarf up to my nose and inhale her sweet floral scent—my cock hardening—I do something I absolutely should not do. I get up and walk over to the window that faces hers, unlock it, and open it up wide.

A cold blast of air swooshes in, rattling some papers on my nightstand and the T-shirt I have hanging over the arm of the sofa in the sitting area. My body erupts in chills, and I shudder quickly only to push the frame as high as it will go, staring out in the darkness of night.

I know her window is open a little, even if her room is bathed in shadows.

I know because I checked—as I do every fucking night—when I first came up.

I'm obsessed with her. I don't even know how or when it happened.

I don't know her, not well anyway, but it's like something inside her speaks to something inside me, and whatever that something is, it will not be denied.

All my brothers had various girlfriends growing up, and I was no different in that, but I hadn't found any woman appealing enough to tempt my full attention until I met Reese.

I met her and thought... *her*. She smiled at me, and I spent the following six years of my life devotedly by her side. We had Stella, and Reese gave up dreams, and I was in school for impossible hours. Yet, our love was never questioned. It never wavered.

It was all that other stuff that challenged us.

There was so much I did wrong. Took for granted. Allowed to happen.

Now... I don't deserve a now. Certainly not with her. Elle.

She's had it bad. I don't have to know the details to know that. I'm the opposite of what she needs. I'm not a good man. I do not deserve someone like her coming into my life. And because of that, I won't confuse her or lead her on when nothing will ever come of it.

It was a mistake to offer her a ride. Now I'm avoiding her as I've vowed to do. But that doesn't stop me from jerking off with her scarf over my face and visions of her behind my eyes.

I'm the worst sort of pervert.

Guilt... why don't I feel you? You've been my constant companion since the day Reese went into that lake. Maybe even before that. But here, now, doing this? Where is my guilt when I need you most? I am not a worthy man.

Still, I strain, listening while staring out into a dark expanse I have no business searching, wondering about her.

The most tempting of goddesses I've ever encountered. My vixen, as I've called her in my head.

Guilt?

No, I don't feel you, and that loss, that ache, might be the most powerful source of my current agony. What happens when I stop feeling it? When I allow the idea of another to intrude? To take over? By letting go of my guilt, it's like I'm letting go of Reese, and that's not something I can ever do.

The light flickers on in Elle's bedroom, startling me out of my darkness. She's there, walking around, getting ready for bed. I can't see her all that well, just slightly obscured images through thirty feet and empty branches. But I can see enough. Her hair is down, curtaining her shoulders and the delicate blades of her back. She's wearing a white tank top and some kind of skimpy shorts.

The sweetest thing I've ever seen. Infuriatingly beautiful.

I need to step away.

I have no business watching her like this, her scarf still in my hand.

But seeing her like this has triggered something in me. Forcing me past drawn lines I knew I'd eventually cross. Hating the intrinsic knowledge that it was, truly, only a matter of time.

"Elle," I whisper, and not even two seconds later, her head whips in my direction as if she heard me call her name. Impossible, but there she is, walking to her window. She draws her curtains farther back and opens her window the rest of the way. She's squinting out into the night, searching for me, and I flip on the lamp on my nightstand, bathing me in soft light.

Her body straightens, her lips parting when she finally sees me, registers what I'm doing.

She doesn't speak and neither do I. I just stand here, gazing at her, same as she's doing with me. I move closer, right up against the window, and she does the same, magnets drawn to each other.

Her eyes flicker, her hand coming out to touch the screen.

"I thought you said you don't do this anymore."

"I don't."

But I am tonight, and we both know it.

"Are you going to stay?"

I shouldn't, but I can't make myself leave this window either.

She notes the scarf in my hand, and I bring it up to my face, smelling her while she watches. Another beat passes, and then she steals my breath as ever so slowly her hands grip her tank top, drawing the fabric up and over her head. She drops it to the floor, her deliciously perky breasts springing free, and I involuntarily groan, my cock pulsing with the need of her.

I rip off my white T-shirt, my skin on fire as her hands slip over her breasts, tugging on her nipples before trailing south, over her taut stomach, to the hem of her tiny shorts. My hand matches her motion and before she can, I yank my pajama pants down, kicking them away and sliding my hand into my boxer briefs, squeezing the base of my cock.

"Take them off," she calls out, and her voice. Her sweet, honey voice is like a shot of lust straight to my balls.

"You first," I challenge, and she doesn't hesitate. Her shorts slide down her supple legs, and there she stands in her window, completely nude, bathed in light, shivering ever so slightly. From the cold or what we're doing, I don't know.

But fuck, I want her.

I want to tear this house apart. Rip the window from the wall and claw my way into her room. The separation is driving me mad, and I pound the side of my fist into the glass, rattling the upper pane. I stare down at the six-foot fence and the tree that separates our houses and then back up at her, contemplating everything.

Frustration roars through me.

I want the taste of her on my tongue, smell her body in my nose, feel her skin on my fingertips. Not just the remnants of her on her scarf.

But that can never happen. Not again.

Rooted in place, the hand holding her scarf against the window, the other touching myself. I won't go to her. I won't pretend this could ever be more than living out a fantasy. Playing an erotic game with a forbidden woman. Our boundaries are set before us, and we're doing this, both knowing the score before we play.

So I lower my briefs and watch as her eyes cast down, taking me in. I do the same, wishing she were closer so I'd have a better view. I jerk my cock as her fingers glide across her smooth mound, dipping in between her legs. Desperate, I want to call out a million dirty things to her. Tell her every damn thought I'm having, but they're not words you can shout out into the night when anyone walking by or with an open window could possibly hear.

Instead, we hold our tongues, lost to our own sounds, as we pleasure ourselves to the other. The head of my cock is coated in precum, and I use that for lubrication, wishing it were the cream of her pussy all over me. She's wet. I'm not close enough, and I can't smell her, but her fingers glide in and out without resistance, her breasts heaving with her every hefty breath.

She lifts one breast, toying with it, squeezing it, pinching her nipple as her fingers move faster, in and out, then circling her clit. She cups her pussy and grinds into her palm, and my cock pulses as if I can feel the soft, wet heat of her around me.

Her head falls back, and I stroke myself harder, so overcome by what we're doing—the vision of her—I'm not sure how much longer I can hold out. Pleasure races up my spine, tightening my balls, and I grunt when she bites down into her lip.

No! I want to shout, *don't hold back. Let me hear you.*

My cock grows impossibly harder while I fist it, stroke it, twist my wet hand up and down and all around, harder and harder, imagining it's her wet cunt making it feel this good.

Remembering all the ways she liked it when I put my tongue up her hot channel, flicked her clit with it, fucked her pussy with my impossibly hard dick. She was insatiable that night, wanting more, loving every way I touched her.

I want to do so many things to her.

Blindfold her pretty eyes while I bend her over—her palms on the floor—and fuck her hard. Wrap my hands around her neck as I stare into her trusting eyes that know I'll make all this pain feel so fucking good. I could spend hours doing this with her. Hours of touching her. Tasting her. Licking the sweat from her body and coming to moans as they flee her lungs.

I have thought of her in every filthy, depraved way imaginable.

And none of it is enough.

She's getting close. Her hand that was on her breast is now braced against the window frame, her head bowed, leaning against it as she works herself. But her eyes. Her eyes are open and on me, on my hand as she works herself up, so close. And just when I can't hold off another second, she cries out, and I catch it.

That sound.

It spurs my own orgasm, and a raspy groan wrenches the air, out into the night, trapped between us.

I can't touch her. I'm helpless, restrained by boundaries and lines I know I can't cross. I can't. Too much is at stake. So I stroke my cock faster, my balls drawing up, and I come all over my chest and abs as I watch her fingers pry every ounce of pleasure from her body.

A pleasure I won't feel. A pleasure I cannot taste.

A pleasure I'm rabid to feel beneath me, a smile I'm furious I cannot fully see.

"Elle." There it is. I say her name again. She's still standing there, naked, breathing hard, so stunning my chest squeezes painfully. Right as the cold breeze hits the cum on my body, freezing me over.

What did I just do with her?

God, I really am an asshole.

There is so much beautiful life in that bold, sexy woman. I'd rather die than snuff that life out. I am bad news for her. And she undoubtedly deserves better.

I say one thing, and I do another, and it needs to stop before it's too late. Before I've done something I can't undo.

This won't happen again.

As if sensing my thoughts, she straightens her body, brushing her hair back from her face. She's waiting for me to say or do something, and I do the only thing that will save us both. I lower my gaze and take a step back, shutting and locking my window once more.

I heave a breath and then turn off the lamp.

Her light turns out a second later, and everything inside me *hurts*. A turmoil I've never experienced before pounding through me. A fiery warpath leaving nothing but destruction in its wake. Charging thoughts I can't give a voice to.

Wishing, for the first time in all these years, I were a better man. A man who deserved a woman like her. *My* vixen. A man who didn't fear all she could possibly represent.

And destroy.

I've been on edge since I woke up this morning, and it has nothing to do with what Landon and I did last night. Or the way he fled the scene as quickly as he could, like a thief in the night, leaving me standing there naked with my light still on and my window still open. Squashing all that bold, empowered bravery I had been rocking by seizing my sexuality and getting myself off with him watching.

No. I'm telling myself I'm on edge because today is my first cooking lesson with Stella, and I'll eventually have to see the heartless bastard otherwise known as her father after. Though he can officially keep the scarf.

I was lonely last night.

A bit sad and a little lost. When I walked in, I could have sworn I heard a noise outside my window. Then his light was on, and he was there, staring at me like I was his reason. Only I'm not, and it was foolish of me to think otherwise.

The girl sitting in the seat behind me already holds that title.

But I didn't realize that until after.

In the moment, I had this heady excitement sizzling in my

veins. I wanted to bring him to his knees. Rock his world. Stupid. So. Fucking. Stupid. I've tried to convince myself that I'm proud of what I did. Screw him. I got off, and it was hot. And the majority of me knows this. Owns this. Revels in it.

But there's that other part…

"Thank you for giving us a ride," I say again to Bridget.

She waves me away as we turn left, leaving the grounds of the school. "It's my pleasure. I can't have you two walking home in the rain. But I will just gently mention again that you need—"

"To buy a car," I finish for her. "Yes. I know. I'm working on it." Sorta. Not really. I haven't decided what I'm going to do about my parents. I texted David about it, and he said my family deserves what they get and that he had allowed them to bully him longer than he should have with how things turned out. Whatever that means. I didn't press it.

But my mother does. I got another phone call this morning from her that I ignored. Thankfully, she didn't leave a voice message. Oh, and to add to things, my sister randomly texted me. Four years since my wedding—the last time I saw or spoke to her—and now she texts? She asked where I was living because she wanted to come visit me.

That can't be good. Last I heard, she was running with a motorcycle gang and got herself arrested for breaking and entering, and larceny. Needless to say, I did not reply. I'm ignoring the world outside of this small Boston suburb, and that's all there is to it.

"Stella, hon, what are you and Miss Wilde making tonight?"

"She calls me Elle after work hours," I correct, and Bridget flashes me a Cheshire grin I can't quite read.

"Chicken pot pie," Stella replies. "It's my dad's favorite, and I looked up some recipes. I also have carrots, onions, and peas that I've grown in my garden and greenhouse we're going to use in it."

"I was thinking we could make a biscuit topper for it instead of using pie crust." I spin around in my seat to find Stella. "Maybe it's the Southern girl in me, but I miss real biscuits and haven't had an excuse to make them since I moved up here."

She nods like that's the best idea ever, and I turn back around, some of my uneasiness ebbing. Today will be fun. I love cooking, and I can't wait to use fresh veggies and now make biscuits. I don't have to see Landon. The girl lives next door. I can just send her home with a dish all ready for him.

He had my scarf in his bedroom. Was he—

I mentally shake myself. Nope, not going there.

"You'll have to let me know how it turns out," Bridget says, stopping at a traffic light in town.

The leaves are already falling. All that beautiful gold, orange, red, and yellow lining the streets and sidewalks. I haven't had this... well... ever. It's beautiful. The air has a crispness to it you feel in your bones. It makes me want to snuggle up under a blanket and read a book by the fire, which I plan to do one night soon. With a glass of wine in my hand, naturally.

"Oh, hey," Bridget goes on, pulling me away from the window. "I'm having a dinner party at my house on Saturday. Mostly faculty and a few friends. Will you come?"

I throw her a side-eye, my expression sour, already knowing where this is going. Her tone isn't hiding anything. "I don't want to be fixed up."

Bridget's head whips in my direction, her eyes wide as she feigns incredulousness. "Elle..."

Yeah. She doesn't even follow my name up with anything else. I cock an eyebrow at her, and she groans, slouching her rigid posture until she's practically falling into me only to straighten just as quickly so she can move us through the light.

"I mean it."

"Fine. But there might be a few single men at my dinner." She rushes on with a pleading tone when she catches my murderous glare. "They're great guys. Smart. Good-looking. Well"—she laughs—"some of them are very good-looking. Others"—she shrugs—"not so much. But the one I want you to meet is absolutely gorgeous. And a super nice guy to boot. If I weren't married, I'd date him."

"The ink on my divorce is barely dry."

She glances in the rearview mirror, then smirks without looking at me. "But it is dry and that hasn't stopped you so far."

"Bridget!" My jaw drops.

"I don't mind you talking about dating. I think you *should* date."

I flip around to Stella, pointing at her. "You do?"

She giggles lightly, and I can't stop my smile. This girl does not give out smiles all that often. Much like her father in that respect.

"Yes. You're smart, fun, beautiful. Any guy would be lucky to date you."

"You're excellent for my ego. I'm going to write that down on a Post-it and keep it by my bed." I give her a wink, only to scrunch up my nose. "But life lesson, Stella. Blind dates are the worst. Trust me on that. When you're allowed to start dating, avoid them like the plague they are. And remember the words you just said to me because you could have been talking about yourself."

She gives me a look and a shrug that suggests she's absolutely indifferent to the notion of dating. "My dad says I can't date until I'm twenty-five."

"Smart man," Bridget and I both say together, forcing laughs from all of us.

"Besides... I think I like girls. But that stays between us."

Well, that's a bomb I didn't see coming, and I wonder if her father knows that one.

"Our lips are sealed. But girls can go on blind dates with

girls. Doesn't change a thing, though admittedly, I'm a little jealous of you, Stella. Women are easier than men."

"Have to agree with that," Bridget jumps back in. "So help me push this along, Stella. I don't want you to see your smart, fun, beautiful teacher get sucked into an anti-men vortex just because she's newly divorced and wasn't so happy before that. Am I right? She deserves to have some fun. Meet some new men. *Good* men," she emphasizes. "Men who will treat her like the goddess she is."

I snort out a laugh, leaning over to plant a kiss on my friend's cheek. "Thank you for that."

"She's right," Stella agrees, and I groan dramatically, sagging down in my chair. "You should go to that dinner party and meet some new people."

She is right. They both are. But still. I'm just not there yet. At least with the dating part. I went from living in hell with a man I was constantly on eggshells around to sleeping with a guy who treats me like a rental car—there for his pleasure cruising, only to dispose of me when he's done with the ride.

Single Elle is just fine. More than fine.

And I have a bad habit of growing attached like a stray cat you feed only once. It doesn't take a therapist to figure out it's because I got very little love or attention at home growing up. It's part of what made me such easy pickings when David came along, though I'll admit, at first, he was nothing short of Prince Charming, and I was his princess.

"Fine. You've both convinced me. I'll go if you promise not to try to set me up. The last thing I want right now is a man. I'm working on me. I don't have any desire to get involved with anyone."

"It's a deal. I won't actively try to set you up."

I roll my eyes, knowing just what that means.

～

"THAT'S PERFECT. Keep slicing the carrots like that." I watch Stella for a second and nod. "Awesome stuff. I'm going to slice up the chicken because that's the gross, boring part." Raw meat —poultry especially—gives me the skeeves. "What made you want to garden and learn how to cook?"

"You're going to think I'm lame."

I turn my head over my shoulder and level my gaze at her. "I swear, I absolutely will not. If you tell me, I'll tell you the truth about why I wanted to be a history professor."

A barely detectable twitch of her lips builds my intrigue.

"When I was a baby, my parents used to call me the human garbage disposal because I would literally eat anything they gave me. It became a bit of a game with them. Everyone got in on it, even my grandparents' chef, Sophia. My mom liked to cook, and the only memory I have of her—well, I'm not even sure it's a real memory, maybe more something I've been told enough times that it feels like a memory, but I swear, I have flashes of it—I was standing on a chair in the kitchen when she was making dinner, and I kept stealing food off the counter and eating it whenever she wasn't looking." Her hands still as she stares down at the chopped vegetables spread out over the cutting board. "I don't know. It makes me feel closer to her. I like growing things. Watching a tiny seed grow into life that can feed people. It's fun. All of it is. Being in the greenhouse and growing food and cooking it."

I swallow past a lump in my throat. "That's not lame. That's actually the least lame reason for doing something I've ever heard."

Her bright eyes flicker over to me, yet another rare smile on her lips, and I can only hope that in doing this with her, I'll be treated to more of them.

"Now you have to tell me."

"Have you ever seen *Indiana Jones*?"

"The movie? No. It's not really my thing."

"I'm going to pretend you didn't say that. Otherwise, we can't be friends. We'll watch it one night. I swear, you'll love it. But I was obsessed with those movies when I was younger. Indiana Jones is a history professor, but he also got to go on adventures and experience history. That was my dream."

"But now you teach middle school."

I laugh at the deadpan way she says that. She's so like her father. "Now I teach middle school, which I enjoy more than I thought I would. Probably because I get to hang with some cool, smart kids." I give her a hip bump. "But maybe one day I'll go back to school and get my Ph.D. and I'll be Doctor Wilde, adventurer."

Now that I'm done with the chicken, I wash my hands, dry them, then add butter and olive oil to the large Dutch oven, showing Stella how I let it melt and then add the vegetables with some salt and pepper, sautéing them.

I hand her the slotted non-stick spoon, and she takes over, a quick study as she mimics my technique perfectly. "Where did you learn how to do this?"

"Food Network," I quip because it's partially true. "My nana also taught me a lot. She liked to cook and bake Texas-style, so I grew up doing that with her. I also did most of the cooking for my family, so anything she didn't teach me, I taught myself. Then when I got married, my husband demanded that whenever we were home, I cook healthy meals for him."

"There is a lot in that last statement I want to question."

I meet her eyes briefly before turning back to the stove. Quiet Stella is incredibly perceptive. "That goes for both of us. Unfortunately, I didn't question enough when I should have. Yet another life lesson: Don't change who you are for someone else and never let anyone steal your backbone. Like those girls in school. They only have power over you if you let them have it."

"You said something similar to me that day, but it's easier said than done."

"Of course it is. If it were easy, it wouldn't take courage. But courage gives you strength, and strength gives you confidence, and confidence can take you anywhere."

She gives me a soft smile, the kind that says she likes that, and then we get to cooking. Talking about food, and while the pot pie bakes in the oven, I grade papers while she does her homework. It's the weirdest relationship I've ever ventured into. Obviously, I love kids or I wouldn't have become a teacher. But still, weird.

That said, I had a lot of fun today, and if the smiles and giggles coming from Stella were any indication, I think she did too.

When the pot pie is done, I remove it from the oven and set it down on my stove for it to rest. "I think your dad will like this."

"He'll love it. It's his favorite. Probably because my mom used to make it a lot."

Something stirs inside me. "They loved each other a lot."

It's a statement, not a question, but she nods all the same. "Yeah. They met in college and had me a few years later. Said I was the best surprise that's ever happened to them."

"I believe that."

"I don't remember my mom much at all, and I don't remember my dad before she died. I just know he was different. At least that's what my grandma and uncles say."

I believe that too.

"He blames himself for her death."

"Oh. That's..." I don't know what that is. The worst thing I've ever heard?

Unfortunately, all this depressing fun bursts like an over-inflated bubble when Stella's phone chimes with a text. She picks it up and informs me her dad just got home. We peek out the window and sure enough, it's still raining.

"He offered to come get me but said he'd be a few minutes. He's on a work call."

"That's fine. I'll walk you. This is heavy and hot. I don't want you to carry it."

Armed with oven mitts and a forty-pound tank that I swear could have single-handedly defeated the Nazis in World War II in my hands, otherwise known as a bubbling hot Dutch oven filled with pot pie, Stella leads the way, holding the umbrella over both of us as we march across the lawns to her side porch, where she punches in a code, and the door unlocks.

I follow her, my heart in my throat, hammering so fast it's a wonder I can breathe past it. She shakes out the umbrella, places it against the wall by the back door, then we track through the mudroom, back hall, past a half bath and a large butler's pantry—my total wet dream—until we reach the kitchen where I set the heavy as hell pot down on the stove.

"Wowzers, that's heavier than the pig I had to carry during pledge week," I gripe. Stella throws me a confused look, and I wave her away. "Never mind and may you never know about it. You shouldn't have to reheat it if you're eating it within the next half an hour. Today was a lot of fun. Thanks for cooking with me, and I'll see you at school tomorrow." I remove my mitts and head back in the direction I came.

Stella takes a step toward me, trying to cut off my escape, appearing anxious and crestfallen. "You're not staying to eat it? You have to stay and eat it with us."

I shake my head. "Nope. It's all for you. Let me know how it turned out."

"But what will you eat?" Stella persists, following me as I walk backward in the direction of the mudroom, wanting to get out of here before I see *him*. "There is so much of it, we'll never be able to finish it all."

"Don't worry about me. I have plenty I can eat. But you did great today. You're seriously a natural chef. Think about what you want to try for Wednesday, and we'll make it happen. Just text me tomorrow so I can figure out what ingredients we'll need to get."

"We did all this cooking, and you're not even going to try it? That's not right. No, you have to stay. You have to."

I open my mouth to argue with that when I sense him behind me. All the hairs on the back of my neck stand at attention as an unwelcome current zaps through me. *Him.* So much for my clean escape.

"Dad, tell her. She has to stay and try this."

Yup. I was right. I feel him brush past me. His blue scrubs-clad arm grazes my shoulder, and it's like that current of energy finds the spark it was searching for and now my entire body ignites. Just from that one simple touch. I flex my hands, trying to shake it off while wondering if it would look ridiculous to turn and make a run for it.

I don't want to see him. Not after last night.

Let me amend that, not after the way it *ended* last night.

The stinging force of his rejection shook me harder than it should have. I'm not even sure what I wanted him to do, but shutting me out—literally—felt like the ultimate blow my already rocked self-esteem did not need. He made me feel cheap and used. Even a simple good night or a stupid wave would have sufficed, but what I could see in his expression and then him slamming his window shut told me everything I needed to know.

Now I need to get away from him before I do something crazy like kick him in the nuts. In front of his kid. I maintain my focus on Stella, though I feel Landon's eyes burning into me like a blowtorch.

"Stella, if she wants to go," he says, his too hopeful voice trailing off at the end, and yup, now is the time to run. Asshole.

Heartless wanker. Sexy devil. I'm not a girl who hates all that well, but yeah...

"Right. Have a great night."

I spin to flee just as a hand grasps my arm, stopping me.

"What I was going to say is, if she wants to go, we'll have to find a way to stop her."

My eyes close, and my breath freezes in my lungs. "That's not what you were going to say," I mumble so only he can hear.

"No," he replies in the same low tone I used. "But it's what I should have said. It's what I was thinking. Stella is absolutely right. You cooked all this food for us, and I'm being rude. Stay and eat with us. You don't even have to talk to me."

What is he doing to me? And why am I powerless to stop him? *Run, Elle. Save yourself.*

"Please," he tacks on, and that's my undoing. His stupid please.

I twist and peek up, finding his beseeching green eyes hidden behind his glasses. So handsome I could die just from looking at him.

"It's just dinner."

I glower. I know that. I know it's not anything more. That's the problem, as I nod and agree to stay when staying is the last thing I should do.

16

After an impossible day of rounding in the hospital, dealing with difficult patients who refuse to make necessary lifestyle changes and wet-behind-the-ears residents, I should be exhausted. Only today I was lit with a fire no amount of caffeine could provide and no amount of grueling work could extinguish.

Shame. Anticipation. Obsession.

Whatever you want to call this insidious, venomous snake inside me. All day it's been biting holes in my armor, slithering beneath my skin, and making me moodier than I typically am. All because of *her*.

Honey hair, hazel eyes, tight-fitting black pants that hug her thighs and ass, cream turtleneck that does the same with her perfect tits... she's going to be my ruination.

"Do you want a glass of wine?" The wariness in her eyes and the stiffness in her posture are keeping my voice soft. My movements light. I fucked up, and for once, I care. And I hate that I care. The way she wouldn't look at me. The way her eyes stuck on Stella, the kitchen floor, the hallway she was desperate to flee into.

Anywhere, but not on me.

I hadn't realized what my own need to run last night did to her. I hadn't thought it through. It's clear she took it as rejection when it was simple self-preservation. I was trying to save us both. Doesn't she see that?

No.

I hurt her when she's already been hurt enough, and there's no excuse for that.

So against my better judgment, she had to stay.

Stella all but pleaded with her. Elle giving up her free time after work for Stella, teaching her how to make whatever it is they made that smells out of this world amazing, and making my daughter smile when she smiles about as often as I do, makes this even more complicated.

I can do random women. Women who aren't in my life or near my daughter. Women who likely fuck me because I'm an Abbot-Fritz and nothing more—whether they think it's me or Luca they're getting. I doubt any of the women I've been with in the past nine years have cared, but Elle did. She cared a lot that I lied to her.

More complications.

She's easier to tolerate when I'm rude and dismissive.

"Yes, please. Thank you."

Yes, please. Thank you. Where is her bite? Her sassy retort? Nothing seems to hold this shooting star down for long, but last night did something to her.

It did something to me too.

Opening my wine refrigerator, I pull out a bottle of white wine and pour each of us a glass, then some milk for Stella because she drinks it with everything. "What did you make?" I ask, using the oven mitt Elle's small hand was just in to remove the heavy red top off the dish.

"Chicken pot pie with a biscuit top," Stella exalts with a noticeable bounce in her step, pride beaming from her. I roll my head over my shoulder to catch her eye just as she sits down at the bar.

"You made that for me?"

She's smiling from ear to ear, nodding voraciously, and I can't help but return it when she looks at me like that. The girl I would burn the world down for, suffer through this misery we call life for. Fuck, she's the reason I get out of bed every day when getting out of bed feels like the worst idea ever. I see so much of her mother in her when she's like this. Happy and carefree, and that knot that perpetually resides in my stomach feels simultaneously lighter and heavier.

"Bellas, you made this? It looks unbelievable." The biscuits golden brown and flaky. The pot pie creamy and bubbly.

"Don't sound so shocked."

"I think designing and building that greenhouse was worth every penny."

She snorts. "You love to design and build stuff. You should have been an architect or a carpenter. I just gave you an outlet."

"In my next life, I'll come back as Jesus."

Elle snorts out a laugh. "Did he just make a joke? Like an actual joke?"

"I'm capable of them every now and then."

She shakes her head. "No. I would have noticed. That's most definitely the first I've heard."

"Maybe you don't find my jokes funny. But if memory serves, I made you smile *several* times the first night I met you."

Color stains her cheeks as her jaw unhinges while her eyes simultaneously widen, only for her to curb her reaction just as quickly. Her initial shock morphs into a two can play at this game raised brow.

"Will the real Landon Fritz please stand up."

Touché. "Fine. You win. Let's just eat."

Elle gets out of her chair, and I wave her away.

"You cooked. I can serve and clean up."

"Very honorable of you."

"I like to think so. Bellas, tell me about your day," I ask, scooping a large heaping of the pot pie and setting it on a plate before handing it over to Elle, who takes it with a smile that momentarily rattles my brain.

"Well, let's see. My English teacher is having us read *Othello*, which is like meant to be socially impactful or whatever. I get that, I guess. But I've read it already, and I can't stand how Othello's jealousy and distrust and Iago's lack of real benefit or written motive for being such a villain ends up being the catalyst for killing poor, loving, trusting Desdemona. I don't plan to waste my time with a reread."

I hold in my chuckle. This girl.

"You're too smart for eighth grade," Elle notes. "You're like that in world history as well, and I happen to know you already take all honors courses. Have you thought about doing more independent studies instead of sitting through uninspiring lectures?"

I pause, dish in my hand for a very long beat before I slide it in front of Stella while staring at Elle, wondering at *her* motives for suggesting such a thing.

"What do you mean?" Stella asks, a scrunch to her brow.

"Stella, you just explained complicated Shakespeare to me on a very adult level. Your English class bores you. I watch you in honors world history. You're bored there too, and whenever I try to trip you up by calling on you, you consistently give me very intelligent and astute answers. So, have you thought about choosing a topic within these subjects that interests you and applying for independent study instead?"

"I'm in eighth grade. Typically, that doesn't happen until high school, right?"

"Imagine you're Indiana Jones, Miss Fritz. What does this world of adventure have to offer you?"

Stella raises her filled fork of steaming pot pie, hovering it over her plate, and then casts her gaze to me. "Dad?"

I shrug, not happy that Elle didn't approach the topic with me first before discussing it with Stella. She's not her mother. I'm her father. That's how this fucking goes. I don't care how well she cooks. I scoop up a plate for myself and then take the seat on the other side of Stella instead of the one beside Elle.

"I think it's worth a conversation," I hedge. "But I'd like to discuss it with your teachers more before we figure out a plan. You might not like all that free time. You already spend too much time alone." Which she does. Pulling her out of the classroom and away from her peers might not be the best for my girl. Intelligence and boredom aside.

"Can I think about it?"

Elle grins around a bite of food. "Of course. And if you don't want to do it now, you can always change your mind later. But your father is right. I should likely discuss this with your other teachers first and then him before we figure out the logistics."

After that dinner commences and everything this woman does pisses me off.

She makes humming noises when she eats. She laughs a little too loud with a smile that lights up her entire face. Stella makes a point of telling me how the biscuits are Elle's nana's recipe and how her nana knew what she was doing in the kitchen—Elle leans over and plants a kiss on the side of Stella's head. I swallow every morsel on my plate because it's very likely the best thing I've tasted in years short of her pussy.

"Will you stay for dessert?"

"Miss Wilde needs to get home for her early day tomorrow, and you have homework."

I get the most you're a motherfucker glare from both these women—Elle for calling her Miss Wilde while suggesting she needs to leave. Stella for parting her from her new BFF in the name of homework she finds completely unchallenging, monotonous, and not nearly as enjoyable as spending the evening with Elle. I get it, but I did my good deed for the day and asked her to stay for dinner. Now I need her to leave.

"I finished my homework."

"I'm sure you have reading to do."

"Not really."

I give up.

Keeping my distance under the guise of doing the dishes, Stella takes an enthusiastic Elle into the living room to show her our family album. But instead of doing the dishes as I should, I'm lingering in the back hallway. Watching like a creeper. Listening like a stalker.

"How long were you married for? My parents were married for almost five years. My dad says he would have married my mother the day he met her, but I know they got married because she was pregnant with me."

Well, fuck a duck and screw a kangaroo, and I'm about to burn down the goddamn zoo. That's not entirely true. I would have married Reese with or without Stella. She just sped things up a bit.

"I was married for three and a half years. But looking at these pictures, Stella, I can tell you that your father means what he says. It's very obvious your parents loved each other."

"Why did you get divorced?"

Stella, always so tactful.

"Because the man I married turned out not to be the man I thought he was."

"What do you mean?"

There's a long moment of silence, and I wish I could peek my head around the wall to get a glimpse of Elle's face. She clears her throat. "Just what I said. He's a professional golfer, and we traveled the world together. We fell in love quickly and married quickly. And for a while, in the beginning, it was heaven. Then things changed between us, almost overnight, and I didn't like the man he became. He wasn't treating me the way I believed I deserved to be treated."

"Why do I get the feeling you're about to tell me another life lesson?" Stella smarts, and Elle laughs.

"See what I mean about you being so smart? I didn't even have to proposition it that way. But yeah, that's a big one. Tell me more about your mom. What's this picture?"

And why does she want to hear that?

Why does her wanting to know about Reese and asking for Stella's sake make me want, crave, desire, cling to her even more? She's so good with Stella. So natural and not even close to jealous of Reese. She's not trying to compete; she's trying to love and understand my daughter.

That's when I do peek. Ever so subtly, pressing myself against the wall, watching their profiles, just out of sight.

Elle points to something I can't see, and I watch, strung out like a junkie, as Stella shifts in right beside her newest hero and shows her pictures of her mom. "That was the first time I tried solids."

"And this one?"

"My first time sledding."

"Looks like y'all were having a lot of fun. I had no idea your dad has that many teeth."

I roll my eyes at her sarcasm, though she can't see me do it.

"Your parents took a lot of pictures."

"My mother was obsessed with them. She wanted to be a photojournalist when she was in college. I have her camera. I just don't know how to use it very well. Besides, pictures aren't really my thing."

"Cooking and gardening are?"

"Like they are for you."

My breath catches, my hand covering my chest.

"Well, thank goodness your mom was into photography, otherwise you wouldn't have these. She took stunning pictures.

And that smile, Stella. I think your dad was right. You do look like your mom. Especially when you smile. So beautiful. Both of you." They flip pages in the worn album, the plastic crinkling. "What's this one?"

"A selfie of us from her phone my dad had printed. That was the last picture taken on her phone. She died the next day."

I can't stop my reaction. I march into the room, staring down at my wife's smiling eyes. The way she stared at our girl. Eyes that tell me I'm a fucked man, and I don't deserve any happiness because she doesn't have any for herself. She took pictures of Stella because she couldn't take pictures as a photo-journalist. She was home with Stella while I was in medical school. I stole her dream. I stole her life.

Reese texted that picture to me when I was in class and at the time, I didn't think much about it. Reese used to send me a lot of pictures of them. It was a hey, we're here, remember us.

Then she was gone.

"Upstairs, Stella. Now. You need a shower."

"Thanks for the hygiene update, Dad." Stella rolls her eyes derisively as she stands, giving Elle a hug that makes me want to die just a bit. "Thank you for today. I just... thank you. It was so much fun. Are we still good for Wednesday?"

"For sure." Elle smiles like the first flicker of dawn after an endless night. "Just let me know what we're making so I can get what groceries we need. You were a culinary genius today."

Stella runs up the stairs, and the moment I hear her door slam shut, Elle closes the photo album with a heavy *clap*. "Can I help clean up since you were too busy spying on us to bother?"

"Why did you leave your husband? Did he hurt you?"

Setting the album down on the coffee table, she rises, adjusting her sweater and turning to look at me. I hate how long she's taking to answer, and with every second, my blood pressure climbs.

She takes a few steps in my direction. "Yes. He hurt me. Just not in the way you think he did."

"How do you think I think he did?"

She doesn't answer me. "Stella told me you blame yourself for your wife's death."

The force of her words has me shuffling back until I'm leaning against the doorway once more, needing its support to hold me up. I didn't realize Stella knew that, though I'm not surprised either. In a way, I'm relieved. I think. It's not a story you ever want to tell your child. But it's one thing for her to know I blame myself and another for her to know the reason behind that.

"That's because I'm the reason my wife is dead."

I wait. I watch. No flinch. No words. She doesn't say, I'm sure that's not the case or we all feel responsible when we lose someone we love too soon or whatever other bullshit there is to throw at me. No glancing toward the door to run out. Instead, the woman I'm desperate to get rid of saunters across the room until she's leaning against the opposite side of the doorframe from me, staring up at me with her swirling hazel eyes.

In a heartbeat she pushes away from her side and into mine, onto me, her hands on my chest, her body leaning against me, her chin tilted up, and her lips... her lips are so damn close.

"I would have stayed with David. I would have stayed forever. I tried. I did everything I could think of to make him see me and treat me the way he did when we first met. Every-thing I could possibly change about myself to make him happy, I did. But he never was with me, and by the time I walked out the door, I had nothing left in me to give either of us. He never hit me. But his words hurt a hundred times more than his fist ever could have."

"He's an oozing bedsore who deserves daily pain for the rest of his life," slips out before I can stop it. Something I wouldn't mind providing. The thought of him verbally abusing her has my molars gnashing together so hard I'm shocked I'm not cracking them. I'm a cardiologist. And an Abbot-Fritz. Destroying him before killing him would be a breeze.

"Maybe. But I don't regret that I stayed and tried, and I don't regret that I left when I couldn't try anymore."

So fucking brave. So much life glimmering in her pretty eyes. How could anyone ever try to extinguish it? For that alone, he should suffer.

"I fought with my wife the night she died." I swallow thickly, my hands going to her hips, gripping her. "I came home from class, exhausted, needing to study for a midterm the next day, and Reese asked if I could make Stella dinner, give her a bath, and put her to bed so she could have a break. I lost it on her. It was a breaking point I hadn't realized I was reaching, and I yelled. Said awful things. Made her cry." I swallow again, this time audibly as I lick my dry lips. "And then finally I told her to go. I told her to leave the house if she needed a break that badly, and she did. She got into her car in a rage, lost control of it on a patch of ice, and ended up trapped in it at the bottom of an icy lake."

Elle's chin quivers, her eyes glassing over with emotion. I haven't said those words aloud to anyone since Reese's funeral. I sat at her graveside with my parents, brothers, and sister surrounding me, and I told them the unforgivable thing I had done. How I had wished it were me who was dead and not her.

I still feel that way. I'll always feel that way.

"My best friend drowned in a lake when I was fifteen. We were camping, and I didn't wake up when she left our tent."

My grip tightens. "Do you blame yourself?"

She shakes her head. "Not anymore. Blaming myself won't bring her back and it won't change the fact that I didn't wake up. I wish I had. I'd give anything to go back in time, but I can't. So I remember her and miss her instead."

"It's not the same, you know. I am the reason Reese is gone. You're not the reason your friend is."

Elle looks as broken as I feel. A big, fat tear hits her cheek, and I don't know if it's for her horrible past or mine.

My lips find it anyway, my tongue licking it away, tasting its saltiness. Absorbing her grief. I cup her jaw, angling her face, my thumb swiping along her bottom lip. I hated her pain when I first saw her because it so closely mirrored my own. We're so alike and yet so different.

She is the beautiful, strong side of pain. The dawn after the endless night of darkness. A new breath of life I was never able to find for myself.

Now as I stare into her eyes, my world shifts. My axis thrown off-kilter. I can't even explain what it is or how it does. All I know is that I'll never be the same again. Because of her.

My lips strike flush with hers in time to muffle her sob. In this second—and just for this second—I feel like I deserve this. This woman.

I'm here to take away her pain. To erase her heartache.

It's a purpose I never imagined I'd find.

And whether she's aware of it or not, she's peeling my layers back. Slicing my solid resistance up into bite-sized pieces before devouring them. She's filling me with something else I can't explain.

Hope maybe?

It sends a shudder through me, a growl from my lungs as I deepen our kiss. Needing to consume her the way she's consuming me. All my trumped-up, bullshit, pathetic attempts at dislike I pretended to feel for her are gone.

My hands comb through her long, silky strands as my tongue invades her mouth. Our lips move together, soft and wet. A breathy sound—so achingly sweet and tragic—emits from the back of her throat before diving into mine.

I swallow it down. Desperate. Hungry. Ravaged and needing her. *Her.*

Elle's hands fist my shirt, her body angry and impatient at my refusal to let her closer. I can't do that. No matter how much I want her, our reality is unchanged. I'm not what she needs. Even if she is *exactly* what I need. Someone who has me *feeling* again.

I break the spell. "You need to go."

"Tell me why."

I hold her face in my hands. "Isn't it obvious?" *I'm going to fall in love with you if you stay.*

"Maybe I want it spelled out for me."

I shake my head. I can't do that.

"I forgive you."

"What?" I choke on the word.

"I forgive you for giving me Luca's name. I understand why you did it, and I forgive you, Landon. I forgive you for shutting off the light and closing your window on me so quickly last night too. I forgive you."

I choke again, my hands all over her, and I dip back down, kissing her sweet mouth, her jaw, her neck. I pull away and open my eyes, finding her breathtaking marbled irises staring straight into mine. I don't look away. I don't hide. She forgives me, and I give her everything. If only just for this moment.

"You shouldn't forgive me."

"But I do. I forgive you."

My eyes clench shut. "You have to go," I growl into her.

She doesn't argue. She knows. "Next time, come and pick Stella up at my door. Now that I forgive you and no longer hate you, I'm starting to like you. A hell of a lot more than I should."

I already like you a hell of a lot more than I should.

She's breathing heavily against me, her tits squishing into my chest, my heart hammering back, unable to be kept at bay. My dick is a steel pipe pressed between us, and I straighten, pushing her back. Keeping my eyes shut. The loss of contact more excruciating than I thought it would be.

A soft kiss on my lips and then she's gone. Out the side door with a click, and I should have walked her home. Made sure she managed the distance between our doors safely. Ensured she didn't get wet from the rain.

But then I would have followed her inside. I would have lifted her up and wrapped her legs around my waist. I would have mauled her against the closest surface because the idea of finding a couch or her bed would have been preposterous.

She would have stared at me the way I've been staring at her—with unmistakable want and need. We would have broken furniture and laughed about it as I fucked us both into mind-melting pleasure.

That's why she had to go.

Because if she stayed, I would have chosen her. I would have chosen to keep her. And then what would I do when I remembered she's not someone I can keep for myself?

17

Staring into my closet, I have no idea what to wear tonight. Bridget said casual, but it's also a Saturday night dinner party. Where I wasn't looking forward to this before, I am now. Especially after this past week.

Stella came and cooked apple cobbler with me on Wednesday, but other than when Landon came to pick her up, I haven't seen him. I've kept my window shut. Curtains drawn. It's been weeks since our night in the hotel. Nearly a week since he's kissed me, and I can still feel his lips on mine. His touch on my skin.

And until that goes away, I'm resigned to keeping my distance.

He can be brutally harsh in an almost excusable way. Maybe it's his tone. Or demeanor. Or his honesty. Whatever it is, I found myself forgiving him even before I knew his excuses. Lord knows I have baggage, but that man invented the term. He doesn't want anything to happen between us and neither do I. He doesn't want complicated, and that shit is my new kryptonite.

So how do I stop thinking about him?

I decide on a red silk blouse with gold faux buttons up the back, a black miniskirt, sheer stockings, and above the knee black suede boots with a pointed toe, insane heel, and red soles. Every time I wear these boots, I feel alive, beautiful, and sexy, and that's exactly how I want to feel tonight. Even if it's just a simple dinner party at my friend's house.

I blow out my hair, giving a softness to my natural waves, and then apply a touch of shimmer to my eyes along with black liquid eyeliner and red lipstick.

Bridget's husband isn't set to pick me up for another twenty minutes or so, and just as I'm sitting down to go over a few quick lesson plan changes I'm making to the sex ed class, my phone rings. David. I owe him nothing, and yet he keeps calling. Why? I don't understand it.

I haven't picked up since the last time I spoke with him, and yet he persists.

The call dies only for him to immediately ring again, and I'm so very done with this game.

"Why do you keep calling me?" I snap as I answer.

"Why do you keep picking up?"

I sigh. "I don't. This is getting out of hand, David."

"You haven't blocked me yet. That tells me you like it when I call."

"Thanks for the pro tip. I'll be sure to block you. Bye now."

"Don't hang up," he yells frantically into the phone. "This is important, Elle."

I roll my eyes, getting out of the chair at my desk in my office, which is really just an unused bedroom, and walking back across the upstairs hall toward my bedroom. "You always say that and it's always the same thing."

"No. This time is different."

I scoff incredulously into the phone. Of course he thinks it is. With a bounce, I fall back onto my bed, my heeled feet on the floor. "Tell me now because after this, I'm blocking you."

"I wish you wouldn't. I wish you'd give me a second chance."

I can't do that. I gave him a hundred second chances. A thousand.

"Spit it out, David."

He sighs. "I'm only telling you this because I love you. Please remember that. I love you. I've always loved you. From the second I saw you in that crowded bar serving drinks, I knew it was you. You hear me, Elle? It's you. So when what I have to tell you hurts even more than I've already hurt you, please know that was not my intention and hold on to everything I just said."

My hand covers my heart, my breath trapped somewhere it can't escape. "Okay." It's a fractured whisper.

"Your parents have been threatening me. Now they're threatening to bring you into this if I don't comply with their demands."

"Which are?"

"Money. They want back the money I took from them."

"Why were you paying them in the first place?"

He's silent for the longest of moments. Then, when I don't think I can take any more, he says, "I've already lost you, haven't I? There's no way I can ever win you back?"

"No." A tear escapes, but that's the only one I'll let go.

"I cheated on you about six months after we were married."

My eyes close, and my body trembles, but it doesn't kill me the way I thought hearing something like that would. I had wondered for the last two years of our marriage if he had a woman on the side. If that's why he treated me so poorly.

"It was a one-time thing," he continues amidst my silence. "It never happened again after. I swear it to you. It was at the charity tournament in Palm Springs. The one you didn't come with me on because you were home with the flu. I flew out there alone, played the tournament, and then had a bit too much to drink after. I went back to my hotel room, and someone was already there waiting for me. A woman who I thought was you."

"What?" I gasp the word.

"It was Cat, Elle. She looked different than she did at our wedding. She looked just like you. Her hair was done exactly like yours, not short and platinum blond like it was at our wedding. I swear, my head was spinning so fast, and truly I thought it was you. I thought you had flown out to surprise me. She was wearing nothing but a bra and a thong, and she started kissing me. Touching me. Getting me naked."

"David..."

"I didn't realize it was her until... Fuck, Elle, I was so messed up. I was... behind her and I saw her rose tattoo and realized it wasn't you."

"You had sex with my sister?"

I think I'm going to be sick. My sister? Why would she do that to me?

"Did you stop when you realized?"

He's silent, and that silence tells me everything I ever need to know. And if I thought my heart couldn't break again, I was so very wrong.

"Your parents caught us right after I realized it was Cat. They were there too, though they never mentioned a thing to either of us that they were coming. It was a setup from the start. It had to be. I even suspected they drugged me, but I have no proof of that as I never went and got a test. Anyway, the three of them threatened to tell you if I didn't pay them."

A hiccupped laugh flees my chest, my eyes closed, and I can't move.

I hardly know what to say. My sister fucked my husband— very likely after drugging him first—in a hotel room. My parents were in on this. They *blackmailed* my husband after catching him cheating on me. I knew they were horrible people. All of them.

But I never... I never would have imagined...

God, everything inside me hurts.

I swallow down my tears and ask, "They blackmailed you for that long?"

"Yes. I knew you'd leave me if you ever found out, so I paid them. Three hundred grand a year, Elle. Half to your sister and half to your parents. And slowly, their demands grew along with their threats. I became resentful. Angry beyond all measure. I blamed you for what I did, and I blamed you for what they were doing to me. I know I treated you poorly. I know I said and did things that hurt you. Hell, I did them *to* hurt you." A heavy sigh. "I'm so sorry, Elle. I ruined the best thing that ever happened to me."

An apology doesn't erase what he did. For years I tried to be rubber, impervious and flexible and hard so nothing could stick to me. But I wasn't rubber. And I wasn't impervious. David had me questioning everything about myself. Hating everything I saw when I looked in the mirror. I was weak and ashamed and lonely and scared.

For years.

I was that beaten-down dog who kept coming back, needing love and affection, and never receiving it. I've been that dog my whole life, first with my family and then with him.

"Why are you telling me this now?"

"Because now they're threatening to tell the world I cheated on you and that's why you left me unless I give them two million dollars."

"Jesus... David."

"I can't do this anymore, Elle. I can't. It's been eating a hole in me for years. They're messing with my career. My life. They already ruined my marriage, and now they want this too."

"What do you expect *me* to do?"

"You don't owe me anything. I know this. But if you could talk to them, try to reason with them, I'd be forever grateful. I'll pull back. I'll leave you alone. I'll give you the space you deserve. I owe you that and more. But if it gets out that I cheated, especially with your twin sister, the press will come after both of us."

He's right. I've gotten random calls from random news affiliates asking for comments or interviews, and that's with them all believing we separated amicably. I don't want to be in the spotlight anymore. I just want to move on with my life.

I never replied to Cat when she texted me. What could she possibly want with me now? To tell me what she did? To try to extort me for money?

"I'll talk to them," I promise. And it will be for the last time. I'm done with my family. Forever. I am *not* that dog anymore.

I never had a prenup with David, and in the divorce, he gave me three million for keeping my mouth shut. I haven't spent his money. I signed an NDA and a contract promising I would never speak poorly about David publicly. I hate my parents and sister for what they did to him. For what they did to me. It doesn't excuse David's behavior. Not by a longshot. But they're just as guilty as he is, if not more.

"Thank you, Elle. Truly. You were a wonderful wife, and I did not deserve you. I'll always love you."

And with that, he hangs up.

The phone slips from my ear, and I lie here, staring up at the ceiling in my bedroom. Would David and I still be happy if none of that had happened? It's a stupid question, and it makes me feel stupid for even wondering. The man cheated on me with my sister—though it does feel a bit strange to think of it that way, especially if he was drugged. But he treated me worse than stepped-in dog shit, and there's no excuse for that.

The irony, if he had told me what had happened, I likely wouldn't have left him. And I would have severed ties with my family a long time ago. The only reason I'm going to speak to my parents about this is because I want this all to be done.

"It's my new life, dammit!"

That's when the doorbell rings. The sound jars me up and off the bed with a whoosh of flying hair and uncoordinated limbs. Fuck. I forgot all about the damn dinner party, and now Bridget's husband, Roger, is here to pick me up.

Only when I drag myself downstairs, plaster a smile on my face I don't even close to feel, and swing the door open, I'm greeted by someone I did not expect. Well, someone I not only didn't expect but have never met before.

"Elle?"

"Um. Yes?" It comes out like a question.

"I take it by your expression Bridget didn't tell you I was picking you up."

Fucking Bridget. "Nope. I was expecting Roger."

He chuckles, running a hand through his blond hair, his brown eyes sparkling as they take me in. He's cute. Really cute. I'll give my friend that much for her subterfuge.

"That makes this slightly awkward. I'm Aaron Brady. I work with Roger."

"You're a lawyer?"

He smiles, showcasing a set of pearly whites. "Yes, but you can't hold that against me. I'm one of the good guys."

I scrunch my nose. "Isn't that what all lawyers say?"

"It is, but in my case, it's true."

Cute and charming. I am so not in the mood for any of this.

"So I'm supposed to trust you that my friend actually sent you here to fetch me?"

"I did know your name and address. But if you'd like to call her for confirmation, I'm happy to stand here and continue to look at you. It's not every night I get the pleasure of meeting such a beautiful woman."

Cute, charming, and a flirt. His list grows. No getting out of this night now.

"What are the names of Bridget and Roger's boy and girl?"

He grins. "Nice try with the trip-up. They have twin boys, Michael and Christopher."

"They do indeed. Nicely done, Aaron. Let me just get my things."

I wish I had time to take a shot of something to settle my nerves, but unfortunately, I don't. After grabbing my purse and making sure my phone is in it, I lock everything up and step out into the cool autumn night. Aaron drops a possessive hand to my lower back as he guides me to his waiting Audi SUV, and I'm too numb to do much about it.

"Do you do this a lot?" I question. "Get suckered into picking up strange women?"

"Actually, this is a first, but I'm not complaining. In fact, I think I'm going to have to thank Bridget for setting this up."

"I made her promise not to set me up."

A warm laugh hits the air. He's clearly not put off by my sour mood. "Then forget I said anything. I'm recently out of a relationship, and she said you are as well. Maybe she just figured we could use a friend in a similar situation."

"Maybe. Bridget likes to play Emma whenever she can."

"Huh?"

"Emma. Jane Austen. Emma's character fancied herself a matchmaker in the story. Never mind..." I trail off at his bewildered expression just as my eyes catch on something off to my left, my head twisting to take it in and settling on Landon.

Our eyes lock.

I freeze for a moment, my steps faltering. He's standing in his driveway near his car, keys poised in his hand, almost as if caught off guard by seeing me. His dark eyes assess me without giving a hint as to what's going on in his head. Slowly they slide down my body, linger on the short hem of my skirt and boots on my thighs until he finds Aaron's hand on my lower back. Then they narrow, harden, before slingshotting back up to mine, searching me for something as his lips twist into a scowl.

Enmity burns from him, a fire blazing in his green depths encased in black frames.

The man is a visual growl, rocking me to my core before all emotion flees his face—an unreadable mask once more—leaving my mind spinning in confusion and frustration. My stomach tightens, and my heart pounds.

As if this night couldn't have gotten any worse.

Aaron gives me a small push, still talking about something I'm not listening to.

He's oblivious to the stare-down I have going with my neighbor, who's still tracking my movements with careful attention. I want to tell him this means nothing. That I don't know this guy, and it's not really a date, but then Landon turns away, stalking back toward his house, dismissing me with his cold indifference as he calls out for Stella and Layla, telling them they're going to be late.

Two seconds later, the girls bolt out of the house. I force my gaze away, trying to catch my breath. Just before Aaron can open the car door for me, Stella calls my name.

"Elle!" she yells across our lawns. "This is my best friend, Layla, I told you about."

Awesome timing, Stella.

I twist back to meet them, forcing yet another smile. The girls come bounding across the expansive lawn, stopping about ten feet away. Landon's boots crunch along the grass, but he holds back, even if his eyes are glued to me once more.

"Hi, Layla," I say with a warm smile. "It's so nice to meet you. Stella has told me everything."

Layla giggles, her long blond hair swinging around her narrow shoulders, though she has about a head of height on Stella. "You too. Stella doesn't shut up. She told me all about your cooking lessons. Can I come too one day? Are you doing it Monday? Because I can totally do Monday."

"I'm fine with that if Stella is because, of course, I'd love to have you join us." I look at Stella, who is one giant, beaming smile as she jumps up and down, showing more enthusiasm than I've seen in her before.

"Yes! That would be the coolest."

"Awesomesauce," Layla squeals along with Stella. "We're headed to my surrogate grandparents' compound for dinner even though it's Saturday, and we normally do family dinner on Sunday. Stella is like my BFF and kind of cousin-in-law. It's complicated."

I laugh lightly, turning to Aaron, who is patiently waiting by my side, a small, amused grin on his face as he watches the girls. "So I've been told."

"Is this your boyfriend? He's super cute," Layla goes on, and I want to die. Behind them, Landon stiffens, his fists clenching at his sides as his gaze drops down to the grass.

"No," Stella answers. "She doesn't have a boyfriend." She turns to me. "Right?"

Aaron laughs while I awkwardly shift my weight, wanting the sidewalk to open up and swallow me whole. I was wrong. This night just got worse.

"No, I'm not her boyfriend," Aaron replies for us. "Just her date for dinner tonight."

Shoot. Me. Now.

"I thought Mrs. Belay wasn't going to set you up at her dinner party."

Thanks for pointing that out, Stella. Right in front of your father and my non-date.

"Well, she likes to pretend she's Emma."

Both girls nod in understanding because both girls are avid readers.

"Seems I'm going to have to read Emma," Aaron muses.

"Clearly I'm behind on my women's fiction. You said it was Jane Alsen?"

Stella and Layla cringe, and I fight mine.

"We should go, or we'll be late," I say before this moment gets worse. "Have fun at your grandparents', ladies, and I'll see you for cooking Monday. Just text me what you want to make. Night."

I say that last word to Landon. But he's already storming off toward his car, his back to me.

"See you," Layla calls out. "Have fun on your date."

"Thank you." Aaron's voice is light, oblivious to any of the tension strung tighter than a high-wire between Landon and me. Hell, I'm not even sure he noticed Landon was there lurking. "Sweet kids." He's still smiling his perfect smile as he helps me up and into his car.

I pull out my phone from my purse, tempted to text Landon, but what would I say? I don't owe him anything. Not any sort of explanation. He kissed me, but he told me to go. I all but put myself on the line, telling him I forgive him. He's made it clear nothing can ever truly happen. The dance between us has been all that's occupied my mind, and I'm tired. So tired of fighting a winless battle with that man.

So tired of everything, I just want to go back inside and crawl under the covers, never to come out again.

I think back to the other night in his house. *"You need to go." "Why?"* He had stared into my eyes with so much pain. *"Isn't it obvious?"*

Yes. It is obvious. I understand everything. All too well. Some men are just too far gone to ever be retrieved. And after the blow my heart has taken these past few years—hell, the blow it's taken tonight—I'd be wise to listen to him. To keep my distance.

But that look in his eyes just now.

The way my heart pounded.

I glance out the window over at his driveway, searching, and finding him standing beside his car door, staring straight at me as if he was waiting for me this entire time. He shakes his head when our eyes meet and gets in his car, slamming the door shut.

I can't fix him. Not with all the glue or tape in the world. Frankly, I have enough mess of my own to deal with without trying to navigate someone as intense and complicated as Landon Fritz.

"You ready?" Aaron asks as he starts the car up.

I turn to him with a forced smile. "Sure. Let's go."

18

____

The whole way to my parents' house, I don't know how to unlock my jaw. Or unclench my fists from around the wheel. Layla and Stella are gabbing away like teenage girls, but the topic is all about Elle. They're analyzing everything from what she was wearing—that fucking skirt and those boots—to the way the guy touched her back, to the way he looked at her, to the fact that the guy called himself her date.

Her date!

And just what the absolute motherfuck is that?

A date! Hell, I can't even contemplate women, let alone other women, and she's...

"Dad, watch out," Stella yells, and at the last second, I catch Gulliver's glowing eyes hitting my headlights, and I swerve, narrowly missing him, my brother, and a row of my mother's rose bushes. I slam on the brakes, gravel and rocks shooting every which way. The second the car's stopped, Oliver's pissed off scowl fills my window as he slowly taps on the glass.

"Taking the driveway at fifty? Really? And with my kid in the car?"

Shit.

"She's not your kid."

"Might as well be. You also have my niece in there."

I grunt.

That's as good as I've got right now.

"Do you plan to move so I can get out?"

"I thought that was kind of fun," Layla counters, giggling. "Like doing donuts in the mud. You know, since you didn't kill Oliver or my dog. Did I ever tell you about the time I nearly killed all of us when Oliver let me drive his Jeep?"

"Yes," Stella and I say together. "Only about fifty times," she finishes.

"Good times," Layla agrees, opening her car door and jumping out. "Let's eat. I'm starving, and your grandma told me she'd have Sophia make that sausage tortellini thing I like. There's a party in my tummy, so yummy, so yummy," Layla sings, doing some kind of swinging arm dance thing, and Stella laughs because that's a lot of what they do together. Layla talks nonstop, and Stella laughs because Layla is all wild energy, and Stella is contained shyness. Somehow these two work, though, the closest of friends and now practically family since I know Oliver is itching to make the fake engagement ring on Amelia's hand the real deal.

Oliver steps back, and I exit the car, slamming the door shut with more force than intended.

"Rough day?" he quips, and I sigh, not in the mood for anything or anyone.

Only the truth is, it wasn't a rough day. It was a relatively good day. I watched the Red Sox destroy the Yankees and secure their playoff spot. I played around with the schematic for my dream house—one I haven't touched in years—for the day when I can actually bring myself to sell the house we're living in and move. Stella and Layla were upstairs together or in the greenhouse after Layla spent the night last night.

All was good.

Then Elle had to walk out of her house looking like sex in heels with a guy beside her. A guy who had his hands on her back and referred to himself as her date. I'm tempted to ask Oliver how he stands it. Feeling this insane over a woman. He loved and lost and now here he is, years later and in love with Amelia. Happy. He's so fucking happy. When the hell was the last time I was happy? Thankfully, Gulliver takes over and jumps on me, slamming me back into my car with his weight while slobbering his dog breath all over my face.

"Down, Gulliver," Oliver commands, giving his leash a good tug. "Come on, boy. Down." Another lick followed by another tug, and the dog finally relents. "I'll be honest with you, man. I saw my life flash before my eyes just now, and there's too much missing from it. I have a lot more shit to do. So how about you try not to kill me next time."

"I'll make every attempt."

"Mom looks good today."

Awesome. That's precisely what I needed to hear. I'd smile at that if smiling were possible.

I close my eyes, leaning back against the cool metal of my car, rubbing my hands up and down my face. I need to get a grip. This woman is messing with my head. She's become the line between obsession and hate I'm trying not to tiptoe, and yet I have no idea how to flip her switch off in my head now that it's been turned on.

"I have a problem."

"I can see that."

"I'm ready to kill someone I don't even know."

"Do you want to take my car or yours to do it?"

I grin. Fucking Oliver.

"What's her name? The one who has you this tied up in knots, since I'm assuming she's not the one you want to kill?"

"Ellery. Elle."

"Your neighbor Luca told me about? The one who laid the public smackdown in the coffee shop?"

"One and the same."

"Are you fucking her?"

"Not since that first night in the bar."

"So fuck her again then and be done with it."

You'd think it would be that simple. Especially when that's how it's been for me since Reese. Any woman I ever felt compelled to see more than once never made it past the second round. By then, anything that had made my dick think it wanted more from them died. But Elle is smart and so damn sexy. She's feisty and sweet and vulnerable.

And every time my lips press to hers, I feel like a teenager with his first crush, who finally got the girl.

She knows what I did. Both to her and to Reese.

And she forgives me.

I'm fucked.

Oliver's smirking at me. "You're fucked, huh?"

I chuckle mirthlessly. "You reading my mind now?"

"It's a talent we've had to acquire since you're a man of few words. Come on in. Spend the evening with your family and forget about the girl."

"That work for you when you tried it?"

"No. When they get under your skin, they're there to stay."

"Thanks," I mutter.

He slaps my shoulder.

"It's what brothers are for. What's so different about this one?"

"She doesn't care that I'm Landon Fritz. She yells at me and doesn't take my crap in any form." *She sees the real me and wants me anyway. She forgives me.*

"Ah. I get it now."

Glad one of us does.

Grabbing the back of my shirt, he hauls me up and off my

car. My baby brother drags me along, across the driveway, down the front path, up the porch stairs, and into the main house, only for me to be instantly wrapped up in my mother's bone-thin arms before she places twin kisses, one each cheek. A Hermes scarf covers her bald head, but any time she leaves this house, she has a wig on.

Octavia Abbot-Fritz, Boston's reigning queen, is all about appearances, and since she is essentially the Joneses everyone tries to keep up with, that will never change.

"Oh, Landon. So happy you're finally here. Come, we're having drinks in the solarium." She smiles, leading me deeper into the house, through one room after the other. She's smiling tonight, and there's more color in her cheeks than the last time I saw her. "Oliver, will you please put Gulliver somewhere he won't break things? I love your newest fur baby, as Amelia calls him, but he broke a chair in the library your father purchased for me at an auction last year. He's not happy and needless to say, I'm not either."

"Where would you like me to put him?"

Gulliver gives a loud bark as if asking the same question his owner is.

My mother points to the right as we reach the back sitting room. "How about in the garden room? He can't get into too much trouble there, and if you leave the doors open and his long leash on, he can go outside on his own."

"Fine."

Oliver walks off, leaving me here with my mother. "Honestly, I just want him to look at the space now that it's been cleared out. I'm hoping he and Amelia will get married in there since it leads straight into the ballroom."

"They're not actually engaged."

"Yet, Landon. They're not actually engaged *yet*. They're living together, and she's still wearing my grandmother's custom-made Harry Winston diamond ring."

I smirk. "You're diabolical."

"When it comes to my children, Landon, I make no apologies. A mother has to do what a mother has to do. Especially a mother of five boys and a daughter who loves testing my every nerve. Besides, if Oliver won't marry Amelia there, then Carter *will* marry Grace there. *Before* she delivers my grandson. I swear, at this rate, I will have to arrange Kaplan's marriage. Who knows what trouble he'll get himself into since that seems to be the theme for all of you. Rina unfortunately will end up eloping in Las Vegas of all places. Brecken already asked for our permission to marry her but said she'd never agree to a real wedding." My mother rolls her green eyes. "I believe Brecken has already purchased tickets to Vegas for that very thing. I'll have to plan something after the fact and try not to cringe as I do."

"At least you know Grace won't say no to you and your scheming."

"My girl wouldn't dare."

Grace and Carter told the family last week they're expecting. First Rina, then Oliver, and now Carter. Three of her six children are in love. My mother is in seventh heaven and best of all, it's giving her not just another grandchild, but more reasons to fight her cancer. And with the way she looks tonight, it seems to be working.

"Ah, he's here." My father comes up, giving me a hug and a smack on the back. "Thank God. Come hide and have a drink with me. If I have to listen to your siblings go back and forth over baby names and TMI OB appointments any longer I'll—"

"You'll what, Dad?" Luca interjects.

"Cut you all out of the will."

Luca laughs. "Right. Sure. Then who will carry on your legacy?" Luca gives me a big once-over. "You're missing someone. Where's the stunning Ellery? I thought for sure she'd be here with how Stella and Layla were telling Sophia about their grand cooking plans for this week with her and how beautiful she looked tonight going on her date. I guess that date isn't you."

I give him my best fuck you face.

"Ellery?" my mother questions, her face lighting up like a bloodhound catching a scent. "Is this the woman Stella has been going on about? Her teacher who cooks with her?"

"That's her," Luca confirms. "Only she's so much more than that. Isn't she, Lan?"

I scratch my nose with my middle finger since my mother is looking at him and not me.

"What is this?" my father jumps in.

"It's nothing," I answer with finality in my voice, hoping to shut this down now. "She's my neighbor and Stella's teacher, and Stella has taken a shine to her. That's all."

"Is it, though?"

Goddamn him. I glare. "Will Raven be joining us tonight?"

My father chuckles, and my mother makes a tsking sound in the back of her throat. "Not this again."

"Except if Luca has his way, it will never end."

"You promised you weren't bothering her, Luca."

"*Bothering her*? I'm not."

My mother makes another sound. "She's been through enough thanks to you. When will you leave that poor girl alone?"

"Never," Luca states simply. "Now, how about that drink, Dad? The good stuff before dinner, and I'll tell you everything Landon refuses."

"I'm going to go check on the girls. Make sure they're not getting into too much trouble with Sophia in the kitchen." My mother offers me a sly wink as she saunters off in the opposite direction from us as we head toward my father's study on the other side of the house.

"She's not going to let that go," I grumble.

"No. She's not," my dad agrees as he shuts the door behind us. "Nicely done, Luca. If you want a free shot at him, Landon, I'll pour the bourbon with my back to you both."

"Sounds fair." Without warning, I jab out, hitting Luca in the arm. Hard. Harder than I typically would. I don't go for the gut, and I definitely don't go for the face, though I'm tempted on both. Right now, I'd like nothing more than to unleash this pent-up fury on a punching bag, but I'd rather not send my brother to the hospital before dinner.

"Twat, that hurt." Luca rubs his shoulder. "If I didn't have surgery Monday morning, I'd hit you back."

I accept a glass from my father. Vodka with a splash of lime and three ice cubes. My father's bar in his office is fully stocked, including an icemaker. Luca gets his favorite bourbon, and my dad sips the same.

"No, you wouldn't," my father cuts him off, guiding us over to the leather couches and chairs in his sitting area. "You pulled a move, and you know it."

Luca smirks as he sits in the chair opposite me and my father, who took the couch. "A move? No. A ploy? Yes. Absolutely."

I close my eyes as I take a sip of my drink. It's smooth and sour with a small bite on the end, just how I like it. Tonight wasn't supposed to be about her. But it's all about her. All the time. Even today, during my good day, I had to fight against the lure of thinking about her. Wondering what she was doing.

What is it about *her* when it hasn't been any others?

"Not tonight, Luca."

"And not tomorrow or the night after or the year after," he snaps sardonically. "But you look like shit. Like a man strung out on a woman while pretending the opposite. I should know. I perfected the art."

That's because I am.

"Are you done yet?"

"It's time, old man. It's time to live a little, and I don't just mean your occasional hookups. Roll the dice, play a hand, and see what happens."

"So says the man chasing after the woman whose heart he broke," I comment in a bored tone, though I'm clutching the tumbler so tight I'm shocked the crystal isn't shattering.

"Yes. Exactly."

"What is all this?" my father presses as I sigh deeply.

"Landon met his match. Well, his second match. He slept with her before knowing who she was."

"I'm not sure what that means. Who she was. Is that code for gold digger?"

"No," Luca answers. "That's code for Stella's teacher and his new neighbor. And his match since she's that too. She doesn't take his shit or mine. It's awesome. Plus, he mentions her, Dad. I'm not even sure he realizes it, but whenever we talk on the phone or even text, he always drops her name somewhere in the conversation."

"No, I don't." *Do I?*

"You've met her, Luca?"

"Yup. Super hot. Smokin' body. Small, but perky tits. Just how Landon likes them. Great ass too."

"Shut up about her, Luca," I grumble under my breath. I'd throw my glass at him if it weren't such a waste of much-needed alcohol.

He ignores me. "Plus, she's smart as hell, not to mention sarcastically funny. She totally ripped both of us apart without even batting an eye. She's perfect for him, Dad."

"For fuck's sake," I snap. "Stop. I don't want to talk about her. You only met her once for ten minutes. There's no way you can know any of this."

Again, I'm ignored.

"The cherry is that Stella is in love with her. I only wish she had come around sooner. This woman has our poor Landon just a touch more than infatuated with her. And struggling with it, as you can see."

I open my eyes to find my brother waving his hand in my direction.

I don't even bother to deny any of it. Likely because of the company and anything I say will stay here in this room. "My infatuation with her will pass."

"And Stella's?"

I glance at my father. "Hers' too. The woman will grow tired of pandering to a thirteen-year-old and move on. She's a renter. A brand-new teacher. The fact that she's Stella's teacher right there means nothing can happen."

"Single?"

"Just divorced from David Chambers." I don't tell them he was verbally abusive to her because it's not my story to tell. It's Elle's, and I won't betray what we shared last week.

"The golfer?"

I nod.

My father leans forward, resting his elbows on his thighs as he rubs his chin, thinking. "And she's Stella's teacher?"

"Yes."

"And teaches her to cook too? And you already slept with her before knowing all this? Interesting."

"Not really. Are we done yet?"

My father and Luca stare at each other, still ignoring me. "I didn't realize this was the same woman Stella's been telling us about. I also didn't realize it was the same woman you slept with."

"Mystery solved. Now we can all move on with our lives."

Except the two of them have a silent conversation, and I don't like where this is headed. In fact, it makes me stand up off the couch, needing to head for the door.

"What's the worst that can happen if you try with her,

Landon?" my father calls out just as my hand hits the knob. "You fall in love with her? She falls in love with you?"

"Yes," I answer easily because it's true. My head falls, my eyes closing, my chest clenching so tight I can hardly draw in air.

"Sounds awful," Luca deadpans. "All that being happy and in love stuff."

"It's not that easy, and you know it."

"No. I *don't* know it. Couples fight and guilt is a motherfucker. I've said this a hundred times before to you, brother, but I'm saying it again now because I think now more than ever you need to hear it. You loved Reese with your whole heart and would have never intentionally hurt a hair on her head. The road was icy. You didn't make it that way. What happened to her was a tragic accident. *An accident.* You would have died in her place a thousand times over and no one, including Stella, questions that."

"Shut up, Luca." I spin around, practically snarling at him. He can say whatever he wants, but it doesn't change the fact that Reese is dead because I yelled and told her to go.

"He's right, Landon. You know he is. You made mistakes. We all make mistakes because to be human is to error. But at some point, you have to forgive yourself and move on. Not just for you, but for Stella. She loves you, and we love you. But her happiness is so interconnected to yours. Why do you think she's latching onto this woman so tightly? A woman she's only known a month?"

I know why. I just can't bring myself to think it.

"You deserve happiness," he continues. "You deserve it all and so does Stella. The only one who blames you for Reese is you. Do you hear what I'm saying? Not Stella or any of us. *Forgive yourself, Landon.* And after you try that, maybe you should also try saying fuck it and give it a shot with this woman. Don't let her become another regret. Forget the fact that she's Stella's teacher. That can be figured out."

I picture Elle with that guy tonight. The one whose hands I wanted to break for touching her. Whose face I wanted to bloody for smiling at her the way he was. With interest and intent. This possessive kill-anyone-who-touches-what's-mine thing is new for me. A bit unsettling at that, but there all the same. Refusing to be denied. No matter how hard I try, I can't suppress my fixation with her.

Which means I either continue to make a futile attempt at pushing it away and eventually grow more insane than I already am.

Or I do what my brother and father suggest.

Is that possible for me? Can I forgive myself for what happened with Reese? Can I actually say fuck it and see what happens?

The kitchen smells like heaven, and I find my friend standing over a roasted pork loin, slicing it up into perfect equal pieces. "You're such a bitch," I start, and Bridget smiles, wholly unrepentant.

"I've been called worse."

"You were supposed to send Roger. Not a strange dude to pick me up."

"Roger was busy."

"Right. So that's why Aaron said you set this whole thing up, and he thinks it's a date?"

Bridget huffs at me, setting down the electric knife. "Go over and grab those rolls out of the oven before they burn, would ya?"

I slip on the oven mitts that are on the counter and retrieve the rolls that are perfectly golden brown. Another second and they'd be hockey pucks. I set them on the counter, then take it upon myself to drop them into the cloth-lined breadbasket.

"You needed a date."

"I did not need a date. We talked about this. I'm working on me."

She rolls her eyes while plating the meat on the platter. "While falling in love with your neighbor."

"I'm not falling in love with him." Not really anyway. "Subsequently he saw us leave."

That piques her interest as her head pops up, her brown eyes growing rounder. "He did, huh?"

"It's a mess, Bridge. A mess. All of this is. David called tonight before your arm candy came and picked me up. The things he told me..." I trail off, shaking my head, my stomach roiling as I think about our conversation. My parents and twin sister set up my husband for blackmail. How do I make sense of that? I legit don't know.

"More threats and abuse?"

"No. He knows it's over. It was about my parents and Cat."

"Fucking assholes," she grumbles as she tosses the roasted vegetables with salt and pepper before pouring them all onto a serving dish around the pork. "You'll tell me everything later?" She checks, and I nod. "Don't let them get wind of who your neighbor is. Billions trump millions any day, and they'll be all over Dr. Fritz in no time flat."

Yet another reason I should stay away from Landon. Those reasons are mounting faster than a champion food eater scarfing down hotdogs.

"I like him, and I wish I didn't, and then you sent this cute guy to pick me up, and Landon was there, and he and I are already..."

She looks up, tongs poised in her hand.

"I just... I need a breather, you know? I need a moment to think and get my head on straight. It's like life is coming at me from all sides, and I don't have the right racquet to swing and smack it away with."

"What?"

"Shut up. Pretend like that made sense and be my friend."

"Okay." She holds up a consolatory hand. "But Aaron is

drama-free and totally stable and normal for whatever that's worth."

"Knock it off. Whatever you're trying to do, please stop now."

"I'm sorry. I won't try to set you up again. But keep an open mind about Aaron. He's... normal."

"When has normal ever been something I liked?"

"That football player you dated sophomore year was normal."

I snicker. "He was not. He was the quarterback. He plays professional football now."

"You clearly have a type. How does Landon fit into that?"

I think on that for a second before lifting my head in her direction. "Maybe because he's the opposite of that? I mean, he's tall and built like a tank. But... he's smarter. Rigid and unrelenting one second and yet so soft and tender the next. Especially with Stella. I think my type is my problem."

"And now you're in love with a famous billionaire. A broken single dad doctor. You're a Lifetime Original Movie waiting to happen, and I do not mean that in a good way."

I get her meaning and then some, and I sag, dropping my elbows to her counter while Bridget puts the finishing touches on dinner.

"I'm not getting together with him. I just don't want to get together with anyone else."

"Fine. I get it." She squeezes my shoulder. "I do, and I'll back off on setting you up. Let's go eat before my masterpiece gets cold."

The dining room is filled with Bridget's people. Aaron, of course. Bridget's husband, Roger. Two of Bridget's friends, Brenda and Mariel, from her book club, and five people who work at the school along with their spouses. I see why she set me up with Aaron. Everyone is here with their spouses or significant others, except for Aaron and me.

"Red or white?" Aaron asks, his eyes chocolaty brown and warm like a freshly baked cookie. He's cute. For a lawyer. But he played ball in college. I can already tell that, though I know zero about him. Clearly, I do have a type. The professional athlete type.

"Red, please."

He pours me a glass of Malbec and takes the seat beside me, dropping his arm over the back of my chair and leaning in close. "Bridget said you cheered for the University of Miami's football team."

Yup. I called it.

"I did. Did you play?"

"Michigan. QB1."

My eyebrows shoot up. "And you didn't go pro?"

"My senior year, I blew out my knee. Dropped me back to the fourth round of the draft. I played for two years in Minnesota but never made it off the bench. I retired and went to law school instead. But I bet we were on opposite sides of the field together at one point though I believe I'm older than you by a couple of years."

"Probably," I agree.

"All right, everyone. Let's eat." Bridget sets the final dish down on the large dining room table before lifting her wineglass and holding it out. "In honor of my best friend moving to town, how about we toast to new friends? Welcome to Wilchester, Elle. We're so happy to have you as part of our team and part of our town."

I blush a tomato shade of red, holding my own glass up. "Thank you so much, Bridget. That truly means everything. I would not be here without you." I laugh lightly. "It's been a whirlwind since moving here, but it's also been so special meeting y'all. Cheers."

"Cheers," they all say, taking sips of whatever they're drinking.

"So tell me, Elle," Bridget's friend Mariel starts as she polishes off her half-full glass of wine in one large gulp. "Is it true you're married to that professional golfer, David Chambers?"

I choke on my sip of wine.

"You're *married*? To David Chambers? The golfer?" That's Aaron.

"Didn't he win The Masters this year?" some random husband whose name I don't remember asks. "I heard those guys pull in several million a tournament. Plus all their endorsements. Is that true?"

"He's so handsome," Brenda, the other woman from the book club I haven't met yet, states. "And obviously rich. If you're married to him, why are you here with Aaron?"

"I read in Intertainment that she left him. Probably because he was stepping out on her," Caroline—a fellow teacher, I might add—hisses under her breath—and not quietly—at Brenda.

"I heard he hit her," Emily, another fellow teacher, retorts, and Caroline gasps, covering her mouth with her hand, and that's when everyone stops talking for approximately three seconds while they stare at me expectantly. Probably checking me for a black eye they somehow missed.

"Zip it, Emily. You're making up rumors you know nothing about."

"If you have the inside scoop, Bridget, why don't you tell us?"

I shake my head, staring down at my plate as I shuffle food around with my fork. "I'm not married to David anymore. We're divorced." I raise my eyes and narrow in on Emily. "But David never hit me. I don't know where you're getting your information from, but that's not true." No, he was just a lying, belligerent asshole who allowed himself to be blackmailed by my greedy parents and crazy sister and grow resentful. Can this night please end?

"So you're divorced? As in single?" Aaron presses, shifting closer to me and staring earnestly into the side of my face.

I nod and catch his triumphant grin. At least someone's happy. This feels more like the small town in Texas I grew up in. A place where no one knows how to mind their own damn business and gossip is a bigger sport than football and shooting. Not like New England where people are notoriously toted as cold and indifferent. Right now, I'd certainly welcome the latter.

"Are you back on the market then?" That's Mariel, her gaze casting from Aaron to me in one swift, fluid motion. "One man's loss is another's gain."

I lick my suddenly dry lips, lifting my water glass and taking a hasty sip. I should have expected this. I don't know why I didn't. I assumed I'd get a question or two, but nothing like this.

"No." I meet her gaze head-on. "I'm not interested in dating right now." I set my glass down and raise my head high, refusing to cower or let them know they got to me. My reasons, my life, my choices are my own, and I'll be damned if I let anyone here make me feel bad about them. But of course, my simple response only brings on a new set of back and forth.

"But why did you leave him if he didn't hit you?" That's Brenda again. "He's so handsome. And rich."

Thank you. I believe you already made that point.

"Divorce is a sin," Mariel hisses, again trying for under her breath and not achieving it by a mile.

"Last I checked, so is gossiping and lying." I raise an eyebrow, but she just grins back at me. I want to roll my eyes at everyone here but settle for taking another bite of something on my plate. I couldn't tell you what it is.

"Is that what I'm doing?" she retorts. "Because from what I read—"

"Oh, can it, Mariel," Bridget snaps. "According to you, everything is a sin, and last time I checked, you're in no place to throw stones. You're just being a bitch, and I'm in no mood for it. Besides, this is Massachusetts, not Kentucky."

"But that's where I'm from."

"I'm aware. And if you're going to be judgmental over a situation you know nothing about, then maybe you should go back there."

I offer Bridget a grateful smile, and she winks back at me.

"Now. Let's talk about sex ed, baby. Because that's the hot topic for Elle."

I bark out a laugh, falling back in my chair and taking my napkin with me to cover my mouth. "Yes. Help!"

After that, things get easier. Sort of. There are no more questions about David or me. I get used to the loud commentary of her friends. The multiple bottles of wine being poured aids in that. Aaron sticks close to my side, engaging me in conversation for most of the evening. And I'll be honest. He is engaging. Smart and quick-witted.

And when he offers to drive me home, after my second glass of wine, I let him. I give him the chance Bridget suggested I give. I even allow him to walk me to my door and wait behind me while I unlock and open it up. I turn to face him, staring into his brown eyes.

He's adorable.

A guy I would totally crush on if I didn't have such a stupid heart.

"Can I call you?"

He steps in, his hand wrapping around my lower back, his lips drawing close.

"I... Aaron, you're great..."

"But you're not ready yet?" he finishes for me, and I nod sheepishly. Cute and engaging, but there's no spark.

"Yes. I'm sorry."

"Don't be. I'll try again in a month." He gives me a wink before planting his lips on my cheek, then he leaves, heading down the path toward his car. I watch him get in, acknowledging the wave he sends me before shutting and locking my door up tight.

I sag against it, my hand on my chest. I survived.

That's when the door pounds against my back. Three times. *Whap. Whap. Whap.*

I flip around, wishing for about the fiftieth time since moving in that this door had a peephole or a nearby window with direct access to the front porch. A Southerner would have never done this. Maybe I'll ask my landlord if I can install a Ring.

"Who's there?"

"Open up, Elle. Now."

My skin breaks out into hives. Or chills. It's hard to tell which they are because I'm covered in them and itchy as hell.

I flip the lock and swing the door open. Landon is there, his glasses on, his hair a disheveled mess of artwork, his green eyes mossy and turbulent. "Did he kiss you?"

I blink repeatedly at him. "Pardon?"

He grips the doorframe. "Did he kiss you good night? Did his lips touch you?"

"Um." I lick my lips, flustered. "Yes. I mean, no. He kissed my cheek but—"

Landon's hands hit the back of my hair, his mouth on mine before I can even comprehend how he moved so fast. I stumble back a step and suddenly I'm twirling through the air, landing hard on a surface I don't care enough about to open my eyes and figure out what it is.

"I hate that he touched you," Landon growls into me, and I swear my panties are now soaked with that admission. "I've been thinking about you all night. Going crazy. I never go crazy, Elle."

God, after the evening I've had, I need this more than my next breath.

He hikes my legs up, spreads them open wide, and rips the hell out of my stockings, right at the crotch. I figure that means it's open season on clothing, and I attack his shirt, snapping buttons across my foyer. My hands dive into the open space where those buttons used to be, feeling the planes and ridges of his chest and abs.

His body.

Lord, I am an unrepentant sinner of a woman when it comes to this man and his body.

Deft fingers skim over the skimpy material I'm choosing to call a thong tonight, and my head slams back, banging into the mirror and the wall as pleasure explodes through my body. I wince.

"You okay?" he mumbles into my lips, his tongue diving back in, twirling with mine before sucking on it. I whimper. Especially as his fingers continue to tease me over my panties.

"Are you asking my pussy or my head?"

I open my eyes and arch up to meet his gaze. He's smiling. And his smile... this rare, uninhibited one?

"Your head. I have plans for your pussy and trust me when I tell you, I intend on taking good care of her. But I'd prefer it if she was the only thing that got banged against the wall tonight."

A breathy laugh escapes my throat. "Another joke. That's two."

"I told you I'm funny."

I shake my head as his mouth drops down, sucking and kissing on my neck in a very distracting way. "No. I don't think anyone ever said you were funny. Though that one wasn't half bad."

"Elle?"

"Yeah?"

His eyes quirk up, meeting mine. "You gonna keep talking about my jokes or can I get you naked now?"

I giggle. "Naked away."

In the next second, my blouse is ripped up and over my head, leaving me in my red lace bra. Landon groans, dropping to his knees and pushing my thighs up higher, hooking my boots over his shoulders. My breath hitches, one hand diving into his hair, the other gripping the edge of the entry table I'm precariously perched on. This thing is not meant for humans to sit on it. It's a good thing I've got a small ass.

He slides my panties to the side and stares at me. "Oh, Elle. You're a sexy, dripping mess for me."

My eyes seal shut, my lungs emptying as his lips cover my clit, sucking on it before his tongue plunges up inside me.

"Holy... ah!"

"Fuck, you taste good. That's right. Grip me and hold on because there's no way I can slow down now. Not with you tasting this good."

With his hands on my ass, he tips me back farther, nearly bending my body in half, catching most of my weight as his mouth devours me. His tongue thrusts, flicking back and forth, in and out as he fucks me with it. Over and over, setting a punishing pace that has me rocking into his face and side to side and ripping at his hair and moaning. He tears his glasses from his face, tossing them somewhere before returning to me, squeezing my ass cheeks, and spreading me wide so he can eat every inch of me.

The mirror behind my head sways dangerously, but I can't focus on anything other than what his lips and wicked tongue are doing to me. Words and sounds tumble from my lips, the heels of my boots digging into his back as he brings my body up higher and higher. Closer and closer.

His fingers replace his tongue, and he shifts, drawing back a few inches, his carnal gaze locked between my legs, watching as his fingers slowly drag out of me only to push back in. It's wet and dripping, and this feels so good my back bows, thrusting my tits up and out. His free hand finds my bra, ripping one cup down and exposing my breast.

The thumb of the hand that's fucking me rubs my clit in deliberate circles, and I swear, stars dance behind my eyes. How does he do this so well?

"Landon," I pant, needing, wanting so desperately to come I'm nearly crazy with it.

"So beautiful," he rasps as he looks up at me, his eyes everywhere, as if they can't decide which part of the action they want to focus on the most. "You have no idea how badly I need you." He growls. "No one fucking else gets this." He leans in and kisses my pussy before licking me from my opening all the way up. "No one. You're mine, Elle. Mine."

He cups my breast in his large hand, groaning when he feels how hard my nipple is against his palm before sliding it up my chest and wrapping around my throat as if he's proving his point. I am his. No one else's. He gives me a possessive squeeze without cutting off my air, and it drives me wild in the best of ways.

I cry out, my voice slightly garbled against the force of his hand on my windpipe. Warm, wet lips dive back in, sucking and playing with my clit while he finger fucks me into a frenzy. Those expert fingers do dirty things to me, crooking to find my inner sweet spot only to pull back and toy with my opening, rimming it. All the while his tongue and lips are feasting on me, alternating between sucking and flicking my clit, ravaging me.

He licks his fingers that are coated in my arousal, then plunges them back in, finger fucking me faster and faster before thrusting his tongue up along with them. "How much can you handle?"

Oh God. No one has ever done this to me. Had both their tongue and fingers inside me at the same time. Licking and plunging. It's so many sensations all at once, and I open my eyes, watching him do it. The sight practically has me coming on the spot, and he must feel it. Feel how close I am. Feel my pussy clenching around him.

He blows on me and I moan, writhing uncontrollably.

"Come, Elle. Come now for me." The stubble on his jaw grazes my inner thighs, and with one final flick of his tongue on my clit, I explode all over him just as he commands, screaming out to God, Jesus, his mother, and likely his father too.

I have no idea.

All I know is that I ride his face through this wonderfully never-ending onslaught of glorious spasms and somewhere, in the back of my lust-muddled brain, I feel the mirror slide, sway, slip out from behind my head, and then *crash* as it collides with the floor. I jerk, causing the table holding me up to wobble dangerously and then pitch forward. One hand flees Landon's hair, desperately holding on to the falling table. My other flies out, searching for a wall or something to stop my momentum, only there's nothing to grasp on to and a different sort of shriek flees my lungs.

Landon curses, yelling my name as my body topples forward and goes down.

Fuck! That's all I can think as I slide my fingers from Elle's dripping pussy just in time to dodge a falling mirror that narrowly misses my left arm. I bounce up onto my feet in a crouch as the thing shatters beside us, and the table starts to shake and then tip forward. Elle goes flying, screaming louder than I just made her, which only pisses me off more.

I need to up my game for the next round.

But before that can happen, I somehow manage to catch her mid-fall, twist us, and drop her on top of me, breaking her fall while keeping her away from the shattered glass that now lines her floor. We're both panting for our lives, a total disheveled mess of ripped clothes. Elle's bra is only covering one perfect tit while leaving the other exposed right up by my mouth. Her skirt is hoisted to her waist, her panties askew with my hand on her ass as I hold her against me.

"What the hell—"

Only she's laughing, angling her body up to meet my eyes with a playful, contented smile. One I immediately return, my tongue swiping out to lick at her sweet little nipple because it's there and why not.

"Well, that happened," I deadpan, and she laughs harder. "Don't worry, I'll replace everything."

I sit up, taking her with me and wrapping her up in my arms, holding her tight against me. Her bedroom is upstairs and down a long hallway. Her family room is like ten feet away. Impossible. If I'm not inside her in the next thirty seconds, I'll die. That's how badly I need this woman. I wasn't exaggerating before.

I need her.

"Oh my God," she says with a breathy laugh. "We broke the mirror. Like shattered it. And the table..."

My teeth scrape down her neck, lingering on her pulse. It's thrumming with excitement. Desire. Post-orgasmic arrhythmia. *Yes.* I suck deeper, harder, licking up her neck until I'm breathing heavily into her ear. Flipping us around, I set her on the floor and crawl on all fours over her, dropping my weight so I can feel more of her against me.

"Landon! The glass," she squeals as some of it crunches beneath my shoe. And that's another thing. That squeal is also louder than the one she just gave me.

I kick aside broken pieces of mirror, grateful we're both still wearing our shoes, and then lift her up and off the floor only to slam her against the coat closet door.

"Problem solved."

"Thank God." Her long legs wrap around my waist, her heels digging into my ass. She hums into my mouth as she kisses me, grinding herself mercilessly down on my dick, still trapped in my jeans. My thigh holds her up, my dick begging for freedom as my hips tilt into her, dry fucking her the way she's doing to me.

But it's not enough.

Nowhere close to enough.

I need to feel her, be inside her. Reaching up under her skirt, right over her soaking pussy, I rip her panties to shreds. She gasps, her head falling back against the door as I slip my fingers back inside her. Showing her, telling her without words... *Feel that? Feel how good that is? No one else will touch you here but me.*

My mouth continues to claim hers, my tongue tasting every inch of her. She's sweet and hungry, and I could kiss her without boredom forever. *Forever?* That seems crazy and irrational and is not something I can think too deeply about at the moment.

Her hands climb down between us, fumbling with my belt, then the button of my jeans, and finally my zipper. Tugging the denim down my hips the best she can until my cock springs free. She fists it in her small hand, stroking me up and down as I grip her ass, squeezing the fuck out of her cheeks, knowing I'm more than likely marking them.

I love that visual and wish I could see it, but that will have to wait. Using my other hand to line myself up with her pussy, I slide the head of my cock up and down through her wetness, and with one thrust, I'm home.

So deep inside her there's no her or me, it's only us.

This.

I thrust up, a slow glide, her juices coating my dick making me slick and hot, and this feels so goddamn good she's all I can focus on. My eyes roll back as I seat myself all the way inside her and still. Needing a second to catch my breath. God. Has it ever felt this good?

I want her to moan my name again. Scream it this time for the cheap seats in the back. I want the world to hear. *I'm* making her feel like this.

Her head presses against the door, her chin tipped back with her eyes closed. She's absolutely stunning like this. With me inside her. Clutching my shoulders with her nails digging in as I fill her up over and over. I can't look away. I can't close my eyes and succumb to the exquisite pleasure. She's breathtaking, and I'm ruined.

I might have been that first night I met her.

Pulling out on another slow drag, I slam up into her only to do it again and again. Each thrust up is harder. Each slide out a little slower. It's driving her mad, and her nails dig in sharper with a plea for more.

"You feel it? You feel what this is?"

"Yes," she moans. "I need more."

"Take what you need, Elle. Fuck my cock until you see stars."

She bounces on me, meeting me thrust for thrust as I quicken my pace, pistoning in and out of her with smooth, hot strokes. Her tits jiggle, and I lean down, capturing the exposed one between my lips.

"Fuck yes," she cries as I sink my teeth into her peaked bud. "More. Harder. Deeper," she chants.

Jaw locked, I power my hips into her, higher, deeper—as deep as I can go. Giving her exactly what she's begging me for.

Her face falls into my neck as I hold her up, screwing her into the door with a constant *bang, bang, bang.* It's loud and rough, my body coated in sweat. And as much as I love holding her like this—so close—feeling her surround me, I need to take her harder, and I can't do that without hurting her back against the door.

Sliding her off me, I set her on shaky feet, flip her around so her hands go onto the door for support, and bend her forward. I make sure she's steady, rubbing her ass, squeezing it, and slapping it once. She moans, and I do it again.

Jesus, I'm going to hell. This sight.

Her skirt is pushed all the way up over her ass. Her pink

pussy is wet and swollen. Her boots—goddamn those sexy boots.

She's my ultimate erotic dream, and I tell her so as my palms continue to run along the globes of her ass, unable to stop touching it. She wiggles, urging me to take her again, needy and impatient. I give her another good, hard slap, then slam back into her.

She screams, her head flying back, her hair along with it. I smack her once more and set a punishing rhythm, holding on to her hips as I slice in and out, faster and faster, harder and harder. Our hips move as one, our skin tacky.

"This ass."

"Smack it again."

Holy hell. I smack her ass with each plunge in, rubbing it as I pull out, listening as she whimpers and moans and calls out to me and God. My dirty vixen is oblivious to what she's unleashing inside me. My cock strokes in and out, the friction of taking her like this shooting explosions of pleasure up my spine. My breath is choppy, and I grip her hair, turning her face so I can capture her lips.

We're sloppy, but she tastes so good, and I need more. Just more. I'll never get enough of her. Not of the way she feels or the sounds she makes or how incredible she tastes. None of it. She's my beginning, and she'll be my end.

Unable to hold off much longer, I reach around, finding her slick clit and rubbing her in time with our thrusts. That's when she loses it. Her body writhing, screaming, swearing. Her hands scraping down the door she's barely clinging to. My other hand releases her hair and wraps around her stomach, holding her up, pressing her against me as she comes over and over, her pussy clenching my cock so tight I wheeze.

And when I can't take it anymore, when her body sags, I come with a roar, my forehead dropping between her shoulder blades. Whole body shakes ripple through me as I still my hips and spill myself inside her, unable to care about the repercussions of that when I absolutely should. I already got one woman pregnant before I meant to, but this is different. I'm not a twenty-year-old boy. I'm a thirty-three-year-old man who wants to mark this woman with my cum.

Who wants to watch as it drips out of her.

I'm claiming her, no going back now.

I flip her around, press her into the door, and kiss her good, long, and hard. We're both still breathless, panting into each other's mouths, but I can't get enough of her.

My forehead drops to hers. "How did this happen?"

"Are you asking about you storming into my house like a possessed demon, the mess we created, or the insanely hot sex we just had?"

I grin against her lips. "Yes. Come with me." I lead her through her house, searching for the powder room. Her house is smaller than mine, and the powder room is easy to find just off the kitchen. I grab a clean hand towel and turn on the warm water, watching her reflection in the mirror, same as she's doing with me.

Her face is red, her hair wild with tangles, but there's a softness to her hazel eyes. A vulnerability I'm all too familiar with. I ring out the towel and then wipe between her legs, cleaning her up. She gives me a slightly embarrassed look, but I don't care. I have to go soon, and I want to make sure she's okay before I do that.

My lips meet the crook of her shoulder, and I tug her back against me. "Are you okay?"

"Are you?" she retorts, and I nip at her flesh.

"No. But I think I will be." I hope. I watch as her eyes close, her head falling back against me.

"Me too."

"Can I draw you a bath before I clean up the glass and leave?"

"You don't have to—"

"I know I don't."

"It's late. I'll just shower after you leave."

I drop the towel in the sink and wrap my arms around her, holding her against me. Feeling like I can do this. Feeling hope for the first time in so long. I thought about everything my father and Luca said. All through dinner. The entire ride home. While waiting for Elle's date to return her home.

I'm saying fuck it, rolling the dice, and taking a chance. It's terrifying, and the guilt I can't help but feel threatens to overcome me, drag me down, and suffocate me. It feels impossible, but I won't know if it truly is until I try.

And I want to do that with her.

"Are you upset I can't stay?"

"I don't know," she whispers. "I know you can't, but I don't know what this is and I'm honestly afraid not only to ask but of what the answer will be."

"Because you want this to happen or because you enjoyed the sex but aren't ready for more than that?"

"Yes," she says, throwing my non-answer back at me.

I kiss a trail up her neck and hold her tighter to me. "I don't know if I'll be good at this. And if I said I wasn't struggling, I'd be lying to you. So how about that's the promise we make? No lying. We take each day as it comes, and we see how it goes."

She breathes out a sigh. "I can do that."

"Good." I reach up and squeeze her tit that's still out of her bra.

She laughs. "I was wondering when you'd notice that."

"I never stopped noticing. I was just trying to be a gentleman and clean you up."

"I think breaking furniture, slapping my ass, and screwing me against my closet door doesn't quite speak to you being a gentleman."

"A gentleman on the streets and a freak in the sheets, then?"

She laughs, spinning in my arms. "You're getting cute with the jokes." She reaches up and pecks my lips. "How about we go clean up that mess so you can get home to Stella."

"She's asleep. I wouldn't have come otherwise. Incidentally, I'd rather her not know what we're up to."

I get a small, jerky nod for that. The kind that tells me she has a lot on her mind. I do too, but I don't leave her until I've cleaned up the mess we made, making sure every last piece of the broken mirror—thankfully most of it was in big pieces—is gone. She kisses me goodbye at the door, but it's quiet and brief. And as I walk across the lawn back to my house, step inside, and lock the door behind me, setting the alarm and heading upstairs, I wonder if anything will ever feel normal again.

Elle feels right in a way I wasn't prepared for. From the second I saw her, everything with her has been a struggle and a fight to resist. To the point where what happened tonight almost feels inevitable.

I'm hoping it's the same for her.

That even though we're a disaster in the making, we don't end like one.

I stop in at Stella's door, listening against the wood. It's quiet, and I open it a crack, peeking in on her. Stella is on her side, sound asleep, tucked tightly under her mountain of blankets. I open the door wider and step inside, looking around.

I don't come in here often. It's Stella's room, and she's a thirteen-year-old girl who values her space and privacy. Her rainbow nightlight Layla bought her after Stella came out to her glows through the room, casting a warm, comforting light. I love that she has that. People who love her no matter what.

Stella's walls are almost bare. In fact, other than her bookshelf filled with books, there isn't much here. I bought this home because Reese loved it, loved how close to town it is, but I've always had dreams of building something for us. A fresh start I was never able to comprehend but have found myself sketching more and more of this dream house in the last few weeks.

Would that make Stella happy?

If I bought a big plot of land she can grow whatever she wants on? Help design and decorate her room however she likes? I cross the large bedroom, running my fingers over her hair.

"I love you, Bellas." My chest tightens as I stare down at my girl. "I miss your mom. I wish she were here. You need that. A woman in your life. Someone you trust. Someone who will hold your heart and hear your words and keep them both safe. I try to be that someone for you, but I know you need more."

I press my lips to her forehead. She needs more.

Is that why I'm so drawn to Elle? Because of the way she is with my daughter? The way my daughter is with her? No. I was drawn to her before that. Now I'm a planet, orbiting her. She's a sun I never cared I was missing until she shined her light on me and my daughter.

Closing the door behind me, I walk down the hall, glancing down at my ruined shirt with a smile. And when I look back up again, Elle's light is on in her bedroom. She was waiting for me. Her window is closed, so I don't bother opening mine, but she's standing there in a skimpy pink tank top and matching shorts. Her skin glowing and her hair wet from her shower.

I fucking love her dark blond hair and those bright hazel eyes.

She's radiant, and I'm falling. So hard I don't think stopping is an option anymore.

I blow her a kiss, and she smiles before shutting out her bedroom light, so I do the same. In the darkness I go about getting ready for bed, taking a quick shower to wash off the sweat and sex still clinging to me, brushing my teeth, and then getting into bed.

I plug in my phone and catch the text I missed.

Good night :)

Elle.

I reply with the same. Catching myself smiling once again. She's the air I haven't breathed in so long. Life I never wanted to live again. I'm addicted. Addicted to her. To this feeling. To just plain old *feeling* again.

Now I just have to make sure I don't fuck it up. For any of us.

"Dance it out now, girl," I sing to Stella, who's shaking her butt around the kitchen, both of us bopping our heads to the beat of Wild Minds. "God, I love this song." I hold up the wooden spatula in my hand that's coated in homemade marinara and sing the final notes of this ballad along with Jasper Diamond.

"My uncles know them," Stella announces as the song comes to a close and an Ed Sheeran song comes over the Alexa. I freeze, wooden spoon in mid-air.

"Your uncles know Wild Minds?"

She shrugs like it's no big thing, and I'm sure to her it's not. Her uncles are billionaires. Hell, her father is a freaking billionaire too, which I guess by extension makes her one? I don't know how the money train works with these people. I grew up in a middle-class home in a middle-class neighborhood, and anytime I went and spent more than five hundred dollars on anything the first year I was married to David, I broke out in a cold sweat and hives.

"Yeah. I mean, Uncle Kaplan did some charity work with Jasper Diamond, and Grace was going crazy because Uncle

Carter took her to meet them at their last concert here in Boston."

"Grace?"

"Uncle Carter's... girlfriend, I guess." Another shrug as she mixes the ricotta with the spices and herbs she added for the lasagna we're making. "They live together, and she just told us a couple weeks ago she's pregnant. But I've known her my whole life because she's Uncle Oliver's best friend."

Wow. That's a mindfuck. "Cool," is what I come up with. This family, man. There is a lot to them. I wonder if I'll ever meet any of the others aside from Luca. "All right, let's layer this lasagna up, and then I'll put it in the oven so you can go study for your math test."

She groans, but that's why we're in her house today cooking instead of mine. It was not my plan to do that. Landon and I had initially agreed all cooking would be at my place. But Stella asked if we could do it here so she could study here since all her things are already here, and it's not like I could say, sorry, hon, your dad doesn't like me in your house, and my relationship with him is a hot mess of complicated.

And is that even still true after what went down Saturday night? We texted some on Sunday, but I haven't seen him since he left after our furniture-breaking sex. I texted him to let him know what Stella wanted to do, but I never heard back.

So yeah. I'm a little wary about being here in the man's kitchen, making a mess, and rocking out on his Alexa. I don't pretend that the sex meant more to him than simple jealousy and scratching an itch and getting it out of our systems. We're not a couple. This is not a relationship. Hell, we're not even friends.

I feel weird being here.

"I hate math," she grumbles as we make a layer of partially cooked lasagna noodles over the sauce. I would have liked to try making homemade noodles, but I'm not a miracle worker, and there's only so much time to get this done in.

"I know, but it's a big test."

"Calculus sucks balls."

I snicker. "You're the smart one taking advanced calculus. That's high school level stuff there."

"I know. I just want high school to be easy, so I'm loading up now." She pauses for a second before going back to adding the layer of meat on top of the ricotta. "Do you think high school will be easier? I mean, do you think I'll make friends? Find people who like me for me? Layla will be there, and she has friends, but I'm not Layla. I'm not as fun or outgoing as she is."

"First off, I think you're a lot of fun. I have a blast every time we hang out. But all I can say is I hope so. The high school is bigger, which means new kids. New opportunities to make friends."

"I don't care if I grow boobs, but all the girls make fun of my flat chest."

"You're thirteen, Stella. Most of those girls have flat boobs themselves. They're just looking for anything they can use against you because you intimidate them. You're beautiful and smart and for better or worse, your family name brings out the suck-ups and jerks."

We finish the lasagna and cover it with foil, and I get the lovely task of lifting the heavy dish into the oven to bake. We already made a salad—using a million fresh veggies from her garden and greenhouse—and the garlic bread.

"I haven't come out yet to anyone in my school."

I nod. I already figured this. "Do you want to?"

"I don't need anyone making more fun of me."

Oh, this poor girl.

I shut the oven door and reach out, bringing her into my chest, hugging her close because sometimes, that's all you can do. Be there for someone when they need it. I rock her gently to the music playing in the background.

"You do it in your own time when you're ready. And whenever you decide that is, you have the love and support of an amazing family. Plus Layla. Plus me. When people make fun of you, that's a reflection of themselves. Not you. It's *their* anger, *their* insecurities, *their* crap. You feel me on that? It's them taking their crap out on you. You are special and wonderful, and I'm so proud of you for owning who you are. Whether you choose to share it with anyone else or not is your call to make."

"I know. I just..." She hugs me tighter, and I fight my threatening emotions before they get the best of me. "I just want to meet new people in high school."

I kiss the top of her head. "I want that for you too." More than anything, I want that for her. I give her another kiss, a tighter squeeze, then I release her with a soft smile. "All right, homework time. For both of us." I wink, and she giggles, grabbing her bag off the floor and running upstairs.

And now I feel even weirder than I did twenty minutes ago.

But I can't leave. Not with the lasagna in the oven and frankly, I don't want to. I want to see Landon. Try to get a read on him so I can temper my own expectations.

Settling in at the counter in the large kitchen, I listen to music while reading over history essays. And when there are ten minutes left on the lasagna, I pop the garlic bread in the oven and take the salad out of the fridge. I don't plan to stay. Not unless he asks me himself.

That's not what this was about, but I can't help the hope as it blooms inside me.

Removing the foil from the bubbling lasagna so the cheese can finish melting, I check my watch. It's nearly seven, and I still have so much homework to grade. Essays take forever, especially written by middle schoolers. Even if they are on Roman gods. I mean, how easy is that? Might not be actual history, but to the Romans who believed in their gods fiercely, it is. Picking a god and explaining how he or she impacted the daily lives of the Romans and why they were so important to their culture is a pretty cool assignment.

If I do say so myself.

After doing one last paper, I tuck all my papers back in my bag and set it off to the side. The lasagna smells like another form of heaven, and as I open the oven, armed with oven mitts, my stomach grumbles, and my mouth pools with saliva. It looks better than it smells.

The timer I set on Alexa goes off just as I'm lifting the dish out of the oven. "Alexa, cancel the timer."

"Smells great in here," Landon says behind me, and I scream, startling so bad I jump and spin around on instinct. The heavy tray of lasagna sloshes in my hands, seeping over the edge of the dish and onto my oven mitt, burning me through the thick cotton. But it's heavy and before I know what's happening, it goes crashing to the floor.

Sauce, noodles, cheese, and meat go flying, splattering every possible surface. The dish smashes, breaking apart and adding to the horrific mess.

For a second all I can do is stand here in abject horror, taking in the carnage of ruined dinner before my eyes. What have I done? Blood rushes through my ears like a freight train, blocking out all other sounds. Landon is standing there, saying something to me, but I can't handle it.

"I'm so sorry."

I drop to my knees, ripping off the mitts and going for the broken dish first. I have to clean this up. *Stupid, ungrateful bitch. Look what you did, you clumsy cunt. You can't even make dinner without fucking it up. Is there anything you do right? Anything? Useless. That's what you are, Elle. Fucking useless.*

"I'm so sorry."

Hot sauce burns through my pants and onto my knees as I

gather pieces of the dish, setting them off to the side. How will I ever clean this up?

"Elle. What are you doing? Stop."

I shake my head.

"Stella, out of here. It's okay. Everything is fine. Go back upstairs and order a pizza for all of us. I've got this. Go."

Landon's words crackle in my periphery, but I can't quite make sense of them. All I see is the mess. All I hear is David in my head as my vision sways and a haze washes over me.

What the fuck is wrong with you?! How could you have fucked this up? How could you possibly be this fucking stupid? A child could have done a better job. I should have married someone with half a brain instead of you. Worthless. Ugly. Ungrateful. Stupid. Bitch.

"Elle!" Landon's voice booms right in my face, and I snap up, taking him in. He's incensed, and I can't stop the sob as it flees my lips, my whole body trembling. "Stop!"

"I'm so sorry. It was an accident. I'll clean it all up. It'll be like—"

My words cut off, air whooshing from my lungs as I'm lifted off my knees, off the floor, and dropped onto the counter. "Elle, look at me."

I can't. I can't stop staring at the mess. His hand is on my cheek, forcing me up. His green eyes invade, his face inches from mine, demanding I see him.

"I don't care about the fucking mess. You're covered in sauce, you've burned your right hand, and your other is bleeding. What were you doing trying to clean that up like this?"

Tears start pouring from my eyes. I can't stop them. I can't speak. I can't answer.

"Oh, Elle." Landon's hands wrap into my hair, and he takes my face, burying it in his shoulder. "It's just a mess. That's all that is. It can be cleaned."

I shake my head against him, clenching my eyes shut. "No." He doesn't understand. I don't understand.

"Yes. It was my fault for scaring you, but what were you doing trying to clean that up with your bare hands?"

"I... I..."

I don't know what that was. It was like I was back in my kitchen in Florida, and David was screaming over me. But I'm not there anymore. I'm here with Landon, who's holding and shushing and comforting me.

"Come with me."

"What—"

Only my words cut off again as I'm suddenly lifted off the counter and carried like a bride. "Stella, stay in your room," Landon orders as he marches up the stairs like I weigh nothing.

"Is Elle okay?"

"She's fine, but I need to clean up the kitchen."

"I ordered pizza."

Pizza. No. It was supposed to be lasagna. "I'm so sor—"

"Don't you dare tell me you're sorry. Not one more time."

Landon carries me down the hall, through his bedroom, and into the master bath, which is easily twice the size of mine. He sets me down on the counter and shuts the door behind us. He goes for my pants, moving me around as he removes them, sliding them carefully down my legs.

My knees are bright red, and I can't tell if it's from sauce or burns. They don't hurt. Nothing hurts because everything is numb. I've hated how David treated me for a long time, but in this moment, I truly, genuinely hate him for what he did to me. And I'm not even talking about the cheating with my sister. Fuck the cheating and fuck her.

This is different.

This is inside me.

Water is running, and my shirt is now gone, and Landon is standing silently in front of me, wiping my legs and arms with a cool cloth. He's twisting my hands, examining every inch, and when he wipes at the blood oozing from a cut, his eyes bounce back and forth between mine and my hand, checking to see if he's hurting me.

It stings but not enough for me to flinch.

"The burn isn't bad, and the cut doesn't require stitches."

I blink. I nod. I swallow and stare into Landon's eyes, so filled with worry for me. He's not mad, and he's not yelling, and he's not David. He's not David.

I lick my lips, feeling another tear drip down my face.

"He used to yell at you if you made a mess?" he surmises.

"Yes."

"Bad?"

"Yes."

His eyes darken, and his jaw clenches, but he doesn't ask anything else about it. "Bath or shower?"

I shake my head. "I need to go back—"

"No. You need to get yourself together and washed up. Then I'm going to put ointment on your burn and bandage your cut. After *I* clean up the kitchen."

I open my mouth to argue, when his lips press to mine, kissing me hard to shut me up.

"I don't want to hear it. No arguing with me. Once all that is done, we're going to have pizza. Together."

"Landon... I..."

His hand is in my hair, cupping the back of my head. "I don't care about the mess. I don't care about my kitchen or anything else. I care about you. You hear me? You. You are perfect to me and nothing that happened downstairs matters. Got it?"

Tears threaten again, and I do my best to push them back, though I know at least one more must leak out because his thumb is there, beneath my eye, to brush it away.

"Shower or bath?" he asks again, and why didn't I meet him first? My whole life would have been different if I had met him first. Then I remember my family and what they would have done to him, and my blood runs cold. I'm a mess, and I should go. I bring nothing but trouble and destruction with me, and he and Stella have been through enough.

But I want them anyway. And now that I know what my family is capable of, I'll protect them from them.

"Shower."

"Good girl." He kisses my lips, then my cheeks, then my forehead. He leaves me, starting up his shower before returning and helping me off the counter. "I'm going to get you something clean to wear. Come downstairs when you're ready, okay?"

"Thank you."

He smiles softly at me, brushing the tip of his nose with mine, and then he's gone, leaving the bathroom. How can my heart feel so empty and so full at the same time? I remove my bra and panties, step into the warm but not hot shower—the doctor thinks of everything—and finally feel the sting of my cut and burn.

I don't know how long I stay in here, and I don't hear when Landon returns with clothes for me to wear, but he must have because when I get out, there are pajama pants, a T-shirt, and a sweatshirt waiting for me.

Not my scarf, I note, and I wonder where he has that stashed.

It brings a smile to my lips, and I go about getting dressed, swimming in his clothes that are ten sizes too big but smell like him. He kept my scarf; I'm claiming at least this T-shirt as mine. Opening the door, I enter his bedroom, unable to help myself as I look around.

It's a lot of grays and whites, minimal and contemporary, yet cozy somehow. His bed is made pristinely, not an item out of place. And his light gray walls boast framed black and white pictures of buildings—some I recognize, some I don't. Architecture. The images are gorgeous, captured with an artistic flair, and I wonder if his wife took these.

Stella mentioned she was into photography.

I walk over to his desk, though I know this isn't his regular office. That's downstairs and filled with computers and books and things. He has renderings of a house, each a little different, but all big and beautiful. The detail on them is incredible, and I was unaware he could sketch like this.

The doorbell rings from downstairs. "Dad, pizza is here," Stella calls out, and I hear her door open, her feet pounding down the stairs.

"I got it," he yells back, and I smile. They're so normal and yet so not. I love that about them. How real they are to me when the world views them as something else entirely.

I open the door to head downstairs, but Landon is there before I get very far. Only this time I don't jump. "You okay?"

"Better."

He smiles, his eyes dancing around my face before giving me a once-over. "I like you in my clothes."

I like me in his clothes too.

He holds up burn ointment and a Band-Aid.

"They're fine, Doctor. No need for the extra treatment."

"Ah, there's my girl. Always giving me sass. What did I say about arguing with me?"

He takes my hand, applying the Band-Aid first to the cut that's barely even a cut and definitely not bleeding anymore. Then he goes for the burn, applying some white cream to it, which I'll admit, feels good. And when he's done, he kisses my booboo over my Band-Aid, and I fall just a bit harder.

"Hungry?"

Not for pizza. I think my eyes give that away because he leans in and kisses me. He kisses me good and hard, only pulling back when we're both breathless.

"Pizza. Stella is waiting on us."

"The kitchen?" I ask.

"All cleaned up and whatever I missed, the cleaning people are coming tomorrow anyway, so we're good."

I'm falling so hard for you, Landon Fritz, you won't be able to get rid of me. That's how deeply I want to bury myself in your heart.

"Thank you."

He shakes his head. Plants another kiss, then shifts me so he's behind me as we walk down the hall. "Can I sneak over tonight?" he husks in my ear before we reach the stairs. I turn back to him and catch him staring at my ass. I give it a little wiggle, and he smirks, swatting it.

Yup. Totally done.

"I'll leave the front door unlocked for you."

I get a pinch this time for that, then we join Stella in the now cleaned kitchen. We eat salad—thankfully that was unharmed—and pizza and laugh like nothing happened at all. Like I didn't ruin dinner and subsequently have a breakdown.

Whether they know it or not, they're healing places inside me I didn't realize were still damaged. This. This is what I want. *Mine*, I think. They're mine, and I want to keep them. If I didn't know that already, I sure as hell know it now.

22

I have a huge favor to ask. That's the text I get shortly before I leave my house to head to the grocery store. Naturally, the sight of Landon's name on my screen makes my heart leap in my chest because I'm stupid like that. Or at least a glutton for punishment and heartache.

Is this of the sexual variety? If not, I operate purely on a bartering system.

The text goes through, and I grab my keys off the counter in the kitchen. It's Columbus Day, and school is closed. I woke up early, did some stuff in my garden, shopped a bit online, read for an hour. It's been heaven.

A heaven I haven't wanted to rock by calling my family. I've been avoiding that. It's been more than a week since David's call, and I haven't found the will to confront them yet. I mean, how do you have that conversation? Their betrayal has been sitting like a boulder on my chest, a minefield in my head. It's like I'm going through the stages of grief only on a never-ending loop and at light speed. I need to sort out my thoughts a little more before I speak to any of them.

But this week... this perfect week... it's been sex and heat and sneaking around and fun. So much fun with Landon that I don't want to disrupt any of that. I don't want to diminish it with their evil—they've taken enough from me already.

How about I barter for sexual favors if you do this one for me first.

Now my interest is piqued. What's so important?

Come outside and you'll see.

I stare at my phone, mulling it over. It sounds ominous, but after last night and the deliciously sore way I woke up this morning, I think it's safe to say I'll pretty much do whatever the man asks of me.

Walking through the downstairs to the front door, I go to check my reflection in the mirror Landon replaced not even two days after we broke the first one. I smile and blush a little, my core clenching. Ever since the lasagna incident a week ago, everything with Landon has been unexpectedly amazing. All of it. The words he's said and the way he's handled my body. That night and then this entire week since has felt like a turning point. A shift.

Something potentially more than just sex.

Is that even what I want so soon after my divorce?

Shaking off those thoughts, I unlock the door and peek my head out, glancing in the direction of his house. A laugh hits my lips. Landon is standing right there to the side of my door, his arms folded across his chest, his legs crossed at the ankles as he leans against the siding. He studies me, and I give him a second look.

"Luca."

He grins like a Cheshire Cat. "Glad you remember me. You're quick to pick up which one of us is which."

"I'm a twin myself. We catch subtleties others miss."

"Landon never mentioned that."

"Probably because I haven't mentioned it to him yet."

"Admit it, you guessed so easily because I'm the best looking of all my brothers."

I roll my eyes, and he smiles, showing off his perfect white teeth.

"Still, I wasn't sure he'd take my advice. Certainly not so quickly, but it's good to know he did."

I shake my head, my brow scrunched. "Huh?"

"You sexted me thinking it was Landon since I confiscated his phone when he wasn't looking. But you did it in a way that suggested you two have gotten busy since I saw him last, which was like ten days ago, and he hasn't mentioned a thing to me."

I blush redder than the Red Sox jacket he's wearing. "*You* texted me? Why?"

"You never answered if you'd help me out. I have a favor, remember?"

I sigh, leaning my arm against the doorjamb. "And you said you'd barter for sexual favors." I raise an eyebrow.

"I meant I'd barter with Landon for those. Act as a liaison. As beautiful as you are, my heart belongs to another, and I'd never go after any woman my brothers are sleeping with."

"What's the favor you need?"

"You have to agree to do it before I'll tell you."

I laugh lightly, shaking my head. "That's not how favors work."

He taps his chin, his expression teasing. "No. I could have sworn it was. So that's a yes, right? Just so we're on the same page?"

"Luca—"

"Ellery," he mocks my reprimanding tone, but he's not budging. He's all devious, man with the plan grins.

I sag. "Fine. What do you need from me?" I'm going to regret this; I can already tell.

"Come with us to the Topsfield Fair."

I blink at him. "*That's* the favor? Going to a fair?"

He holds his hand up like he's not done. "With all of my siblings and their significant others and some of their friends."

"Oh." I shake my head. "Yeah, thanks, I'll pass."

"Too late. You already agreed." He pushes off the siding of the house, coming forward to grab my hand and drag me away from my door. "Don't stress it. We can announce our secret love after everyone has had their requisite corn dog. It's safer that way for you. They'll eventually grow to accept you. Our love is strong."

"Wait." I pull out of his grasp. "Does Landon know you're doing this? He won't like it. He won't want me to come." We're supposed to be a secret, dammit. And going to a fair with his family is... a big deal.

He rolls his eyes impatiently. "Of course, he'll want you to come." Then he dips his head as if he's reconsidering that. "Once he gets used to the idea, he'll be glad. I think. He's just too stubborn and self-flagellating to take the initiative and invite you. But the truth is, Landon doesn't know I'm surprising you like this, and if I know my twin, which obviously I do, he's going to be pissed. So let's shake our asses and get a move on. Everyone is waiting for me because I told them I had to make a quick phone call to the office first. But you can't say no because you already said yes and since this little subterfuge is actually all for Stella, who asked you to join us. We both know you won't say no to her."

"God, you and Landon could not be any more different."

"True, but irrelevant. And did you miss the part where everyone is waiting for us?"

Not us. Him. This could go one of two ways, and I have a feeling despite this week, Landon won't be happy I'm tagging along. That alone might make it worth it. I get off on ruffling his feathers, if for no other reason than he's irresistibly endearing when he's miffed at me. I like his grumpy side, I'm learning.

Especially when he's all growly and looks at me like he's picturing me naked.

"You're sure?"

"Positive."

"I need my purse and to lock up."

Luca groans. "Do it quickly."

By the time I grab my purse and change into riding boots instead of the cute flats I was wearing, Luca is glaring at me.

"I said quick, gumdrop. That wasn't quick."

My eyebrows hit my hairline. "Gumdrop?"

"Colorful. Sugary sweet. No?" he questions, bewildered at my expression.

"No. Gumdrops are disgusting and should never be a term of endearment, let alone considered a proper candy."

He rolls his eyes. "Jesus. Only a woman would analyze that so deeply."

Truth.

"What does Landon call you?"

I laugh. "Elle. He calls me Elle."

"Fuck, he's so boring. I'm shocked he doesn't insist on calling you Ellery. If I didn't love him more than my own life, I wouldn't be able to stand the guy. Weird how you went to bed with him thinking it was me all along." Luca winks at me.

"Not another word on that, Luca. Ever. Again."

He nudges my side with a cocky smirk I'm positive makes women's panties melt from their bodies. We walk across the lawn in the direction of Landon's Range Rover that's idling in his driveway. Landon's head snaps up when he senses people approaching his car, and a deep frown hits his lips when he notices me walking alongside his brother.

"This was a bad idea."

"This was a great idea. Did you know he's started working on his dream house blueprints again? Talk about boring. The man makes blueprints and schematic sketches, but he hasn't touched it in years, Elle. Until now. He has fire in his veins again, and if he occasionally needs a nudge to keep that fire from snuffing back out, I'll do whatever I have to do."

I think I love Luca Fritz. I think he's the brother everyone in this world should have. Why couldn't my twin have been like this?

Luca opens the back door for me where Stella and Layla are seated, but before I can climb in, I reach up and give him a kiss on his cheek.

He touches his cheek where my lips just were. "What was that for?"

"For everything you're doing." I wink at him. "And to keep that fire going."

He grins when he hears Landon muttering under his breath. He was watching us in his side-view mirror. Without a word or a greeting to Landon, I slide in beside Stella, who gleefully pushes herself into the middle seat.

"You're coming with us?" Stella squeals in delight as she buckles her seat belt.

"Yup. I sure am. Your father was kind enough to invite me to join y'all today."

Luca snickers, and I meet Landon's scowl in the rearview mirror with a smile.

He can scowl all he wants, but the man had his face between my thighs last night along with what is likely his favorite appendage. If turning into a douchebag asshole is his routine after every time we have sex, then a come to Jesus chat is headed his way right quick.

I am not that girl anymore. The one who lets herself get walked all over.

I know I should hold back. Play the I just got divorced and this is a rebound card. But I can't make myself swallow that pill. And now I'm mixing metaphors. Just fantastic.

But this man does things to my heart. To my body. To my

mind. Is what I'm feeling real or is it just a byproduct of not feeling like this for so long when I was supposed to? Is my heart that desperate for attention that it'll cling onto the first man to come along who catches its attention, or is Landon the guy I've been missing all this time?

I shouldn't have said yes to today, but a fair appeals to my Texas-girl heart. Especially the one who's growing to love fall in New England along with the girl sitting beside me and the man sitting in front of me.

"I can eat my weight in fried dough," Layla informs me, pointing out the fact that she's wearing pants with an elastic waist.

"That's me with nachos or anything else Tex-Mex food related. You should see me with Texas chili and cheddar jalapeño cornbread." I groan. I miss real Texas chili.

"Wow. That sounds so good. Can we make that when I come over again with Stella to do cooking class?"

"Sure. I used to make that once a week at least. It was my daddy's favorite."

That's when *I* scowl. Daddy. The fuckwad hardly warrants the endearment or title.

I have no idea what to do about my parents and the predicament they thrust both David and me into. I don't want them to push our marriage and its misery out into the public eye. I've already been ignoring calls from press, and that's without any scandal attached to it. But in this week, my parents, despite their threats, haven't leaked anything to anyone.

Forty-five minutes later, we park in a grassy lot beside a fleet of other luxury cars right on the side of the entrance to the fair. "Looks like we're the last to arrive," Luca notes, and I glance around the lot, spotting a group of people standing off to the side speaking with a man wearing a uniform.

"Did you rent the entire place out?"

Landon shakes his head at me in the rearview mirror. "No. We just made some arrangements, is all."

Arrangements. Such a billionaire thing to say. It's funny, I almost forgot that not so insignificant detail. With Landon, it's easy to forget who his family is because he seems so far removed from all of that. He just strikes you as a wealthy guy.

It makes me like him more. Not because of his money, but because of how he doesn't flaunt it the way so many do. I ran in circles with millionaires and billionaires, and showing off their wealth is what they did. It's what they lived for. Like the size of their bank account was their only measure of worth.

Landon doesn't care about any of that because he has nothing to prove to anyone.

His cool, sophisticated arrogance is a weapon no doubt most are intimidated by. His family's wealth outrivals nearly everyone's in the world. And yet he's this guy. A single dad who built a greenhouse for his daughter, does the dishes himself, and spends time with his family, taking them to the fair. His priorities are life goals so many overlook in the name of greed and power.

The passenger door is opened for me, and Landon takes my hand, helping me out, his intense gaze clinging to my face. He doesn't say anything. No comment about why I'm here, interloping on his family day. He just stares for a second longer, then shifts his focus over my shoulder to the group of people I was just marveling at, watching as Stella, Layla, and Luca join them.

The door shuts behind me, and I turn, unable to do this with him. I wanted to ruffle his feathers, but now that I'm here, I'm the one rattled. I feel a tug on my pinkie finger, holding me back a step as Landon loops his through mine. My heart gives a quick lurch in my chest as he squeezes.

"Hi," he says, and I can't fight the resulting smile at that if I tried. Or the way my insides swoop and swirl like the rides I'm watching in the distance.

"Hi."

"I should have been the one to invite you. Not Luca. I was afraid it might be pushing things too fast for us, so I didn't."

So that's what that frown in the car was for.

"I can be here for Stella."

"But what if I want you to be here for me too?"

Damn him. My heart...

"You look beautiful."

I swallow hard. "Thank you."

"Will you let me win you a stuffed animal and then make out with you on the Ferris wheel?"

I close my eyes and blow out a controlled breath through my nose. "How could a girl ever turn down an offer like that?"

He gives my pinky another squeeze and releases me.

"Come on, Elle," Luca calls out. "Come meet the whole fam-dam-ily and our extended group of miscreants. They already know all about you. Good gossip travels quickly. Especially by text."

"Fucking Luca," Landon snarls under his breath, but a laugh escapes all the same.

"How are you twins?" I ask as we crunch our way over the mostly dead grass, maintaining a distance I'm desperate to erase.

"In the womb, I got all the brains, looks, and brawn, and he got all the leftovers."

I laugh again. Landon makes jokes that shouldn't be funny, but because they come from him and he's so deadpan about them, they slay me. Or maybe it's just the man doing that. He gives me a wry smile that lights up his eyes, and just like every time he smiles at me, I want to press my lips to his to know what it feels like against them.

He has the sexiest smile I've ever seen.

When I met him—the real Landon, not the fake Luca—he didn't smile. Or talk this much.

I've pretended not to notice, but I do. I make him smile and talk, and he makes me feel special because he shares those things with me. I'm in dangerous territory. I need to listen to my head, but my heart has always had its own agenda. When it loves, it loves wholly and without restraint. It's always been my greatest weakness, but one day, when the situation is just right, I know it will be my greatest strength.

But today is not that day.

23

A thousand eyes are set on me. Then on the woman walking beside me. Then back to me. It's like watching the US Open tennis final, and it's all tied up. The anticipation is killing me, and I'm on the edge of my seat, terrified and excited. My heart is hammering in my chest, and I might be sweating a bit.

Why?

I'm nervous about introducing this woman to my family. To people I loosely consider friends because they're good people and have always been good to my people. The last time I brought a woman to meet my family, I ended up getting her pregnant a year and a half later and marrying her.

And then losing her.

I've been trying for the fuck it approach, but that's really more Luca's and Kaplan's style than it is mine. I'm not good at it. I'm pissed my brother invited her, and I'm grateful my brother invited her. I want to grab on to her with both hands and never let go, and I want to shove her away and never look back.

Last Monday did something to me. Her reaction to the ruined lasagna did something to me. And for about the hundredth time, I wanted to hop on a plane and kill her moth-erfucker of an ex-husband. More importantly, it made me want to take care of her. To bandage all her battle wounds and remind her just how strong she is.

She's changed me.

But what does being with me—really being with me—mean for her job? For her being Stella's teacher?

For me?

I can't fall in love with this woman and not have it turn my entire life upside down. Am I ready for that to happen? Is it already too late?

Luckily I don't have to open my mouth. Stella does it all for me, claiming Elle as her favorite teacher and neighbor ever as she introduces her to Rina and Brecken, Oliver and Amelia, Carter and Grace, Kaplan, then our friends, Halle and Jonah, Aria and Wes, and Margot and Drew.

The women take over, swallowing Elle up with questions and compliments. Amelia and Rina are like hawks—I figured they would be—informing Elle that she's their saving grace. That they've heard all about the cooking classes, and they want in too. Elle takes it all in stride, with smiles and laughs and welcoming open arms. But it doesn't stop there.

"Halle, Aria, and Grace are all pregnant," Rina announces. "They can't go on any rides with us, and Margot is chicken shit and refuses."

"I'm not chicken shit. I get fucking motion sickness. If you want to hold my hair back while I puke all night, then I'll go on rides with you."

"Um. How about we not do that," Drew pleads. "My car hasn't been the same since Margot was sick the last time."

Margot slaps Drew's arm, and he wraps her up, holding her close and kissing her forehead.

"You know you weren't supposed to tell the world I'm preg-nant," Aria exclaims with a good-natured puff as we follow our private guide—and security detail because we need that here— toward the entrance. "I'm like barely pregnant."

"Oh." Rina does an impression of an owl. "Right. Totally forgot that point with all the pregnant women around here. So sorry." She turns back to Elle with a grimace. "Forget I mentioned that."

Elle laughs, pressing a hand to Rina's arm like they're already old friends. "I don't know what you're talking about. I'm not wishing anyone congratulations. I swear. Not to sound rude, but if y'all can't go on the rides, then why are you at a fair full of them?"

"The food," they all say in unison before cracking up.

"I'm from South Carolina," Halle states, shifting in beside Elle. "Texas?"

"Texas. But I don't hear much of an accent from you."

Halle winks a blue eye at her, tossing her copper penny hair over her shoulder. "That's because I've pretty much lost it all unless I'm drunk, which obviously I'm not anymore now that I'm pregnant. Aria and I have been trying to get Grace to be our OB, but she's refusing."

Grace groans, likely because this has been an ongoing thing. "That's because you're my friends. I can't be your doctor. Just like how I won't allow Carter to be mine."

"Doesn't stop me from trying," he remarks, pressing his palm over Grace's small belly. "It's my baby, I don't see why I can't deliver it."

"Because you can't. The last thing I want is your face between my legs during that particular moment."

"Are y'all doctors too?" Elle asks the other women.

"I'm a nurse," Rina states with pride. "The only Fritz child who is not a doctor. Margot is a nurse with me. We work in the same hospital as Oliver, Carter, and Grace. Halle is a nurse practitioner. Aria an artist."

"An artist? What's your last name?"

"Um... Well, I paint under Aria Davenport, but now I'm Aria Kincaid."

"Oh my lord." Elle reaches out and grabs Aria's hand. "I own one of your paintings. I mean, I used to. I suppose my ex-husband does now, but we purchased it from a gallery in New York a few years back. It was beautiful. You're so talented. I can't believe I'm getting to meet you in person."

"You did? Wow! That's amazing. Thank you."

"Someone seems to be the belle of the ball," Amelia teases, coming in beside me. "And you seem to be watching her like a man who can't tear himself away."

I peer down at my tiny redheaded one-day sister-in-law. Have I been doing that? Watching Elle like I can't tear myself away?

"I don't know what you're talking about."

She grins coyly up at me. "Oh, I know. But it's still a good look on you. For whatever that's worth to you."

"I second that," Oliver agrees. "I get it now. Why you say she's different." His green eyes hit mine. "She is."

"You're all rushing things. It's been ten days."

Oliver snorts. "But who's counting?"

Amelia shakes her head. "No. It's been much longer than that. Six weeks from what Luca told us."

"My lovely fake fiancée is right. For better or worse, you've been different since the night you met her. You've just been pretending otherwise."

We walk through the gate, the unmistakable sounds of the fair all around us. People shouting, kids laughing, roller coasters rumbling, winners of games being called out with obnoxiously loud buzzers and bells as their backdrop. The air is filled with the scent of fried food, popcorn, and hay as multi-colored lights flash from every direction. It's sensory overload, and my kid loves it as she belts out a squeal of delight, grabbing onto Elle and Layla and running off without even asking me or telling me where she's going.

Elle throws me a glance over her shoulder, her expression letting me know she's got her.

"We'll go with them too," Amelia promises me before she and Oliver jog off to catch up to them. One of the private security guards we hired does the same, and I relax a little. The last time we all went somewhere public, we were photographed relentlessly. Hounded for autographs.

I never understood our appeal, but Amelia likes to remind us we're celebrity influencers in this city whether we like it or not.

"So, is it love or just lust?" Kaplan asks, falling in beside me as we walk. I don't reply because I don't have to, and knowing him, he doesn't expect me to anyway.

"She's great," Rina says as we stroll around, checking out the various attractions and games without stopping at anything in particular. "Stella chatted my ear off about her the other night on the phone. But I didn't expect her to be here today. It's a surprise. A nice surprise, but still a surprise."

"Take that up with Luca," I tell her.

Luca gives an unrepentant shrug. "She's perfect for him."

"Are you two...?" Carter trails off.

"Bumping uglies?" Brecken finishes for him, and I give him a look. "What? Since when are we not grown-ups and able to ask the obvious question?"

"Since you just used the term bumping uglies," Grace retorts.

Brecken laughs, holding up a conciliatory hand. "You're right. I should have said fucking."

"Or maybe the better question would have been to ask if they're together?" Rina pokes Brecken in the side.

"Can we not?" I droll in a bored tone, already knowing none of them will listen to me.

"No," Kaplan and Luca say together.

"I want to sell the condo at the Ritz and buy a house in Rina's neighborhood closer to the hospital," Carter declares, changing the subject. "Grace says she's not ready to move again so soon."

My lips quirk up into a smirk, and I throw him a grateful look.

"Then do it or not but stop talking about it already," Kaplan grouses. "I want to hear more about the pretty Texas honey my brother is fucking."

"Why? Because now that Landon is into someone, that means you're next?"

Kaplan blanches at what Rina said, and we all chuckle under our breaths.

"Shut your face, baby sister. That'll never happen."

"Until it does. Look at Landon." Brecken points at me.

"I'm going to go find Stella," I announce, needing space because this will all start again, and I'm not ready to talk about it. Talking about it sets it on a different level when all I'm trying to do is get from one moment to the next, and unfortunately, that doesn't always feel possible. Elle and I have a lot of strikes against us already and now that she's met my family, this thing between us feels real when I'm not sure either of us was ready for that.

"You mean you're going to find Elle," Luca calls out with a laugh in his voice as I saunter off. I flip them all off.

I'm trying not to think. Just go with it and see what happens.

Something I've never been particularly adept at.

I could text Oliver or Amelia to find out where they are. But as I wander through the massive fairgrounds, staring at my phone, I pull up my text chain with Elle, scrolling through the conversation she had with Luca when she thought it was me.

Sexual favors, huh?

I could go for that.

Sex. Can we keep it just that?

I shoot Elle a quick text, and she informs me they're all about to get on the pirate ship ride. I head in that direction, having been to this fair every year since I was kid. Even when we did rent out the entire thing. We didn't this year or last year. Just asked for half the crowd while paying for double the loss in revenue.

The fair organizers were only too happy to comply. I paid for it myself because I want Stella and Layla to have free rein of the fairgrounds without being stalked. And before you start questioning that, it's fucking real.

Stella and I live in a small town twenty-five minutes outside of Boston.

But anytime I take her out in the city, her face ends up in tabloids like she's a celebrity kid.

This has also started happening with Layla since Oliver and Amelia got together—their relationship alone made national news—which has also led to Oliver bringing in security— Amelia has no clue about this—to follow them whenever they go anywhere, ready to step in as needed.

I've said it before, and I'll say it again... money breeds madness.

By the time I reach the pirate ship, Oliver, Amelia, Elle, Layla, and Stella are already on the ride. Their arms held up high in the air as the ship swings like a pendulum, screams hitting the impending dusk air.

I watch as Elle and Stella share glances and smiles and laughs and screams. It has me smiling like a fool. Like a guy falling for a girl and a father happy his kid likes the woman he's falling for.

I don't know how I could have ever imagined this thing between us being just sex.

"I want to deserve her," I whisper to overly fragrant, cool air.

"She's not you—she'll never be you—but could she be the next best thing for our girl?"

Would she even want that?

The ride ends, and I watch as they shuffle off, still laughing, breathless in their fun. Elle catches my eye, and I swear she blushes, biting her teeth into her lip and giving me this adorably shy-girl vibe. She's still so uncertain. So damn sexy.

"Anyone hungry?" Oliver asks, and Layla squeals out a hell yeah because Layla could eat constantly if allowed.

"I saw the grilled cheese guy right beside the fried dough guy over there." He points somewhere I'm not looking—I'm too busy staring at my girls. "Stella Bella, there was also that loaded baked potato guy nearby."

Stella whoops into the air, Layla style. One of Stella's favorite foods is loaded baked potatoes. She's tried to grow potatoes but to no avail. If I told her we were moving to Idaho tomorrow, she would not fight me on that.

"You coming, Dad?"

I stare at Elle.

She gives me a look.

Followed by a smirk.

I shake my head.

I turn to Stella.

"I think I'll take Elle on the Ferris wheel first. You stay with Layla, Uncle Oliver, and Aunt Amelia." I wink at Amelia, who just laughs it off at this point considering she and Oliver aren't actually married or even engaged for real.

"Come on, girls," Amelia calls out, taking Layla by the arm and pretending to give her a rough tug. "I'm starving. Do you see all this fair food? How will I sample it all if we don't start now?"

"Solid point," Layla agrees. "Stella, I bet I can eat a potato faster than you can."

"Anyone vomits in my car, you're all grounded," Oliver declares.

But they're walking away. They're leaving me here with Elle. Elle, who is sauntering slowly up to me, her head canted, her hair now knotted in a braid over her shoulder, her eyes glimmering in the waning light as they promise all the naughty things that have my mind racing and my cock hardening.

"Hey," she says impishly.

"Wanna go for a ride with me, beautiful?"

"You're awfully friendly today, Dr. Fritz."

"I thought I was pretty friendly with you last night when I snuck over, Miss Wilde."

She takes my outstretched hand, and it's like all my missing pieces suddenly fall into place. I don't even care if the world is photographing us. I just care about her. *Her*. Her smile is my salvation.

Holding her hand, my lips silent, I find the Ferris wheel, and when the guy running it sees me, he nods his head and holds the small line back, allowing us to immediately climb into the next waiting car.

"You have some clout," Elle notes as we take our seats, both of us on the same side of the metal car, causing it to tip back and sway a bit.

"Does that bother you?"

She considers this for a moment, staring out into the forest that surrounds the grounds of the fair. I take her hand, toying with her fingers. "No. I think it's amazing how you all clearly have each other's backs. Protect each other. I never had that with my family. They're greedy and cutthroat and dangerous."

That piques my interest as I stare into her profile.

"Your parents?" She mentioned her mother a couple weeks back.

"My parents. My sister. All of them." Her head flies back in my direction. "But I don't want to talk about that, Landon. Not yet. I want you to make me feel good on this ride. The way you said you would."

Fucking hell.

The car we're sitting in jerks, the ride starting to move, only to stop again as they allow people into the next car. I lean in, knowing we're bathed in shadows, and press my lips to hers. "I'd love nothing more than to make you feel good." *Forever.* There's that word again. Do I mean it, or have I been so emotionally dead for so long that I'm latching on to the first woman who forces me to breathe again?

I can't decide if it matters or if I even care because in the next second, my mouth engulfs hers, pushing her into the unforgiving back of the car, causing it to rock even more. Only neither of us is at risk of breaking anything tonight.

She's wearing jeans, and I shove her hips forward, thrusting her legs open wide. "Undo your button and zipper for me. Show me what color your panties are."

Her breath audibly catches, her eyes wild on mine before they fling every which way, scouring the darkening night for anyone who might catch us.

"Do it," I demand. *Give me your trust, Elle, and I'll give you all the pleasure in the world.*

She slouches down farther, undoing her jeans but not lowering them.

I glance down, pushing aside the top flaps of denim. "Black." My favorite.

My fingers toy with the lacy top, fingering the skimpy material, rubbing it between my thumb and pointer finger.

"I hate that you're Stella's teacher."

"I could likely get fired for this. It's a private school, and they have strict rules. Especially when it comes to the Abbot-Fritzes, I imagine."

I shake my head. "I'd never let that happen. If I had to speak to the school, I would."

"If you do, I'll castrate you in your sleep."

I chuckle. So fiery.

My hand flies into her hair, cradling the back of her head as my mouth dives back in, kissing her like I mean it. Like this is our moment, and I refuse to squander it.

"Does that mean you'll touch my balls?"

She laughs. "Your jokes are getting better."

"It's you."

It is. I'm smiling and quipping jokes for the first time in years. Hell, I have a living, breathing, beating heart for the first time in years.

"All my siblings love you," I mumble into her lips. "Stella loves you. You're not getting fired."

"Good to know," she rasps into my mouth, her hand clutching my bicep, her nails digging in, pleading. Adrenaline heats my blood. We're actually doing this. Right here. Out in the open. On a ride where anyone—if they looked closely enough—might be able to see us.

The ride moves, casting us higher and higher into the air that's growing darker and darker by the moment. From up here, all we can do is peer down at the lights. At the sounds. At the fun.

My lips trickle along her jaw as I take a deep inhale, licking her soft, sensitive skin before blowing cool air on it. She shudders and shakes, a whole-body tremble I feel everywhere against me.

"You're under my skin." She says it like a warning.

I cup her face in my hand, forcing her eyes to mine. "Under your skin is my new home."

Another tremble as my lips fall back on her neck, and she reaches out, gripping my shirt in her fist. My hand slides between her lacy panties and her skin, heading south until I find her bare pussy lips. She's so soft, I take a second just to stroke her like that. She whimpers into me, and I go lower, bypassing her clit to drive her crazy while finding her wet opening and delving a finger in, fighting her constricting jeans.

"Always so wet for me, Elle," I murmur against her.

"Landon."

My name. It sets me on fire. "I'm going to finger you until you come. But can I sneak out again tonight and fuck you in your bed after Stella has gone to sleep?" I haven't had a good night's sleep in over a week, and I regret nothing of it.

"Yes." A hum. A moan. A plea.

A thrill shoots through me as I twist my hand as best as I can, two fingers diving into her hot, wet channel, my thumb rubbing her clit. She moans, her head falling back, and I stare at her, watching her face, enraptured by her pleasure.

I fuck her like this. The wet sound caught between us, my fingers coated as she grows hungry and sexy, desperate and needy. Grinding, rolling her gorgeous hips into my hand. My lips feast on her neck, the top of her chest over her shirt. I can't reach her tits, but I want them. I want them so bad. I can fit one entirely in my mouth and God, you have no idea how hard that makes me.

To the point where I'm grinding against her side, finger fucking her with smooth, fast-paced strokes. Hitting her spot. I feel it every time I do. She whimpers and moans and jerks and claws, and I try to stifle her sounds but watch her like this because it's everything, and I find it nearly impossible to choose between that and my lips on hers.

The Ferris wheel goes around, our car on the descent as air whooshes past us, the fair so close, but so distant. "Elle," I whisper in her ear. "Tonight when I come over, you're going to sit on my face. I'll hold you down on top of me, my tongue in your delicious pussy. My finger in your ass."

She trembles, my fingers picking up their pace, fighting so hard against the sturdy fabric of her jeans.

"I want you to ride me after that. I want to watch your beautiful tits bounce. Your eyes staring down at me, euphoric in pleasure."

"Landon." She's clutching the fabric of my shirt now, balling it up in her fist. My girl loves dirty talk. Her head on my shoulder, her legs scissored open in the car as we glide around and around, my stomach swooping with the motion of the ride. "I'm..."

She cries out, and my lips descend upon hers, muffling her every sound, swallowing them down for my own. To keep. To cherish. She comes so hard, all over my fingers, the sensation making my cock leak in my jeans.

Her body loses tone, and I slip my hand from her pussy, past her panties, and out of her jeans. I lick my fingers clean—holy hell, I wish I had eaten her out—and I zip and button her up.

"You are my vixen. My demon. The woman I refuse to let go of now that I've caught you."

"Then don't," she rasps, her voice hoarse. Shaking with aftershocks or fear. I do not know which. "Don't let go, Landon. I don't know what this is, but I want it. But I feel like I should keep my distance."

"I can't let you do that. Not anymore." The alpha, the fierce protector inside of me, won't have it.

"There's so much you don't know. My life... it's such a mess right now." She hiccups out, biting into her lip to stop what I think might be a sob. "I don't know how to trust anymore. Everyone I ever thought I should..." Her eyes glass over with emotion.

"My beautiful Elle." My lips hover over hers, our eyes locked. "I promise I'll do everything I can to change that."

24

Landon never ended up winning me a stuffed animal, but after the orgasm he gave me and the words he spoke to me, who cares about a piece of fluff made in a sweatshop? The whole way home, I'm buzzing with aftershocks of him. With a growing need for more.

But the girl sitting in front of me overshadows all this sweet anticipation.

Stella is oddly quiet, her face twisted toward the window, practically giving her father her back as she rides shotgun. Landon glances in her direction more than a few times, clearly picking up on the vibe she's putting out.

I'm not sure what happened.

We were set to leave the fair, all of us meeting up by the front entrance surrounded by security, since people were snapping pictures of the Fritz clan. But Stella looked upset, holding close to Layla and refusing to talk about whatever was bothering her when Landon asked.

Now that we're almost home, I can't help the paranoid thoughts that she's upset about me. That she's figured out—or someone told her—that her dad and I are... crap, I don't even know *what* we are. But I'm worried that whatever this is between us, Stella isn't happy about it.

We pull into Landon's driveway, straight into one of the bays of his three-car garage. Before he even has a chance to shut down the car, Stella unbuckles herself and darts out of her seat.

"Bellas?" Landon calls out as she slams the door behind her.

"I'm going to bed," she yells back, and just like that, she's flying through the door to the house and is gone.

"Shit," he mutters, running a hand through his hair. "Let me walk you home, and then I need to go figure that out."

I shake my head as I get out of the car. "No. She's obviously upset about something. Go talk to her. I can walk next door on my own."

He hesitates, clearly torn. "Do you think she knows about us?"

Us. If only now were the time to question just what that means.

"I don't know." I lean up on the balls of my feet and plant a kiss on the corner of his lips. Then I walk out of the garage without waiting for him.

"Will I still see you later?" he calls after me, and I pause without turning back. I'm in so much danger of losing my heart for good to him, and if his daughter doesn't approve...

"Text me after you talk to Stella."

Then I shoot out of the garage and across his lawn, not quite running, but not walking either. But just as I reach my door and blow out a relieved breath—one I don't even understand—my phone chimes in my purse.

I quickly tug it out, though I should know better than to assume Landon is already texting me. He's dealing with an upset Stella, and now it seems is when I have to put out my own family fire.

Cat: **I heard all about your divorce. So sorry, sis. Call me. I want to come visit and help you.**

God, what a duplicitous bitch she is.

I guess I can't avoid this forever.

Shutting and locking the door behind me, I drop my purse on my kitchen counter and immediately go for reinforcements in the form of liquid courage. As I generously pour the gold, fruity liquid into my wineglass, I dial her up before I can second-guess or even think about what I'm going to say to her.

Cat picks up immediately. Her voice—so shockingly similar to mine—rings through my phone as I switch her to speakerphone and set it down on the counter.

"Hey," she exclaims, surprise and delight in her voice. "It's so good to hear from you. I wasn't sure you'd call after the last time we saw each other."

"You mean when you got trashed at my wedding and hit on every rich guy there, whether they were married or not?"

She laughs like it's the funniest thing ever, and I take a hearty sip of my wine. "Well, that's not exactly how I remember it, though the details are fuzzy for me. Sorry about that. I should have called and apologized back then, but things have been... busy, I guess, for me."

Oh, I imagine they have been.

"What have you been doing, Cat? Mom and Dad never tell me anything." Not that I ask anymore.

More laughter, and it's impossible to tell if it's fake or not. If she hears the edge to my voice, she's clearly ignoring it. "A little of this, a lot of that. You know how it is."

Not really, and that's the vaguest fucking answer I've ever heard.

"The folks told me about your divorce from David."

I take another sip, gripping the glass in my hand as I stare down at my phone. "And what did they tell you?"

"That you walked out on him six months ago. Without telling anyone."

"Yup."

"Are you doing okay?"

Now it's my turn to laugh because the bitch doesn't have a drop of sympathy in her voice. "I'm great."

"So, how did it end? I mean, Mom and Dad said David's really upset about it. That he wants you back. They mentioned you got a settlement out of him, so I guess it's not like you need him now."

My eyes bug out of my head. David. That fucking cowardly swine told them about the money I got in our divorce. No wonder Cat is calling me. No wonder my parents have been texting relentlessly and nothing has been printed in the tabloids. They're holding out, hoping I'm now their lucky golden ticket.

Fuck them.

"And I heard you drugged him, fucked him, and then you and our loving parents blackmailed him for years."

Silence. But now I'm grinning like the Cheshire cat because that felt good. I flip off my phone as I take another sip of wine, but somehow my glass is empty, so I grab the bottle from the fridge to refill it. Giving my sister a minute or two to figure out her next move.

"You still there, sis?" I chide.

She clears her throat. "Yeah. I'm still here." She laughs some more, but now it's sardonic, and I know this is where things are really going to get bad. "I didn't think he'd ever have the balls to tell you. The man was so pathetically lovesick and broken when he realized what we were up to."

Hmmm.

"Do you care so little for me?" All of you, I want to add, but don't bother. Hell, I don't even know why I asked. It's obvious they don't.

"You and I were never going to be besties, Elle, and I needed the money. Mom and Dad were in just as dire straits as I was. You had yourself a nice, cozy situation, and we took advantage."

"I'm aware. You ruined my marriage."

"The way I see it, you're sitting pretty with a few million dollars. You're better than David ever was, anyway. Miss perfect princess who always had it *so* easy."

Fuck you!

Because easy? No. No, I didn't have it easy. Not even a little. I had two parents who barely registered I existed. A twin sister who couldn't stand me. A best friend who drowned when I was a teenager. A husband who verbally abused me for the better part of two years. So no. Not fucking easy, sister.

"How's this since we're past the bullshit part of our conversation? You give me half the three million you got from your divorce, and we won't splash around your husband's misdeeds with your twin publicly. Think of the scandal and embarrassment that would cause." She emits a fake gasp.

I glare down at my phone, leaning against the counter when what I really want to do is hang up and block her number. "It would cause a lot of both. I already know this. But I'd rather eat shit from the press than give a penny to any of you."

"I need this money, Elle," she presses quickly, her voice taking on a desperate note. "Giancarlo will not be patient much longer. Or maybe I should just give him your address and settle the score that way. I doubt he'd care which one of us he breaks."

I shake my head. "Who the fuck is Giancarlo?"

"My bookie and boss. Who do you think, you stupid bitch? We didn't all have cheer scholarships and rich professional golfer husbands. Some of us had to do the best we could with what we had going."

"My heart bleeds for you. Truly. You should call Hallmark

and sing them your sad song. Maybe they'll pay you for your bullshit by turning it into a movie."

"I owe him big. It's no fucking joke. David's money was helping me pay that down. Now that's all gone because of you, and you're being cavalier with my life. He'll kill me, Elle. Without even caring, he will."

My eyebrows hit my hairline, unaware my sister was gambling again. I knew she had gotten herself in some trouble years ago—when I was at University of Miami she was betting on games—but as far as I knew, that had all been cleared up, and she had stopped. Actually, it was my parents who cleared it up for her, now that I think about it. Interesting.

"How much do you owe him?"

"Five hundred grand."

I whistle through my teeth. Jesus.

"Now you see why we did what we had to do and why I need you to do this for me. Mom and dad helped me. Why can't you?"

I can only shake my head as words fail me.

"Is that why they helped you with David? Because you already put them in the hole once?"

Silence and then a sigh.

"After he's paid off, I'll use the rest of the money to disappear somewhere, and you'll never hear from me again. I promise. Mom and Dad can figure their own shit out. They still have ways of earning and an income from Dad's pension. They were just mooching off David because they could. But I need this, Elle. I fucking need it, or he'll kill me."

So she keeps saying. But how on earth can I trust what she's saying is true?

Then again, I think it is. I think she's in some real deep shit with this guy because all her life people have bailed her out when she needed them to.

Lifting my glass to my lips, I polish off the rest of it before chucking the glass in the sink, listening as it shatters and glass sprays everywhere. My hands meet the counter as I stare dejectedly down at my phone.

What do I do now?

What the hell do I do now?

These people ruined my life. Care absolutely nothing for me. But she's my sister. My twin. And suddenly I'm the difference between what... life and being murdered? I can't do nothing and allow her to die. I'd never be able to live with myself.

But I don't want to do this. Be another person to bail her out. I don't trust her. I don't trust that she won't still try to sell what happened between David and me to the press. I also don't believe that this guy will actually kill her.

"Send me his information, and I will speak with him directly about what you owe. If I determine you're not trying to play me, I'll pay him the money. In exchange, you'll keep your mouth shut and leave me the hell alone. You get nothing from me, and we are done. That is my only offer. Take it or leave it. Because from where I'm sitting, a little press ain't looking so bad compared to your life."

"I can live with that."

"If you betray me again..."

"I won't. I promise you, I won't. What about Mom and Dad?"

I laugh bitterly, head thrown back and everything, all psycho mode. "They're not my problem. They're yours. You can let them know that I'm done, and I never want to hear from them again. If they go to the press, I will not pay your debt. If any of you talk after it gets paid, I will tell the whole fucking world what you all did. I'll cry sob stories on television, and if I can manage it, get you all arrested for extortion. Understand?"

"Yes. I'll tell them."

"Send me his info and lose my number."

I disconnect the call and drop my head to my counter, letting it all out. I scream and pound my fists and *rage*. Does anything good ever last? Am I not deserving of a new life and a fresh start and some fucking happiness?

I shriek at the top of my lungs, howling out curses.

"I fucking hate all of you," I bellow, pounding my fist again, but refusing to cry. I will not do it. Not over them. My parents knew the trouble Cat was in, but instead of coming to me and explaining the situation, they helped her set up my husband for blackmail.

Pushing off the counter, I storm out of the kitchen and up the stairs, ripping my clothes off as I go. I bypass my room and head straight for my shower, flip it on to scalding hot, and get right in. The water sears at me, and I collapse to the tile floor, gripping my soaked hair in my hands, my forehead pressing into my knees. I'm panting hard, nearly to the point of hyper-ventilating.

I will send this Giancarlo guy his money.

I will never speak to my parents or my sister again.

And with any hope, this fucked up situation and any remnants of my old life will be done with forever. Then I can move on. Put everything I have into this new life.

I blow out a shuddered breath. God, never have I needed anything more than I need that to be true.

25

A strange noise startles me out of my semi-conscious state. After I lost it in the shower for a bit, I dried myself off and climbed into bed. I have no idea how much time has passed. If I fell asleep or not. But... there's that noise again.

What the hell is that?

It's like a *ping*.

Sitting up, I comb my hands through my snarled hair and glance around my room. My light is on, and I squint, blinking a few times as I adjust to it. Everything looks fine. Nothing seems—

Ping.

It's coming from the window, and I immediately leap out of bed, nearly smacking my hip into my nightstand as I do. I narrow my eyes, straining to see, and finally land on the dark form of someone standing outside, beneath my window in the grass. For a second, my heart thunders thinking it might be someone like David or even that Giancarlo character, but instinctively I know it's not.

Unlocking the window, I fling it up and open, momentarily stunned by the blast of cold as it hits my... naked body. Awesome.

I hear a chuckle beneath me.

"I tried calling and texting you a dozen times and after being reduced to playing the role of a teenager, this is how you open the window?"

"What are you doing out there?" I hiss, crouching down so no one can see me even though my window isn't facing the street.

"I'm sneaking out, remember? Come let me in."

The playful tone of his voice tugs a smile to my lips.

"Go to the front." Before he can answer, I shut and lock the window, shivering and rubbing my hands up and down my bare arms that are now covered in gooseflesh. I throw on the first thing I find, a tank top and boy shorts I had tossed over my chair, then fly down the stairs only to realize what I must look like. And I haven't brushed my teeth.

Dammit.

"Are you there?" I whisper-shout through the door.

More laughter, and it makes my aching heart sing. "I'm here."

"Good. I'm unlocking this door, but you have to give me a minute or two before you come upstairs."

"Is this some sort of kinky hide-and-seek game you're trying to play, or are you being self-conscious? Because I already saw you, and I can tell you you're fucking beautiful."

"I showered but didn't brush my hair or teeth."

"Oh, Elle. I don't care about any of that. You're perfect."

I snort. "Did *you* brush your teeth?"

He's silent for a beat. "I might have."

"See? I need a minute."

I unlock the door, then sprint for my life back up my stairs, more winded than I should be. I don't think walking four miles a day back and forth to work is keeping me in the shape I'm used to. I hear the front door shut with a resounding click of the lock flicking into place and go for my toothbrush first. That is until I see my hair.

Holy rat's nest, Batman, we're in trouble.

With one hand on my toothbrush and the other on my hairbrush, I attack both with clumsy precision.

"Elle?" Landon's impish lilt rings out through my bedroom, and I nearly choke myself on my toothbrush.

"Just a minute," I murmur around the suds of toothpaste before spitting into the sink and rinsing my mouth out. Then I finish up with my hair and give myself a quick once-over.

"You know we don't have to play this game with each other, right? The one where we primp and preen and pretend we're not ourselves."

He has a point, but bad breath isn't something I'd like to risk right now.

Working past the sudden swarming hive of nerves in my stomach, I fling the door open and find Landon right on the other side, waiting for me, his hands gripping either side of the frame. Over the past ten days, I've done some incredibly naughty and dirty things with this man in this very room, and yet suddenly having him in my bedroom tonight, staring at me like that, I feel like a shy virgin. Unsteady and unsure of how to proceed.

I'm so very lost and out of sorts, but his eyes tell me I don't need to be. They tell me I'm everything he's been searching for and with that, I step out of the bathroom and remove my tank top, dropping it to the floor.

His breath comes out in a rush as he stares unabashedly at my breasts before trickling down my stomach. My hands follow his gaze, catching on my boy shorts and lowering them before kicking them away, baring me completely to him once more. A grunt hits his lips as he licks them, worshipping me without touching me.

"God, Elle." It's all he's got before he steps forward, and his lips fall on mine, his hands to my hips where his fingers caress the dips and slopes of my skin.

I'm desperate for him—I'm always desperate for him—but I'm also done playing games or being uncertain. I step back, my hand on his chest, holding him at bay.

"I don't want to be this high school Lifetime movie steamy HBO Max fantasy book drama Netflix original show anymore. You need to want me, Landon. Me. Not the sex. Not my pussy or even my tits. Me. Because I have so much family drama, my life has turned into a Nicholas Sparks kinda bullshit."

He blinks at me more times than I can count. "You lost me a bit."

"I'm not a fuck toy. I'm not a screw and toss."

His hand runs through my hair as he stares into my eyes. His other hand comes up, cupping my cheek. "Do you know why I was so harsh with you after that first night we met?"

"Because you're a grumpy bastard?"

He smirks. "That was part of it. But I knew the second I saw you in that bar that night that there was something about you I couldn't resist. I was afraid of your power to change my life. To change *me*. And you did, Elle. You changed me and now that I know what being with you feels like, I'm never going back to being that guy again."

My heart flutters in my chest.

"I want you with a ferocity I never knew was possible. My heart hadn't beat in nine years until some pretty girl in a bar looked at me with these hazel eyes that tore straight through me, reminding me I'm not the heartless man I believed I was. You're the air in my lungs and the smile on my lips. You're my missing piece."

His forehead meets mine, our noses pressed before he dips

and kisses me again, this time with such aching tenderness and patience and devotion my toes curl and my hands clutch his shoulders for support. His tongue sweeps in, tasting me, exploring my mouth, driving whimpers and sighs from the depths of my soul. He nips at my bottom lip only to treat the top one to the same divine torture that has my heart racing and my body growing warmer.

This is no ordinary, urgent kiss. It's not an I need inside of you this second or I'll die kiss.

It's how lovers kiss.

And it manages to sweep me off my feet. Literally as Landon lifts me into his arms and carries me over to the bed, setting me down and climbing on top of me. I clutch the hem of his sweater, attempting to tear it off, but it gets stuck on his muscled torso, and he's forced to break our kiss to reach behind his head and remove it for me.

Why is that so sexy? That move that guys do?

I ask him, and his only response is to chuckle at me, but that smile... His smile makes my chest clench with wonder. With hope and possibility. Impatient hands fumble with his belt, uncoordinated as I undo the metal buckle, then the button of his jeans and zipper all the while his mouth explores my neck with hot, wet kisses.

Reaching down, he wrenches his belt free from his pants with a *whoosh* that snaps through the air, but he doesn't remove his pants the way I need him to.

"Landon," I whine, growing impatient, tugging on them like a child after a denied toy.

His lips layer with mine, his body held up by his hands as he stares straight into my eyes. "Do you trust me, Ellery Wilde?"

"Yes," I answer honestly. I don't have many I trust right now, but I do trust him.

His tongue darts out, licking the seam of my lips, and I lean up, attempting to deepen the connection when he pulls back, creating distance. The hand still holding the belt comes up and suddenly I feel the cool, smooth texture of leather gliding up my stomach, between my breasts, along my neck, and across my cheek.

"How much?"

My breath audibly catches.

"Enough for you to allow me to tie you up?"

I swallow thickly and nod, still staring into his green eyes that are dark, his pupils totally blown with lust, yet he's still so in control. The bulge pressing into my lower half, unfortunately stuck behind his jeans, grows harder, igniting an insatiable craving to shoot through me. My empty core tightens, impossibly wet.

Right now, I'd do anything this man asked or commanded of me.

"Yes."

"Has anyone ever done this to you before?"

I nod. David did a few times, but it did not excite me half as much as the idea of Landon doing it does.

"Christ, you make it so hard to breathe." He kisses me, deep and hard and with a lot of tongue. And as he does, he shifts his weight back onto his knees while his hands capture mine, lifting them above my head. My wrists are pressed together and then bound as the leather wraps around over and over before securing them with the buckle.

Breaking the kiss, he surveys his handiwork, testing my circulation—ever the conscientious doctor—and my ability to move. When he's satisfied, he shifts me, sliding me up the bed until I'm in the center, and climbs off, standing up.

The leather is rough and tight, and I'll most definitely have marks on my wrist, but right now, looking at him, I don't care about any of that. His smoldering gaze rakes me in, inch by inch in a slow, primal show of dominance. A flush creeps up my flesh, puckering my skin with goose bumps and hardening my nipples.

"Fuck. Look at you. Never have I seen a more beautiful sight."

He shakes his head as if it's too much, then lowers his jeans, leaving him in only his boxer briefs. His cock is gloriously hard, tenting through the cotton, and he gives it a small rub, his eyes going to half-mast as he does. I'm so desperate for him to touch me, I'm barely hanging on.

I lick my lips, panting, and attempt to sit up, but he's not having any of that as he pushes me back down.

"I want to taste you," I complain. I haven't done that. Had him in my mouth. Sucked him down my throat until his eyes roll back.

I must have said all that aloud because his eyes clench shut, and he's doing some sort of breathing thing, muttering what sounds like the names of weird heart conditions under his breath.

He points at me, lowering his briefs to the floor. "Open your mouth."

And just like that, I might come a bit as I do exactly as he says. Only, he doesn't crawl over me and shove his dick in my mouth the way I expect—clearly my previous experiences with this have tainted my expectations. Instead, he climbs on the bed, kisses my cheek, and straddles my head but facing the other way.

"You're not to move your hands," he tells me, then before I can do much of anything, his cock hits my lips, and I swipe out my tongue, desperate to taste him. He's thick and long and sexy. Just the sight of him like this has me—

"OH MY GOD!" I scream when his lips capture my already pulsing clit and suck it into his mouth. That I most certainly wasn't expecting and since my lips are pressed to his dick, he groans when he feels the scream against it.

"I need my hands, Landon."

"No, baby. Just your sweet mouth on me while I eat your sweet pussy."

Fuck. How in the hell am I supposed to do that when his tongue is plunging into me? He seems to understand my dilemma because he angles his hips and starts thrusting into my mouth. I'm helpless. Bound and helpless as he starts fucking my mouth, his thighs on either side of my head, his knees dipping into the mattress. He slides past my tongue, all the way until I'm gagging and choking, trying to suck on him to regain some of the control he's not allowing me to have.

Meanwhile, his tongue and fingers are everywhere. He had mentioned he was going to sit me on his face while he played with my ass and even though the positions are reversed, that's exactly what he's doing to me now. His tongue is in my pussy. The fingers of his left hand rolling my clit, playing with it while a finger from his right hand, wet from dipping in my pussy, toys with my forbidden ring of muscles in the back.

His chest and belly are over mine, his heat seeping into me, his weight bearing down without crushing me. It's total sensory overload in the best possible way. I moan around him, my hips canting of their own volition against his mouth as I try to take his cock in as deep as I can without suffocating to death.

He pushes that finger past my barrier, forcing my muscles to relax, and holy hell, I feel full. So full. Especially when two fingers from his other hand replace his tongue, and he starts fucking me with them all at once.

"Fucking hell, that's the sexiest, dirtiest thing I've ever seen."

I wish I could see it too. I'm desperate to but lose that train of thought when his tongue flicks my clit. I'm out of my mind. It's too much and so good and so lewd and forbidden, and I'm getting tighter and wetter, my skin on fire, and I'm nothing but pure, carnal pleasure.

Landon doesn't stop.

He keeps going, bobbing his dick in and out of my mouth, the taste of his salty precum like a palate cleanser before the dessert course, and I want it. I want it all. I want him to feel as good as he's making me feel.

Drool dribbles all over my cheek and chin as he groans and grunts and tells me how good my mouth feels while he continues to eat me out and play with me until I'm so worked up, I lose focus on what I'm supposed to be doing and come with an even louder scream than before.

My body arches up into him, my nipples grazing the light smattering of hair on his chest, heightening this sensation more. I lick at him, playing with his tip with my tongue, but I'm coming so hard stars and fireworks and fucking unicorns are dancing behind my eyes as wave after wave of absolute bliss spirals through my every nerve ending.

Finally, after years, I sag, boneless and flayed, on my bed. I must have blacked out because when I open my eyes, Landon is right above me. "You're not your dick. How did you get there?"

He laughs. "I'm going to wash my hands. Don't move."

"I won't."

"We're not finished."

"Okay."

He grins and kisses my lips, and I close my eyes once more. A few minutes later, the belt on my wrists loosens, blood rushing back into my fingers, and I clench my fists several times to regain circulation.

"Did I hurt you?"

"I liked it."

Suddenly I'm lifted and placed under the blankets, but then he's back on me, hovering over me. "Open your eyes, baby."

I smile dopily up at him. "Tonight is the first time you've

called me anything other than Miss Wilde, Ellery, or Elle. Your brother thought it was weird that you didn't have a pet name for me."

He rolls his eyes in the darkness, the blanket surrounding us, his hands twining with mine as he sets them on my pillow up beside my head. His hard, heavy cock presses between us, and heat flares from within me once more.

"My brother has a lot to say about me and what I do. More importantly what I don't do. But I'd rather not talk about Luca in this moment."

"How did you know it was him I was talking about?"

"Only Luca or Kaplan would say something like that, and I took an educated guess."

"I like your family."

He smiles, his nose brushing mine. "I like that you like them. But for fuck's sake, can we *not* talk about them right now?"

"What do you want to talk about then?"

"You. I'm going to make you come until you pass out. Then, after that, I might eat you out once more before I'm forced to leave you."

"I love it when you talk dirty to me."

"I wasn't talking to you. I was talking to your pussy."

An unexpected laugh shocks the air as it leaps from my lungs. "God, your jokes are getting so good." Kinda, sorta. Still dorky, but I love them. And I totally love him.

"I want to fall asleep with the sweet taste of your cum on my lips. On my tongue."

Oh. So joking time's over. Because my clit just pulsed, and my core just convulsed with that.

His thick length slides between my thighs, grinding up, slipping through my wetness, and hitting my spot just so. Lightning zaps around the room, practically electrocuting us, but I'll burn alive for him if he keeps touching me like this.

"You're my fucking goddess, Ellery Wilde. Let me touch you. Let me fuck you. Let me taste you until the absolute last second I can."

Then he shifts, slides down my body, and thrusts up, straight into me so effortlessly it's like he was always made to be inside me. And the best part, we haven't even gotten there yet.

26

A moan splits the air between us as my hands squeeze hers. She feels so good. So tight and wet and warm sheathed around me. We're doing this without a condom again and since I know she's on the pill—I saw them in her bathroom the other night and like the responsible adults we struggle to be with each other, we had the talk—there is no way I can ever take her while wearing one again.

My eyes stay locked on hers, open and watching the magnificent woman beneath me. My knees press into the mattress, our chests mashed together, sweat clinging between us as I move inside her. Pump harder. Grind deeper. I can't get deep enough and now that feels like a challenge. Her legs wrap around my ass, her head falling back into her pillow, her chin lifting as she loses the battle and closes her eyes.

I take her bottom lip between my teeth, dragging and sucking on it. The way she tastes and the sounds she's making build my movements to savage proportions. My thoughts are primal.

Mine, mine, mine, chants through my head.

What is it about her that does this to me? That makes me

fear I could lose her at any second? That has me fucking her harder, trying to chase those demons from my mind and prove myself wrong? I can't lose her. Not to anything.

"Elle," I rasp into her mouth, angling my pelvis so I hit her clit with each pound I'm slamming into her. "I'm going to fuck you until you forget your name. Until all you know is what it feels like when I'm inside you. You feel it?" I thrust harder, and she cries out, nodding, her mouth seeking mine in a sloppy kiss. "Mine, Elle. Fucking say it. You're mine."

Her eyes snap open, searching my face in the darkness. "Yes. I'm yours."

Thank fuck.

I adjust us, releasing one hand and cupping her ass, lifting her up higher and sliding back in all the way to the hilt. Her pussy convulses around me, and I know she's getting close. I know it's seconds before she's coming all over my cock. Her flushed body and the lust-drunk look in her eyes and greedy pussy tell me everything.

I hook one of her knees over my shoulder, release her other hand, grip her hips, and take her like a man who has found heaven. My tongue swipes at her nipple, flicking it as best as I can before sucking her entire tit into my mouth, all the while I move inside her, skin slapping skin. The bed is banging into the wall and yet, still, I'm not deep enough.

"Not yet," I grit out, and she whimpers.

I pull back, practically up on my knees now, and stare down at where our bodies are connected. My cock glistens, coated in her, sliding in and out, and it's so fucking hot I nearly come just from that.

"How much can you take, Elle?"

"Touch me. Please, touch me. I'm so close."

Her hands are on the headboard now, holding on, grappling at the fabric like it will save her. It won't. Tonight I possess her body. It's mine. I almost wish her wrists were still tied. I'd love to take her ass. To watch what my cock looks like in that hole, but I'm already so worked up, I won't last, and when I fuck her there, I'm gonna wanna last as long as I can.

A rumbling groan vibrates my throat at the thought.

"So many things I'm going to do to you."

My finger finds her slick, swollen clit, but before I can stop myself, I slide out of her and cover her pussy with my mouth.

She screams out, her hand ripping at my hair as if it's too much for her. She tells me that. That she can't, but she will because I want her to come like this, and then I want to fuck her into another orgasm. My cock is a wet, leaking mess, angry I took it from where it belongs, but it'll make my own orgasm that much better.

I suck on her, swirling my tongue around her clit over and over before sucking it back into my mouth. I don't play with her dripping opening, though I know she's desperate for that. No, my cock will fill her up, but first...

"Come, Elle. Come for me, baby."

"Oh, *fuuuuck!*"

I flick her clit back and forth, scraping it between my teeth, and that's when she loses it. Her nails on my shoulders scratching at me as she twists and writhes and undulates and begs and moans and screams out my name while squeezing the hell out of my head with her knees.

My girl is loud, but there's no one else to hear us, so I tell her I want to hear it all and, just when she starts to come down, I release her clit, reposition my cock, throw her leg back over my shoulder, and slam into her.

"Holy hell, Landon," she wails, her back so arched it's as if she's bent in half the wrong way. With a hand on her tit pinching her nipple, the other on her hip, I dig into her as deep as I can go.

I lick my lips. "I could eat your pussy for hours."

I could. That's seriously how much I love doing it.

"Fuck, Elle." My breathing is choppy, ragged, sweat dripping from my forehead, but I don't stop. The friction. The feel of her body—hot and so damn addictive—I want to stay buried in her forever. "So fucking good."

My fingers find her clit as I stare down at her, my vision hazy with endorphins, but her eyes are glued to mine. Locked in a soul-stripping, mind-bending connection unlike any I've ever experienced before. I'm owned and possessed and so fucking deep there's no space between us.

Her body trembles and shakes as she starts to come again. I fuck her through it, my thumb still rubbing her clit, bringing her higher until I can't stand it another second, and I come with a roar, shooting myself inside her. My vision goes fuzzy and sparkly, crackling on the edges, and I heave in a gasping breath as my body stills. My cock pulses and pulses as her walls suck every drop from me.

I collapse on top of her, rolling us until she's now on top of me, and close my eyes, my fingers in her hair, unable to catch my breath.

"Good thing you bothered to brush your hair," I murmur a few minutes later, still half-dazed as I get caught in a snag, working it out gently with my fingers.

She giggles against me and goes silent, her hand over my heart, both of us happy and sated and sleepy and what wouldn't I give to be able to fall asleep just like this only to wake up and do that all over again?

I lift her up, carrying her into the bathroom. It's unfortunately nearing midnight, and we both need sleep after more than a week of very little. "Can I shower with you?"

She laughs like that's the dumbest question ever and makes me set her down so she can start the water.

"I hate this. I hate showering and leaving. I hate not waking up with you in my bed beside me."

She doesn't reply, and I step in behind her, wrapping my arms around her waist, dropping my chin to her shoulder.

"We could fix that, you know."

I know I'm likely moving too quickly, that this all happened so fast between us—zero to sixty in no time flat—but it's as if now that my heart has learned how to beat again it only wants to beat for her and doesn't care about time or rules or anything else.

It just wants her.

Her hands twine with mine over her stomach, and I close my eyes as hot water cascades over us.

"My sister slept with David."

The words stun my eyes open, blinking at the tile wall. I tense, and she feels it because her fingers release mine, tickling my forearms, trying to relax me.

"My sister is my twin. I don't think I told you that yet, but she is. Identical. Just like you and Luca, though absolutely nothing like you and Luca. We're night and day and oil and water. I was the good girl, and she was the rebel, always getting into trouble. She had ruined our wedding. Got drunk and made a lewd speech and then proceeded to hit on every male there, whether eligible or not. I hadn't spoken to her since until tonight."

"And she told you she slept with your ex-husband?" I'm a lot stunned and even more confused. What sort of sister would do that, close or not?

"No. David told me the Saturday night before I went on my date."

I grunt. That was only like nine days ago. It feels like a lifetime with how much has happened.

"David was at a tournament I didn't attend because I was at home sick. He had too much to drink at the bar, or more likely it seems my sister drugged him somehow, and when he went back to his room, I was there. Only it wasn't me. Obviously, but he didn't realize it, or so he claims. It was Cat, and she was naked, and they started having sex, and then he realized it was her, and my parents were there."

"Your parents?" presses incredulously from my lips.

"They all blackmailed him, Landon. For two years. Threatened to tell me and ruin our marriage, so he paid them off. Only they did ruin our marriage." She sighs.

"Elle." I don't know what to say, so I just hold her tighter against me. Her family set up her husband and blackmailed him? The fuck? I can't wrap my head around that, only I can. Not from my family, but I'm an Abbot-Fritz and yeah, people do all kinds of insanely fucked up things in the name of a dollar.

"There's more, Landon. My sister is involved with some guy. Some bookie or something. She's in deep for five hundred grand with him."

Now I really stiffen, my heart galloping in my chest. Is that why... has she been... No. She wouldn't.

"I'm going to pay him myself," she declares, and I can't help but sag a little at that, and I hate that that's where my head went, but again, Abbot-Fritz and that's just how it goes. "I told Cat I'd pay him, so he doesn't kill her, but that I'm done with them. All of them. I know I likely shouldn't bail her out after what she did, but I can't sign her death warrant either. Anyway, I had her tell my parents I was done with them too. Threatened not to pay or to go to the press and sing a sob story if they ever spoke about what they did publicly. But you're a Fritz, Landon."

I swallow, my mouth bone-dry. "I'm not following." Except I am, and I don't like where this is going.

She spins in my arms, licking her lips and staring up at me as water rains down on us. "I worry if my family somehow found out we're involved... that they'd..." She can't even finish her statement, and I understand why—and am grateful for it. She's worried about me. About Stella. About what they could do to us. The fact that she's talking to me about it, not after my money, but concerned for it and me, tells me all my instincts about her are correct.

I cup her face in my hand. "I know how to take care of myself."

She shakes her head against me. "They're ruthless. Look at what they did to David."

"If this is your attempt to get rid of me—"

"No. But I need you to know what I come with. What I potentially come with. I'm hoping they'll slink away into the shadows. I threatened a lot, but my parents get nothing out of this, Landon, and that's what scares me."

"I don't scare off that easily."

But I'll do my own research into her family. Something I should have done from the start but didn't. I looked into her. Into her ex-husband. Now it seems I have more than just Stella and my family to protect. She thinks her family is ruthless. She has no clue.

She's never crossed a Fritz.

Money can buy a lot of whatever you need, and I happen to have plenty of it.

"David was horrible to me," she whispers after a very long, quiet moment. "I was constantly on eggshells, nervous and jittery whenever he was home. Everything I did, I found myself questioning how he'd react. And nothing I ever did was good enough. Everything I am was an affront to him. I was too ugly. Too stupid. Too careless. Not grateful enough. Not perfect enough. He let me know it too. Any chance he got." She licks her lips, her eyes tilting up to mine. "It's why I was so upset when you slammed the window shut on me. It was like everything he always told me I was hit home in that very moment. I wasn't enough."

Fuck. Just fuck. How could I have been so stupid and reckless?

"It was me who wasn't enough. Not you. I never felt

deserving of you. Not from the second I saw you, even until now. I'm trying. I am. I want to deserve you. I want to deserve this." I press my lips to hers. Press them on her chest over where her heart thrums. "I've hated myself for so long, Elle. I was furious with Reese that night. I thought she had the easiest gig in the world, being home with Stella while I was spending interminable hours in med school and studying. I was wrong. She was home and happy with our girl, but she also had dreams I didn't take into consideration. Aspirations beyond what her life was, and in truth, Stella had been going through a rough toddler patch. She was difficult, and Reese did need a break. But instead of recognizing that, I yelled. I yelled and told her to go, and she did, and she died."

"Regret is such a strange thing, isn't it? The power it wields. The way it scars. David loved me, and you loved Reese. And I think, truly, if time were malleable, we'd correct our errors instead of learning from them. But that's history, right? History teaches us to talk about it so we never forget or repeat what should never be repeated."

Her hand is on my cheek the way mine is on hers. I stare into her eyes, holding them for so long. Searching their depths. Reveling in their secrets and mysteries that are only mine to discover.

"Maybe this is our second chance at getting it right."

"I want that," she tells me. "All of what you said. I want to wake up beside you. As much fun as sneaking around this week has been, I don't want to do that forever. But I still think we should keep this a secret. From everyone. I don't know what would happen to my teaching position, and there's Stella to consider and my family and—"

I shut her up with a kiss because I have too much on my mind right now to fight with her. She wants to keep us a secret, and she's probably right. For a little while longer at least, but if this thing is going where I want it to go, then I'll have to tell

Stella, and I won't be able to keep Elle a secret because I don't *want* to keep her a secret.

I kiss her, reassuring her until my kisses and reassurances turn into lust and passion, then I take her once more in the shower before I wash her hair and her body, then I'm forced to kiss her sleeping lips good night to sneak back out into the cold, dark night and into my house. I shut the door behind me, the warmth and comfort of my home a relief as I lock everything up and set the alarm.

But as I walk through the first floor toward the stairs, I halt in my steps, stunned at what I find waiting for me.

27

I feel caught as my teenage daughter sits on the second to the bottom step, waiting for me. Such an odd role reversal, but here it is. Stella was upset when we came home from the fair, and no matter how hard I pressed, she refused to tell me why. After locking herself up in her room, she was asleep when I left.

Or so I thought.

I will admit, this is all new for me. I never snuck out. It was impossible from the compound. The security in that place is insane. It's a million miles to anything from there, and well, I never had a good reason to try. I have no idea how this is supposed to go or what I'm supposed to say to my thirteen-year-old as she stares me down like she's getting ready to yell and then ground me.

"Were you with Elle?" She looks impossibly hurt.

Oh boy. I take a seat on the step beside her. "I thought you were asleep."

"I was faking it."

"Why?"

"You didn't answer my question."

I swallow and stare into my daughter's eyes. My wife's eyes. "Yes. I was with Elle."

"Are you... are you... having sex with her?" She swallows and blushes, her gaze falling a bit from mine, but she leaves that heavy question hanging between us.

Shit. Sometimes it's awesome being a single dad to a daughter. This is not one of those moments.

"Yes." And please God, don't ask me to elaborate on that.

She nods and falls silent, staring at the carpet on the stairs between us, and I have no fucking clue what to say.

"I thought you didn't like her. You were always kind of mean to her. At least when she first moved in."

"I tried not to like her."

"Because of Mom?"

My insides tighten. "Because of a lot of reasons."

She nods, and I find myself staring down at the top of her head, wishing she'd look up so I could figure out what she's thinking. "I know why you blame yourself for Mom."

My lungs empty, and my chest clenches like it's caught in a vise.

Now she looks up. Straight at me. "Uncle Oliver and Uncle Carter told me."

I nod. That's all I've got. In a way, I'm relieved they did because how do you tell your daughter you're the reason her mother is dead? On the other hand, it should have come from me, and it should have come a long time ago.

"Why did they?" It's likely the wrong question, but I'm curious.

She leans forward, bringing her feet up to the first step and dropping her elbows to her thighs. A frown pulls down her lips as her eyes train toward the front door, and fear grips me. The thought of losing my daughter's love is the most crushingly terrifying thing I've ever experienced, and I lost my wife.

This is why I never told her. This. This right here. I can't breathe, and my heart feels like it's beating out of my chest, silently begging her the way I am.

"I saw you walk off with Elle. I saw you take her hand, and Uncle Oliver noticed I did. We met up with Grace and Uncle Carter, and I heard them talking about it a little when they didn't realize I was listening. They talked about how relieved they were that you were finally putting the past behind you and moving forward."

"Bellas—"

"I asked them why you blamed yourself for Mom—that I had overheard from Grandma and Grandpa a few years ago— and Uncle Carter and Uncle Oliver told me about the fight you had with her that night. The things you said."

Emotion clogs my throat, and I do my best to clear it, but her utterly despondent tone and expression break me in two, and a tear slips down my cheek before I can stop it. My head falls in shame, my heart cracking open, bleeding out.

"I didn't know how to tell you. Bellas, I'm so sorry."

She swivels in my direction and takes me in, our faces only illuminated by the soft glow of the small lamp on the entryway table. "I told Mercedes Smart that she was a stupid, insecure bitch, and I hoped she died a painfully slow death."

I startle back an inch. "What?"

"She was teasing me. Making fun of me for things I'd rather not tell my dad, but I said it to her. I was angry and upset, and I lashed out. Shouted something I didn't mean to her."

"Honey, I—"

"I know you loved Mom. I know you wish it had been you instead of her. I overheard that too."

Fuck.

"We all say stuff we don't mean." Her eyes shift back and forth between mine. "I don't blame you for what happened to her. You didn't mean what you said, just like I didn't. It just took me a little while tonight to figure that all out in my head."

More tears fall, and there's no way I can stop them. A shudder wracks through me, and I grab my daughter, dragging her to my chest and holding her firmly against me. She grips my shirt with her small fists as her body trembles and jerks while she cries softly against me.

For a few minutes, I rock her, hold her, cry with her, feeling so blessed and undeserving. Feeling a lightness I haven't felt since the day she was born. She'd make her mother so proud, and I know Reese is watching us now, feeling this with us.

"I love your mom, Bellas. I always have, and I always will. I miss her." Especially right now. I'd give anything for Reese to see Stella like this. Growing up and so sweet and smart and beautiful and perfect.

"I miss her too. I wish I had known her."

A bite into my lip to stop a sob. "I wish that too. So much."

"I know, Dad," she whispers into me, her voice hoarse. Pulling back, she wipes her tear-soaked face, and I do the same with mine while keeping her close to my side, pressed into me. Her watery blue eyes lock on mine. "But now you love Elle too?"

I lick my lips. "I think I might, yeah."

"Are you going to marry her?"

Christ on a cracker, how do I answer that? "I don't know, Bellas. It's far too soon to think about that. She's recently divorced, and we've only been... we're not exactly..." Fuck, I don't know what to say. "It's new, and we don't want to rush anything. I don't want to rush her. Does that make sense?"

"I guess so."

"She also wants to keep it quiet for now."

Her eyes sparkle up at me as I run my hand down her long, long hair. "Because of me? Because she's my teacher?"

"Sometimes I forget just how smart you are. That's definitely one reason."

"I'm happy it's her."

Now I get choked up again. "Me too."

She drops her head onto my shoulder and the two of us sit here, lost in our thoughts.

"You have school tomorrow. Or I guess it's today now."

"And you have work."

"We're both going to be tired then."

She giggles, and never has a sound made me smile the way this one does. "I went into your office earlier. I saw the plot of land on your computer. The blueprints for the house. It's not just sketches anymore. It's actual blueprints."

"Oh?" That catches my attention.

"The land is six million dollars?"

I chuckle at her shocked tone. "It is."

"But there's no house on there. That's just the land. You'd have to build the house."

I kiss the top of her head, breathing in her sweet, clean scent. "It's a lot of land, and this is Boston. What did you think of it?"

She looks up. "Will you build me another greenhouse?"

I press another kiss, this one to her forehead. "Bigger than the one you have now, yes. And with all that land…"

She climbs onto my lap the way she used to when she was a little girl, and I just about lose my shit again. My arms snake around her, and I hold my baby because when the hell will I ever get this chance again? She's growing. So fast. Too fast.

"Do I have to be a doctor when I grow up?"

I laugh at her scrunched-up, grossed-out expression. "It's the Fritz way."

"Uh-uh. Aunt Rina is a nurse."

I grin at her I got you there expression. "But she's still in the medical field," I tease.

"Daaad," she whines with a sing-song inflection.

"It's medicine or bust, kiddo. Sorry."

"Then I'm running away tonight."

I pinch her side, and she smacks at me, but my tone grows serious. "You can be whatever you want to be as long as you're happy. That's all I ever care about."

"Then I think I want to be a chef. Open a restaurant called Stella's that serves food I grow."

"I think that would be incredible." And I do. Truly. She's an Abbot-Fritz and has a trust fund bigger than the gross national income of some small countries. She can make all her dreams come true and then some.

"I guess I might like the idea of moving and building that house. Can we show the land to Elle?"

I lean back against the step, my eyebrows at my hairline. "You want her to see it?"

She turns her head fully in my direction and nods exuberantly, her bony butt digging into my thighs, and I adjust her on me. "I love her too."

God, this girl.

"I'd be okay with it if she was my stepmom one day."

And now I'm about to cry like a pussy again.

"We'll talk about it another day. Like I said, she might not be ready for all that yet. Us Fritzes are a lot to take on."

"I think she could handle it."

"I hope so."

Maybe I shouldn't have said that out loud. Maybe I shouldn't even be thinking along those lines, but I did, and I am, and fuck it. I want it. I want it all, and I want it with Elle.

"I'm beat, and you need to get some sleep."

She groans like the teenager she is and climbs off my lap, standing up and stretching out her limbs as a yawn hits her lips. Without waiting for me, she trudges up the stairs, heading for her room, and I follow, pulling her in for another hug in front of her door because I'll never get enough of them.

"Night, Bellas. I love you."

"Love you too, Dad."

She shuts the door, leaving me out here, and it's almost as if I don't know what to do with myself now. I never thought I'd feel like this again. Never dreamed of it because I never wanted it.

"Thank you, Reese," I whisper and walk down the hall to my room.

It's pitch-black in here, but I find my way to my window and stare out toward Elle's dark one. She's asleep. Barely stirred when I finally dragged myself away. It was torture, and I miss her already. Wish I were back in her warm bed with her sweet body wrapped around mine.

This thing between us is tricky. But now she's ours, and I'll do whatever I have to do to keep her that way.

28

"**P**enis," I say with a loud, unmistakably confident voice. "Vagina. Breasts. Testicles."

Everyone in the room either blushes, giggles lightly under their breath, or both.

"Come on," I cajole. "It's your turn. Say those four words and say them loud and proud."

Nothing.

"Y'all, we can't talk about sex until you're comfortable with the parts of your anatomy, and I will not allow slang in my classroom. So, let's do this. Penis. Vagina. Breasts. Testicles. Sing 'em out now."

More giggles, but then some of the wise-ass boys take this as their moment to shine and start shouting them out. But since that's the point of this exercise, for once, I encourage them. The fact that I'm standing in front of twenty thirteen and fourteen-year-olds yelling out penis and vagina is not a scenario I saw coming when I left David.

But now, I'm gonna be honest with you. I'm so here for it.

"Remember, my room is Vegas. Let's preach this out so we

get all this awkwardness over simple words out of our systems. Then we can get to the good stuff."

"Like sex?" Justin Thompson asks, his eyes trained right on me. Yeah, the little shit likes to flirt with his much older teacher.

"Like sex," I reply, staring straight back. "Do we need a little encouragement?" I grab my phone that's sitting beside where I'm perched on the front of my desk and unlock it. I already have the song cued up, so I hit play, making sure the speaker is as loud as it can go. Salt-N-Pepa's "Let's Talk About Sex" blasts through the room.

I hop off my desk, grab the large bag of Hershey Kisses I had hiding behind me, and tear it open. If the awesome '90s hip-hop beat doesn't get the kids going, sugar certainly will. So much for wellness.

"Pop Quiz hotshots," I say, stealing a note from *Speed* as I walk down the center aisle. "What happens if someone asks a question in this class?"

"We listen and answer respectfully. No making fun of anyone," Candice, a goody too-shoes if ever there was one, answers.

I toss her a chocolate that she fumbles and has to dive for. "That is correct. Are we going to make recommendations, jokes, or inappropriate comments on things like vibrators, dildos, lubricants, or best techniques for masturbation or sexual positions?"

"Um. No?" Katherine Ford answers it like a question, but I'll give her credit for being brave enough to answer that one in the first place and toss her a candy.

"That is also correct. If you have specific questions you'd rather not ask aloud, you can drop them in the questions box I have at the front of the room. I am the only one who will read them and feel free to leave them anonymous if that makes you more comfortable. I will answer questions I deem appropriate as they come along. Anything inappropriate will not be answered, so save it if you're going to use it as a mechanism for being lude. Nothing embarrasses me and nothing rattles me."

"Will you demonstrate sex for us? I'd love that action. Hell, I'll do it with you. I don't care if the class watches us."

I spin back around in Justin's direction. Fourteen going on dipshit. "Justin, disrespectful and misogynistic comments like that will land you in prison one day. Note to yourself, women do not like to be harassed or made to feel uncomfortable about their sexual safety or their bodies. Do better or I'll speak with the headmaster and your mother."

I flip back around, not giving him a second's more attention.

"Back to penis, vagina, breasts, and testicles. Shout it out for me and make sure I can hear you over the song."

I return to my desk, hopping back up and crossing my legs at the knee. The kids go at it, screaming at the top of their lungs and thinking they're just about the funniest things ever. But the truth, they need to get it out of their systems. I can't have them snickering or laughing or blushing every damn time I say vagina.

Just as the song cuts out only to start again, the door swings open, and a teacher I don't know all that well, but who was at Bridget's miserable dinner party, pops her head in, looking not too pleased with me.

"Everything okay in here?"

"Peachy keen and cherry pie. We're just working out our sex ed jitters."

She glances about the room at all the kids and then back at me. "Right. I forgot that was starting today. How much longer are we shouting this for?"

"I think we're done for now, but I have two other classes today."

She groans. "This will be a long day."

Tell me about it.

She shuts the door behind her, and I return to the class. Sex ed is supposed to last for over a month. I think this will be the longest month of my life. Still, it will take a natural disaster tearing the school from its foundation to dampen my good mood. Because while we're talking about sex in here, I'm getting all the action in the form of my hot neighbor.

Hot, furniture-breaking sex. Stolen kisses and ass spanks. Public orgasms. Crazy, dirty, bondage sex. Cuddling and kissing and sweet lovemaking sex. All the sex, all the different ways. He snuck over again last night—though he told me Stella caught him Monday night and knows all about us—and we screwed like the few hours of separation were a few too many. We couldn't keep our hands off each other and when it was over, he kissed my lips, told me I was beautiful and that he hated to go and wished he could stay.

I swooned.

His damn sated, goofy, remorseful smile had me swooning.

I feel like a teenager. Sneaking around. Keeping secrets. It's a dangerous thrill I can't help but crave more of.

I'm a smitten sex kitten riding reverse cowgirl on a sex train headed for fucked station. It's why I'm not allowing myself to think too deeply on anything or I'd end up talking myself out of it and what good would that do me? I figure at this point I've been hurting for the better part of three years. What's a little more hurt if that's what this amounts to in the end?

Only this time, I don't think it will end like that. I think we're headed for something a whole lot bigger and better. Fingers crossed.

I hit stop on my phone before the song keeps going and lock it. But not before I pull the pathetic move of checking for new texts. None. Not that I should expect any. The man is at work saving lives. Yep, full-blown teenager again.

"Welcome to sex ed in case you missed what your wellness class has been transformed into for the next month. Despite us fooling around"—I point around the room with a stern finger at the kids who start to laugh—"no pun intended. This is a serious class with some important information that no joke can hopefully keep you from making life-altering mistakes."

"Like what? Babies?" Candi Foster asks.

"That's one." I toss her a chocolate. "But how about STIs or sexually transmitted infections? They can be a gift that keeps on giving if you get the wrong one or it goes untreated. And unfortunately, you can be infected with one and have no knowledge of it, passing it along to other partners."

I get a lot of sickened looks and scrunched noses.

"See what I mean? And none of this is limited to hetero-sexual sex, so regardless of who you're into, safe sex is univer-sal." That little nugget is for Stella, who is sitting in the back corner of the room, quiet as a church mouse—likely because she knows what I'm doing with her father, so that makes this a touch awkward—though I'd never call her out or even glance in her direction. As far as I know, Stella has still not come out to her classmates. Just her family, her best friend/cousin of sorts, Layla, and me. Then again, I highly doubt she's the only LGBTG+ person in this class and definitely not in this school.

"Have you ever had sex?" Dalton Royce, Justin's BFF, ques-tions with a knowing grin. He thinks he's tripping me up. So young. So foolish.

"Yes," I reply. "I was married for three and a half years."

"So he's the only guy you've been with?" he presses.

"My sex life is absolutely none of your business and far from pertinent to your learning."

"My mom says women who have multiple sex partners are sluts."

I turn my attention away from Dalton, over to Mercedes Smart, who's glaring at me as if she thinks I'm a slut. Likely because she has a crush on Dalton and Justin and every other cute boy in this school. She's also the head bitchy girl who likes to harass Stella for being flat-chested and 'socially weird' as she calls her. You can imagine how much I like this girl.

"The word slut is not only derogatory and shaming, but it also sets women's equality back. Men are not typically called such harsh words when their sex lives are thrown under the microscope. Degrading a woman in such a way, or any way, is among the worst offenses you can do, and it is not something I will tolerate in my classroom or anywhere. If I ever hear cruel or intentionally hurtful language being used by anyone about someone else, whether in this classroom or anywhere on school grounds, it's an automatic detention."

I glare, raising a pointed eyebrow at her, and she sits back in her seat, visibly jarred by that.

"Now that we've gotten formalities out of the way, let's get started."

The bell rings twenty-five minutes later, and I nearly fist pump in the air and woot out a cheer. Yet another thing I can high-five myself for getting through in my first year as a teacher. And I think I did a good job with it too. Stella throws me a small smile on her way out, and I take that as a win too. The rest of the day is a variation of the same. Only now I have a better grasp on what to expect, so it goes smoother than the first class did.

And when the final bell sounds and everyone packs up their things, I sag in relief, settling behind my desk, content to grade some essays before going home, opening some wine, snagging a hot romance book, and taking a bath with it.

But two hours later when I get home, I find something waiting for me. Something that has my breath audibly catching and my hand covering my mouth, trying to stifle the sound.

Sitting on my front porch by the door is a giant bouquet of

flowers in a pretty glass vase with a white envelope leaning against it.

I make quick work of unlocking my door, setting my stuff down, and then returning for the heavy flowers. It's loaded with sunflowers and orange roses and white hydrangea and deep purple orchids and calla lilies. It's the most beautiful arrangement I've ever seen, and I spend a moment staring at them, breathing their fragrance in before I go for the card.

It's an actual card, not just one of those generic things the florist sticks in.

A thick, plastic card slips out, landing on my counter when I open the main card, and I find myself gasping once more because it's a gift card to a very high-end kitchen supply store.

Something to brighten your day and make you smile.

Love,

Landon

I pant out a breath. Then another. He put this all together himself. Wrote the card himself too and then had it delivered. Just to brighten my day and make me smile. I can't remember the last time someone did something like that for me. Made me feel this... special to them.

I pick up my phone, debating if I should call him or not. It's only a little after five, and I don't know if he's at work still or driving home, so I decide on a text.

Thank you. This was the best surprise to come home to. My smile is uncontainable.

He replies almost immediately. **Open your door and show me.**

My brows pinch in as I read over his text only to jump six feet in the air when I hear a knock on the door. He's here. Gripping my phone tighter, I squeak out a girlish squeal, only to just as quickly rein in my over-exuberance. It's not easy. It's a damn chore.

I'm a total slut for him. No shaming there. I wear that title proudly.

The man makes my heart thunder, my belly flutter, and my mind turn to goo.

I skip—way too quickly, might I add—to the door and fling it open wide.

Landon is wearing his glasses, dark slacks, and a pale blue button-down shirt, the sleeves rolled up to his elbows. His green eyes are sparkling, so much lighter than I think I've seen them.

"I snuck over here first before going home when I saw you reach your door. You like the flowers?" he asks, smirking at me, his gaze devouring.

"I love the flowers." I lean into the doorjamb, putting us only inches apart.

"I thought about getting them from Stella's greenhouse but was afraid of her wrath if I pillaged her flowers."

And I'm in love. All over again and again. He was going to pick the flowers for me himself?

"You didn't have to do all this. The gift card. It's too much."

His whole body dips in until it presses against mine, barely inside my door. His lip captures my bottom one. "I would have gotten you more, but I think it might have scared you."

"Are you falling in love with me, Landon Fritz?"

It's meant to be a joke. Something light, to ease the coiling tension that's burning low in my belly, threatening to consume me. But he doesn't take it that way. And when I realize this, realize he's not denying it or pulling away or running back to his house, but rubbing his nose against mine with an achingly wonderful and slightly nervous grin on his lips, I thread my fingers through his hair and close the inches between us, kissing him hard, with a passion I'm tired of fighting.

I don't care that he's my student's father. I don't care that he's my former asshole neighbor. I don't care that I only left my husband not even eight short months ago or that I should stay away from him because I worry about my family getting their greedy meat hooks into him.

I just care about how he makes me *feel*, and right now, I'd rather die than give this up.

This perfect man. This perfect moment.

That is until the perfect moment bursts, and everything instantly goes to hell.

29

___

Blinding light flashes from directly beside my face, blasting my eyes open and forcing my head to turn in the wrong direction. In the direction of the motherfucker who's snapping our picture. Again. With a douchebag, I got your shit on camera smile.

Fuck.

Motherfuck.

This slimy motherfucker—and yes, I know I'm dropping motherf-ers like Stella pops Skittles, but can you blame me—is leering at Elle, a dirty, grimy smile on his ugly mug. "Ellery Chambers, who's the new man? Is he why you left your husband David Chambers or was it because he cheated on you?" He thrusts a phone into her face, and she jumps back, slamming her head into the doorway.

She doesn't even wince. That's how stunned and terrified she is.

But then, the guy turns his eyes on me, and I realize I know him. That is to say I've seen him at events and things all over town. And when he realizes that he, too, knows me, it's game over. His eyes widen with Pulitzer-caliber excitement.

"Landon Fritz. You're Landon Fritz."

I almost wish he had thought I was Luca, but I suppose my glasses are a bit too telling.

His smile turns positively sickening with glee, and his camera comes up again. It wasn't from his phone, which I find almost weird, but I react—stupidly, I admit that—and grab it from his face, rip it over his head, and smash it to the ground.

The guy starts screaming at me. Threatening lawsuits and First Amendment rights and screw him. My hands are on Elle, and I'm tearing her from her doorway, shutting the door behind us and running us away from the guy at a full sprint. He's getting pics on his phone now. I know he is. He's not telling us so, but I'm not stupid. I know how this works.

When Reese died, the media were relentless.

It was like the fact that I had just lost my life and my soul and was actively bleeding out without signs of stopping was ultimate fodder for their vampirish ways. They camped out on our lawn. On the sidewalk. Tried to climb my goddamn six-foot fence. They trailed us everywhere. Attempted to get Stella—poor little, tiny, baby Stella who was not much more than a toddler and who had just lost her *mother* to talk to them. They had no boundaries. No respect.

They never have, but when they catch a scent?

I slam the door shut behind us, locking it up and setting the alarm. The big alarm. The one that has motion sensors in the grass and blares loudly when someone hits a certain perimeter.

"Landon?"

That's Elle, and I think that's all she's got because she stops there. She's horrified. And worried and looks more than just a little guilty. She hasn't seen me like this, but I don't just have one girl to protect now, do I?

Slipping my phone out of my pocket, I make the call. It rings once, and Mr. Fairchild, my parents' house manager, who was also a former member of MI6, answers. "Dr. Fritz?"

"I need security to come to my house and escort us to the compound immediately."

"They'll be there in fifteen minutes, sir."

He disconnects the call because he has work to do. Knowing him, he'll be here himself—like he was back then, by our side—until this is resolved.

"Stella, we have a code gray," I yell out into my house. "Get what you need and nothing else. Move. You have five minutes."

She doesn't respond, but I hear her moving upstairs.

"Landon?"

I blink, noting Elle's frightened tone, and spin back around, facing her.

"What just happened?"

"We were photographed."

"I get that. But what's all this?"

"They'll hurt you."

Doesn't she understand? That's what they do.

"Landon. It's okay."

I shake my head. It's not. Once they get involved...

"Look at me."

"You don't understand." I won't let them get to her.

A hand is on my face now, and all I can see is her, but that's because everything else around her feels fuzzy. "Tell me."

"They nearly ran us off the road on our way to the funeral. They followed Stella for months. *Months*, Elle. Me for longer. They wanted us upset. They wanted their soundbites. They wanted to see us broken and then break us further."

She steps into me, pressing herself against me, her soft eyes clinging to mine, forcing mine to cling back. Desperately. "They can't break us now because we're no longer broken."

I exhale on a shudder.

"What about your family? That guy knew about David cheating. That wasn't random."

Her eyes bounce back and forth between mine, then drop

to her phone that's still clutched in her hand. She breathes harshly through her nose, then makes a call. I watch her, but she spins away from me, facing the back hall.

"Did you break your promise or was this Mom and Dad?"

She listens. Then sighs.

"I paid the bastard, Cat. I paid him yesterday. I talked to the monster for an hour, then I paid him. So what the hell happened?" She listens again, her hand going to her hip and her head dropping. "What the hell do you mean they're here?!" she yells. "I told you to tell them I was done."

She growls at whatever this Cat—her sister, I presume— says on the other end.

"Well, now it's all fucked up, and it's not just me and David who they dragged into it. Disappear, Cat. I mean it. I'm more than done with all of you."

She disconnects the call, then storms back toward me, only she's not coming for me; she's headed for the door at my back. Her hand hits the knob, and I loop my arm around her waist, spinning her around.

"What the hell do you think you're doing?"

"Going to clear this mess up. My parents are out there with that guy. They had started this mess before I even spoke to Cat. She claims she didn't know, and when she told them I was done, evidently they weren't having that."

"You can't go out there."

She thrusts her finger past me. "My parents are out there, Landon. I'm going to stop this."

That's when the perimeter alarm goes off, blaring through my house. My phone lights up instantly with a call from my security company, and I give them the all clear because I don't want the cops showing up. Not yet. I want to handle this myself.

But first, I want to get Stella and Elle out of here.

Except Elle isn't waiting. She's flying past me, heading through my house and going for the front door. Goddamn her!

"Elle, stop!"

"No," she yells back, not slowing until she rips the front door open and storms outside like a tornado ready to mess some shit up.

Whoever tripped the alarm is nowhere to be found, but that doesn't stop her. Especially when she spots a white sedan parked one house down from hers. She runs toward it, and immediately three people step out. The paparazzi guy, and a man and woman who appear to be in their mid-fifties or so. The man is tall but round and portly, with a ruddy complexion I've seen more times on chronic alcoholics than I can count. He looks absolutely nothing like Elle. But there's no mistaking the woman is Elle's mother.

They have the same eyes and the same frown and the same coloring.

"What the hell did you do?!" Elle screams at them, not even caring that she's doing so out in the open.

"He broke my camera," the stupid asshole says, pointing at me. "I've called Intertainment. They're going to sue you."

I grin at him, following closely on Elle's heels. "I'd love for them to try. You forget I have a restraining order against you assholes."

He blanches as he should because I do. Like I said, money can buy you just about anything, and I have a lot of money. I have a restraining order against Intertainment and several other bullshit internet rags, magazines, and newspapers that forbid them from coming within a hundred feet of my house or Stella without my explicit, written permission.

"I-I-I didn't know you lived there," he stammers.

I just shrug lightly. "So who tripped my alarm then? The police will be here shortly. You can figure it all out with them." That last part is obviously a lie, but he has no clue about that. He heard the alarm. No mistaking that.

He turns purple and instantly dives back in the car, shutting the door and peeling out of here, leaving Elle in a standoff with her parents, who suddenly don't look as smug and confident as they did when they stepped out of the car.

"I paid off Cat's debt. Why are you doing this to me? Haven't you taken enough? Caused enough damage?"

Elle is less than a foot from them now, but her voice hasn't lost any of its fire.

"You paid off Cat's debt," the man growls at her. "You took care of her, but what about us? What about what we need? David's money was keeping us afloat. Without it, we're destitute. You owe it to us, Ellery. We're your parents. You lived under our roof for eighteen years. We fed and clothed you."

Elle laughs. And it's the most are you kidding me bitter laugh I've ever heard in my life. "Is that a joke? What you need?" she snarls sardonically. "You think I give a rat's ass what you need or the fact that you think I owe you for biologically being my parents and providing legally obligated bare necessities? You blackmailed my husband! All of you did, and you didn't care when I cried to you and told you how cruel and awful David was to me. You told me to suck it up and deal because he was my husband. I don't give a crap what you need or what you feel entitled to. You are no longer my parents. You are not my family, and I'm done with you. All of you."

"Except now we know about him," her mother says, pointing to me. "We looked him up. Just now after Kevin told us who he saw you with. He showed us the pictures he took of you two running away after he smashed Kevin's camera, so I'm guessing he doesn't want to be photographed. If you give us the same amount you paid Giancarlo, we won't make trouble for him. Or his family."

Oh, hell to the fuck no.

Except Elle just shakes her head like she's done with all of this. "I'm calling the police. I'm filing a restraining order, and I'm telling them how you extorted money from my ex-husband.

You people are sick. You really, truly are. I don't even know what to say to you anymore. I don't know why you're here or what you were hoping I'd give you, but threatening Landon and his family is one hundred percent not the way to get me to do anything."

"We need that money, Ellery!" her father yells, spitting and turning redder by the second. "Cat took us for everything we had. Every last penny. We lost our car and our condo. Now we have nothing, and you will pay for that. You will."

That's when two very different things happen almost simultaneously.

The first is three large, black, identical SUVs come racing down the street, two parking in my driveway, one in front of my house. Fairchild steps out along with other security, some of them I know, some I don't, but that's not surprising. We're a large family with a large security force on retainer, and anyone with Fairchild, I trust.

I point to my house, and he flies in, going straight for Stella.

The other thing that happens is Elle's father starts profusely sweating when he sees the cars, likely thinking they're here to arrest him. But then he grabs his chest and starts wheezing before falling to his knees. His wife shrieks, but he doesn't stay on his knees for more than a few seconds before he collapses to the grass, unconscious because he's likely having a heart attack.

"Dad," Elle screams, still standing, frozen in place, her expression aghast despite what just transpired between them. The wife collapses on top of him, yelling his name (Paul) and shaking him, slapping his face, doing anything she can think of to wake him up.

"Elle, go with Stella and the security team to the compound," I tell her as I run to her father, practically shoving his wife off. She starts to yell at me, trying to rip me away, when Elle springs into action.

"Mom, let him go. He's a doctor."

Elle pushes her mom away, and the woman falls into the grass, staring at me with wide, unblinking, anxious eyes. Elle takes a few steps back, and I get to work, checking his carotid and listening for breath sounds. He has a pulse, but it's thready, and his breathing is barely there. Any second, he's going to code, and I'd rather him not do that in front of his daughter.

"Elle, go with Stella and Mr. Fairchild," I command again, twisting up and forcing her gaze. "Now. No arguing. I need to know you're somewhere safe. I'll take care of your father. Go!"

I nod at Fairchild, and he's there, grabbing Elle's arm. Stella is watching me as she climbs in the back of one of the SUVs, a security guy on either side of her. I can't do much about that now, but I need Elle to go too.

"Landon..."

"I've got it. Please, Elle. Go."

She swallows and bobs her head, casts a fleeting glance at her mother, then back to her father, over to me, and runs for the SUV.

"I've called paramedics," Fairchild informs me. "They're en route."

"Thank you. Keep them safe."

"With my life, sir."

I know he will. My father saved his life once, and he's spent his life returning the favor.

Just as they pull away, I lose Paul's heartbeat, immediately starting CPR. I swear if he dies on Elle's grass...

"What medications is he on?" I ask his wife, whose name I still haven't gotten.

"Nothing," she sobs. "He doesn't take anything. You have to save him."

Of course he doesn't. But I'd bet my license he has high cholesterol, hypertension, and possibly type II diabetes. "How much does he drink a day?"

I glance over at her as I internally count to thirty compressions in my head, then tilt his chin up, plug his nose, and give him two rescue breaths before immediately going back to chest compressions. She doesn't answer, and that's not a good sign.

"Is he going to die?"

Now it's my turn not to answer, but luckily, I don't have to. Within seconds the ambulance arrives, taking over CPR for me and getting the defibrillator on him to deliver a shock. But this day is far from over.

PAUL COMES to in the emergency room. It only required one shock in the grass to get his heart going again, plus a boatload of IV drugs and some oxygen. Once he was stabilized, we sent him straight up to the cath lab, and it took them not even ten minutes to figure out that three of his major coronary arteries are blocked and unable to be stented or treated medically.

Now we're back in the trauma room, keeping him here because his heart rate likes to flirt with V-Tach despite the meds we're giving him to stop that from happening. He catches my eye, noting that I'm running the show in the trauma room, and doesn't say anything.

"His wife just arrived," Linda, the head nurse in the trauma room, informs me. I made his wife take an Uber—I paid for it —to the hospital because there wasn't enough room in the ambulance, and doctor trumps wife.

"Perfect," I tell her. "I've got this." I nod to all the nurses, the resident, and his med student. No one argues. No one questions. This is my hospital. I don't typically work in the emergency department all that often unless I'm on call and am needed down here. Mondays and Thursdays I round on the floors. Otherwise I'm in the office seeing patients, but they all know me.

More importantly, they know my name, and they know my dad.

Everyone clears out just as... "What's your name?" I ask Elle's mother.

She gives me a wide berth as she cautiously enters the room, her wary gaze flipping back and forth between her husband and me until she's standing up by his head. "I'm Betty."

"I'm Dr. Landon Fritz, but I know you already know that."

Paul is on a gurney with an oxygen mask over his mouth and nose, hooked up to IVs and telemetry. I can see every move and twitch his heart makes.

"Is he going to be okay?"

This woman, who seemingly cares so much for her husband, even for her other daughter, cares nothing for Elle. I can't even fathom it, but I see it all over her. The hard glint in her eyes. The steel rod of her spine. The animosity and spite that is pouring off her in waves.

I stand on the other side of the gurney, bearing down on them and making my power and presence felt. "I saved your life today," I tell Paul first and then Betty, not bothering to answer her directly. "Everyone in this room knows it. Your heart is beating, and you are breathing because of me. Because I didn't let you die. If you ever come near Ellery, my daughter, me, or any of my family again, you'll quickly learn I'm capable of a whole lot more than saving lives."

I let that threat hang heavy in the air between us.

Then I take a step back and plaster a smarmy smile on my face. "And because I'm positive you won't dare challenge that, I'm bringing my father in to perform your coronary artery bypass graft surgery."

Betty gasps, covering her mouth, and then reaches for Paul's hand. He coughs into his mask, his heart giving a few extra charged beats before it reluctantly goes back into sinus rhythm.

"Lucky for you, he's one of the best cardiothoracic surgeons in the world. But, like me, he doesn't suffer threats against his family or loved ones well, so I wouldn't try anything. Certainly not with him cracking your chest open to repair your heart. Once you're in recovery and healing, I'll be sure to check in on you prior to your discharge. After that, I expect we'll never see or hear from you again."

Betty licks her lips—Elle does that, so it throws me for a second—then nods resolutely. "You won't."

"I didn't think so."

I catch movement outside the trauma room and leave the two of them here to deal with all I just dropped in their laps. Pushing through the door, I find my father leaning against the opposite wall, reviewing the chart on the computer, dressed in scrubs.

"I haven't gotten to meet her yet, but your mother tells me she's lovely," he says by way of a greeting.

I collapse against the wall beside him. "She is."

"You're keeping me from dinner with my wife and granddaughter, as well as the woman who stole my son's heart. I hope these people are worth it to you."

I grin, rubbing my hand over my mouth. "They're not. But she is."

"Then I guess I can't let the man die on the table?"

A chuckle slips past my lips. "Not worth the resulting lawsuit. They're everything you always warned us about."

"But not her."

Even though it wasn't a question, I answer, "But not her."

"Then go to the compound and reassure her that her father won't die tonight. I've given Fairchild the all clear, but I think Stella is still a bit shaken up."

"I'm on it and thank you."

"Anything for you, my boy. Anything." He slaps my shoulder, then goes straight for the trauma room. "Mr. and Mrs.

Wilde, I'm Dr. Fritz. That is all you're allowed to call me, and I will not tell you my first name. You're lucky my son cares enough about your daughter to even bother bringing me in here tonight to save your life."

I laugh as my father keeps going, but I don't care enough to stay and listen. My ladies are waiting for me.

30

I feel so strange being here after everything that happened today. Stella and I were whisked away like the first family under an immediate national security threat. They're the Abbot-Fritzes, and they're not normal people. I realize this, but I guess I just didn't *realize* this. I mean, who has a security team on speed dial?

That was a trip.

That and my father dropping dead on my front lawn. That was something too.

I expect Octavia Fritz to hate me on principle. She should. My family threatened her family today. But the second Stella is done hugging her grandmother and relaying what went down, the beautiful woman with the adorable blond wig parts her arms like the Red Sea and envelops me in a crushing hug like I'm the Egyptians who were racing after the Israelites.

I'm not sure that makes sense, but it's been a day, and I think a modicum of slack should be awarded my way.

"You are everything Luca and Stella said you are and more."

I can't help but smile at that. "With the exception of Stella, that's not as comforting as you might think it should be."

She laughs, her green eyes sparkling, and now I know where her boys—except Carter, whose eyes resemble decadent dark chocolate—and daughter get it.

"No. I imagine it is not. Luca was always my troublemaker. But he'd never say anything he didn't mean, and everything he told me about you was not only kind, it appears was right on the money."

Money. I flinch at that, and she notices, giving me the warmest of smiles as if to say, you're okay now, you're one of us. Landon told me the other night about his mom. How worried he is about her health. How scared he is of losing her. I had told him once that I'd take his mother over mine any day, and now more than ever, I mean that.

She is the family glue, lovely and gracious and kind.

"Are you worried about your dad?" Stella asks as they lead me through the house—house is a loose term for palace—until we reach some sort of room that's not quite a dining room but clearly some meals are eaten here. *A breakfast room?* "You don't have to be. My dad will save him."

Oddly enough, I'm not worried about my dad. I mean, I don't want him to die. I'm not that sort of evil. But I don't want to hear from him again so...

"I have no doubt your dad will save him."

"And my grandpa. He went to help too."

Great. I'm sure that will fly like reindeer at Christmas in this family. "Will he be upset about working so late into the evening?"

Octavia—she insisted I call her that—places a hand on my forearm. "The man lives for surgery. Since I became ill, he's unfortunately had to cut back his hours, so having any excuse to cut someone open, he'll take."

Oh. Well. I'm not sure what to say to that. Evidently, my father is getting cut open tonight, and my boyfriend's father is doing it. What a motherfucking day.

"Are you hungry?" a woman wearing black slacks, a white button-down blouse, and a soft smile comes in and asks. "I'm Sophia. The Fritz family's chef. Stella's been telling me you've been teaching her to cook."

I blink and stand up, somehow feeling like I'm stealing this woman's thunder with that, though I think that might be in my head since she seems genuinely delighted by this. "Yes. Every Monday and Wednesday."

"We should do a lesson here. All together. I'd love to be part of it."

"You would?"

She laughs at my flabbergasted expression. "Of course. It would be fun. We'll have Layla come too and make a party out of it. From what my little birdy here has told me, her uncles and aunt are very jealous they haven't gotten to taste any of her creations."

I'm totally about to start crying. "I'd love that."

"Wonderful." Sophia gives me an even brighter and warmer smile than she was two seconds ago. "So... hungry?" She checks with the other two women I'm with.

"Starved. Like... could eat a bear starved."

Sophia rolls her eyes at Stella. "Tell me something new, kid. But dinner is ready unless we're waiting on Dr. Fritz and Dr. Landon."

Dr. Landon sounds so weird and formal, but I guess she's the family chef, so it makes sense? I don't know. I have zero frames of reference with this kind of money. These people put rich people to shame.

"I believe Dr. Fritz and Landon will join us later. Would you mind putting supper together for us?"

"Not at all. I'll be right back with it." She winks at Stella, then leaves. And wow. Just wow. These people are the nicest ever. Not a snooty bone among them. I hate that that's precisely what I envisioned despite having met the other Fritzes, but yeah.

I fall back into my chair, staring out the back window at the magnificent grounds that seem to go on forever. That is until a hand over mine startles me back to the room. "A drink, dear?"

"Does it sound bad if I say yes?"

Octavia laughs, and it reminds me so much of when Rina did. They look so much alike, and I hope I get to know Rina better.

"Not at all." She rises out of her chair and now I feel awful. I assumed she'd have someone do it for her, but nope, this woman is walking across the room—it's a freaking mammoth room for what is likely a third eating room—over to a bar I hadn't previously noticed."

"What's your poison?"

"I will honestly drink whatever you're making."

"Stella, should we give her our special Shirley Temples?"

Ummm... that's not exactly what I was hoping for.

"I think she'd love them," Stella replies, and now I can't say a word.

"Mine is adjusted slightly from Stella's, and I'll make yours the same. Does that sound all right?"

Oh, Octavia Fritz. You are a very special woman. "That sounds wonderful."

"I figured you'd agree with that." She returns with three glasses—crystal glasses on a silver tray, no joke—for all of us. "This one is yours, my sweet." She places the very obvious Shirley Temple in front of Stella. "These are ours, Ellery, but yours might have an extra punch of ginger beer in it." She winks conspiratorially at me, and I think I love Landon's mother.

"Thank you and thank you for welcoming me into your home so graciously."

"It is truly—and I mean this from the bottom of my heart—my pleasure. To better days ahead of us now that you're with us."

"I will absolutely drink to that."

Our crystal clinks with that perfect crystal sound, and we each take a sip, and yep, this is some form of a Moscow Mule with a lot of vodka and a splash of lime and grenadine, and a few cherries thrown in—likely for Stella's benefit.

But it's when Stella remarks, "Yeah, my dad is in love with you, so now our whole family is," that I choke on the vodka that is now burning a hole through my esophagus. Thank Jesus it wasn't a cherry or a Heimlich would have been necessary.

"What?" Stella asks, perplexed by my reaction. "He told me he was."

"Stella, honey, I'm not sure your daddy has told Elle that yet, though. I think that's why she's so surprised."

I nod. I gasp.

"Does that mean you don't love him back?"

"Good question, Bellas," Landon says, entering the room. "I'm curious about that myself." He drops into the empty chair beside me, all smiles and grins and freaking hot sexy man. "Does your choking mean you don't love me back, Elle?"

Bastard. He's really going to put me on the spot like that. In front of his daughter, who is my student, and his mother, whom I just met. I glare, and he chuckles, patting my back and kissing my forehead. Right here. At his mother's... some kind of eating room table.

Once I'm able to catch my breath, I go for my water, taking a hasty sip.

"Your dad's going to be okay," Landon announces, and the change in topic is giving me whiplash. "He had a heart attack. One of his coronary arteries was completely blocked and another two were severely narrowed and unable to be stented. My father is performing bypass as we speak. He'll spend tonight up in the CCU and then about three or so days in the hospital before he's discharged. I'll see him again prior to that and get him set up with a cardiologist close to his home and that will be that. I have their word on it, and I believe this time, it's true. In any event, I'll be keeping tabs to make sure."

"Thank you." My chin wobbles, and I suck in a breath. I don't want to cry. Not here.

He takes my hand. "You're welcome. It's been quite a day. Are you okay?"

"I am now."

A smile lights up his face and wow, this man and his smiles. They dazzle my insides.

Without thinking too deeply about it or second-guessing, I lean in and hug him, dragging him to me. And when his ear is by my mouth, I whisper, "I love you." Because some things for the first time need to be said in privacy. Well, semi-privacy because I'm positive Octavia and Stella heard it.

Especially when Stella squeals and claps and bounces up and down in her seat.

Landon abruptly rises from his chair, taking me with him. "Mom, please ask if Sophia would mind keeping our plates warm. I need to speak with Elle alone for a minute."

"Of course."

Only her smile could power up Times Square after a blackout.

He plants a kiss on top of Stella's head, then he's dragging me along, through room after room, to the point where I'm already lost. I hope he doesn't expect me to find my way back by myself. We fly through a music room, loaded with instruments, up a back staircase and down a hall until he opens a door and practically shoves me inside it.

Before I can get my bearings, he's pressing me back into the wall, getting right up in my face. "Did you mean it?"

I blink rapidly and nod. "Yes. I meant it. I love you. You're the one who hasn't said it yet after putting me on the spot. Twice now."

His hands clutch my face, his fingertips brushing through my hair, his eyes wild and locked on mine. "Ellery Jane Wilde, I love you. I love you for forgiving me for unforgivable things. I love you for your smiles and your warmth and your laughter. I love you for how you love Stella. I love you for pumping life back into my dead heart and reminding it how to beat again. I love you for your spunk and bravery. I love you for—"

I cut his words off with my lips, practically climbing the man like a spider monkey. I can't get close enough. One hand is in my hair, the other under my ass, holding me up and pressing me into the wall as he kisses me. And kisses me. With tongue and teeth and lips and heat and so much passion, it suffuses my every molecule.

His lips drag down my neck, sucking and biting.

I gasp. "Landon, you're going to mark my skin."

"I know."

"We're at your parents' house."

His warm breath glides over the trail of wet skin he's leaving behind, and I tremble in his arms. "I don't want to stop. I need you."

His mouth dives back in, and any remaining objections die on my tongue as his sweeps across it. His hands are all over me, tugging at my shirt, palming my breasts, squeezing my ass. Mine can't be contained either as I grip at his shirt and grapple with his pants. Our kisses are sloppy and wet, our movements frantic.

He breaks contact to tear my shirt off, but instead of attacking me again, he pauses, staring straight into my eyes. "I know you've been through a lot. With David, with walking away from him, with your family. I know this. I also know I'm not easy. I come with a family of my own that is no small undertaking. And I have a child. A child who's just hitting her teenage years. I know I'm a lot, and I know you've been through a lot. But I'm asking if you'll choose us anyway."

And just when I didn't think my heart could be any fuller.

I place my hand over his chest. Over his pounding heart. "Everything I went through led me here. And there's nowhere else I'd rather be. Ever."

His mouth slams back down against mine, our hands frenzied as we remove piece after piece of clothing. His fingers slip between my legs, finding me wet, and with a growl, he spins me around, and we go tumbling down onto a bed.

"Whose room is this?"

His head pops up, and he glances around. A chuckle rumbles his chest. "Kaplan's. I've never fucked on Kaplan's bed." He grins. "Then again, I've never fucked on my bed either. This is all new for me."

His fingers glide along my drenched heat, and I moan, falling back on the bed and no longer caring where we are. Pleasure ignites through my limbs as I climb on top of him, sinking down, taking him fully inside me.

Nothing matches the feel of this man inside me. Nothing ever will.

He thrusts up, and we both groan, but time is not on our side, and our movements become dirty and sloppy, quick as both of us chase our release with fingers and mouths and pants and moans. He fucks me like a beast. Like a man who'll no longer be denied. And when we're done, both breathless and smiling, he dresses me.

Piece by piece, he puts me back together. Same as I do for him.

"You ready for dinner with my parents?"

I laugh, shaking my head. "They're going to know."

"All they care about is that I'm happy. I'm a little too old to care about their thoughts on what I do behind closed doors."

"This wasn't the way I wanted them to meet me."

His hands are back on my face as he lifts my chin up to meet his eyes. "I know, but like I said, you made what we all thought was impossible happen. Nothing else matters after that. It's you and me now. And this is our second chance at getting it right. No more regrets."

EPILOGUE 1

Four Weeks Later

"You seriously won't tell me where we're going?" I ask grumpily, my arms folded over my chest, though I don't think I'm fooling anyone. I think both Stella and Landon know I'm not the least bit put out over whatever surprise they have planned for me.

"Patience, love," Landon says, reaching over and pulling my hand away from my body so he can play with my fingers. "We only have another five minutes before we get there. Do you think you can manage that?"

I glare at him, but again there's no heat to it. "I'm not a child."

"You're way more impatient than I am, and I'm still considered a child."

"That's because you're a breed of your own, Stella. We cannot all have your grace and perfection."

She snorts from the back seat, but then follows it up with, "That's probably true. Justin Thomas told me I'm a queen and should start acting like one. That if I choose, with my beauty, brains, and breeding, I could not only rule the school but the world."

"Is that because you stood up to Mercedes Smart?"

I glance over my shoulder in time to catch Stella's shrug, but she's grinning with pride.

"Probably," she muses. "I don't think she expected me to sit down with her and explain that her words didn't bother me anymore, and that I believed them to be a reflection of herself and that because of that, I was worried about her."

It was a shining moment, and I'm still so proud of Stella for it. Mercedes broke down into tears and told Stella how she was just jealous of her because all the boys secretly had crushes on Stella, and Stella is a Fritz, and yada, yada, yada. Now they're quasi friends.

Landon and I exchange quick glances. "Did he ask you out?" Landon asks after a quiet beat.

"He did, but I told him he wasn't my type."

I snicker. "Did you tell him just who your type is?"

Stella laughs. "No way. The look on his face at being rejected was far too precious."

"You're evil, Stella. And I think I like it."

"Me too," she agrees. "But only because he makes sexual advances on you at school."

"He does what?" Landon barks out, his head whipping in my direction.

I roll my eyes and cock a brow. "He's fourteen, Landon. He's pushing boundaries and testing limits because clearly he doesn't get a lot of those at home. He's entitled, but he'll learn. His mother was useless when I tried to speak with her about it at fall conferences. I got the boys will be boys response, which just encourages rape culture. Anyway, for every inappropriate comment, I deduct a point from his final grade and give him a detention."

"Do I need to talk to his father? I know his father. He's a mental and physical weakling. I can crush him with very little force."

I squeeze his hand. "Slow down there, Thor. I can more than handle a fourteen-year-old boy."

He grunts in dismay but doesn't argue further. He knows I can more than handle myself. He saw me go postal on my parents in my yard, and when I told him about my conversation with the infamous Giancarlo, he was impressed. And annoyed I didn't talk to him about it first, but truly, it wasn't his battle to fight or win for me.

My father came out of surgery well and after five days was discharged from the hospital. After that, I have no idea. I haven't heard from any of them. Not David. Not Cat or my parents. That's my old life, and I'm done with it.

But after everything went down, I decided I needed to talk to the school about my relationship with Landon. And Stella, since she's not just the daughter of the guy I'm with. She's so much more than that to me, and I needed to make my position on it all known. Bridget was worried about it. Even offered to come with me as moral support, but if they were going to fire me over that, then so be it.

I can always find another job.

I can't always find another Landon and Stella.

No one gets you for the crime, they get you for the cover-up, and that's not what I wanted to have happen. I needed to be the one to tell them before they inevitably found out. Not much was done about it. Not as much as I thought would be anyway.

Stella is already an A student in all her classes, and I offered to have any tests, papers, or assignments I've graded reviewed by another teacher. They declined and just told me as long as I don't show favoritism to her, then it should be fine.

I never have, and I never will. At least not at school.

Landon takes a turn off the road and suddenly we're bumping along a gravel path that's cut deep into the woods. "If you're taking me here to kill me, you should know I don't go down without a fight."

Landon throws me a quick wink, but then releases my hand so he can safely steer us down the road that winds its way along until we reach a massive clearing with a bunch of orange flagged stakes stuck in the ground. He parks the Range Rover off to the side, then pivots to me.

"We're here."

Only he sounds a little breathless, his suddenly guarded eyes holding mine.

Stella hops out of the car, and Landon does the same. I unbuckle my seat belt, then Landon is opening my door for me, helping me down and retaking my hand. Most of the trees are bare, their leaves scattered across the earth, my boots crunching into them as we follow after Stella, who's running around, weaving in between sticks.

"What is this place?" I ask, no longer able to contain my curiosity.

"It's going to be our new home," Stella screams in delight, casting her face up to the fall sun that doesn't provide a lot of warmth in the cold air.

"Your new home?" I survey the sticks that, now as I examine closer, seem to outline a boundary. A seriously huge boundary at that.

"These are the foundation sticks," Landon tells me. "When they start digging, this is where they'll do it. Then they'll build the house over it."

"It's..." I'm at a loss for words as I release his hand, walking deeper into the space and looking around. There isn't much out here, but we're also not far from the town we live in. Maybe a ten or so minute drive. "You bought this land?" I spin back around to find Landon watching me intently. He gives me one short nod. "How many acres is it?"

"Twelve."

My eyes widen. Holy hell. Twelve acres here? I know what the house I rent is worth—what land is worth in this part of the country—and I cannot begin to fathom what he spent on it. The soft sounds of a forest surround us, and if I listen closely, I catch the gurgling and splashing of running water in the not too far distance. A brook or stream likely. It's quiet and peaceful and the air is fresh and sweet.

"This is the house you designed? Your dream home?"

Another nod.

"When do you break ground?"

"Next week. I want them to get the foundation done before the ground freezes. Once that's done, they can do the framing and everything else over the winter. But, well, there are other things to consider."

He swallows the distance between us in five large strides, joining me in the center of what will one day be a house.

"What are the other things?" I ask, my mouth going dry at the intensity in his expression as he stands tall over me.

"What the kitchen should be like. You know, since you and Stella like to cook so much. If we should have a second office. One for you. And then other things. Things like what you've always dreamed of having in your dream home."

"You want to know the things I want in my dream home for yours?" My eyebrows hit my hairline.

He takes my hand, pulling it away from my trembling lips. "Yes. Because Stella and I are hoping that when it's finished sometime in the late spring, you'll move in with us. And then it won't just be my dream home or Stella's. It'll be ours. All of ours."

My breath catches. "What if I want a wraparound front porch?"

"Done."

"And a four-season sunroom in the back that looks out into the woods beyond with a wood burning fireplace so we can watch the snow fall and stay extra cozy warm?"

He grins at that. "Also done."

"Landon..."

"I mean it, Elle. I want this to be our home. I want this to be the start of us."

"And I want a pool. And siblings," Stella calls out to us as she continues to run and dance along the sticks. "A younger brother and possibly a younger sister, but I'm undecided on that last one."

"You don't get to decide what they are. You get what you get."

"But Uncle Carter said that sometimes people can decide what gender they want their child to be."

Landon groans, rolling his head over his shoulder and catching her eye. "If Elle and I ever try for a baby, I'd like us to do that the natural way, which means no choosing gender."

"Ewwww!" she cries, covering her ears and closing her eyes. "Gross. TMI, Dad. Just ew."

I laugh, sinking my teeth into my lip when Landon turns back to me.

"Are we going too fast for you?" His eyes beseech mine. "I know this is a lot to take in. But there's no pressure, and the house won't be done for about six or so months, and then you can dec—"

I cut off his rambling with a kiss. Climbing up on my tiptoes, I wrap my arms around his neck and press my lips to his. I kiss him so he knows I want this. I kiss him so he never doubts again that this is my dream too. A home with him and Stella. One day babies—boys or girls or both.

All of it.

"I want at least two kids. One day, but not yet. And I like the idea of my own office."

He smiles against me. "Yeah?"

"Yeah."

In the next second, he's sweeping me off my feet, swinging me through the air until we're both breathless with laughter. He tugs me into his chest, his lips planted in my neck.

"I love you," I whisper.

"I love you too. Today. Tomorrow. Always."

EPILOGUE 2

L uca
Unedited and subject to change

THE WOOD PLANKS of the steps leading from our private beach up to our Martha's Vineyard home dig into the soles of my bare feet. But it's got nothing on my shoulder that's twinging and kicking up like a bull at a rodeo. I've been so miserable since I got here, I hardly recognize my own reflection and the pain isn't helping to improve my mood.

Neither is how weak I still feel.

They talked about this in med school.

Patients going into depression after a major injury or illness.

I have no illusions that's what this is. I just never considered it would happen to me. On either of those accounts.

My shoes dangle from two fingers. My other hand brushes back the windswept strands of my chestnut hair that cling to my face. It's too long, but finding the energy to do something about it isn't high on my priority list. At least not until I can get the greenlight to go back to Minnesota.

Tonight was fun, though. Kinda monotonous, same old shit as it always is, but fun. My brothers and baby sister all flew out to the island, and I would be a fool to believe it wasn't because I'm here for the foreseeable future. They're worried about me. *I'm* worried about myself, and it shines through.

What will I do if I never fully recover? If I can't go back? If I can't continue and finish my residency?

If I can never operate again?

And as if fate enjoys the kick to my ass, my shirt sleeve catches on a random nail that's sticking out of the wood railing and my shoulder jerks.

"Fuck," I hiss as I rub over the barely healed scar, aggravated with just how tender the wound and the surrounding tissue still are. "Heal. I command you to heal."

I snicker, a little buzzed and a lot annoyed that I'm still hurting despite the joint I smoked and the two strong drinks I nursed tonight. Carter stayed at the bar. So did Kaplan and Oliver. Landon didn't even attempt it, having gone to bed likely when his nine-year-old princess Miss Stella—my favorite girl on the planet—sacked out for the night.

He doesn't know how to leave her and that's an entirely different matter.

So different from my reason for being banished to our parents' estate on The Vineyard in the middle of my goddamn neurosurgery residency at The Mayo Clinic.

Which brings me back to my aching shoulder.

And the music I hear, a lulling distraction luring me away from the break in the path where it diverges between the main house and the pool, tennis courts, garages, and staff residences. For a moment, I freeze, unsure exactly what I'm hearing. A violin? Cello maybe?

But from where and from whom?

I amble toward the music, too depressed to go to bed with my thoughts and too bored to bother trying to fuck one of the local chicks.

Boring. So boring. It's not even their fault. It's purely mine.

But that sound. That achingly, mournful, exquisite sound.

It rattles my bones in the best of ways. It calls attention to my muscles, urging, begging them to follow it. To capture it. To listen more intently. I've never heard this song before—though far from a classical music expert. This feels more modern.

The sound leads me to the garage. All five bays are closed, but there is a light glowing through the upper windows and no matter how high I jump, I can't quite make out who is there. Trying the side door, I find it unlocked and as quietly as possible, I turn the handle, slipping inside and shutting it behind me with a soft click.

The air in the garage is thick, heavy with humidity, and I roll my sleeves up to my elbows.

The music is coming from the other side of the garage, and I weave my way around the large Jeep, Tesla, and Mercedes convertible only to stop dead in my tracks for a second time, my breath stalling in my lungs at the sight before me.

Hot damn.

A woman is sitting on a folding chair, her black-as-night hair hanging over the back of it, her face flushed and tacky with sweat. From this angle, I'd swear the only thing she's wearing is the large cello sitting between her spread thighs, but as I edge closer, I notice a paper-thin, gauzy white, flowy top that stops just below her ample breasts and matching tiny shorts.

Her eyes are closed, her head bowed as one hand moves swiftly and fluidly up the long neck of the instrument while the other gracefully drags the bow along the strings. Carefully, I keep to the shadows along the doors, angling for a better position to watch her. She hasn't heard me yet and though I feel as though I should know her, that I've seen her before somewhere, I'm coming up at a loss.

Another step and then I stop, standing here like a creeper as she plays the cello in a way I've never heard or seen any instrument played before. The way she draws each note from it, coaxing its exquisite moans like a lover, has me entranced.

Or maybe that's the woman.

Because just looking at her has my dick hard as steel when it hasn't shown interest in anything or anyone in over a month. Calling her simply beautiful is practically an insult. Words haven't yet been invented to describe her and she hasn't even opened her eyes yet.

Or looked up.

But I need her to. The urge to see her face and what she looks like when she discovers me here is oddly compelling. Then I might need to fuck her. Work whatever bizarre magic she's weaving out of my body. Unless she's Rina's friend or something. Shit. She is at my parents' estate and judging by the way she's dressed and her comfort playing cello here, she belongs.

I clear my throat, but she doesn't catch it. In fact, she's so lost in her music she doesn't notice me until I grab a random old deck chair and drag it over to sit beside her. Then she starts. Almost violently, she practically falls off her chair as her head flies up and her gaze snaps over to me.

Startling blue-green eyes land on mine and something strange and foreign stirs in my chest, squeezing ever so slightly. She blinks rapidly—her eyelashes a thick, black fan across her creamy cheeks—as she adjusts herself on her chair and licks her pillowy lips nervously.

"Luca."

Now it's my turn to blink. "You know me?"

A flush of crimson creeps up from the top of her cleavage to the roots of her hair. "Well, yes, sir. I mean, it's been a while, but

I... of course. That is to say, I knew you weren't Dr. Landon." She shakes her head, flustered. Clears her throat. "Did I wake you with my playing?"

Sir. She called me sir. And Dr. Landon? *The fuck?*

I study her closer. Raven hair. Caribbean ocean eyes. Knock-out body.

Shit. Raven hair. Raven. How could I have not recognized our house manager's daughter? Double shit. Morgan Fairchild has been with our family since around the time Kaplan was born. He and his wife both, but she died shortly after Raven was born. If he knew the thoughts I was just having about his daughter, he'd kill me. Literally since the man is former MI6.

"Raven."

If possible, her blush deepens.

"It's been..."

A long time. I swear, she was all braces and big glasses and looked nothing like this the last time I saw her. She was also—

"Four years," she answers for me, gently setting her large black cello down along with her bow into an open case beside her chair. "Since you and Mister Landon graduated medical school. At least, that was the last time we spoke." Embarrassment consumes her features, and she looks down. But I'm caught on that four years ago thing.

"Raven, how old are you?"

"Eighteen."

Her answer rocks something inside me and I lean forward, my elbows hitting my thighs as I pin her with a stare I can't explain.

"And how long have you been eighteen?"

Her head tilts at my odd question, but I wait her out, needing to know just what level of depraved son of a bitch I'm hitting.

"Three months."

My gut sinks.

"I turn twenty-nine in two weeks."

Why am I telling her that? I'm nearly eleven years older than her. She's a teenager. Essentially part of our staff, who are more like extended family. I shouldn't feel this sort of... disappointment? Is that what that is?

"I know when your birthday is, Luca, and I know how old you are."

A smirk hits my lips at the 'duh' way she says that. "Is that right?"

She stares innocently at me, but there is something else there. A glimmer in her eyes. Something that tells me she likes how thrown off I am by our age difference. Almost as if she can see my ill-placed desire for her and wants to play with it, twirl it around her fingers.

I'm Luca, but Landon is Dr. Landon. I lean back in my chair, rubbing a hand over my mouth as I consider her. If she's at all embarrassed about her blatant lack of clothing, she's not showing it as she cautiously waits for my next move while not removing her gaze from mine.

Such a gorgeous contradiction—shy and brave—I find my smirk growing against my better judgment.

"You're a lot younger than I am. Does our age difference bother you?" The way it bothers me.

She laughs now, the sound a sexy rasp. Her voice is like those sea salt caramels Rina made me eat earlier with her. Smooth and creamy, yet with a zinging coarseness on the end.

"Should it?" She laughs harder at my expression. "I've been told being eighteen is considered a legal adult. I can vote and fight for our country and..." She leans forward, cupping her hand around her mouth as if she's about to tell me a secret. "I don't even have to ask my daddy's permission before I want to go do something I shouldn't."

My dick jumps excitedly at that proposition, but I tamp it down. She's bold. Beautiful. And impossible. The first woman to get my dick stirring in over a month is as forbidden to me in just about every way a woman can be. Gotta love that irony, but that doesn't mean I'm getting up and walking away either. She's a winless game I can't help but want to continue playing.

"Is that what has you out here? You no longer need permission to be up past midnight?"

A shrug of her shoulder, her hands twining up in her hair, lifting the heavy strands off her dewy neck. It also lifts the bottom of her crop top and I catch the hint of the heavy undersides of her breasts. Holy damn, that's insanely fucking sexy.

"Are you flirting with me?" I tease when she doesn't answer.

"Possibly. Does that bother you?" she asks, throwing my question back at me.

I chuckle under my breath. It fucking should. "Not even a bit. I'm just glad you've stopped calling me sir and haven't referred to me as Dr. Luca. But you never answered my initial question."

She tosses her hands up, the strands of her hair falling around her. "I couldn't sleep. What's your excuse?"

My eyes snap back up to hers. "I decided I was done for the night and didn't feel like going to one of the parties my siblings were headed for."

"No woman for Luca Abbot-Fritz to end the night with? Has such a thing ever occurred before?" She gives an exaggerated gasp, covering her mouth as her eyes widen.

"You mock me, Little Bird, thinking you know me so well. You knew it was me and not Landon as well as my birthday, age, and evidently my fuck habits. What else do you know?"

Aqua eyes sparkle, lit with challenge as she matches my position, crossing her legs at the knee, her arms across her breasts forcing them up just a bit and revealing a hint of more cleavage. Cleavage I have absolutely no business looking at, but her rare and exquisite form of beauty makes it impossible not to notice.

"I know you sleep shirtless, only in your boxer briefs. I know you like to run ten miles before the sun comes up because your eyes are sensitive to light, and you don't want to run with sunglasses."

"Wait, wait, wait," I interrupt, holding up a hand. "How do you know I only sleep in boxer briefs?"

She winks at me without answering. "I know you take your coffee with a touch of cream and no sugar because you prefer hazelnut coffee and feel that's sweet enough. I know you know every line from the original three Star Wars movies and likely all the newer ones, even if you hate one, two, and three. I know you also have a coveted secret stash of Star Wars figurines but brought only five of your favorites with you when you left for college. I know your heart shifts as quickly as your eye, favoring a new woman every week. I know your greatest love is your family and that you'd give your life for any of them without a second's hesitation."

I stare at her. Utterly floored. "Raven Fairchild, how long have you been stalking me?"

"Nearly all my life."

A laugh bursts from my chest. "And why is that?"

"If you're looking for someone to pad your ego with compliments and batting eyelashes as they throw themselves at you, you're talking to the wrong girl."

"You know, you're nothing like the girl who stuttered at the sight of me, saying sir and Dr. Landon."

"That was all before you looked at my boobs."

I choke out a cough, hacking up my lungs. "Christ, woman. You're going to kill me."

"What are you doing here, *Luca*?" she emphasizes my name. "Looking for a quick, easy lay?"

"If I wanted that, I'd be at the party right now. Instead of here with you. But the fact remains, you know an awful lot about me when I know so little about you."

"You mean like how you didn't even recognize me tonight?"

"Caught that, did you?"

She raises an eyebrow.

I shrug contritely. I should have recognized her. Maybe I wouldn't be sitting out here with her then. As close as I am. Intrigued and unable to force myself to get up and walk away as I should.

"You saved my life once. Do you remember?"

I rack my brain for a moment and then answer, "When you fell in the pool, and I jumped in after you?"

She nods, staring down at her lap, her fingers twirling an errant string on her tiny shorts. "I was running back to the staff house and tripped over something in the yard. I sprained my ankle and fell into the pool at the same time. I was in so much pain I could hardly swim and was struggling to reach the side. You jumped in. Dragged me out."

"Then I spent the rest of the afternoon watching Disney movies while you were bundled up under a blanket in front of the fire. I think I also made popcorn and ordered pizza."

A smile lights up her face. "You did."

"What does that have to do with the stalking?"

Her head falls back, her long hair along with it, and I admire the column of her neck. How graceful she is. She doesn't look or act eighteen. That's for damn sure.

"I developed an adolescent crush that day." She rights herself. "But don't worry, old man. I gave up that ghost a long time ago."

My hand hits my chest. "Old man?"

She scrunches her nose. "So old."

"I'm wounded."

"I've been told."

Any warmth or amusement I was feeling instantly dies inside me as ice runs through my veins, making my body shudder and my shoulder ache as if to remind me of the real reason I'm on this island. She leans forward, her fingers stroking over my hand, a tender look in her eyes, along with a soft smile. No pity and it's a relief.

"Walk me home."

It's not a question, but I stand all the same, swallowing thickly. I flip my hand around, grasping hers and helping her up. She doesn't release me as she goes for the massive cello, nor does she allow me to take it from her when I attempt. Instead, she silently holds my hand as we exit the garage, the warm, salty wind hitting us with its briny tang, blowing our hair and clothing about.

And when we reach the front door of the staff quarters at the back of the estate, she gives my hand a squeeze, meets my eyes for a flicker of a second, releases me, and walks inside, shutting the door behind her. No goodnight or see you around.

I chuckle to myself, rubbing my hand over my mouth.

Well, that was unexpected as hell. Kind of fun. A lot dirty—at least my thoughts were. Raven Fairchild. Yes, definitely unexpected. And inappropriate...

I have no idea what that was. All I know is I can't do it again. Not with her. No matter how much I want to.

THE END

THANK you for reading Doctor Heartless! Doctor Playboy, Luca's and Raven's story will be coming summer of 2022 and is loaded with plenty more Fritz men and the women who they fall head over heels for. If you haven't read the previous books in this series, keep going for a sneak at Doctor Scandalous.

I am planning to release the first 20% of the book (the history) exclusively in my newsletter prior to release. It will be available as part of the entire story upon release, but if you're anxious for a taste of Raven and Luca's story before then, make sure you sign up HERE!

END OF BOOK NOTE

Hey everyone! Thank you so much for taking the time to read Landon's and Elle's story. I sincerely hope you enjoyed it. I know it was a bit different from Doctor Scandalous and Doctor Mistake, but that's also partially what I loved about it. It's a big city, billionaire romance that felt more like a small town, single dad romance. It's sort of all of those things.

When I first started this series, I knew Landon's was going to be a heartbreaking story. Grief and guilt are funny things. They're clingy and needy and wreak havoc. A lot of this story I felt was about healing and forgiveness. Not just for ourselves, but for others.

When we allow ourselves to forgive, that's when the healing can truly begin. It was an emotional story to write. I definitely shed a few tears, especially during Landon's chat with Stella on the stairs.

Okay, enough of the heavy stuff. I want to thank my gorgeous betas, Danielle, and Patricia as well as my early readers, Joy, and Gina. I have no idea what I'd do without you. You help me give these books the life they deserve.

To my husband and my girls. Thank you for putting up

with my mood swings during the writing of this book. You are in every beat of my heart and I love you all endlessly.

And to you, lovely reader. Whether you're new to me or not, thank you. I could not do any of this without your love and support. Thank you for taking a chance on this family and this world.

Much love!!

XO

Julie Saman

Catching Sin

Darkest Sin

Standalones:

Just One Kiss

Beautiful Potential

Forward - FREE

DOCTOR SCANDALOUS

Oliver

I'm walking toward the gates of hell. And they charge for admission.

"Oh, Oliver..." Christa Foreman greets me with a slow once-over, her pastel-pink lips curling up into an impish grin. She's aptly named, because our senior class president was no joke when it came to strong-arming and manipulating her fellow classmates into getting what she wanted. "It's so good to see you. Wow. I mean, I see your pictures in magazines and on social media every now and then because I follow you, but you're way better looking in person than I remember from high school."

"Um. Thank you?" It comes out as a question, my head tilting in her direction.

"Sure. No problem." She licks her lips, her long, fake eyelashes batting faster than a butterfly's wings at me. "Are you here alone tonight?" She giggles as a flush creeps up her cheeks. She's married. Can we just say that? "I'm only asking because I need to know how much to charge you. I got stuck collecting money until the event coordinator can get her shit together." She huffs out a flustered breath, rolling her eyes derisively. "Anyway, it's a hundred per person. Should I put you down for one or two?"

And this is where I hesitate. Not over the money. The money is not an issue.

"Just give me a second."

Christa stares longingly at me, licking her lips. "Sure. I'll give you all night."

"Right." Because I have no idea what else to say to that. I don't remember Christa being so overtly interested in me when we were in high school. Then again, that was ten years ago, and I was most definitely taken. Which is both the main reason I don't want to be here and the main reason I came. But now I'm starting to reconsider everything.

I have nothing to prove by being here.

Not to *her*, her douchebag husband—my former friend—or anyone else.

I should just go. Maybe meet up with Carter, who I already know is going to our favorite bar, and get lost in a night of fun. Nothing about this hellhole will be fun. And in truth, I could really use a drink. A quiet one. It's been a shitful week. Too many patients. Not enough time. Oh, and finding out that your mom's cancer is back is always a winner.

I slip my phone from my pocket and shoot off a text to my best friend, Grace.

Me: Sorry, babe. Not gonna be able to make it.

The message bubble instantly dances along my screen. **Grace: It's not a choice, honey pie. Everyone is already asking when you're going to get here. Everyone.**

And instantly I'm tempted to ask if *she's* asking. In fact, my thumbs, who seem to have a mind of their own, start to type that very question until I tamp them down and rein them under control. Of course, she's asking. That's what she does.

She continues to hunt me down with terrorist-level determination, even all these years later.

She's likely giddy at the prospect of rubbing her picture-perfect life in my face without even caring that she's the last person on the planet I want to see tonight or any other night. Hence why now is the perfect time to leave.

Me: Don't care.

Grace: Yes, you do. Come on. I know you're already dressed for tonight. Carter sent me a text.

Carter. My traitorous brother.

Grace: Just come inside the hotel. Come up to the reunion. Have a drink with me. See the people you haven't seen since high school who will fall at your feet the way they did back in the day. Oh wait, they still do.

Me: You're doing a shitty job of selling it there, sweetums.

Grace: Everyone will think you're a pussy if you don't come.

Me: Nice gauntlet drop.

Grace: I thought so. Now get your ass over here!

I growl out a slew of curses under my breath, still seriously contemplating fleeing for the sake of my sanity, when I catch sight of a short, curvy redhead in a tight, backless black dress, higher than high heels, and fuck-me red lips that match her hair walking up to Christa. She's as late as I am, and before I know what I'm doing, a smile cracks clear across my face.

I know her instantly.

Even if it's been ten years since I've seen her. A guy never forgets the girl who gave him his first boner. A first-ever boner in class, I might add. We were twelve and she bent over to retrieve her fallen pencil when a flash of her training bra caught my eye. Instant erection.

I was pretty smitten after that moment, as you might imagine.

"Amelia," Christa greets her, her face now lacking any of the warmth it had when she was talking to me. "I had no idea you were coming."

What the fuck? You'd think in the ten years since we graduated from our annoyingly prestigious prep school that the rich girls would get over the self-created, mean-girl bullshit they had with the scholarship kids.

Amelia turns redder than her hair, and she takes a small step back before straightening her frame and squaring her shoulders. "Well, I'm here. Graduated same year as you. I even received the invitation in the mail. Must have been an error on your part," she finishes sarcastically.

"Uh-huh. It's a hundred-dollar entrance fee," Christa snaps, taking far too much pleasure in announcing that sum as she purses her lips off to the side, giving Amelia a nasty-girl slow once-over.

"A hundred dollars?" Amelia asks, though it comes out in a deflated, breathy whisper.

"Yup. Sorry," Christa sneers with a sorry-not-sorry saccharine sweet voice. "No exceptions. Not even for the kids who were on scholarship."

And that's it. Before Christa can say anything else that will make me want to throttle her, I walk over to Amelia, wrapping my hand around her waist. "Sweetheart," I exclaim. "You made it. I was starting to get worried."

Amelia jolts in my arms, her breath catching high in her throat as she twists to face me. Then she looks up and up a bit more because she's about a foot shorter than I am even in her heels. Suddenly, two sparkling gray eyes blink rapidly at me, and my heart starts to pound in time with the flutter of her lashes, my mouth dry like I've been eating sand all night.

"I'm sorry," she says, confused, her parted lips hanging just a bit too open for us to be selling this. "I think you must—"

I lean in, my nose brushing against her silky red hair that

smells like honeysuckle or something sweet and I breathe into her ear, "Just go with it."

She swallows audibly as I pull back, staring into her eyes and wondering how a color like that is even possible when she smiles and robs me of my breath. *Whoa.* That's unexpected.

"I didn't mean to worry you..." She trips up, biting into her lip like she's searching for a suitable term of endearment. Or maybe my name? I guess it is possible she has no idea who I am. We didn't exactly run in the same circles, and I just came up to her and wrapped my arm around her. "Oli," she finishes with, and I blow out the breath I didn't even realize I was holding.

"It's fine. I just didn't want to go in without the most beautiful woman in the world on my arm."

Amelia gives me that stunning smile again, this time with a blush staining her cheeks, and I marvel at how it makes her eyes glow to a smoky charcoal. Goddamn, she's fucking sexy.

"Wait," Christa interrupts. "You're with her?" She points at Amelia.

"I sure am," I declare without removing my eyes from Amelia's because those eyes, man. They're just too pretty not to stare at. "I'm a lucky bastard, right?"

"You're with him?" She turns that finger on me.

"So it seems," Amelia replies, her tone a bit bewildered, though there is a hint of amusement in there, too.

"But. You're. You. No. You're Oliver Fritz," Christa sputters incredulously. "And she's Amelia—" Her words cut off when I throw her my most menacing glare, already knowing the exact nasty nickname she's about to throw out. Why certain women feel the need to degrade and belittle other women, I'll never understand.

I slip two one-hundred-dollar bills from my wallet and toss them at Christa. "Have a good night," I say instead of what I'm really thinking. My fingers intertwine with Amelia's, and then

I'm dragging her past Christa, down the long corridor with the paisley rug and gold walls, toward the ballroom.

I guess I'm going to my high school reunion after all.

The second we're out of sight of Christa, Amelia yanks her hand from mine, stopping in the middle of the hall and turning to stare up at me. "You remember me?" she asks and then shakes her head like that's not what she meant to say.

"Amelia Atkins. You were in most of my classes from the time we were in sixth grade or so, on."

"Right. What I meant to say is, thank you for stepping in back there, but it really wasn't necessary."

"Maybe not. I'm sure you can handle yourself with women like Christa. But it felt wrong to stand there and watch that go down, doing nothing. I can't stand women who feel the need to hurt others just to make themselves look and feel better."

She folds her arms over her chest, giving me a raised eyebrow. "And yet you dated a woman who did exactly that all through high school."

Touché. A bark of a laugh slips out my lungs. "Can't argue with that. Hell, I dated that same vicious woman through college too. Adolescent mistake. What can I say?"

Still, at the mention of that particular woman, an old flair hits me straight in the chest. My fingers find my pocket, toying with the large diamond solitaire set in a diamond and platinum band I stuck in there tonight. It's *the* ring. The one I nearly gave to said woman who was screwing around on me with my friend, Rob. A lesson in betrayal I've never forgotten. It's why on certain occasions, I carry it with me.

A reminder to never get too close again.

"Sorry," Amelia says, withering before my eyes. "That was insanely rude of me. I don't even know why I said that. Christa got my hackles all fired up, and I just took them out on you instead of her, like I should have. Damn, some women seriously suck, right?" I can't stop my chuckle, though I think she was being serious. She stares down at the rug, shifting her stance until she's leaning back against the wall opposite the closed doors where the reunion is taking place. "Look, I wish you hadn't paid for me. Money and I aren't exactly on speaking terms at the moment. It's going to take me a while to pay you back. But I *will* pay you back. I just don't have that kind of—"

My fingers latch on to her chin, tilting her head back up until our eyes meet. "I don't care about the money. And I don't want you to pay me back." She opens her mouth as if to argue with me, and I shake my head, cutting her off again. "I mean it."

She huffs out a breath. "Well, thank you. That's very generous. But if this is how this night is already starting off, I'm thinking maybe I should just go. Hell, I shouldn't even have come here in the first place. I don't know what I was thinking. My sister talked me into it, and I thought..." She shakes her head. "Never mind. It's stupid."

I prop my shoulder against the wall so I'm facing her, folding my arms while I stare at her because I can't seem to help myself. "Why is it stupid?"

"You really want to know?"

"I really want to know."

Those big eyes slay through me, slightly glassy with emotion. "Because no one in there wants me there. You heard Christa. I was fooling myself into thinking that I could waltz in here ten years later and everyone who treated me like garbage growing up would finally see me for me. That they'd finally realize we're all on an even playing field now that high school is over. It was going to be like putting all my old bully nightmares to rest once and for all. Only, nothing has changed. I'm still the girl wearing thrift store digs who couldn't even afford to pay the entrance fee."

Wow. That's...

"Can I tell you something?" I ask.

Her hands meet her hips. "You mean something to rival the

way too personal verbal diarrhea I just spouted at a man I haven't seen in a decade?"

She's trying for brave and strong, and even sarcastic. But she's sad. I can see it in her eyes that bounce around my face, almost as if she's not sure she wants to know what I'm about to say. No one wants to be slammed back into their high school nightmare. She wanted to walk in there and make all those assholes eat their words.

I want that for her too.

I like Amelia. I always have. There was something about her that just got to me on a weird level I never quite understood. She was sweet and nerdy and quiet and reserved. So understatedly beautiful. Her hair was all wild with red curls. Her glasses a touch too big for her face. Her body small with her ample curves hidden beneath her ill-fitting prep school uniform.

And looking at her now, after hearing what Christa was saying to her...

In truth, I do remember people being that nasty. Though now I'm positive it was a lot worse than I knew about if Christa's reaction to her tonight is anything to go by. I only heard comments here and there that I didn't pay much attention to, nor did anything to stop. Even if I never directly contributed to it, by not stopping it, I was part of the problem.

That's on me. And it's not okay. I should have done more to protect her. I should have said something.

"Something like that. You told me yours. Now I'll tell you mine."

"Alright."

I step into her, bending down like I'm about to tell her a secret when really, I just want to be closer to her. Smell her shampoo that makes my cock jump in my slacks. Feel the heat of her body as she starts to blush from my proximity.

"I don't want to be here either. I got talked into it by my friend, Grace, and now here I am."

Her eyebrows knit together. "Why wouldn't you want to be here? You're a doctor. You were the most popular guy in our class. Captain of the football team. Everyone loved you. Still do, if the tabloids are anything to go by."

I suck in a deep breath, ready to tell her something only my family and Grace know. "My ex is not only in there with her husband, my former friend, but she's pregnant. Likely going to be delivered by either my brother or my best friend since she sought them out to be her OB. How's that for irony?" I roll my eyes. "The only saving grace I have when it comes to Nora is that she never knew I was about to propose. I had the ring in my pocket, ready to drop down onto one knee, but before I could do anything, she told me she was in love with Rob and that we were over."

Amelia sucks in a rush of air, her eyes flashing. Her hand shoots up, covering her parted lips as she stares at me with a combination of shock and sympathy. "God. That's awful."

"The real kicker of all that is I had made a lot of sacrifices for her. A lot. Nearly everything I wanted I had given up for her with the exception of medicine. But I chose NYU to be with her instead of playing ball at Michigan. I finished college in three years instead of four because she said the sooner I can complete med school and residency, the better. Then, on the fucking day I got into Columbia for med school and was set to propose, she informed me she had been cheating on me for the better half of six months."

Six. Fucking. Months!

"Jesus, Oliver. I'm so sorry. I never heard anything about that."

"That's because no one knows, so if you wouldn't mind keeping that to yourself, I'd appreciate it. The last thing I want is for that to hit the press next."

She reaches out her hand, touching my arm and giving me a squeeze. "Of course. I'll never tell anyone. I don't blame you for not wanting to go in there. It seems we both felt like we had something to prove by showing up tonight."

That's not the reason I came tonight. But Nora is the main reason I didn't want to go in. I've successfully avoided seeing her for years. In truth, I've been over her for a long time, just not over what she did to me. Most of my bitterness and resentment is on me. I should never have made those sacrifices for her.

I gave up pieces of myself I can never get back.

But Amelia deserves more. She always has, and she never got it. She deserves to have people look at her and treat her with the respect they never did. They owe it to her. Hell, I owe it to her. I don't want her to leave tonight the way she is now.

"I only wish it had turned out better for us," she continues. "But I think my carriage has officially turned back into a pumpkin and I should just cut my losses and head home. Tonight can't possibly end the way I had envisioned it."

Like a bolt of electricity flowing through me, suddenly I'm giddy with an idea that is quite possibly the most ridiculous idea in the history of ideas. Christa nearly swallowed her tongue when she thought Amelia was my date. So maybe everyone else will react the same way if that's what they see. Bonus for me—I'll have a hot as hell woman on my arm and maybe Nora will leave me alone.

More than that, I *want* to go in there with Amelia. I want to spend more time with her tonight. And if they don't like it or think less of me for it, well, I don't give a shit.

But Amelia being my date isn't enough. Not with my reputation. They'll just assume I'm using her, because ever since Nora and I split up... I've been somewhat of a player. A fact the media loves to report on. Hell, my face is splashed across the internet every other week, showing me with a different woman each time. Not in the last few months or so, but it's been the standard of my life since Nora. It's the way I keep from getting hurt again.

And the media reporting on it all? Well, that's the standard of all my brothers' lives. It comes with being a Fritz and living in Boston. We own this city. We're royalty. For better or worse, that's how it is.

But if Amelia and I really want to make an impact tonight... if I really want to make all those assholes who hurt Amelia choke, and Nora—who still calls me to tell me *all* her 'happy' news—realize that I've finally and officially moved on from her... it needs to be more than just people thinking I'm dating Amelia.

They need to know she's something special. Believe she's something special *to me*.

My fingers dig back into my pocket, locating that ring. Looking at her... plotting this insane idea... I'm hit with the fact that I know it will change everything. Both for her and for me.

A deviously crooked smile curls up at the corner of my lips.

Yeah. I have an idea, alright. And I think I can get Amelia to go for it. It's only for a few hours anyway. What could go wrong?

Grab Oliver and Amelia's scorching hot fake engagement romance, Doctor Scandalous now!